Jeffrey Robinson is the ... ... of a dozen books of fiction and non-fiction, including *The Risk Takers*; its sequel *Minus Millionaires*; the biography of Saudi Arabia's former oil minister, *Yamani - The Inside Story*; *Bardot - Two Lives*; *The End of the American Century*, an account of the chilling hidden agendas that underpinned the Cold War, and *The Laundrymen*.

Born and raised in New York, he lived in France for twelve years before moving to the UK in 1982.

Other books by Jeffrey Robinson

Fiction

The Ginger Jar
Pietrov and Other Games

Non-Fiction

Bardot - Two Lives
The Laundrymen
The End of the American Century
The Risk Takers: Five Years On
Rainier and Grace
Yamani - The Inside Story
Minus Millionaires
The Risk Takers
Teamwork
Bette Davis: Her Stage and Film Career

Jeffrey Robinson

THE MARGIN OF THE BULLS

WARNER BOOKS

A *Warner* Book

First published in Great Britain in 1995 by
Little, Brown and Company
This edition published in 1996 by Warner Books

A CIP catalogue record for this book is available from
the British Library.

ISBN 0 7515 1440 3

Printed and bound in Great Britain by Clays Ltd, St Ives plc

Warner Books
A Division of
Little, Brown and Company (UK)
Brettenham House
Lancaster Place
London WC2E 7EN

In the margin of the bull,
the merchants too had many years' indulgence,
but none from guilt as well as punishment.

William Langland, Piers the Ploughman

Pour Fifine et Jean
Le Gracieux

Chapter One

One way to judge a man's success is by the number of times he's been bankrupt. Although it doesn't take a genius to go broke the first time, when he's gone belly up two or three or four times, if nothing else, it means there are people who believe in him enough to pay for his next ticket on the merry-go-round. By definition, I reckon, the guy is successful.

Yet, if that were the sole criterion, I'd be ruled a failure.

Another valid indicator – at least in my country, America – is the left breast pocket of a fellow's shirt. Truly successful men don't have left breast pockets on their shirts because they don't buy their shirts off the rack. Instead, they've got embroidered initials there. The general rule of thumb is, the better the shirt maker, the more subtle the lettering. Two letters is correct. Three is crass. Four is definitely "bubba" – the kind of thing you see on some used car salesmen and just about all politicians who come from states beginning with vowels.

The reasoning behind the theory is simple. The more subtle the embroidering, the less a man feels he has to prove. The less a man feels he has to prove, the more successful he must be.

Unfortunately, my initials on a shirt don't work because it's too easy to mistake BR for something dim-witted like British Rail. Although I once had two

1

shirts made with initials stitched into the left cuff because I'd seen Cary Grant wearing a shirt like that and I reckoned if it was all right for Cary Grant, it should be all right for me. However, Pippa argued, the rules that applied to Cary Grant did not apply to the rest of the world's male population – with the possible exception, she said, of Mel Gibson and Eric Clapton – which means now, none of my shirts have my initials anywhere. But then, they don't have left breast pockets, either.

Needless to say, these things are often a question of culture. In the UK, where I've lived for the past 24 years, success is frequently judged by what people call you. If you are known simply as Mr Radisson – as I am – you may be successful but you're not officially successful. If you are called Sir Bayard – as I am not – everyone knows that you're at least successful enough to have made the proper donations, or to have pushed the proper buttons, which is often the same thing. Yet, it isn't until the Queen whacks her sword on your shoulder and dubs you Lord Radisson of Pennstreet PLC – as I shall never be – that you have formally arrived.

For my money, the best general yardstick of success is the number of telephone lines a man has within arm's reach of wherever he's sitting.

It's the old joke about Muck, driving down the highway in his Rolls Royce, when he gets a call from Meyer, his biggest rival. Meyer explains he's just installed a fax machine in his Roller and wants Muck to know that. But Muck says, sorry, he doesn't have time to be impressed because his other car phone is ringing.

Studying this in detail – I daydream best when I've got such serious matters to ponder – I've come to the conclusion that success has nothing to do with the actual number of telephones someone has. Nor should the person with the most lines automatically be crowned the most successful. The trick is to have the correct number of lines, which I surmise to be six.

My first two lines are for regular incoming calls. By

having two, there's always one free for a more important call. The third is a line that rings only in my office, giving certain people with whom I do business access to me without going through my secretary. The fourth is reserved for my use – no one knows the number so I can always dial out. While the fifth is a private fax line, because there are times when documents must come to me directly – documents I wouldn't necessarily want anyone else to see.

And then there is my sixth line – my private-private line. No one knows the number except Pippa and Peter. No one answers it except me. And I always answer it, no matter what else I'm doing – as I did when it broke into my early afternoon daydreaming on 5 November 1991.

I'd been leaning all the way back in my chair, with my feet up on my desk, contemplating the relationship between life and baseball. I'd just asked myself, how has the Infield Fly Rule changed the course of Western history, when it rang.

Certain that it was Pippa, I kept my eyes firmly shut and answered it with, "Tell me what you're wearing."

Peter whispered, "Stockings and a suspender belt."

I dared, "Black or red?"

He purred, "So it is just my body."

"It used to be," I confessed. "Now it's just your money."

"Funny you should mention that because money is why I'm calling."

We usually spoke a couple of times a day. He'd ring me early in the morning, unless he was "working a lass" – as he so colloquially referred to it – and I'd phone him in the evening to tell him what the day was like. I'd been out of the office all morning, but I'd spoken to him the day before so I knew he was in Paris, where he now spent most of his time, working lasses. "You? Money? I can't believe it."

"Ask where I am."

3

"Paris, France."

"That's not a question, that's an answer. Anyway, you'll never guess, so I'll tell you. Las Palmas."

"What happened to Paris, France?"

"Her name is Hélène."

"That's just a pansy way of calling someone Helen."

"That's right, Hélène, as in, is this the *visage* that launched a thousand *bateaux*? She's a Dior model, about nine feet tall, and I picked her up after a catwalk show yesterday. I told her I'd take her any place in the world that she wanted to go and she said, Las Palmas."

"You offered to take a girl with legs up to her ass anywhere in the world and she chose the Canaries? How old is she, 15?"

"Older," Peter insisted.

And then the two of us said, at exactly the same time, "But not much."

We'd had this conversation a few million times before. "16?"

"Hélène is not why I'm calling."

"17?"

"Almost 19, okay?"

"*Almost* 19? Does she know how *almost* old you are?"

"Listen, I'm not calling about Hélène, I'm calling about Ro-bear."

"Is that her convict brother or her motorcycle gang member boyfriend?"

"Ro-bear, as in Max-well."

"You picked him up in Paris too?"

"No, but they're about to pick him up not far from here. Like a few miles out to sea."

"Who?"

"Ro-bear Max-well."

"No, I mean, who's picking him up?"

"I presume it's the local version of the United States Coast Guard."

4

I suggested, "Let's start all over again. You and Ro-bear Max-well are working a Dior model who's in the United States Coast Guard?"

"You want to make some money or not?" He said, "I'm in Las Palmas with this French bird, and the whole town is going crazy because Captain Bob isn't here."

"You'd have thought they'd be singing with joy."

"I'm saying not here, as in not here, even though his boat is. He's not on it. He's missing."

"Maxwell missing?" What a thought that was. "Where is he?"

"That's what all those air-sea rescue guys in their nifty multicoloured helicopters want to know."

"You think he skipped? Is it summer yet in South America?"

"No, I think he fell overboard. That's the rumour. I think he's dead."

My eyes opened and my feet came off my desk. "Jeezus!"

"So," Peter asked quietly, "do you sincerely want to be rich?"

"What a good idea." I grabbed my TV's remote button. "I'll get onto it right now."

"We're at the El Castillo."

"I'll phone you later."

There was nothing about Maxwell in the teletext headlines on BBC1 or ITV, so I switched to the share listings page on Channel 4. At 1 o'clock, Maxwell Communications was trading at around 138 pence.

My watch said it was now 1:25.

Roderick wouldn't be in his office yet because Nassau is five hours behind London. And except in the summer, when he came in very early to avoid the mid-day heat, I knew I'd be lucky to find him before 3 o'clock my time. The problem was, I didn't know if I could wait that long. My gut was telling me to let Roderick do this but my head was saying, it's now or never. So I mumbled, what

5

the hell, and phoned the most trustworthy of the four stockbrokers we used.

"What about Maxwell Communications?"

"Toilet paper," Adrian O'Neil replied immediately. "No one wants it. Wait a minute." He found it on his screen. "Opened at 139. It's going nowhere fast. Call it ... 137–139."

"All right," I said, "short two million. It's on the Tivoli Court Trading account. The agent in the Bahamas is Roderick Hays-White. He's the one selling."

"No problem. Hold on." He shouted something to someone across the room, punched some keys on his computer, then came back to me. "The best I could do is 137."

I said fine, and the deal was done.

A year ago, those same shares were as high as 241 pence. But they'd been slipping steadily ever since. *Sotto voce* on the street was that Maxwell had built himself a house of cards. However, because of the British libel laws, no one dared repeat it too loudly. If he was swimming with sharks – literally this time, instead of figuratively – I was willing to bet that every Hooray-Henry from Holborn Circus to Gran Canaria would soon be shouting, I told you so.

I got on the intercom to Patty West, my secretary. "Hold everything."

She said, "You've got a 2 o'clock with Mr Von Slingerland from Gold Assay."

"Reschedule. I'll let you know about the 3 o'clock."

"And I've got Derek from Touche Ross on the line if you want to take it."

Guys flogging metals and the world of accountants would just have to wait. "I'll get back to everyone later," I said, and clicked off.

To keep a close eye on the market, I dialled my computer into Reuters real-time share price service. I put Maxwell Communications in the centre of the screen and sat back.

By 2 o'clock, there was still nothing on any of the teletext services, although Maxwell's share price was definitely slipping.

So far so good.

Most people think that when you get into the market you always want to see your shares go up. They think it's only when prices rise that you make money. And yes, if you bought IBM or Polaroid in 1955 and held on to them, you've made piles of dough. But long-term investing in blue chips and short-term punts on anything and everything are not the same game. In the short term you want movement. Up or down doesn't matter as long as there's action. All you have to do is choose a direction. Right now, Peter and I were betting that Maxwell's shares would continue heading south.

When my screen showed the shares at 129–131, I phoned Adrian again. "What's going on? Who's selling?"

"Wait a minute." There was the usual commotion in the background. I tried to hear what he was saying to the guy next to him, but he cupped the phone. Then he put it down, called to someone across the room, then cupped it again before coming back to me. "It's Goldman Sachs. Rumour is they've just unloaded."

If that rumour was true, I was willing to believe that they must know something. If they knew what I thought they knew, other people were about to find out about it too. I told him, "Sell two more for us."

"Hold on." He punched some keys, shouted numbers to someone, came back on the phone to say, "Hold on Bay. Just a second," then shouted to someone else, "How many? Are you sure? Thanks." He said to me, "Bay, it was Goldman Sachs. Two point two. That's not confirmed but that's confirmed. You didn't hear it from me. I've sold another two for you but couldn't get more than 129. What's happening?"

"High tide," I volunteered. "Where's Mirror Group?"

"Let me see . . ." He punched a few more buttons.

"It's 77–78. Looks like it's off a half. Been that way all day."

"No action at all?"

"None."

No action means no profit. "I'll pass. But I'll call you back."

"Are these for you or Tivoli Court?"

"Always Tivoli Court," I reminded him. "Always Roderick Hays-White. He's the one who called. He's the one who's dealing. This has nothing to do with me. For Chrissake, make sure you've got it right."

"I've got it," he promised. "I've got it."

For the next 30 or 40 minutes, I did nothing more than swing my eyes from the teletext screen to the computer screen, waiting for something to happen. By 2:45, the shares were down to 120–122. There was still no news, but I decided I'd had enough. I instructed Adrian, "Round 'em up."

In the time it took to push a couple of buttons and shout to someone on the other side of his dealing room, he bought back the four million shares I'd sold. "Deal," he said. "Done at 122."

Exactly 13 minutes later, the London Stock Exchange announced that all trading in Maxwell Communications Corp. and Mirror Group Newspapers was formally suspended. Shortly after 3 o'clock, the teletext screen lit up with the banner headline, "Robert Maxwell Is Missing At Sea."

Peter could now afford at least one more leggy almost-19-year-old. For the price of a few phone calls, the two of us had just bagged a fast £440,000.

Chapter Two

I arrived in Britain on Saturday, 21 March 1970, with no place to live and no place to go back to. I didn't know anyone. All I owned was $65, a brand-new passport and a slightly new name.

The decision to leave America was not an easy one. I never told my parents or my sister. I couldn't bring myself to tell Elizabeth. I'd half-planned it for months, and in the back of my mind I was hoping that I could convince her to come with me. But then she and I had one of our usual stupid fights – I can't even recall now what it was about – and so I stormed out of her place, went back to mine, packed a duffel bag, closed my bank account and set out to hitchhike from Baltimore to Toronto.

On the way, I was beaten up by a drunk in a Buick who decided he wanted me to become his woman. I slept rough for two nights somewhere near Rochester, New York, and nearly got arrested for it on both nights. I was stopped at the Canadian border because by this time I needed a shower and a shave and the Canadians knew that anyone my age who looked the way I did was running away from something. They held me there for nearly six hours before they got bored and let me go.

Because I couldn't get a plane out of Toronto for a week, I had to crash in a student hostel and, even though I finally got to shower and shave, hanging out like that for seven days put a serious dent into my money.

The only thing smoking east from Toronto was a charter to someplace called Luxembourg. I bought a round-trip ticket for $109 – it was just a dollar more than the one-way price – and managed to sell the return coupon for $50 to a guy from Kansas who lied that he was an art student on his way to spend a year in Italy. The deal was, he'd pay me on the plane. Luckily, no one bothered looking too closely at the tickets when we filed on board.

It turned out to be his 50 bucks that kept me alive.

I had no idea what I was going to do when I landed in Luxembourg. But I had plenty of time to think about it because, a few hours after we left a cold and foggy Toronto, we made an emergency stop at Gander, Newfoundland, and sat there freezing for nearly 36 hours. A stewardess said it had something to do with one of the engines. The charter company's representative kept making announcements every few hours to say that he was trying to get in touch with someone in Calgary to see what they wanted him to do with us. In the end, he never managed to find anybody. I spent two nights sleeping on three plastic chairs in the under-heated lounge at the main terminal.

When the plane was repaired, 165 very disgruntled people piled back on and sat there grumpily until the pilot found Luxembourg. It was snowing when we landed and I couldn't be bothered trying to find somewhere to stay, so I made my way to the train station and got on the first thing heading for anywhere, which turned out to be London, England.

We stopped in Brussels and for a moment I thought of getting off. But my high school French was non-existent and, anyway, someone in the compartment told me it was a Walloon city. Because I didn't have a clue who or what a Walloon was, I stayed in my seat. I hadn't yet figured out that I'd have to get off the train at Ostend and take a ferryboat across the English Channel or I wouldn't have bothered.

I hate boats.

By the time we got to the dock, I'd somehow convinced myself that it was too late to turn back. I claimed a seat near the men's room and true to form, within minutes of pulling away from the pier, I did what I always do whenever I'm on a boat. I got furiously sick.

Once my stomach was emptied, I went outside and spent the rest of the trip in a cold sweat, clinging desperately to the rail, fighting for any air that didn't stink of car fumes, beer or vomit.

The first I saw of Great Britain was a coastline of white cliffs – which weren't as white as they were filthy grey – under dark skies that were now pounding those cliffs with rain. The next thing I saw of Great Britain was the grimy, congested port called Dover, with cars and trucks honking their horns, inching through massive puddles towards little booths where men in raincoats were screaming at the drivers to get into this line or that line or wait for the next ferry.

I staggered off the boat through the rain and into a tatty Immigration Hall where a handful of sour-faced British Customs Officers were just as wary of me as the Canadians had been. They asked all sorts of dumb questions like, why did you come here? Still green from the crossing, I didn't have the stamina to answer, because I'm afraid of Walloons. So I lied. I said I was coming to visit my grandmother who lived in – the only place I could think of was Piccadilly Circus. They eventually let me through, but probably only because the line of several hundred people behind me was growing increasingly restless. From there, I followed the crowds, as if I'd been programmed, on to a train that deposited me a few hours later at Victoria Station.

I have always loved railway stations – like the ones in those old black and white French films where the whistle of the Orient Express echoes off the high steel beamed ceilings – but this place smelled of popcorn and bubble gum and hamburgers being sold at a tiny stand called Wimpy.

Needing someplace cheap to stay, I waited in line at the Tourist Information desk for nearly 30 minutes.

I hadn't bathed in three days, hadn't seen a bed in as many nights and must have looked exactly like the fugitive that I'd become. Still, a kindly, dark haired woman in a green sari phoned all over town to get me a room. She found one in a boarding house on Sussex Gardens, not far from Paddington Station. I had no idea where that was or how to get there. She said I could take a bus or the tube – the subway, for me – and handed me a map. It was raining badly here as well, but I was too exhausted to care. I needed to save money so I walked.

It took me nearly an hour.

The old woman who opened the door stared at me suspiciously – I must have made quite a sight, soaked as I was – but after I introduced myself as the fellow sent by the Tourist Information lady at Victoria Station, she confirmed that the price of a room was £2 a night. In those days, that was just under $5.

My room was on the top floor with a little window looking out on to the gardens. I wanted to sound cheery and said that her boarding house was just what I'd been hoping for. But she insisted it wasn't a boarding house – "This is a Bed and Breakfast" – and asked how long I'd be staying. I admitted that I didn't have any idea. She insisted on two nights in advance. I gave her $10 as a deposit and promised to exchange money later.

It was 3:30 in the afternoon.

When she left, I shut the door and tried to find the heater. There was a contraption on the floor that looked like a heater but I couldn't get it working, until I noticed that it took coins. But I didn't have any coins and couldn't be bothered going all the way downstairs to beg some from her. So I got out of my soaking wet jeans, socks and shirt and put on a dry sweater. Then I climbed into bed.

At $5 a day I could stay here for 13 days. I tried not to think of what my situation would have been had I not flogged the other half of my ticket in Toronto. But $5 a day didn't take food into account. I guessed that if I could eat for a couple of bucks, I could live here for maybe up to nine days.

I told myself I had nine days to worry about the rest of my life.

Slowly, out of the thick daze that had rolled in across my brain, the thought dawned on me that here I was, in a place where I knew no one, with only enough money to last for nine days.

Then I realized that this was the first time in my life – all 20 years of it – when not a single person in the world knew where I was. Not my parents. Not my sister. Not Elizabeth.

I wondered when I would see her again.

I had no way of knowing at the time that the war in Vietnam would drag on for another few years and that the wounds inflicted on our national conscience would take so long to heal that I wouldn't be allowed home for a very long time.

It was the worst day of my life.

And for the first time since I was nine years old, the first time since the day that dumb dog I'd loved so much died, I cried myself to sleep.

A loud banging on the door woke me.

"You'd better get up," a woman was shouting. "This is last call for breakfast. If you don't come down now, you don't eat."

I couldn't figure out where I was. "What do you want?"

"Last call," she repeated.

My back hurt and my legs felt as if someone had been pounding on them. The bed was too soft and the mattress caved in at the centre. And I was hungry.

I tried to focus my eyes but my head hurt too. My

13

duffel bag was perched on the wicker chair that sat in front of the wobbly wooden table under the tiny window. There was a lamp on the table and I reached for it. But someone must have been trying to save money by using 15-watt bulbs because, when I snapped it on, it made almost no difference.

The room was cold.

I recalled the thing that took coins. Pulling myself out of bed, with the sheets and blanket draped over my back, I crawled across the floor to read the word "shillings".

That's right, I'm in London, England.

But I didn't know what a shilling was.

My watch said it was 9:30, which meant I'd slept almost six hours.

Shillings, I kept repeating. I need shillings. And I need dry clothes. And dinner. And a bath.

There was a sink in the corner of the room and a mirror above that. Still carrying the bedding with me – thinking that I must look like an Indian who'd escaped from the reservation – I went there to see that I needed a shave, too.

That's when the words of the woman pounding on my door came back to me. Last call for breakfast?

I walked over to the window and moved the lace curtains aside.

Christ, it's morning. I've slept all the way through. It's 9:30 in the morning.

I dumped the bedding, shoved my legs into a pair of dry jeans and stepped into dry shoes – my only other pair of shoes. I grabbed my key, locked the door and raced down the stairs.

The restaurant was in the basement, except it wasn't really a restaurant because they only served one meal.

Bed and Breakfast.

I suddenly understood.

The old woman who ran the place gave me a stern look as I stumbled in. "Sorry," I said. "Please, I'm very hungry." I felt like that kid from the Charles Dickens story. Please, sir, may I have some more. "I won't be late again."

There were only a few other people in the room, which was otherwise filled with violet Formica tables and yellow plastic chairs.

"All right, this time," she gave in. "But only because it's your first day."

I had orange juice – it was metallic and terrible – corn flakes, one fried egg, one greasy sausage, two cold slices of toast and two cups of diluted coffee. I never would have paid money for such a lousy meal but breakfast was included in the price of the bed.

I reminded myself, it's free.

And that made it taste just fine.

Because it was Sunday, and everything in London was closed, I took the day to sort myself out. I shaved and had a bath. I also found out how to use the heater. The woman – her name was Mrs Earl – advanced me two shillings and, once I got the thing working, the room warmed up very well. I hung up my clothes, shoved my duffel bag under my bed and took a nap. Later that afternoon I found one of those CHANGE places at the end of the Edgware Road called Marble Arch. A dark-skinned man with an odd accent who was shielded from his customers by two-inch thick glass asked me how much money I wanted to change. My instinct was to go for $20, holding on to the rest just in case. Then I asked myself, just in case what? I pulled all my money out of my pocket and took the plunge. "This is $55," I said. "It's everything I have in the world." He couldn't have cared less. He gave me a few very large bank notes, a handful of strange coins and a receipt. "I need shillings," I told him, forcing one of the bills under the glass. "Let me have shillings, please."

He stared at me. "You want five quid worth of shillings?"

I didn't know what a quid was or how many shillings I'd get, but shillings meant heat. "That's right."

He counted out 100 of them.

Too embarrassed to admit that I'd made a mistake, I shoved them into my pocket and went about my business.

London looked to me exactly the way it always did in Peter Sellers' movies. The roads were crowded with funny-shaped taxis and double-decker buses, all of them driving on the wrong side. The streets were lined with places where you could get a cheap meal – fish and chips wrapped in yesterday's newspaper – which I decided was quaint the first time but pretty lousy every time after that.

When I was done with dinner, I returned to my room, fed plenty of shillings into the heater and went to sleep.

The next morning, I was the first person down for breakfast.

The food didn't taste any better, but by now my head was clear enough to think about other things, like how I was going to spend the first day and the first week and the first month of the rest of my life.

In college, I'd discovered through trial and error that the best places to pick up a girl were art museums and libraries. Art museums were preferable but stalking there required a lot of time and in this situation, I felt, one of the many things I didn't have was time. I'd already used up two of my nine days.

The library routine was easier. But here again, time was a factor because the best time to meet a woman in a library was on Friday or Saturday night around 8. Anyone still sitting in a library at that hour didn't have a date and if you played your cards right, you could separate her from her books by 9:30. That left the entire evening and, in some lucky cases, the entire weekend. My problem was that I couldn't wait until Friday night. I needed to find a place to stay very quickly.

16

The only college I'd ever heard about in England –
besides Oxford and Cambridge – was the London School
of Economics, which meant I had no choice but to work
my Friday night routine there on a Monday morning.

Mrs Earl gave me directions.

It was easy talking my way in and, after pulling a
bunch of books off a shelf, I sat down at a strategically
well-placed table to see who I could find. I spoke with
a girl from New Hampshire who told me where the
student cafeteria was, how I could get a free meal and
that she had a boyfriend. I spoke with a girl from London
who told me she was studying for a masters and that she
lived at home. I spoke with a girl from Germany who
told me she thought English guys were cute, and when I
told her I wasn't English, she moved on to the next guy.
The next girl I met worked part time in the library and
kept wondering what I was studying. I told her I was a
big fan of John Maynard Keynes. She said she preferred
Karl Marx and that ended that.

The day wore on with no success. I gave up around 8
– by now the place was dead empty – went to the student
cafeteria, had a free dinner and walked back to Sussex
Gardens.

I returned to the LSE library the following day. But
Tuesday was no better.

On Wednesday, I met a French girl named Maryse
who told me that she had a Dutch girlfriend whose
name sounded like Yonkers who loved American guys.
But the girl whose name sounded like Yonkers turned
out to look like an American guy, so I passed.

On Thursday, I spent most of the morning reminding
myself that this would work, that there was no need to
panic – not yet anyway – that I still had three nights left
before I was on the street. But I struck out again.

My luck changed on Friday.

The moment she walked by the table where I'd
installed myself, I knew she was the one. I could tell.
I can always tell. I got a slightly nervous feeling, the

same one that used to crawl up inside my stomach when I'd sit in the main library at Johns Hopkins on a Friday night.

I watched her find a seat and waited until she got settled. Then I made my move. I chose the chair opposite hers, smiled shyly and engrossed myself in a very thick book.

It was someone called Anthony Trollope who'd written something called *The Way We Live Now*. I'd chosen it with care because it struck me as a typically British thing to do – toiling through some obscure author I'd never heard of. Except I was finding him unreadable. I can only blame too many teenaged summers spent trying to find the dirty pages in Harold Robbins.

For the next three hours I watched her whenever I could without making it seem too obvious. She worked steadily. I waited patiently. She was short, with long dark hair and wore no make-up. Her jeans were a little too tight for someone with thighs that were a little too big. But that was all right with me. She had that look in her eyes.

I assumed she was English, only because the odds were in favour of her being English. It would take years before I'd hear the expression English ankles. Had I known about it then, I would not have assumed she was English, I would have been positive.

"Fuck," she said.

I looked at her. "Excuse me, was that an exclamation or a question?"

"Fuck. An exclamation. As in, fuck, my pen just ran out of ink." She tossed her Bic onto the table and sat back, running her fingers through her hair. "Have you got a pen?"

I shrugged. "Sorry. I don't."

"How can you come to a library without a pen?"

"I came for the books."

She reached across the table to see what I was reading. "Trollope? Who bothers with Trollope any more?"

"Can't get enough of him." I wondered, "Is it high tea time yet?"

"Trollope and high tea? How long have you been in this place, 50 years?"

"More like 50 minutes."

"I don't want tea." She tried, "Got any grass?"

"No. You?"

She made a face. "I've only got one hit left."

Now it was my turn. "Enough for two?"

There was a long pause while she sized me up. "Sure, why not." And just like that she packed her books and stood up. I thanked Mr Trollope and left him sitting on the table.

Given enough time, I told myself, it never fails. "Where to?"

"Follow me."

I did, for several blocks and up three flights of stairs, to a small studio apartment which she referred to as her "digs". Once inside, she tossed her books on the floor next to the couch, pulled a scrawny little joint out of her dresser, lit it and took the first hit. Then she handed it to me. We got stoned together telling each other stupid jokes – like, how do you know when there's an elephant in the fridge? By the footprints in the cheesecake! And, how many Californians does it take to screw in a light bulb? Six. One to hold the bulb and five to share the experience.

She and I howled with laughter.

After a while she pulled out a bottle of wine.

By the time we finished that, we both knew we were going to get it on. I lifted her out of her clothes, took mine off too, and carried her onto the bed. Later she asked what my name was and I told her, Bay. She said hers was Fiona. I said, hi Fiona, and she said hi Bay, and then we started doing it again.

She was up early the next morning. I found her in the shower. "Not now," she said, pushing me away. "I've got a class."

"When?"

"Later."

"What are you doing for the weekend?"

She smiled. "You."

"Can I bring a change of clothes?"

"You won't need clothes."

I went to Mrs Earl's, checked out and was back at Fiona's for tea time. She found me sitting on the floor in front of her door.

"Fuck," she said.

I wondered, "Is that a question or an exclamation?"

She unlocked the door and motioned for me to come inside. "This time it's an invitation."

I stayed for a month.

For two people who had so little in common, we got on surprisingly well. It turned out she was from someplace called Lancashire, which I learned is south of Scotland. She was getting a masters at the LSE and didn't have a clue what she was going to do with it once she had it. She didn't want to teach. She didn't want to work for capitalists. She figured maybe she'd travel for a while – she wasn't sure whether she'd go to India or Iran first – and then, she thought, she might wind up in Hong Kong to learn Cantonese. I told her I was from Baltimore and had gone to Johns Hopkins. When she wondered what I was doing in London, I answered, "Hanging out." And that was, basically, the extent of our conversation for the entire month.

She had enough money that she wasn't bothered about keeping the place stocked with food for the two of us. She also had a decent, albeit sporadic, dope connection so that, every now and then, she could get some good stuff.

At one point, towards the end of our second week together, I decided to see if I could find some part-time work. I spent two days painting a local Indian restaurant – they paid me £5 a day and allowed me to take home dinner for the two of us. I'd never eaten Indian food and didn't much care for it. But Fiona loved it. Then, I got myself a job waiting tables over lunchtime in a pub called The Double Dutchman. They paid me £3 for four hours plus a pair of cottage pies which they said was my lunch. I brought them back to Fiona. She liked those too.

The third job I came up with while staying with Fiona was the best. It was a throwback to my own school days. I began taking exams for people and writing term papers. In two weeks, I sat exams in first-year economics and third-year political science. I also wrote papers on Adam Smith, the League of Nations and Harold Macmillan's agricultural policy. I'd put the going rate at £15 per exam, payable in advance – that was, admittedly, expensive but it was refundable in case of failure – and £12 a paper, payable in advance, non-refundable under any condition. In almost no time I earned nearly £70.

Because I was now meeting people at the LSE and eating regularly, I was starting to think about moving on from Fiona – trying to connect with someone who liked sex as much but drugs a little less – when one of her ex-boyfriends showed up.

That afternoon I'd picked up £35 from some guy, writing a double-length paper for him on Trotsky – Old Leon would have been proud to know that he was the object of an exercise in pure capitalism – and planned on inviting Fiona out for a meal to celebrate. But when I got to the apartment, I found a fellow in a long leather raincoat hammering both his fists on her door.

"Can I help you?"

He was as surprised to see me as I was to see him. "Doubt it," he replied, "you'd probably want to lead when we dance." He pounded again.

I suggested, "If she hasn't answered by now, maybe she isn't home yet . . ."

Just then the door flung open. "Did you forget . . ." Fiona looked at the guy standing there, then saw me two steps behind him. "Peter . . . Bay . . . Peter . . ."

He smiled at me. "She never could get her appointments straight. Men standing on the stairs waiting on Her Highness. It's exactly like *The Knack* in reverse."

"Hi," I waved to Fiona.

She berated him. "Peter . . . what are you doing here?"

He said, "I thought we'd celebrate."

"Wait a minute," I cut in. "That's what I was going to say." I told Fiona, "We're rich. I wanted us to go out for a meal."

"Peter . . ." She was very flustered. "What do you think you're doing here?"

"I told you, I wanted to celebrate." He turned towards me. "She's always been very emotional about reunions."

"I'm celebrating Trotsky Day," I announced. "You?"

"Our first anniversary," he explained. "She threw me out exactly one year ago today."

"For Christ's sake," Fiona exploded, "stop it." She moved away from the door and the two of us stepped inside.

"Mine's Peter Barry Goddard." He extended his hand.

"You're all three of those people?" I shook his hand. "I've only got two names. Bay Radisson."

He was taller than me, with short-cropped light hair and a very angular face. "Fiona's the best. How long have you been Mr Fiona? I lasted nearly seven weeks. A year ago today."

"Cut the shit," she snapped. "You were the one who walked out."

"No, luv, you threw me out. I specifically remember." From under his coat he produced a bottle of champagne. "I'd hoped to make amends but I see you're already making amends with someone else." He patted my shoulder. "Sometimes love hurts."

I didn't know what to do. "Listen Fiona, if you want to discuss . . ."

"Stay right where you are," she ordered. "Did you get the money for your paper?"

"Yes. That's why I thought maybe we'd go out to eat . . ."

"Wonderful," Peter said. "Fiona dear, get some glasses, we'll just have a little champers here and then the three of us can have a meal . . ." He uncorked the champagne. "See, it is indeed a celebration."

"Oh, fuck," Fiona muttered. And almost as if there wasn't anything else to do, she fetched three glasses.

We drank the champagne, then went in Peter's old Citroen 2CV to a cheap and cheerful place on the other side of town called The Ark. He bought a bottle of Spanish red – Fiona's mood slowly changed from anger to mild annoyance to careful amusement to outright giggles – and paid the whole bill for the three of us. "I made some money in frozen pork bellies," he disclosed.

"Sounds very appetizing," I said.

"It's easy when you know how." He reached into his jacket pocket and pulled out two joints. "Here? There? Anywhere?"

We went back to Fiona's and the three of us smoked Peter's grass. For a while we laughed. Then those two started talking about old times. Then Fiona began to get all misty. Peter opened another bottle of wine and I put my head in her lap. After a while, she leaned over and put her head in Peter's lap. With one hand she stroked the side of my face. Through the haze of all that smoke I could see she was rubbing the inside of Peter's thigh. As I felt her breathing increase – mine too – I slowly reached my hands under her sweater. She let me take it from her, then arched her back and kissed Peter. I pulled off the rest of her clothes. We smothered her with our mouths, the two of us fully dressed, Fiona totally naked. She was in no hurry – neither were we – but eventually she stood up and took our clothes off. Then she moved us to her bed where Peter and I shared her for the entire night.

The next morning, when I woke up – with Fiona

sound asleep on her stomach in between us — Peter's eyes were already open.

The bedding was on the floor.

I felt awkward and didn't know what to say.

He propped himself up on one elbow and started gently rubbing her bare ass. "Kind of makes us blood brothers."

It was the beginning of the most important friendship of my life.

Chapter Three

I moved out of Fiona's place and into Peter's shabbily camp, three-room, fifth-floor Bloomsbury walk-up. After I unpacked what few things I had, he and I sat up for the entire night, smoking dope, telling each other our life's story.

"Her name is Elizabeth," I began. And for the next hour I rambled on about how we met and how we parted and just about everything that happened in between. I told him things about her and me that I'd never told anyone before.

The very first thing he said when I finished was, "You should go back to her."

And right away I promised, "Someday I will."

Then he spoke to me about a girl named Barbara. "She died."

"How?"

"An accident."

"What kind of accident?"

He looked at me sadly, "The kind that isn't supposed to happen to the first person you ever love," then lay back on the floor and stared for a long time at the paint-cracked ceiling. "We were going to get rich."

I stretched out and stared at the ceiling too. "Rich is good."

"Rich is better than poor."

"Okay," I said, "so let's you and me get rich."

"Good idea. Let's get rich."

There was a long silence.

I wondered, "How do we do it?"

He said, "I once read a survey where they asked bankers and businessmen to think of one sure way of getting rich. A third of them answered, rob a bank. A quarter of them answered, marry it. A few said, choose your parents well. The rest said stuff like, win the pools. Only a very small percentage answered, work hard for it."

"I don't think I'd be very good at robbing banks," I admitted. "So okay, I'll go for the marrying it category."

"Sounds good to me."

There was another long pause until I asked, "What do we do in the meantime?"

He shrugged, "Beats me."

I wondered, "Working for it?"

"Nah." He made a face. "Marrying it is better."

"But you work." I started to say it as a statement, then changed it to a question, "Don't you?"

"Of course." He feigned insult. "I work very hard, as it happens. I'm trying to learn how to become a gentleman of independent means."

"Any luck?"

He paused for a moment. "Well . . . it's true that I happen to find myself financially embarrassed from time to time. Which reminds me, as long as you're going to live in the spare room, I'll only charge you £6 a week."

I pointed out, "I don't have £6 a week."

"If you can't afford to pay £6 a week, I might as well charge you £12 a week."

"It's a deal," I said. "With your unmistakable financial skills and my charm, we should be getting rich very quick."

"I inherited most of my repertoire from my old man. That and a 1939 Jaguar coupé which never had any doors."

"Why didn't it have any doors?"

"What kind of a question is that?"

"Sounds perfectly rational to me. I mean, why would anyone buy a car without any doors?"

"He didn't buy it. He won it in a bet. It was particularly significant because it was one of the few bets he ever won. It was also his prize possession. When he went broke, the only thing he wanted to keep was the car. He fought so hard that the bailiffs finally said he could have it. They took the house instead because that did have doors."

"Where's the car now?"

Peter mumbled, "Kind of disappeared."

"Did he sell it?"

"No. I told you. I inherited it."

"So what did you do with it?"

He hesitated, then confessed, "I buried him in it."

"You did what?"

"I buried him in it." He said, "What the hell, I couldn't afford to get any doors for it either."

I sat up on my elbows to gape at him. "You buried your father in a car?"

He sat up on his elbows and forced a smile. "Dead, you know."

"Can you do that?"

"Can I? I did. He loved that car. It was the least I could do."

"What did the people who came to the funeral say?"

"What people? What funeral?"

"What do you mean, what people, what funeral? When you bury someone, that's a funeral."

"We didn't have a funeral. It was just me, my old man and two grave-diggers. And all they said was, hey look at that, a 1939 Jaguar coupé. Where are the doors?"

I didn't know what to say.

Peter finally broke the silence. "He was the most logical man I ever knew. He was a horse player. Which might strike you as being totally illogical. But while standing around betting shops, growing old and shabby in the middle of a blue smoke haze, rubbing elbows with rummies who pissed away their unemployment money and drank their winnings, out of that he developed the Goddard Doctrine."

"The Goddard Doctrine?"

He nodded. "Fundamentals to live by."

"Such as?"

"Such as . . . Class A horses can logically be expected to win Class C races. Class A horses in Class C races can logically be expected to carry the shortest odds. Therefore, never bet on a Class A horse in a Class C race that isn't the odds-on-favourite, unless the owner and the trainer and the jockey have staked their life savings, mortgage and kids' education on him too."

I had to know, "What does that mean?"

"It means that my father had logically concluded, the only sure way to make money is to wait until the race is over, then bet on the winner."

Philosophically, I muttered, "If only . . ."

"No," Peter interrupted with enormous confidence, "Whenever."

"Who takes bets once the race is over?"

"People who don't know when the race started."

As it turned out, that's how Peter was earning his living. Not at the race track but in the commodities futures market, betting only on the winners.

The way he explained it, he was occasionally sleeping with a girl named Tricia who worked for a mildly crooked broker named Norman. One night, she'd described to him how Norman earned lots of money by holding back for just a couple of minutes on a few orders from a few players.

Say a big client wanted to buy $10 million worth of sugar contracts. The first thing Norman did was raid a few of his clients' discretionary accounts and sell some sugar contracts. He might hit ten clients for $10,000 each. A small enough amount to go unnoticed. Then he'd come into the market with the $10 million order. A buy like that might send sugar prices up a few pennies. The instant that it did, if it did, he'd buy back the $100,000 worth of contracts for those ten discretionary accounts. If the market kept going up, that was fine and his clients stayed happy. Most of the time, though, his clients never knew that Norman had traded in and out like that, except, of course, that Norman took his commission on the trades. Norman also kept the difference between the selling price before the big player came in and the buying back price after he'd come in.

Because Tricia had somehow been led to believe that she and Peter might be developing a meaningful relationship – that's what it was called, in those days, when a woman thought a guy was interested in her mind, too – every now and then, when Norman was doing one of these deals, she bought and sold with him for Peter's account. He had to guarantee to put up 10% of the contract value if something went wrong – which he readily agreed to do, even though he couldn't afford to pay up – but, after the first two or three trades on the back of Norman's greed, his own account with the firm had enough in it to provide a little cushion.

"If she loses it for me," he said, "I guess I get wiped out. Except we're betting on the winners so I figure the only way I can lose is if I get caught in bed with her best friend." Now a broad grin swept across his face. "Actually, you might like her best friend."

"Does it get me a trading account with Norman too?"

"We should be able to arrange that." And he did.

Tricia's best friend was called Cecily and, because I spent the next six months being nice to Cecily, Tricia cut me in on Peter's game. He and I didn't earn a lot of money being nice to Tricia and Cecily, but it gave us something to do, it put food in the fridge and it provided us with a little stake on which to base our future.

Complementing my introduction to the world of

commodities, I reinstalled myself at the LSE library, this time to read everything I could about how markets work. One of the things that quickly caught my eye was the price discrepancy that frequently arises for the same commodity in different parts of the world.

The text books call it arbitrage.

During the dark ages of the unregulated early '70s, there was often a sizeable time lapse before prices around the world adjusted to heavy selling in one market or heavy buying in another. It was a very big window that many people jumped out of, without ever having taken time to notice that they were on the 53rd floor. But I soon came to realize that if you waited for your moment – especially knowing a few seconds in advance when one of the major players was coming in to buy or to sell – that when you hurled yourself out the window, there'd be a great big balcony to land on.

To play this game looking like true professionals – despite our raw amateur status – Peter and I bought a shell company from a broker in the Isle of Man called Amalgamated Finance Management, Ltd. We changed the name to AFM, and decided it should stand for "Another Fine Mess", in honour of Stan Laurel and Oliver Hardy. We even had stationery printed with a bowler hat logo, which we thought was hilarious. Next, we got Norman to open an account for AFM with a broker in New York. We then paid the telephone company a fortune – several hundred pounds seemed like a king's ransom to us in those days – to install two more lines in Peter's flat. Every afternoon, around 2:30 London time, he'd get on one phone and I'd get on the other and we'd start checking prices in the two markets. Most of the time there was nothing happening and all we managed to accomplish was to run up our phone bill. But every now and then we'd hook something. Like the compleat anglers we were fast trying to become, one of us would buy while the other sold.

It was slow and painful but through sheer persistence

we began to squeeze small profits out of very narrow margins.

When the girls accused Peter and me of only dating them for their inside information, Peter tried to make a joke that we cared about all of their insides. But they weren't amused. So he broke off with Tricia and I spent one last night with Cecily.

The following day, just to prove to them that they'd made a terrible mistake in ditching us, we took our trading account away from Norman.

Once I'd settled into life at Peter's, I phoned my parents to tell them I was okay. My father was so angry with me that he hung up on me and my mother was so upset that all she did was cry.

I was sorry I'd made the call.

I then thought about ringing Elizabeth, but I couldn't face another scene, so I sat down to write her a long letter. In it, I told her that I loved her and that I was sorry I'd walked out on her and that one day everything would be all right. I asked her to forgive me. I asked her to wait for me.

I never got an answer.

Checking the mail every morning was hell. I'd race down all those stairs and sort through all the envelopes that the postman shoved through the door for everyone in the building. And every morning I'd climb back upstairs, dejected, trying to convince myself that the next day would be different.

I suffered for a week, then two weeks, then a month, then two months. I finally made myself believe that my letter to her had gotten lost in the mail and so I wrote another one. This time I told her that she had touched my life in a way no other human being had and that, no matter what, I would always love her.

Again, every morning, I raced down the stairs. And again, I spent two months climbing back up disheartened, telling myself that she would write.

After two more months of tormenting silence, I plucked up my courage to phone her. I'd decided that, instead of saying hello, the moment she got on the line I was simply going to say, "Please come to London." So I dialled her number and it rang several times, until a man answered.

That startled me.

I stammered, "Is . . . is Elizabeth there?"

He said, "No, but I'm expecting her home soon."

I wasn't sure if that meant her home or their home. I had no idea who he was and I couldn't bring myself to ask. The best I could do was, "No message . . . thank you . . . goodbye . . . I'll call back later . . ."

I spent the rest of the night, and the rest of the week and the rest of the month angry with myself, repeating the promise I'd made to Peter. "Someday I will."

And each morning for the rest of the week and the rest of the month I woke up fearing that, like so many promises I'd made throughout my first 20 years, this one too would go unfulfilled.

Before long, Peter took up with a girl named Phyllis, who worked at the Stock Exchange. There wasn't anybody in my life, so I tagged along, ever the reliable odd one out. While he soon started complaining that Phyllis only ever wanted to have sex in the morning – he told me there was something weird about nighttime that made her viciously nasty and something weird about dawn that made her voraciously wanton – I was trying to forget Elizabeth by learning how the share markets work.

When the secondary banking crisis hit, Edward Heath's government caved in. The Labour Party came back to power and, with it, a pipe-smoking prime minister named Harold Wilson.

Almost immediately, he and his pals wreaked havoc with their misguided efforts to tax the spots off the rich. But the chaos they created made for massive uncertainty in the markets and in confusion there is profit.

We'd grown more and more confident in our arbitrage game over those first few years and found ourselves playing for bigger and bigger stakes. And even if we didn't win every time out, thanks largely to the Labour Party's gross ineptitude we found ourselves winning more than we lost.

Peter and Phyllis split up after six or seven months because, he said, his nerves could no longer stand her nighttime rejections and overzealous morning obsessions. But she and I stayed in touch for a while – in a mutually weak moment, we even had a little fling – until she married a stockbroker, moved to Surrey and began greeting the day by punching out kids. She once promised that she would always remember those four mornings we spent together in the Lake District. And, although I didn't say it, I would always remember her too – not just for the nickname I gave her, "The Dawn Patrol" – but because she was the one who opened my eyes to the fact that, on the London Stock Exchange, accounting periods run two weeks.

It was a licence to print money.

For the purpose of pragmatic bookkeeping, the buying and selling of shares had long ago been divided into fortnightly segments. If you bought on Monday the first – the beginning of the accounting period – you weren't billed until Friday the 12th, which was the end of the accounting period. And then, payment wasn't due for another week, that is, until Friday the 19th. It meant that if you could buy low at the start of an accounting period and sell for a lot more before it ended, without putting up so much as a farthing, the difference was pure profit.

Next, I learned that you could frequently buy on the preceding Thursday or Friday for the new account, which gave you an additional couple of days.

Even better, there was a way to extend the trading period beyond the end of the account, which came in handy when my timing was off. It was called "cash and new" and it meant that I could delay paying for the shares by pushing the deal into the next trading period, simply by sending the broker a cheque for his commission.

Getting my timing right was extremely difficult – it took a pile of reading and a hefty amount of guessing – but every now and then I pulled it off. The first time it worked was with a company called General Traffic. I'd bought 200,000 shares at 14p and sold them ten days later at 18p. We walked away with an £8,000 gross profit.

With my mother's voice ringing constantly in my ears – always put something aside for a rainy day – I shoved most of that money into the bank, as a back-up for whenever my timing was off, which happened often. But then I caught GEC on a wave and made 6p on 220,000 shares and a few months later watched Great Universal Stores take off on a 7p jump while I was holding 180,000 shares. It doesn't seem like a lot of money these days. But it was a helluva lot more than we had before either of us discovered the joys of Phyllis in the morning.

As long as the Labour government seemed so keenly intent on being a pain in the ass, Peter decided we needed a better-structured holding company to keep our money away from them.

And as long as that winter was so filthy, we concluded that the best place to buy a company was somewhere warm, like the Bahamas.

We left London in a snow storm, flying to Nassau first class – thank you Mr Wilson – and for the first few days we did nothing more than sit on the beach, thinking about rum, fruit and life.

It was the closest I'd been to American shores since I'd left the country and every time I looked west, across the expanse of water, I thought about Elizabeth. When I finally admitted to Peter that she was on my mind, he pointed to the phone and said, "You might as well get it over with. Do it now or we'll miss dinner."

I phoned her. But the number didn't work. I checked with information. But she wasn't listed.

"Now you know," Peter said. "She's married."

"I guess." I tried to sound casual about it. "I hope she's happy." But I could see that I wasn't fooling him, so I stopped fooling myself and called my parents, hoping my mother might know where Elizabeth was.

My father answered and we talked, in a stilted way, for a few minutes. It was still painful for him to accept my fugitive status and he urged me to come home. I said I couldn't. He said, "Well then, the hell with you," and passed the phone to my mother. She got on the line and told me he hadn't been well. I asked her if they needed anything. She said no. I asked her if I could send them something, or buy something for them. She said no. Then I asked her if she knew where Elizabeth was. She said, "I heard she got married."

When I hung up I told Peter, "I feel like such a failure. They won't let me do anything for them. And it's too late to do anything for Elizabeth."

"Well then," he said, "maybe you should start doing something for you."

I asked sarcastically, "Any bright ideas?"

He walked to the door of our suite. "How about getting down off your cross just in case someone else needs the wood."

With that he left me to sulk alone – to spend the rest of the day sitting on the balcony staring out at the ocean.

I guess it's true that we don't choose the people we love any more than we choose the dreams we have. That love, like dreams, imposes itself. And even if I have since told other women that I have loved them – there have only been a few – Elizabeth was the first woman I ever said it to. Which is why, in my mind, when I said it to her it meant the most.

I will forever wonder what might have been.

*   *   *

The next morning Peter and I started knocking on doors. Behind one of them we discovered an elegant black man in a mustard-yellow suit, 20 years our senior, sporting the name Roderick Hays-White.

He greeted us in his reception area – where the walls were covered with hundreds of cane-wood framed incorporation certificates – introduced himself, introduced his secretary and handed us his card. It read, "Company Director". So we handed him our AFM bowler-hatted card.

Roderick was the only person ever to get the joke.

He roared with laughter, said, "Follow me," and led us into his private office where, behind his desk, hung a huge gold frame with an original poster from Laurel and Hardy's masterpiece, *Big Business*.

"Now turn around," he said.

The wall facing his desk was decorated with 100 bowler hats.

"I do believe," he bowed, "that we have something in common."

We've been in business with him ever since.

That same afternoon, Roderick incorporated a company for us called Tivoli Court Trading. He folded AFM into that company and then set up a UK-based shell for us called Pennstreet. Next, he backed Tivoli Court Trading into Pennstreet so that we could keep everything we earned away from Mr Wilson and his Chancellor, Mr Callaghan. Over the years, he's continued to spread our assets throughout a tangled web of two dozen companies and private trusts.

Thanks in large part to Roderick – who put us in a position where we could make real money – Peter and I slowly worked our way out of the bush leagues.

Timing might not be everything in life, but it plays a big part.

On our first outing – hidden behind our new-look, tax-efficient duck blind – we took aim at a company called Slater Walker, one of the original conglomerates of the 1960s. I started buying and selling within the accounting period in January 1975 when the shares were at 35p. Beginning with a block of 150,000, I was soon playing with as many as 800,000 at any given time. By March, the Slater Walker share price had nearly tripled.

Mildly put, the market had gone berserk.

One day I bought 375,000 shares, watched the price shoot up 20p and sold that same afternoon. Another time I bought 225,000 shares on a Tuesday just before lunch and sold them on Thursday just after lunch at a 15p profit. In all, over that eight to ten week stretch, we averaged around 24p net profit on the total movement of something close to 2.8 million shares. I couldn't believe how easy it was.

That's when my father died of lung cancer. He was 58.

I thought he'd quit smoking but I guess I was wrong. He was still so angry with me for having left the United States that he'd forbidden my mother or my sister to tell me how ill he was. I don't know what I could have done about it even if I'd known, but I wish now I had. My mother phoned to break the news. The toughest thing was telling her that if I came home for the funeral I'd be arrested. She pretended to understand.

When I hung up, I started to cry. I cried for three days – for him and for her and for me, too.

Four weeks later my mom passed away in her sleep. She was 57.

My sister said she'd died of a broken heart. Sandy said mom had simply been unable to survive without my dad. I told her I couldn't come home for that funeral either. Sandy's husband swore he'd never speak to me again. I mumbled, "Every cloud has its silver lining," hung up, went back to my place and cried for another three days.

Except for Peter – who did the best he could under

the circumstances – I didn't have anyone to turn to. The one person I wanted to hold me – the person I needed the most – was married to someone else. And I didn't even know her married name.

In April 1976, Wilson stepped down and Jim Callaghan took his place. That fall, we scored again with Slater Walker. By then, the bubble had burst and the company's shares had tumbled to 16p. Peter's girlfriend at the time was an accountant who worked for either Price Waterhouse or Peat Marwick, I can't remember which, but one night she told him about a damning report that was about to be published on Slater Walker. The following day, we sold two million shares. Two days later, the report came out and Slater Walker's share price was sliced in half. We bought back our shares at just under 9p. After commissions, we were looking at nearly £130,000.

In November of that year, a peanut farmer from Plains, Georgia, got himself elected President of the United States. One of his campaign promises had been to offer a general amnesty to all draft dodgers. True to his word, Jimmy Carter was sworn in on the steps of the Capitol on 20 January 1977 and, the very next day, he made good on that pledge. He put his signature on the bottom of a single sheet of paper and, just like that, I was a free man. I could go home.

Except, I had no one to go home to.

Somewhere in the middle of all this, Peter and I decided we had to look more respectable, so we set out to hire a secretary. Our want-ad read: "Two young businessmen need one experienced, not-so-young secretary, willing to work very hard for very little." The first person to answer it was a 28-year-old, black, single mother from Brixton named Patty Rowlands who showed up for her interview carrying her three-year-old son, Monroe. I asked her if she could type and she said, "With four fingers." I asked her if she could file and she said, "Even a dim-wit can file." I asked her why she wanted the job and she said, "Because I need the money." I'd never hired anyone before and that struck me as the perfect answer. I told her, "Okay, you've got the job." And for the first two years she was with us, Monroe came to the office every morning too.

It was clear that we were on a roll, so Peter bought a place in Chelsea and I did as well – property prices were terribly depressed – and, once we discovered the joys of real estate, we put a little of our stake into a small, three-storey office building in Covent Garden. In those days, nobody wanted to be there. Except us. Peter liked it because we were only two blocks from the stage door of the Opera House where he expected to meet ballerinas. I liked it because the morning market was very colourful, there were some decent little restaurants in the neighbourhood and because I'd seen *My Fair Lady* with Elizabeth.

Shortly after we moved into the top-floor suite of offices, we bought a 78-year lease on a small two-bedroomed flat in Notting Hill Gate, in West London, which Patty thought was going to be used as a *pied-à-terre* for our clients. As soon as we had the deeds and the keys, I reminded her, "We don't have any clients," and handed them to her. "This is for you and Monroe."

A year later, she announced she was going to marry the man upstairs, Wendell West, a widower from Jamaica with three kids of his own. Peter and I teased her mercilessly about what had been going on in the stairwell for the past 12 months. As a wedding present, we gave her the clear title to the place. We also paid for a contractor to break through the walls, turning their two flats into a really big duplex. She responded by insisting that both Peter and I walk her down the aisle.

I stayed in Britain, an eye-witness to the Callaghan years, because everybody has to live somewhere.

Aghast, I watched as Big Jim reeled from disaster to disaster. He managed to screw things up so badly that, in 1979, the country fired him and brought Margaret Thatcher to power. But then, those were great years for us. Not only did all of this political upheaval create sufficient confusion in the markets to make money, now, suddenly – thanks entirely to Mrs Thatcher – making money was no longer a cardinal sin.

Our record success with Slater Walker was quickly outdone when we heard about a company called Polly Peck. Run by a Turkish Cypriot entrepreneur named Asil Nadir, Polly Peck's shares went – with breathtaking speed – from 5p to 8p to 35p to £8. From there the price eventually made its way to £10, then to £12. It stopped to pause at £20 before galloping to £35. There was no rational reason for such an explosive surge. The company kept reporting swelling profits. But this had less to do with end-of-the-year figures than with speculators gone absolutely wild.

Peter and I did our bit to add to the euphoria and, for a time, we were nearly £8 million ahead in real money and almost twice that on paper. Getting rich on Polly Peck options was like knocking off a bowlful of goldfish with a shotgun. Except that, like many people, we got caught being a little too greedy and lost a big chunk of it when the shares dropped back to £22. They eventually split ten for one and it looked as if the race was on again. However, we had enough sense to beat a retreat – we were nursing singed fingers – content to take a greatly reduced average profit of 42p on an overall movement of 8.3 million shares.

Anyway, by this point – in the early '80s, with Britain in a new mode – I'd concluded that the best way to make real money was to take a few hints from the US.

Guys in the States like the Texan tycoon T. Boone Pickens were making fortunes with little more than sheer bravado. It was called "greenmail". In late autumn 1983, he and a consortium of friends picked up 21.7 million shares of Gulf Oil at $45. Almost immediately, he announced his intention to take over the company, fire the board and run things himself. The board panicked, Pickens unloaded at $80 and netted a profit of $760 million.

So too the British-born Jimmy Goldsmith. He went after the American paper, energy and insurance group St Regis and together with three financier friends – Australia's Kerry Packer, Italy's Gianni Agnelli and England's Jacob Rothschild – he sent the St Regis board into such a state of trepidation that, within a few weeks, they'd turned the consortium's $100 million stake into $150 million.

In my mind, if greenmail was good enough for them, greenmail was good enough for us. Except, of course, no one trembled at the thought of Goddard and Radisson storming into a boardroom. So when Pickens went after Gulf, we started buying shares in a small Dutch refinery called Rotterdam-Henk. Rumours spread that T. Boone was everywhere – it didn't take us long before we got very good at kindling rumours – and those shares went from 14 guilders to 24 guilders, which is where we got out. When Goldsmith went into timber, we found a Canadian company called Brentwood Woods and started buying shares through a purpose-built Caribbean shell. For some reason, the Canadian press came to believe this was another of Jimmy's takeovers. The shares shot up from $2.75 to $9. And we sold.

We dabbled in some newspaper shares, letting the markets think that Rupert Murdoch was interested. We dabbled in a brick company, spreading rumours that it was James Hanson and Gordon White who were about to pounce. And we dabbled in some property, never bothering to deny the rumours that the big players behind the purported take over were really the Toronto-based Reichmann Brothers.

Some of the time, it worked. When it did, shares rose accordingly, we'd take a few points and get out with a neat profit. When it didn't, we'd cut our losses and run for our lives.

Once or twice we got too cocky, like the time we started buying Smith Corona shares on the New York exchange – we had more chips on the table than we could ever have afforded to lose – and tried to make the markets think the predator was Robert Holmes a'Court from Australia. No one believed us and we had to bail out in a hurry. A few months later, Hanson Trust, led by Gordon White, came barging into the market and ran Smith Corona's prices into the stratosphere.

That was the monster that got away. And, like all weary fishermen, I still think about it. Had Peter and I gotten it right, we could have retired in tawdry luxury for the rest of our lives.

Then there was the time Peter was dating a gal who worked for the Press Association. She let it slip that Tiny Rowland at Lonrho was about to unload his stake in House of Fraser, the department store chain that owns Harrods. He'd been building a position for years and, according to her, had grown bored with it. So we sold short, unloading a sizeable block, and spread the word that it was Lonrho doing the selling. I should have known something was wrong when our selling didn't affect the share price by more than a penny. Two days later Tiny fired the opening salvo in what turned out to be a bitter, and unsuccessful, battle for Harrods with the Egyptian Al-Fayed brothers. House of Fraser shares soared and, even though I managed to get us out very quickly, we took a major hit. It then emerged that this particular lady journalist had a flat-mate who fancied Peter. The week before, in the middle of the night, Mademoiselle Flat-mate arrived at Peter's, stripped off in the hallway, tied herself in a red ribbon and banged on the door. Naturally, Peter accepted the gift – he insisted it would have been rude to do otherwise – never thinking that Miss Press Association might someday hear about it. When she did, she threw a sucker punch which landed squarely on Peter's – and my – bank book.

However, it wasn't until we pretended to be Bob

Maxwell that we decided we'd finally found our niche in life.

We launched a dawn raid on a printing company in Edinburgh, our rumour hit that it was Captain Bob, the shares jumped 60% before lunch and we got out that same day. The following morning, those same shares nose dived below the price they'd been 24 hours before, so we hit again. This time the market was a little more sceptical, but we still made 22% by tea time.

Next, we went after a property company with real estate along Fleet Street. The markets again believed it was Captain Bob and we racked up a neat 30% in four days.

Then there was the time when Maxwell met Tiny Rowland with an eye towards buying the Observer Newspaper group. We sold Lonrho short, went long on Express Newspapers and put the word about that the Observer deal wouldn't happen but that the Express Group was his next target.

Spinning rumours about companies of that size was very difficult. Still, we put a lot of chips on the table and let the wheel turn. Lonrho's shares dropped a few points and Express shares went up a few points and we slid through with a narrow margin on a great deal of money. We even managed to keep it within the two-week accounting period.

I immediately realized how extremely lucky we had to be to get away with it. It was much too much like gambling and I don't like gambling. By nature I'm a poor loser. So after that we deliberately dropped back and went for smaller fish.

In all, we did our Bob Maxwell act eight times. Nobody wanted him on their board and the mere thought of Maxwell taking over a company left certain corporate chairmen quaking in their Swiss-made Ballys. The only time we nearly got caught was when we tried to buy into Waddingtons, the game and toy manufacturer.

We started buying before he did, sent word out in the usual way that it was Maxwell and two days later Maxwell actually came into the market to try to take them over. Peter wanted to sell and run, but I said no, we couldn't because, if we unloaded all the shares that some people thought were Maxwell's and he was still in, they'd start wondering who the hell was screwing around with the share price. So we sat there, until the chairman of Waddingtons found Maxwell's Achilles' heel – Captain Bob refused to divulge any information about his Liechtenstein trusts – and the bid crumbled. We got out just before he did and, although we made some money on that one, it wasn't anywhere near as much as we would have made had Robert Maxwell not pretended to be himself at the same time we were pretending to be him.

Chapter Four

The entire country saw Captain Bob get buried on *News at Ten*. His funeral was the lead story that night. It was on the front page of every paper in the country the next morning. And yet many people still worried that, even in death, he had some sort of gimmick up his sleeve.

The joke going around was, don't libel the son-of-a-bitch just in case he too comes back after three days.

When he didn't rise again to stalk the earth for another 40, editorials took the tone that Britain had lost a great character. Sure he was brash, rude, impudent, audacious, brazen, erratic, volatile, frequently obnoxious and predictably difficult. But, they wrote, the City was slightly poorer for his final flotation.

No one at the time saw any irony in the words "slightly poorer".

Beatification turned out to be a non-starter. His empire crumbled – caved in exactly like a house of cards – and his image decayed faster than his flesh. The truth got out that he was a horrendous crook – he must have known it would – and now it was rare to find anyone who wasn't crowing, I knew it all the time.

The joke going around was, when they fished his body out of the ocean, one of the rescue workers spotted dorsal fins circling nearby and wondered how come the sharks hadn't eaten him. The answer was, of course, professional courtesy.

It's academic whether he jumped or he fell or he was

pushed off his boat. Although, had I been a political cartoonist, I would have drawn a picture of the police interviewing the entire crew on the deck of the yacht. I'd have drawn a long line of people, standing at attention, waiting to be questioned – from the captain in his sparkling white uniform to the maids in their frilly costumes – and at the end of the line, I'd have sketched a man in a wet suit with a face mask.

We'd long since convinced ourselves that, if Maxwell ever found out we were so boldly using his name in vain, he'd do one of three things – he'd fall on the floor laughing, or he'd sue us, or he'd fall on the floor laughing and then sue us. So when Patty came in one morning to say Captain Bob himself was on the phone, I was certain our gig was up.

I put on my most reserved voice. "How do you do."

"Will you come to see me." It was difficult to know if he was asking or demanding.

"I'd be delighted," I fibbed. "Is there something I can do for you?"

"It's what I can do for you," he said.

Naked benevolence being, almost always, a one-way street, I wondered, "Are you buying or selling?"

"What I like about Americans is how they get straight to the point. In this case, I'm buying and you're selling."

"Gee, you're pretty good at getting right to the point too, and you're not even American."

"I'm Czech," he said. "We built America."

That took some thought. "I can't recall how many Czechs signed the Declaration of Independence."

He laughed, "My office, tomorrow at 10," and hung up.

When I repeated the conversation to Peter, he warned, "After shaking hands with him, count your fingers."

Arriving at Maxwell House by five to ten, I was duly escorted up to the top floor and directed to a couch in a large waiting area. A tea-lady came by and asked if I wanted something. I said, "As this is Maxwell House, coffee will be fine." She clearly didn't get the joke and served Sanka.

At 10:10 I checked my watch and mumbled, "Fashionably late."

At 10:20 I remarked, "Rude."

At 10:30, when there was still no sign of him, I got up and walked over to the secretary's desk. "My appointment was for half an hour ago."

She nodded politely and said that he would be with me shortly.

At that point a very nervous young man in an ill-fitting blue serge suit arrived, checked in with the secretary and was instructed to take a seat. Oblivious to my presence, he sat where he'd been told to, crossed and uncrossed his legs non-stop and talked to himself. Deep in one-sided conversation, he pointed fingers to reassure his invisible audience that he was serious about this, fiercely mouthing words, although no sound came out. His left thigh slapped down on his right thigh. He banged on his knee to make a point. Then he uncrossed his legs and shifted them, slamming the right one on top of the left one.

I tried to find a tune to hum to keep up with his oddly choreographed dance, and settled on "Chicken in the Straw". It fit perfectly. Then, I tried to guess who he was and what he was doing there. Something about him made me think, accountant. Either neon affects skin tones or they all go to the same barber.

He couldn't have been much older than 23. There was a very shiny wedding ring on the fourth finger of his left hand – he fidgeted with it as if it was uncomfortable – so I surmised it was new.

I decided he was new as well.

My conclusion was, here's a young, recently married accountant, who'd just been hired by Maxwell as an assistant at – I picked something easy – a printing works

47

up north. This, therefore, was his initial meeting with the chairman.

Now his speech made sense.

Sir, I want you to know that I will do you proud and that within five years you can expect to find me on your main board.

It was the speech he'd rehearsed the night before, in bed with his bride.

I'm going to reassure the chairman that I'm his future, that I'll earn my way onto his board because I'm what's happening.

And all the time, propped up on Laura Ashley pillows, she coo-ed for the dynamic man who would someday father her children.

I thought about saying to him, it's going to be fine, don't worry. But now it was 10:40 and I'd waited long enough. I strolled back to the secretary and whispered, "*He* called *me*. In two minutes I'm outta here."

She said, "Yes sir."

That's when the door behind her desk opened and Maxwell appeared. He acknowledged my presence with a nod, then strolled up to the young man who was somewhere in the middle of his soliloquy.

As the portly Captain Bob closed in on his prey, the newly hired, newly married, newly rehearsed accountant shot to attention.

Easily able to intimidate weaker men with his ungainly form, Maxwell towered over the flustered bridegroom, put a finger in his chest and didn't so much speak with him, as lecture him. I couldn't hear everything he was saying – his back was to me – but it sounded as if he was telling the young man that he expected body and soul.

The poor kid never got a word in.

Two minutes later, Maxwell grabbed his hand, shook it brusquely, said, "Thank you for coming to see me," turned and was gone.

Later that night, the kid would perjure himself to his bride-in-Ashley – I gave him a piece of my mind, I did –

and, while she lay there prone, waiting for him, he would secretly plot revenge on the maniacal castrator.

As I was ushered in I reminded him, "You said 10 o'clock British time, not 10 o'clock Czech time."

He put his arm around me, as if we'd been pals for years, and half dragged me onto the huge balcony at the side of his office. "I want to show you something." He pointed down towards Liverpool Street Station. "See that? Trains are moving."

I didn't get it.

Then he swung me around and pointed up towards the sky.

I feared that he was going to say, planes are flying. Instead he came out with, "I'm going to put a weather vane up there. Just like you do in New York."

"I'm from Baltimore."

"If they do it in New York, they do it in Baltimore. That's what I'm going to do here. A weather vane and a clock, so that everyone in the City of London will know the time and the temperature, just like you do in New York."

"Baltimore," I corrected.

It was as if he didn't care about anything I said. "You and I have a lot in common."

I shuddered at the thought. "Weather vanes, Baltimore and the Declaration of Independence?"

"Exactly right." His arm still hung heavily on my shoulder, father-son style. "Neither one of us is British and yet we've both conquered this country." He stopped, then added as an after thought, "In our own way, of course."

"Of course."

"That's why I like you. We're cut from the same mould. Immigrants who have taught the British a thing or two."

"We sure have," I nodded, thinking it was easier to agree with him than ask what the hell he was babbling about. "You said on the phone that you're buying and I'm selling. . ."

"For the moment," he pulled me back into his office, "I'm buying. Coffee? Tea? Cold? Hard? Soft? Anything you like."

He sat me down in an ersatz red leather chair facing his ersatz mahogany desk. All the furniture in the room looked to me as if it had come straight out of a bankrupt hotel. One entire wall of his office was lined with books, none of which appeared to have been read. Behind me, on another wall, were photos of him with everyone imaginable – the Queen, the Prince of Wales, the Duke of Edinburgh, four prime ministers and hordes of foreign leaders – some of them highly suspect, like Erich Honecker of East Germany.

I pointed to the one with the Queen and was very tempted to say what I always say whenever I'm confronted with such vanity. I wanted to ask, do you think she has the same picture in her office? But something told me it would be wasted on him. God only knows, he might have insisted she did. So I came out with the rather dumb line, "You must meet a lot of famous people."

Over the next several minutes he proceeded to list the famous people he'd already met that week. He finished with, "And now there's you."

I reminded him, "But we haven't been photographed together for my office, so it doesn't count. Yet."

"I have my own photographer." Maxwell and I were on totally different wave lengths. "He's on call 24 hours a day. I'll ring him and we'll arrange a photo for your office."

"Let's wait for the signing," I suggested. "That is, as long as you're buying and, it goes without saying, that the price is right."

"I am buying," He fell into his ersatz red leather high backed chair. "And the price will be right."

"Just what is it that I'm selling?"

"Your shares in Chronicle's Union."

50

I stared at him for a couple of seconds. "Chronicle's Union, huh?"

"I want all the shares you've got. No publicity. Just a private deal between us."

"Hmmmm." I didn't want to admit that I'd never heard of Chronicle's Union. "What kind of money are we talking about?"

"They're trading at 65p," he said. "They're worth maybe 70p. I'll pay you 80p."

"That's generous."

"My generosity is only on the table today."

I nodded several times, to show him I was seriously considering his offer. "And you'll take everything I've got at 80p?"

He stood up, signalling the end of the meeting. "I'll pay 80p for up to five million shares."

"And over five million?"

"You're holding more than five million?"

I merely grinned. "And for anything over five million?"

Perhaps thinking I'd outfoxed him with some secret offshore trust, he snapped, "82½"

"You understand that I have to consult my partner."

"And you understand that the offer will be withdrawn at the close of the market tonight."

"I'll ring you with the word one way or the other this afternoon."

"You see," he said, grabbing my hand with his huge paw and shaking it, "we are cut from the same mould."

"We built America," I winked.

He kept slapping my back, all the way to the door.

Phoning Adrian from the car on the way back to my office, I needed to know, "What's Chronicle's Union?"

He answered, "I give up, what's Chronicle's Union?"

"Can you look it up for me?"

"It's not something we follow. Hold on." He came back a minute later. "Turns out to be a newsprint wholesalers in Wales. They've also got a small fleet of vans for newspaper and magazine distribution. It's nothing."

"Fax me whatever you can, please. Right away. And find out how many shares are around. Thanks."

Peter was reading the fax when I stepped into the office. "You and Captain Bob fall in love?"

"It was surreal. He put his arms around me. I mean, he hugged me."

"He wants you."

"Not quite. He wants our chunk of Chronicle's Union."

"This stuff?" He handed me the four pages Adrian had sent. "What chunk?"

"The chunk he thinks we own."

According to Adrian, the only interesting thing about Chronicle's Union was that the fellow who started it was married to a French woman whose family owned a printing works outside Paris called *L'Imprimerie des Hebdos d'Ile de France*. For whatever reason, her shares in the family concern were listed as belonging to Chronicle's Union.

"If that's what Maxwell's actually looking for," Peter said, "why call us? Why does he think we have any? And doesn't he realize that as soon as he tips his hand we go into the market to buy whatever we can?"

"Maybe he does." I thought about that for a moment. "Who knows, maybe he's doing to us what we used to do to him."

"We ought to be flattered."

"Except I don't think that's his game. At least, not this time. I think he wants us to help him get Chronicle's Union. He must know there are shares in the market. Perhaps he figures that as soon as he starts buying them the price will shoot up to 90p or a pound or higher."

"He hugged you?"

"Thinks of me like a son."

Peter said, "So, let's accommodate dad."

Before we took the plunge, we agreed to hedge our bet. I got Roderick on the phone in Nassau and asked him to buy for us whatever shares he could find in the French printing works. We wound up with a little over one million. Then Peter rang Fran Dyer, a broker we often used, and arranged for some traditional options. We bought five million shares' worth of calls, with a target date 10 days down the line and a target price of 68p. It cost us 2p each, or £100,000. We then sold four million shares' worth of puts with a three-month target date and a target price of 58p. We were paid 3p a share for those, or £120,000. That put us slightly ahead, not counting dealing costs. If the price went up, we'd make money on the calls. If the price went down, the puts were there to protect us. Our worst-case scenario was that we could lose £1 million.

Once we'd fixed that, I asked Adrian to see how much Chronicle's Union was around. He came back with six million shares, which he said we could have right now for 66p. Peter thought we should take it immediately, but I felt we should wait until we could buy it on the curb. The London Stock Exchange closes at 4:30 but trading continues until well into the evening, as long as you can get a broker on the phone. The downside to waiting was that he might not be able to find anyone willing to sell and, if he did, there'd probably be an extra penny or two premium put on the shares. The benefit was that buying such a big block – according to Adrian, this represented nearly 29% of the company – meant we could keep it relatively quiet until the market opened the next day. At that point, we'd be required to make a declaration as to our intent. Except, by then, we'd have unloaded the shares and it would be Maxwell's problem.

Adrian assured me that he couldn't see anyone else coming along to take the shares away from us and Peter reluctantly concurred, so we waited.

At 4:45 Peter checked with Adrian to make sure the shares were still available. He said they were, although the price had crept up a couple of points because someone had taken a block of options on them. It was par for the course, as markets are easily affected by rumours. He was quoting 71p. I nodded and, while Peter waited on the line with Adrian, I rang Maxwell. It took a few minutes before his secretary put me through but when she did I told him, if he wanted six million, my partner and I were willing to sell them to him.

"I never doubted you for a moment," he said. "I'll pay you 75p."

Son of a bitch! I reminded him, "You and I might have built America, but I assumed it was on a handshake."

"My word is my bond," he said sternly.

I said just as sternly, "The deal was 80p a share for the first five million and 82½ for everything above that."

"Are you accusing me of going back on my word, young man?"

"Mr Maxwell . . ." If we were going to take our losses, it was better to take them now. "Yes or no?"

"I'm not used to being treated this way."

Peter was right when he told me, years ago, that whoever circumcised Captain Bob had thrown away the wrong bit. "Neither am I. Yes or no?"

"If you're going to threaten me, then the answer is no."

"Fine," I said. "Nice to have met you."

I was about to shake my head at Peter, signalling him to tell Adrian no, when Maxwell blurted out, "80p for the whole lot."

That stopped me. "So you do want them after all?"

"I told you I wanted them. But what are you paying for them, 68? 69? And what will they be worth tomorrow morning when the word gets out?"

He'd known all along that given half a chance to make some money on his back, we'd sweep the streets for him. "Did we build America or just steal it from the Indians? The price is still 82 1/2 for the last million."

Maxwell started to chuckle. "I was right. We are cut

from the same mould. All right. Draw up the paper work and deliver everything tomorrow morning. I'll have a banker's draft ready."

"By my calculation, that comes to £4,825,000."

"It certainly does." He said. "Thank you."

Before he could hang up, I asked point blank, "I take it that means we have a deal. £4,825,000."

He chuckled again. "You take it right."

I nodded to Peter, who now told Adrian to buy the shares.

Our solicitor, Gerald Chappell, arranged the contracts and personally took them over to Maxwell the next morning. When the market opened, the shares were already trading at 77p–79p. After keeping Gerald waiting for nearly two hours, by which time Chronicle's Union edged up towards 90p, Maxwell signed the appropriate forms. An hour after that, a flunky handed Gerald a cheque.

By noon Maxwell had announced his intention to take over Chronicle's Union at 96p a share. That now established, Peter had no trouble selling our call option for £1.34 million and buying back our put option for £1.4 million. We wrote off the difference – £60,000, plus our dealing costs – to insurance. In the meantime, without any money actually leaving our bank account, we'd grossed 9p on the first five million shares and 11½p on the next million which, after costs, brought us an even half million pounds profit.

And that was just on Chronicle's Union.

Two weeks later, when Maxwell launched a dawn raid on the Paris exchange, taking control of *L'Imprimerie des Hebdos d'Ile de France*, the price of those shares jumped nearly 20 francs, which gave us a profit of nearly £2 million.

Peter and I drank a toast to Captain Bob.

And just for good measure, when the bottle was empty, we counted our fingers.

Chapter Five

Christmas in the south of France was an annual tradition for Phoebe Goddard Radisson and Brenna Woolcott Radisson, who came into this world 19 minutes apart, on 23 September 1989.

I'd bought a small two-bedroom flat in Cannes in the early '80s. It wasn't a particularly stylish place, but it was on the top floor of an older building, the elevator worked, it had a great balcony and there was a garage in the basement, where I installed a classic Ferrari California convertible that I kept promising myself to restore someday. The apartment required almost no upkeep and the price was right. So Cannes was where I'd go when I didn't want to be in London.

After the twins were born I negotiated the apartment next door. This time the price wasn't right. I overpaid and knew I was overpaying. But it gave us the entire top floor and I justified the extra expense as a premium. Pippa and the babies moved down that spring so she could be our onsite contractor and chief decorator. With the help of an old drunk carpenter named Narcisse – whose only authentic talent was his ability constantly to dangle a smelly yellow Gauloise from his lower lip – Pippa merged the two flats. She broke through the wall to convert the second living-room into a dining-room, combined two small French kitchens to make a decent sized one – with room enough for a huge American fridge – and took one of the spare bedrooms to make an office for me. Because 1950s French plumbing wasn't quite as romantic as she'd once imagined, she also modernized the bathrooms. I now tell people we have the only six-room penthouse in Cannes with £5,900 worth of bidets.

We're on the eastern end of the Croisette, a few blocks before you get to the new port. In my bachelor days, I thought this was a pretty sexy place to be. But with my 42nd birthday fast approaching, I was coming to the conclusion that the Croisette was too noisy. Peter suggested that man's ever increasing aversion to tumult is directly proportionate to his age. In other words, the Croisette wasn't getting noisier, I was just getting older. Not true, I said. Older is when it takes all night to do what you used to do all night. And in that respect, I'm still younger until somewhere around 2 a.m. He recommended a doctor who could give me a prescription for Vitamin E plus a good price on double glazing.

I never learned to speak much French, although I point good in French. This one, I'd indicate, and hand the sales assistant a credit card. I'm equally fluent in German, Italian and Hungarian.

On a whim, in the middle of a four-day fling with a Danish TV presenter named Jette – a gorgeous blonde with big teeth and lots of hair – I bought an audiotape that unequivocally promised I could master the language in 30 minutes. Half an hour later, I unequivocally knew how to ask for the post office. My lady Viking was ever so impressed.

There wasn't much point in my struggling with any foreign language while I was with Francesca because she spoke everything and spoke it all perfectly. When Pippa entered my life I found I could depend on her A-level French. Except, of course, when we needed to find a post office, which was down to me.

Malika, our Moroccan nanny, usually mixed up French and English with us and French and Arabic with the twins, which is why I'm still not sure what

57

language they speak. Most of the time it sounds like English, but then they slip into some sort of secret patois. At least they understand each other, even if their mother and father don't.

So the five of us flew down to Cannes the week before Christmas and settled in for our three-week stay. The day after we arrived, I walked all over town pointing at presents for the girls, and a couple of things for them to give Malika. The next day I pointed at a tree and all the decorations to go on it. When I got it home I reassured the twins there was no reason to worry, that Father Christmas, whose real name was Santa Claus, would find us in France even if everyone in Cannes called him *Père Noël*. But at 27 months old, none of that made much sense to them.

We gave them their gifts on Christmas morning because waiting until Boxing Day, which was what Pippa was used to doing, never made much sense to me. Naturally, they both got far too much. And because they're twins, they both got the same far too much. I'm not sure when they're supposed to get different far too much, but Pippa also dresses them alike, which worries me, because they're not the same person. I want their individual personalities to develop. Pippa says it's not time yet to separate them. She's read all the books on twins and insists that, when they're ready, they'll make the break themselves. Considering the hell we went through to have them, I trust Pippa to know what she's doing.

That's the way she and I have agreed to run our marriage. I allow her to make all the little decisions, like how to raise the kids, where they'll go to school and where we live, while she allows me to make all the really important decisions, like whether or not the Russians should be invited to join NATO.

If Christmas was for the twins, then the week between Christmas and New Year's was for Pippa.

I found some terrific underwear for her at a specialty shop in one of Cannes' back streets — the kind of store most people only walk into wearing dark glasses — another Hermès scarf for her collection and a pair of earrings which she modelled for me along with the scarf and the underwear. Malika looked after the girls while Pippa and I spent one night at the Moulin de Mougins and another night at the Hotel de Paris in Monaco. Then, for old times' sake, we checked into the Negresco. I even arranged to get the same room we had there the first time.

Finally, it was my turn.

Being a New Year's baby meant that when I was a kid I always got a combined Christmas-birthday gift. Everyone insisted that one present was twice as good as two, except I knew I was only getting half as much stuff as people born in February. All these years later, Pippa also combines Christmas and birthday gifts, so I'm still getting half as much. Although the quality is way up.

There were two boxes and one long tube left wrapped under the tree. I inspected them closely when no one was around, figured at least one of the boxes was a shirt, saw that the other was too wide and too heavy to be a tie, and didn't have a clue what the tube could contain.

To celebrate New Year's Eve and my birthday, Pippa was going to cook a goose. I'd already chilled the champagne. That afternoon, she took our rented Peugeot to one of those huge supermarkets that the French do so well, to stock up on food for the rest of the week. Malika was looking after the girls until 5 o'clock, when she'd be off for three days. I sat on the balcony for half an hour going over some figures for a development we were planning along the Thames called Howe Wharf, but because the weather was so beautiful — it was one of those especially sunny south of France winter days — I convinced myself there was an entire year ahead of me to think about work and that I owed it to myself to end this one with a stroll along the Croisette.

I ambled slowly up the beach side to the old port, where I stopped at a newsstand to buy an *International Herald Tribune* and a *Financial Times*. Then I made my way back to Le Festival where I laid claim to a front row chair.

Say what you will about the French. They name their railway stations after military defeats, and every village in the country has a *Place de la Victoire*, except that it's terribly difficult to recall any French victories. When the Gulf War broke out, they quickly joined the allied forces by sending an aircraft carrier to the Middle East, but in true Gallic spirit they took the precaution of removing the planes first. They are infuriatingly arrogant and arrogantly make a sport out of snubbing foreigners. They demand that foreign films be dubbed into French, except French Canadian films, which they show with French subtitles. They drive appallingly, insist on the right to bring their dogs into restaurants and are the only people on earth who find Jerry Lewis funny. Every French person thinks he or she is born knowing everything there is to know about wine, food and sex. French men are the worst kinds of male chauvinists, although that might be explained by the fact that French women allow them to get away with it. Furthermore, their language is downright bewildering – they claim it's far too subtle for anyone but the French ever to get right – largely because there are many letters they should pronounce and don't, such as the "s" at the end of Paris, and many others they shouldn't pronounce and do, such as the "p" in pneumonia. There is one "you" for someone you know and another "you" for someone you don't – which happens to be the plural of the "you" whom you do know – even though there is only one person you don't know, and no way to refer to plural "yous" whom you do. Equally infuriating, many of their nouns are designated masculine or feminine when there's every reason to suggest they should be the opposite. For instance, hard-on is *la bite*, feminine, and vagina is *le vagin*, masculine. Yet when the history of the earth is finally written, it shall be noted that the French gave us café society. And for that, the human race should be forever in their debt. You can keep pubs. And you can keep bars. Ye Olde Dragon's Arms stinks of stale beer. And I never really cared about all those people who hung out at Cheers. As far as I'm concerned, let the street parade begin and, when my time finally comes, bury me in a French café.

I ordered a meringue and a bottle of Vichy, and when they were finished I mumbled, what the hell, it's my birthday, and splurged for another round. I washed it all down with an espresso and the word game on the comics page of the *IHT*. But I only made it to page eight of the *FT* where a headline stopped me: "Stock Exchange To Probe MCC Dealings."

The story noted that computers, which record all transactions done through the Stock Exchange, had revealed some "unusual" dealing in Maxwell Communications Corp. shares in the hours immediately preceding the suspension of those shares and the subsequent announcement that Maxwell had been lost at sea.

According to an unnamed source, several large blocks had been sold and the circumstances surrounding those sales were being considered "suspicious" by the Stock Exchange Surveillance Unit.

A spokesperson for the Stock Exchange, who refused to confirm or deny the report, insisted that the Exchange never commented on investigations undertaken by the Surveillance Unit or its Insider Dealing Group.

However, the *FT* claimed, while no group or individual had yet been singled out, those share movements in MCC were so extraordinary that the Market Supervision Department already determined that insider trading had, in fact, taken place.

By the time I got home there was a faxed copy of it waiting for me from Peter with a handwritten note at the bottom. "Amusing, no?"

I phoned him in Paris. "I saw it. But it has nothing to do with us."

"I know that. So do you. But what does the Stock Exchange think?"

"Frankly Scarlet, who gives a damn?"

"How about the Fraud Squad?"

I reminded him, "It was down to Roderick and Tivoli Court. Our names don't appear anywhere. Anyway, we weren't the only ones trading. Adrian told me Goldman Sachs was in the game. And I'll bet they weren't the only other ones, either. Best of all, we didn't have any inside information. We've got an airtight alibi."

"Don't you watch *Columbo* reruns? He only arrests people with airtight alibis."

"Come on, we moved a couple of million shares. You don't think we torpedoed the price, do you?"

"Probably not," he said.

"Definitely not." I needed to rub it in. "You must think I'm boring because I'm right all the time but I'm learning to live with it. Now, let's get onto really important things, like, what are you doing tonight?"

"What or whom?"

"I think it's who, not whom."

"That's what marriage does to a man," he sighed. "The first thing that goes is his whoms. I'll ring you tomorrow to wish you happy birthday. It's cheaper than a present."

When Pippa came home — lugging 14 of those annoying little plastic shopping bags with handles that curl into wires and dig into your hands just as the bags get too heavy and begin to tear — I showed her the article. She wanted to know, "What happens if they find out it was you?"

"First of all, it wasn't me." I grabbed the nearest bag, which ripped as soon as I took it, sending two quarts of ice cream rolling across the kitchen floor. "Second of all, there were plenty of people trading that day. Some of those guys were playing for much bigger stakes. We're small fish."

"Small fish sometimes get caught in big nets."

"Actually, I think the expression is, big fish sometimes get caught in small nets." Milk, butter and eggs went into the fridge. "Not to worry because we're in the clear." I put oranges in a bowl and celery in the sink to wash. "If the trades are listed anywhere, they're down as Roderick for Tivoli Court."

"Are you sure?"

"Trust me." There was yogurt and chocolate mousse and Laughing Cow cheese, which also went in the fridge. "I'm sure."

"And if they find out it wasn't Roderick?"

"I'll tell you what I told Peter." I opened half a round of Camembert, sliced off a piece and stuck it in her mouth. "No matter what anyone thinks, we didn't have any inside information."

The twins went to sleep on New Year's Eve, all excited that they were going to wake me up the next morning by singing "Happy Birthday". Left alone, Pippa and I started drinking champagne around 8:30. We got just drunk enough to wind up eating our roast goose in the bathtub. We brought in the New Year by having each other for dessert.

As promised, the girls woke me with a song and breakfast in bed. They helped their mother carry the tray, then crawled in next to me and proceeded to eat both croissants. Crumbs flew everywhere. I was still finding them two days later on the sheets around my ankles. But that was fine with me.

Pippa brought in my gifts and, sure enough, the first box was a shirt. Inside the second was a beautiful silver and gold picture frame with a colour portrait of the twins signed Snowdon.

I had to know, "When did you arrange this?"

She grinned. "I arranged it."

"When?"

"If I tell you all my secrets, will there be any mystery left?"

I inspected the portrait closely. "It's gorgeous." The twins were looking straight at the camera and laughing. "What do you mean, all your secrets?"

"Well, most of my secrets," she smiled, then said, "the next one is my special gift to you."

I ripped open the paper that covered the tube, noticed there were no markings on it which would give away its contents, then pulled off the metal cap at the end. I carefully extracted a huge colour poster of the 1966 Baltimore Orioles World Championship team.

"I love it," I yelled. "This was my first world series. The Orioles beat the Dodgers in four straight. I was there. I saw Jim Palmer beat Sandy Koufax in the second game. And Koufax won the Cy Young Award that year, for the second year in a row."

The twins curled up next to me.

"Look at this." I named every guy on the team. "This is Moe Drabowski. In one game he struck out six guys in a row to tie the major league record. And this was the manager, Hank Bauer. And look, here's Frank Robinson. He was named MVP that year ... that stands for Most Valuable Player ... because he ..."

"Daddy?" Phoebe asked.

"... because he batted .316 and hit 49 home runs." I was so excited with this poster.

"Daddy?" Phoebe tugged at my shoulder. "Daddy?"

"What, sweetie?"

Brenna answered for both of them. "Can we have more croissant?"

Later that day the four of us walked on the beach and watched a horde of rather crazy old men and women – the local Polar Bear Society – take their New Year's dip in the sea. I promised Pippa that I'd find a framer first thing in the morning because I wanted to hang the poster in my little office there. Then we went to Le

Festival and put a serious dent in the French national ice cream supply. We picked at the rest of the goose for dinner and when the girls got into the tub for their bath, I joined them. They both fell asleep that night in my arms.

It was my best birthday ever.

The blurb in the *FT* was the last thing on my mind.

Chapter Six

Shortly after our encounter with Robert Maxwell, I asked Peter, "Ever hear the one about the lady who put all her eggs in one basket?"

He nodded. "Patty Page. A tisket, a tasket. It's one of my favourites."

"Ella Fitzgerald," I corrected. "And I'm talking diversification."

"What for?"

"So we don't crack all of our eggs."

"How about if we just buy a bigger green and yellow basket?"

"We need to protect ourselves. We need a more solid asset base."

"What do you want to diversify into?"

I suggested, "Manufacturing?"

"Too late," he said. "Someone has already invented the better mousetrap."

"How about if his mousetrap factory is up for sale?"

Peter waved, "Have a good time."

In spite of his scepticism, I set out on what would become our first major shopping spree. Because neither Peter nor I knew anything about manufacturing, I theorized that I should look for companies that could, basically, run themselves. I wanted businesses with a product I could draw a picture of because, I knew, if I could draw the product, I could understand it. I decided I also wanted old family firms, now down to the third or fourth generation, overpopulated with bored ancestors who were strapped for cash. My idea was that somewhere, lost in a management structure riddled with nepotism, there was a young buck who was stymied because he didn't have the right blood, who knew how to make the company work, and who, given the opportunity, could earn us all a lot of money. So I put together dossiers on a hundred likely candidates and, after nearly nine months, brought it down to a shortlist of six.

My first choice – the Yorkshire-based Schools Jams and Jellies, makers of Schools Marmalade since 1899 – was the easiest of the lot because the man running the company, Stevenson Schools, didn't want to be in the marmalade business. The 50-year-old great grandson of the founder, his only interest in life was marine biology. I estimated the business was worth around £4.5 million, which in those days was a lot of marmalade. We offered to buy out the family and take over the business for £3 million. Some smart-assed solicitor they brought into the negotiations tossed a monkey wrench into the works at the very last minute, claiming that he would advise against the sale for anything less than £4 million. I convinced Stevenson Schools that his lawyer was screwing things up, so the lawyer got fired and we paid £3.6 million.

The company had a turnover of less than half a million pounds and worked off an 8% margin. Based solely on the numbers, I was therefore getting a pretty tiny return on my money. But I was buying more than pulping machines and a distribution network. Once I got the Schools' family out of the business and fired their top management – whose average age was 55 – I took a close look at a few of the younger guys who'd been held back.

Three stood out. I appointed Charles Patterson, the 32-year-old assistant marketing director to be president and Roger Griffith-Jones, the 28-year-old assistant sales manager, to be marketing director. I put them both on incentive bonus schemes where they could double their salaries by meeting quotas, and then backed away to let them get on with the reorganization.

The third fellow, a strange young man from Yorkshire named Thomas Jonathan Jackson, had been assistant finance director. I'd fired his boss and asked Jackson – who was just 24 – to run finance temporarily, thinking that eventually I would bring in someone with more experience and move Jackson sideways. He was a Greenpeace–Save the Whales–Say No To Atomic Energy–Save the Rain Forests–born-again vegetarian. Not that I have ever had anything against any one of those campaigns on their own, but when you find a guy who is active in everything – and also claims that in a previous life he was Charles Darwin's dentist – you have to start wondering.

I couldn't believe that Jackson had his heart in jams and jellies. But this was a kid full of surprises. He showed up in London one afternoon, saying that he was on a secret mission – I had to promise never to tell Patterson or Griffith-Jones – because he wanted to make me a propoosition. I sat him down and agreed that mum was the word.

In a voice just above a whisper, he said, "I know a way to increase profits perhaps by as much as 50% for a very small cash outlay."

I told him, "This is exactly the kind of thing you should be discussing with Patterson and Griffith-Jones. They run the business, I don't."

He answered, "I recognize my responsibility to the company, and I promise you that I will present my idea to them no matter what you decide. But I want to know, if the idea works, would you bring me to London to be finance director of Pennstreet?"

"You want to come here," I said, more a statement than a question.

"You don't have a finance director."

68

"We're a pretty small operation. I don't know if we need a finance director."

"What about becoming a big operation?"

I thought for a moment. "Do you know anything about the man you were named for?"

"No."

"No one ever call you Stonewall?"

"No. Who was he?"

"Look it up," I said, then mentioned, "We don't use recycled paper."

He shrugged, "You can always learn."

"Patty smokes."

"She can always stop."

"Peter drives a car that belches smoke."

"He'd look great on a bicycle."

"I eat meat."

"You'll see the light."

If nothing else, I decided, the kid had guts. "Okay, here's the deal. You increase those profits 50%, and handle the whole thing inside the chain of command the way you're supposed to, then find someone to take your place, get Patterson to approve of the new guy, and I'll give you a six-month try-out here. If you don't make the cut after six months, you're out, and there's no going back to Schools. If you do, I get to call you Stonewall."

He went home and sold his idea to both Patterson and Griffith-Jones. The way he saw it, there were simply too many people taking a slice of the action between the orange growers and the supermarket shelf. His scheme was to cut most of them out by setting up our own export company in Spain and Morocco and our own import company in the UK.

Through his Greenpeace contacts, Jackson knew a Spanish businessman who put us in touch with a consortium of orange growers all of whom were against using toxic chemicals. We found a like-minded grower in Morocco and another in Cyprus. We struck a deal to take their entire crop, exporting it through a joint venture with that Spanish businessman and importing the oranges through a UK company we set up as a subsidiary of our own Truro Trading.

Our supply of organically grown oranges was less than we were used to, which meant we had to cut back on production, but because we'd dumped the middlemen and because we had what we believed was a high-quality product, Patterson and Griffith-Jones were able to increase the wholesale price of Schools Marmalade to take up the slack.

Our turnover remained pretty much the same, but our profits jumped a staggering 74%. Schools entire line of jams and jellies became the first 100% organically grown label in the UK – this at a time when selling organically grown anything was akin to preaching mystic religion. Turnover has steadily climbed in the 12–18% range and profits have continued to increase every year since, averaging 22–25%.

I kept my part of the bargain and moved Jackson to London for his six-month try-out. Although I continued eating meat, Patty continued smoking and Peter refused to ride a bicycle, I've called him Stonewall ever since.

As he settled into his post as finance director of Pennstreet PLC, I started looking again at my shortlist for a possible second acquisition.

My next choice was the Oppenheim Piano Company. Founded in Germany in the mid-18th century, old man Oppenheim made his name as piano builder to Johann Strauss the younger. According to the legend, it was an Oppenheim piano, in 1866, on which Strauss first played the Blue Danube Waltz. Oppenheim's grandson Ralph managed to get the family out of Hitler's Germany in the very early '30s, bringing with them to England their traditional piano-making skills. Unfortunately for the Oppenheims, they were soon outdistanced by bigger names like Baldwin, Bosendorfer, Bechstein, Steinway and Yamaha. When I approached them, offering to buy the company, they turned me down flat. There was no way they'd sell out. Great-grandpa's name was on the company door and, as long as there was an Oppenheim to run the business, it would stay a family affair.

I said I understood and walked away.

Stonewall took a different approach and scored again. He didn't get us the company but, during the course of our expedition into the world of pianos, he met great-great-granddaughter Susan Oppenheim and on the night of their very first date she moved in with him. They've since organically grown a pair of whale saving, vegetarian kids.

My third choice, a plexiglass manufacturer in Kent, was a non- starter because the family sold it before I had a chance to come calling.

My fourth target manufactured electric switches for the railroad industry. They claimed to have a large contract with the SNCF – the French national railway – but I got the impression that they'd cooked their books to show the French government they were sound enough to win the contract. I immediately backed out, not because the product wasn't good, but because I could see the problems I'd be buying if they ever lost that contract.

Company number five made paving stones. It was owned by three brothers, who'd inherited it from their father. I liked what I saw of the company, although I quickly began having doubts about the brothers. They were each working to their own agenda. The first brother pulled me aside to say – "Just between you and me" – that my purchase of his one-third share of the paving stone business was contingent on my also making an offer for his Vauxhall dealership in Suffolk. Then the second brother pulled me aside – "No need to mention this to the others" – to say that, if I wanted to buy him out of paving stones, I also had to buy him out of a small pleasure craft port near Lyme Regis. By the time I got to the third brother – "How about you and me doing a little deal on our own?" – and heard that he was also flogging a timber yard he owned in Leamington Spa, I decided I never really wanted to be in the paving stone business, anyway.

The last company on my shortlist was the Norwalk Lamps and Fixtures. It was based in Derby and owned by the remnants of the Norris and Lucas clans. Old man Norris, who started the business just after World War I, married the daughter of his biggest competitor, old man Lucas, and put the businesses together. The grandchildren were feuding and more than happy to sell the company to us. We paid £7 million for it – leveraged at 95% with a consortium of three banks – even though they were turning over only 10% of that and not showing any pre-tax profits. On paper, we couldn't afford to keep up our interest payments. But three warehouses came along with the deal, two of which we sold and one of which we put into our own portfolio, and that kept the banks happy while we restructured the company.

Again, I let the top management go and promoted a few of the younger guys. I also brought Roger Griffith-Jones down from Yorkshire to be president. He easily made the transition from marmalade to fixtures, and turned a profit within 18 months.

And again, Stonewall took the oblique approach, coming up with another business for us.

He studied Norwalk Lamps and Fixtures, realized they were overpaying for packing materials and convinced me to buy a small company so that we could manufacture our own cardboard and our own bubble paper. Before long we were also making our own plastic chips – those little white and blue things you keep finding under chairs and behind furniture months after you've unpacked your brand-new Norwalk Lamp.

Within two years we were one of Britain's most successful manufacturers of little white and blue things.

*   *   *

There was never any doubt in my mind that diversification is sound business strategy and that taking a long-term position in manufacturing was one way for us to diversify soundly. But nowhere is it written in the Bible – or, for that matter, in any college-level business administration textbook – that long-term propositions automatically equate to making money.

A guy I once met who went to the Harvard Business School told me that when the Dean addressed the incoming class on the first day he said, "If you want to learn about business, you're in the right place. If you just want to make money, drop out now and get into property."

I related the story to Peter and he instantly conceded that the Dean had a point.

"Students of Huxley and Huxley's students," he stood up, clasped his hands behind his back and strutted around the office with a Groucho Marx stoop. "Many people in property development would have the world believe that they are pushing back the boundaries of the last great frontier, that theirs is the most exciting challenge of all, and that no two deals are ever the same. Except . . ." He pointed his finger towards the heavens . . . "except . . . except . . . of course, buying and selling property is exactly like buying and selling paper clips or toothpaste and, in the end, all property deals are exactly the same. You find a place and get a bank who believes in your numbers, and/or in you, to pay for it. Then . . . then . . . then ladies and gentlemen, you either flog it to the next guy to make a fast profit or you develop it yourself and lose your shirt." Taking a low bow, he said, "Class dismissed," and sat down.

I applauded. "Excellent. Excellent. Just one thing missing, your-professorship."

"What's that?"

"The best thing about the property business."

"You mean, that it's all about money?"

I shook my head. "That no education is necessary!"

73

Chapter Seven

When we first became interested in developing Howe Wharf, Peter stated with great authority that it had been named for Viscount William Howe, an illegitimate descendant of King George I, who'd been commander-in-chief of the British forces during the American Revolution.

"He was a veteran of the battle of Bunker Hill, captured New York City, defeated George Washington at White Plains, Brandywine and Germantown and then went on to capture Philadelphia. Surely such an achievement, at the height of the illegal overthrow by force and violence of the rightful government, warrants a wharf."

I reminded him, "Not where I come from," and proposed instead that the place had been named for Gordie Howe.

"Gordie who?"

"Howe."

"Who Howe?"

"He, Howe, of slap shot fame," I answered. "The guy played 26 seasons in the National Hockey League and wound up with career records for most games, most goals, most assists and most points. A wharf is the least he deserves."

We were both wrong. The property was, in fact, named for Elias Howe, an American inventor who, in 1846, had patented the first viable sewing machine.

This was the site of his original UK factory. Except, there wasn't anything left from his day. Howe's sewing machine plant had, early on, been taken over by a Hungarian corset manufacturer known in the trade as Nagler the Unscrupulous. Having turned down Howe's proposition to provide him with sewing machines, he waited for Howe to go back to America before pinching his invention. Unfortunately, Nagler never got the thread feed right and his machines stitched backwards, which meant, as someone slipped into one of Unscrupulous's corsets, the stitching immediately unravelled. Needless to say, Nagler quickly went out of business. His son-in-law bought the place from the bankruptcy courts, modernized the machinery and tried to keep the art of Hungarian corset making alive. But just before World War I, he failed to understand that the future lay not in girdles but in leggings for the army. So son-in-law now joined father-in-law in Guernsey, living as tax exiles on the money they'd successfully kept out of the receivers' hands.

The factory fell into disuse, until a highly successful legging manufacturer moved in. The self-proclaimed "King of Hooks and Eyes", Phineaus Roth employed nearly 200 people. But then the army changed uniforms. With no orders to sew hooks and eyes into, Roth turned for help to his childhood friend, Leopold Harris, who happened to be Britain's most infamous professional arsonist.

Working out of his family's firm of insurance assessors, Harris provided select clients with a full range of services – everything from torching their building to fraudulently assessing claims in their favour. Harris was eventually arrested and sent to jail. With the money Roth made from his 1930 fire, he moved to Florida.

The lot remained vacant until the beginning of World War II when a property developer with an odd accent, who spelled his name Sir Andrew St John, but called himself Ahn-dray Sinjin, filed papers with the local council for permission to build a tennis ball factory there. As most people's attention was focused on the war effort, no one took much notice of him or his plans. Had they done so they might have discovered that he was a Belgian whose real name was Andre Sardou, that he'd never been knighted and that tennis ball factories don't usually have 55 mirror-ceiling bedrooms and an indoor swimming pool.

He'd only just finished hanging the mirrors when the place took a direct hit from a V–1 buzz bomb.

A warehouse designed to cater to a flourishing Port of London was built on the site in 1953, at precisely the same time that the Port of London stopped flourishing. The electricity was shut off in 1957 and never turned back on.

The decaying remains were owned by a small group run by a fellow named Trevor Bunning. He was a refugee whiz-kid from the '80s – now out of cash – whom the sobering '90s were methodically turning into a caricature of himself. His red designer braces stretched too tightly across his stomach – once taut and hardened by afternoons of squash at the poshest City clubs, but these days an obvious paunch. His suits were wearing at the elbows. Some of his ties were beginning to fray. His matching handkerchiefs didn't always match.

Bunning had been forced to get rid of the company Rolls, to divest himself of his Porsche and to sell his wife's Land Rover. While he'd insisted on keeping his cherished number plate – TREV4 – it was currently attached to a second-hand E-reg Jag. As for his wife's fancy licence plate – 4NIK8 – he'd sold it for £1,500 cash to a friend who thought it was hilarious that his own wife, who didn't get the joke, was riding around with that on her car. He'd also unloaded the company boat and had to buy his way out of the lease on the company Cessna.

Whenever anybody asked Bunning's wife how she was getting on, she'd explain that she'd had to pull their three kids out of Westminster and send them to a much less expensive place, which bothered her because "the other children at this new school are just a bit down-market".

Whenever anybody asked Bunning how he was getting on, he'd tell them with a self-possessed air, "I've been rich and I've been poor and believe me, it's easier to get laid when you're rich."

Certainly there was a marked downturn in the quality of bleach blonde he carted around for his traditional mid-week tryst. In the good old days, he loved to remind jealous friends that the lady of the moment was "between films". Now, he was openly embarrassed when the lady of the moment explained how she was hoping, someday, to run her own salon.

A devout believer in P. T. Barnum's first law of nature – there's a sucker born every minute – Bunning had originally put Howe Wharf on the market for £18 million. That might have been fine had we not been in the midst of the worst slump since 1929. At best, the property was worth only about half that. He knew it. And compounding his misery, so did everybody else. He'd rapidly been forced to lower it to £13 million.

My interest peaked when I heard on the grapevine that he was growing desperate. It's a weakness that particularly attracts me because I believe that the more despondent a guy is, the more likely he is to make a serious mistake.

Like so many of these guys, Bunning had made more than his share of enemies on the way up. Now, true to the old adage, he was meeting them again on the way down. Doors were slamming in his face. It seemed as if everyone was out to get him. But kicking a guy just because he's on the canvas and you assume he can't kick back is a pretty foolish stunt. After all, until he's taken the full ten-count, he might just get up and turn nasty. I've always felt it's much wiser to convince someone who is down to buy back his own dignity by taking ten cents on the dollar. So I did my homework, found out everything I could about

Howe Wharf, and discovered, among other things, that he'd paid £11.8 million. I could sympathize with him wanting to get out with as much of his skin as possible, but the Red Cross and I are two different organizations and only a fool would mistake one for the other.

Confident that I had the right cards in my hand, I rang him to say I could be interested – I emphasized, could be – but only if the price was right.

He said, "It would be wiser if you worried more that the property was right and understood how the price reflected that."

I reminded him, "In this market, there is no such thing as the right property."

He countered with, "In any market, if the property isn't right, your bargain price is a nightmare in disguise."

We met in his office, where he threw himself straight into his spiel. "Only three things count when you're talking about property. Location. Location. And location. And Howe Wharf is all about location. Howe Wharf is where the future is."

I insisted, "Cash is where the future is."

He kept saying, "You've got to see it. The minute you see it, you'll understand."

So we climbed into his car, on what turned out to be the coldest day of the year, and headed towards the Isle of Dogs, to help me understand one deserted building with half a roof and no glass in any of the windows.

I walked around while he stood with his hands in his pockets pretending to admire the view – an unkempt field where shrubs overran what was left of a concrete tract, a river that wasn't commercially dead but was definitely in intensive care, and the outline of a phoenix called Docklands rising out of the ashes of gross neglect.

"It's a loser," I lied, pulling my coat closer around me.

He bellowed, "My arse it is."

"Best if you keep it."

He swung around with a shocked expression on his face. "You said you were buying."

"I said I was looking."

"So look."

"I've seen it. Now I'm freezing. Let's get out of here."

"This is prime cut."

"This is a useless lot in the middle of a useless part of town. Let's go." I hurried back to his car.

"All right," he shouted after me. "Go ahead. Play your macho games."

I turned around. "It had better be cheap."

"I paid 13–5 for it."

I shook my head.

He stared at me, then stammered, "Ah ... I mean ... you know, all in... Yeah, that's right. What I meant was, 13–5 was my all in. That's it. No, I didn't pay 13–5 for it, I paid less, but after all my expenses. . ."

I offered, "Five and a half."

"What?" His face dropped.

"Is that a no?"

He waved his hands frantically. "£5.5 million? You've got to be . . . You must think I'm . . ."

"Thanks anyway." I began walking away again.

"Bay," he called out. "Where are you going?"

"Someplace warm."

"Okay, we'll talk in the warm." He chased after me. "We've just started. Give me a chance at least to get you up to a reasonable price."

By the time we reached his car I'd let him get me up to £7.2 million.

"But that's all. That's my final offer."

"You're driving me to an early grave." He reached out for me, put his hands on my shoulder and whispered, "How much of it can we do under the table?"

"What are you talking about," I asked in full voice.

79

"Shhh." He motioned to keep my voice low. "This is just between you and me."

"There's no one within two miles of us," I continued to speak normally.

"Shhh." He continued to whisper. "I don't know how many sets of books you keep, Bay, but I'm juggling too many plates."

"I'm a public company. . ."

"You've been in the game long enough to know the score. How many small companies like mine do you think could survive with only one set of books?"

"We do."

"Like hell you do. You off shore? The tax man ever see those books? Everyone cheats." His whisper got even quieter. "You can't survive if you play by the rules because the rules are out of whack with reality. When you're trying to survive in the jungle, reality means creative accounting. You show the tax man one set of accounts. The one you live on. And you keep the other set of accounts under your mattress."

I wanted to know, "Do you think you could carry on your accountancy class inside the car. I'm freezing."

We got in, he started the engine and turned on the heater.

"The deal is seven point two," I reminded him. "And everything is on the table."

He barked, "Aren't you a little old to still be a virgin?"

"I'm certainly too old for date rape."

"Ever run up against the tax man? What a thrill." He sat all the way back, facing the steering wheel with his shirt pulling loose from under his belt to show a glimpse of hairy stomach. "In 1987 I got hit for nearly a million quid in back taxes."

"Strange thing to be proud of."

"You can't pay it if you didn't make it."

"Did you pay it?"

"Did I have a choice?"

"Why didn't you fight it?"

"Of course, I fought it. I spent £300,000 on solicitors, barristers and accountants and with all that muscle I was able to force the Inland Revenue down to £800,000. My victory only cost me an extra hundred grand. Sure I got four years to pay it all off. Except they charge interest on top of the outstanding balance. Life sucks when a guy can't afford to be a winner."

"That's what you get for fooling around with two sets of books."

"What are you talking about? This was what they were able to find in Britain. This was the first set of books. Thank God for the other set. It's what kept me out of debtor's prison." He clasped his hands together, pretending to pray. "Thank you Lord for inventing the Channel Islands."

I pretended not to know anything about that.

Now he lowered his eyes to meet mine. "Don't act so bloody innocent. I'm telling you every small businessman in this country keeps double ledgers."

"If you know that, how come the Inland Revenue doesn't?"

"Were you born on this planet?" He forced a belly laugh. "They know about it. They know everyone cheats. But they're also smart enough to know it's a double-edged sword. The more you cheat, the more you have to cheat. Then, when you really need the money, you can't touch it without admitting the sham. They start asking where every sixpence came from and, before you know it, they've got your gonads in a vice. It's crazy. While you're flush they let you dig yourself a really deep hole and the day you come up short you discover they're standing on the rim, looking down at you, sneering, ready to pour in the hot lead."

"Sounds like just deserts to me." I smiled affably. "The best I can do is seven point two. And it's got to be totally kosher."

He shook his head. "I've got to take part of it under the table."

"Sorry."

"I need an even eight."

"Not another nickel."

"You're killing me, Bay."

"Rest in peace, Trevor."

He tugged at his shirt. I could see sweat forming large circles under his arms. "You're killing me. You're killing me."

"You can put the car in gear now Trevor. And not to worry. You'll find someone else. Maybe next time."

"Deal," he barked. "You've got a deal. Okay. You win. It's a deal." He feigned a defeated look. "But I want you to know you're driving me to an early grave."

"At least," I said, "now you'll be able to pay for the hearse."

Of course, Bunning was totally full of shit. It's an obligatory quality for anyone in property. As anguished as he pretended to be, from behind his eyes I could see that he thought he'd finally found a turkey to take Howe Wharf off his hands. I also knew he probably would have settled for a couple of hundred grand less. But it hardly ever pays to screw someone down to rock bottom. Again, it's about a giving a guy the chance to buy back his own dignity. So I let him off the canvas. And I did it knowing how, in his head, he was already rehearsing the story of this battle, already hearing himself crow that he'd beaten me and walked away a winner. He couldn't wait to gloat over this with his soon-to-be somewhat-pacified bankers.

What he didn't know – what he couldn't have known – was that had he held his ground, had he shown even a dash of the gutsy confidence which had singled him out as a star ten years ago, he could have pushed me harder and I probably would have gone a little higher. But the swaggering Bunning of those days was long gone. The '90s version was a schmuck.

He was a schmuck for telling me about his problems with the tax man — for giving someone he was doing business with ammunition that could possibly be fired back at him someday — and a schmuck for getting himself into a position where he had to unload the property at all. The infrastructure being developed for Docklands would make Howe Wharf easily accessible. I was betting that five or ten years down the line all sorts of shops and restaurants would be springing up in the area. I was looking to convert Howe Wharf into the most attractive residential property in East London. What's more, I saw the market as having bottomed out and, at least on paper, felt we could recoup our costs within five to seven years. That would put us into the black just before the millennium.

Coming as close as it would to my 50th birthday, I quietly thought of Howe Wharf as my personal pension plan.

Having committed myself to £7.2 million, I was prepared to shell out another £5–7 million for development and construction. But because I feel safer when I have a cash cushion — you never know what can go wrong — I put together a scheme to finance it with other people's money.

Through various trusts, foundations and offshore companies, Pennstreet PLC was 51% owned by Peter and me. The rest was owned by the public. Buried inside Pennstreet, both Peter and I had private vehicles for real estate. Mine was called Long Beach Properties and was based in the British Virgin Islands. Peter's was Britannica Consolidated Trust, based in the Caymans. Although they were nothing more than a series of bank accounts and two brass plaques hanging in Roderick Hays-White's office, both companies held 20% stakes in Pennstreet, in addition to whatever assets we'd managed to put in there over the years. It was not merely a tax efficient way of doing business — and much less dangerous than Bunning's double bookkeeping — it was a tried and trusted way of keeping a good part of our business private.

On my instructions, Roderick bought us a UK shell company called VisionStar Ltd. into which we funnelled money from Long Beach and Britannica Consolidated to purchase the wharf from Bunning. We then bought an off-the-shelf company based in Delaware, called Yasmine Valentine Inc. and sold the wharf to ourselves for £9.25 million. Next, Yasmine Valentine Inc. sold the wharf for £10.75 million to a shell we'd set up in the Channel Islands called Philippe A Properties Ltd. From there, Britannica Consolidated and Long Beach issued junk paper to purchase Howe Wharf for £11.3 million, which put our original outlay of £7.2 million back in the bank and gave us £4.1 million for development.

Ownership of Howe Wharf was transferred back to VisionStar, cutting off any Caribbean connections to Peter and me. Pennstreet Properties then signed a letter of agreement with VisionStar to buy the wharf for £13 million – the price being supported by Bunning's original prospectus, asking £16 million. As banks like to see companies put their own money in projects, I magnanimously slapped £3 million on the table. All I was asking the bank to put up was £10 million.

It was a dream deal.

We had a terrific property, secretly leveraged at something like 165% and backed up by a small war-chest of cash in the bank. We also had a long-standing and highly profitable relationship with one of Europe's most unashamedly greedy bankers.

Chapter Eight

Shortly after Mrs Thatcher moved into 10 Downing Street, the *Financial Times* did a story on Peter and me as part of a series on small-time entrepreneurs who'd made it through the Labour years, rising from total obscurity to "future star" status. We've always tried to discourage that sort of thing but, once the *FT* turned their spotlight on us, people who'd never given us the time of day were lining up to offer us watches.

There was a fellow named Dudley who wanted us to buy his stake in a goldmine. "Believe me, chaps, at this price it's too good to be true." Unfortunately for him, we'd already learned the hard way that any deal billed as too good to be true, usually is. We told Dudley, thanks anyway.

There was a fellow named Nigel who had a fantastic real estate bargain for us. Fantastic was his word. One problem with it was that, in order to make a killing, we had to get in before noon the following day. We said we might be interested but we'd have to see the property. No time for that he said. We shrugged and called time on Nigel.

There were two young women named Pamela and Priscilla who tried to get us to back a product they wanted to develop that smelled suspiciously like snake oil. When we said it wasn't our thing, they flashed a lot of cleavage and wondered if that was our thing. I later reminded Peter it was the first time he'd ever consciously turned down a still-breathing woman over the age of 18.

There was a posse of City gunslingers in yellow shirts with bold blue polka dot ties who'd put together a penny share fund that couldn't miss. When we said no, they warned us, "You'll be sorry." The fund went from 10p a share to £1.60, at which time they decided that the weather was better somewhere in the Mediterranean. I regretted not having their address because when I heard warrants had been issued for their arrest I wanted to drop them a line asking, who's sorry now.

There was a "can't miss" reinsurance scheme at Lloyd's which we deliberately passed on because Peter and I have always been broadly dubious of Lloyd's. The first time I saw the place — invited there for lunch, taken on the visitor's walk through the dealing room and given a chance to touch the Lutine Bell — I had the distinct impression that I was in the middle of a kitchen with far too many cooks. They even let me sit down in one of the old wooden dealing boxes — about as thrilling as touching the bell — to give me an up-close view of the excitement. Can't you just taste the profits, someone whispered in my ear? I grinned, unable to get the thought out of my head that here was a place filled with people so frightfully anxious to handle my interests, they never bothered trying to convince me that they were as dedicated to my interests as I was.

There was a small broker in the City who was putting together a foolproof fund that hedged currencies. It's the final frontier, he bragged. But the fund was based entirely on discretionary trading — he'd be using his clients' money without asking his clients if they wanted him to use it — which Peter and I knew from our days courting Tricia and Cecily was anything but foolproof.

And there was a fellow named Pancho who had an abandoned cargo of Scotch whisky — 30 containers worth — which he offered us at 15p on the pound. The only problem with Pancho was that he couldn't tell us why he had this cargo, or who owned it, or for that matter, what we were supposed to do with it. We later heard that Pancho got arrested for fraud.

"Having money," Peter decided, firmly ensconced one afternoon in some quaint Poor Richard, wise-sayings mode, "is a lot like being Brigitte Bardot at the age of 25. Great fun. But no prerequisite. On the other hand, I always wanted to be Brigitte Bardot."

I proffered, "The similarity ends with the fact that you both wear shoes. Except she doesn't most of the time."

Peter, however, was unremitting. "Money is the applause a businessman gets for turning in a virtuoso performance."

I conceded, "Not bad."

He asked, "How about, money can't buy happiness, but it can rent a lot of it."

I winced, "Not good."

He raised a finger to make his point. "Money attracts money."

I insisted, "Not true." Or, at least, it was only some-times true. And much of the time it was blatantly false. From our experience, money primarily attracted people who didn't have any but wanted some.

Dozens of courtiers came knocking on our door every month. And I'm hard pressed to think of more than a handful of over-the-transom deals that were even good enough to consider. The notable excep-tion was Clement Marc and his great meat cleaver escapade.

He rang one day, out of the blue, introducing himself to Patty as the recently installed head of the London branch of the Federation of Swiss Cantons Bank. Trans-lated directly from the French, the bank is known internationally as BFCS.

Patty automatically launched into her spiel, advising him that neither Peter nor I any longer took calls of this nature and that, if he wished to approach us with a deal, the only way we would consider anything was in writing, mailed to us, marked for her attention. Whereas she once suggested that anyone who wanted their proposal returned must also enclose a self-addressed stamped envelope – we had to make her understand that we didn't really want to appear that unapproachable – the usual reflex from the usual banker was to argue with her. First he would insist, and then he would demand, to be put through to Peter or me. After all, he would bellow, I am much too important to send my proposal to someone's secretary.

Those guys never got a second shot because anyone picking a fight with Patty was swiftly reduced to permanent banishment.

But Clement, ever polite, responded that he'd be delighted to send his proposal to us, marked for her attention. And the following morning a messenger arrived with a cover letter addressed to her, saying thank you for your time, and I would be most grateful if you would please consider passing this along to Messrs Radisson and Goddard. The next page was his letter to us, which began, "Have you ever considered your future in meat cleavers?"

The way his proposal explained it, Clement had stumbled across a German fellow named Eugene who owned a small British company that manufactured meat cleavers. Eugene's main holding company in Germany was originally in the fanbelt business and somewhere along the line, while expanding into aluminium siding, he'd acquired a Swedish match company that had, for some inexplicable reason, bought this meat cleaver manufacturer 20 years ago.

"This is," Clement wrote, "a fairly typical example of the Pac-Man theory of business. Gobble, gobble, gobble. Take over anything that gets in the way, regardless of who it is or what your own goals are."

Eugene wanted to return to his fanbelt-aluminium

siding roots and when Clement saw that *FT* blurb about us, he hoped we might be interested enough to let him broker the deal for us.

Peter couldn't figure out why we'd want to be in the meat cleaver business. And I had to agree with him. Except that, towards the end of his proposal, Clement made a very strong allusion to the fact that Eugene's meat cleaver company also had a few decent real estate holdings.

Attached to the proposal was a well-designed document that spelled out the virtues of BFCS and, in particular, its experience with small, independent entrepreneurs. Clement also provided references which, with the usual discretion, we were invited to check. I recognized one name on his list – the chairman of a medium-sized pharmaceutical firm – and rang him. He acknowledged that he did business with BFCS because Clement was not a typical Swiss banker. I asked what that meant and he answered, "The bloke is flexible."

So, if only out of curiosity, Peter and I agreed to an initial meeting.

The first thing that struck me, as Clement stepped into our office, was that he didn't look like a senior-level Swiss banker. The gnomes are supposed to have ashen hair and dark, conservative suits. This guy had long black hair which was cut in a way that made his portly face appear much larger. He wore a navy blazer with a striped shirt and a bright-coloured tie that came very close to clashing with his shirt.

He told us – with self-mocking candour – that he'd gotten his masters degree from the Wharton School at the University of Pennsylvania because he couldn't get into Harvard. "My last year at Zurich I spent trying to make the Olympic ski team and my grades suffered. So Harvard said no."

I wondered, "What about the ski team?"

"They said no, too." He shrugged, "Instead, I made the Olympic banking team."

We sat him down, expecting to hear a long self-congratulatory presentation. But all he said was, "We're what you'd call a designer bank. You go out and get any offer you can from any other bank in the world, and we'll better it."

"Any offer anywhere?"

"It's just that simple."

"Okay," I said, "so tell me about meat cleavers."

He shook his head. "I can't. I know how to finance the deal. If you want to learn about meat cleavers, you'll have to go to Frankfurt."

Based on little more than the prospect of an interesting deal – and the novelty of this skiing banker – the three of us flew to Germany to meet Eugene, a wiry little man with a moustache that came very close to being Hitlerian.

Over lunch in a restaurant that Clement took us to because they featured 36 different kinds of wurst – which I whispered to Peter simply had to be the worst – Eugene gave us a heavily accented pitch for a going concern with a warehouse stock of 16,000 meat cleavers. He even presented each of us with a gift of six cleavers – the finest forged steel with designer wooden handles, one size fits all – and showed us a brochure with colour pictures which noted that they sold for £79.95 to the restaurant trade. He calculated that 16,000 of them put the retail value of his stock at £1,279,200. As he normally wholesaled them at 40% off, he priced the lot at £767,520. And that, he said, was what he wanted for the business. However, he warned, we would also have to assume a debt of £330,000.

Despite his comic moustache, he was serious enough for us to take seriously. We told him that if he'd be willing to wait one week, and in that time not negotiate with anyone else for the company, we'd consider making him an offer. He agreed.

On the way back to London, Clement said, "All I want is a chance to finance it for you. If and when, shop around, get the best deal you can, then ring me and I'll better it."

It sounded fair enough, although it struck Peter as an odd way to do business. "So here's a fellow who puts a deal in our laps, which we may or may not go for, without anything more than our own promise to come back to him at some point to discuss possible financing."

"Don't tell me you haven't figured it out yet?" I was surprised at him. "The guy's betting that we're sharp enough to realize there's a better deal waiting in the on-deck circle."

"What's an on-deck circle?"

"It's a baseball reference," I said.

He nodded. "Thanks. That makes everything perfectly clear."

"How about, waiting in the wings? Next on line? Next on the list? A two-fer?"

"What the hell is a two-fer?"

"You know, two-fer the price of one?"

Now he shook his head. "Baseball has a lot to answer for."

There was no need to explain it further because it was so obvious that Clement was working at what the retail business calls a loss-leader. You hook the customer by giving away the first item in order to land him with the next one. Knowing that, we decided the first item had to be worth a very close look. All the more so because I've always believed that when someone offers me a pound coin for 50p, I have an obligation to buy it. Conversely, when someone is willing to pay me a pound for my 50p, I have an obligation to sell it. But in both cases, the first coin I always take out of my pocket is ten cents to invest in shoe leather.

While Peter checked out the company's property holdings – they owned a small freehold plant in Coventry, a warehouse not far from Birmingham Airport and a tract of land adjacent to the warehouse that could be developed – I got on the phone and rang a bunch of large butcher shops. The first thing I learned was that not all meat cleavers are created equal. The next thing I learned was that the reason the meat cleaver business didn't fit into Eugene's consolidated scheme of things was because none of the butchers I spoke with wanted to buy them.

To a man they agreed that Eugene's were well-respected meat cleavers but they were British made and the Japanese pretty much controlled the market. In other words, there was no way Eugene could compete. The Japanese made a better product and, even though they were higher priced, the people who knew the difference – all these guys who professionally cleave meat – preferred the Oriental version.

The next step was to get in touch with some Japanese manufacturers – the cutlery buyer at Harrods gave me some names and numbers in Tokyo – and when I finally reached the sales manager at Katsuura Knives, he told me that his main market was Europe and North America. On a whim, I wondered if there was anyone in Argentina who sold his meat cleavers – Argentina popped into my head only because it's a beef producer – and he said no, they were still concentrating on Europe and didn't yet have plans to go into South America.

I said thank you, decided I didn't need to speak to anyone else in Japan and started phoning companies in South America. Eventually I found someone in Uruguay who not only distributed commercial cutlery, but also spoke acceptable English. I arranged to send him a couple of cleavers and shipped them by air that afternoon. Two days later he phoned to say they'd arrived, that he liked them and that he would be willing to take them off my hands if they were priced to undercut the Japanese products currently being offered to him.

When I asked which Japanese brand was coming on strong in South America, he replied, Katsuura. Realizing that someone was lying to me – either my new friend in

Tokyo or my new friend in South America – I asked him the wholesale price of those meat cleavers. He said they worked out at £57.35 each, f.o.b. Tokyo. I promised him 16,000 at £43, which was 25% less. He offered to take them all at £32. We settled on £36.50. He faxed me that afternoon, confirming the £584,000 deal, which meant I now had a chunk of Eugene's asking price up front.

Except, of course, I had no intention of paying Eugene his asking price.

At that point, I rang Clement and told him that we might go for the deal. He was delighted and asked if I needed finance. I said we were looking for a bridging loan. He said that was no problem. I then told him that I wanted a series of letters of credit in varying amounts between £550,000 and £767,520. And, without a moment's hesitation, he agreed to arrange that for us.

Seven days after we first met Eugene, I was back in Frankfurt, saying that I was prepared to offer £495,000 for his British company.

He brought his price down to £725,000.

I explained the state of the market and the cost of money and reminded him that in a very real sense, in addition to buying a £330,000 debt, I was also buying his problems. However, I said, I'd be willing to come up to £550,000.

Now he announced that, although he'd kept his side of the bargain and not gone looking for any other offers within the agreed one-week period, he'd received an unsolicited proposition a few days ago from a Japanese manufacturer. He didn't say how much, and I specifically didn't press him because I didn't want him to box himself into a corner. By claiming that the Japanese had offered say, £700,000, there would then be no way for him to come down under that.

On the other hand, knowing what I already knew about Japanese meat cleavers, I was willing to gamble that he was lying. So I reached into my attaché case, discreetly sorted through my collection of letters of credit and plunked one down, addressed to him and signed by Clement, for £585,000. I said it was his, subject to contract and that I hoped it matched the Japanese bid.

Poor Eugene was now facing a major dilemma.

If he believed this was my top offer – after all, here was a banker's guarantee made out to him in that amount – he couldn't say that the Japanese had offered more without running the risk of losing the money staring him in the face. Yet, if he intended to accept my offer, he wouldn't want me to believe that I'd outbid the Japanese and might, therefore, be overpaying.

I sat quietly, letting him stew.

Eugene didn't know I'd come armed with letters of credit in higher amounts, so he thought about it for a respectable length of time, pretended to do some calculations, left his office claiming he needed to make a phone call, and returned a few minutes later mumbling something about preferring to have the money now rather than wait on the Japanese. He extended his hand, I shook on the deal and the rest of the paperwork was left to our solicitor, Gerald Chappell.

Clement came through with the money and charged us a quarter of a point less than the competitive rate.

An hour after I bought a British company from a German with a moustache for £585,000, Peter sold our inventory of 16,000 meat cleavers to a South American who spoke English for £584,000. It meant that, when the £330,000 debt was added into the equation, we'd covered nearly two-thirds of the deal.

We shopped around for a few days to see if anyone – including the Katsuura people – might be interested in buying the business without the real estate. When no one came forward, we offered the company to the 18 employees. They turned us down, so we closed it. We said we were sorry to have to do this but if they didn't want to run the business, we didn't want to run it either. We paid them all 10% above the going redundancy rates.

They objected to being put on the dole, but the business was simply not worth saving.

We kept the warehouse, to add to our commercial property holdings, and had no trouble putting it out on a long-term lease. We then applied for and were granted planning permission to divide the property in Coventry. We offered the freehold of the factory for sale – it took about six months and we eventually got £465,000 for it – then sold the adjacent land with commercial development permission for £340,000. When all was said and done, expenses, redundancies and taxes paid, Peter and I came out of the deal with a very profitable warehouse in Birmingham plus £287,000 in cash.

Eugene was happy. We were happy. And Clement was happy, too. In fact, Clement seemed so pleased with us that, as soon as the ink was dry on the meat cleaver deal, he came up with another venture – the one he'd probably been hoping to hook us on all the time – £12 million worth of hunting rifles that supposedly once belonged to Edward VIII.

The way Clement related the story, the man who gave up the throne of England for a twice-divorced American and spent the rest of his life in exile, mainly in France, had secretly negotiated with Stanley Baldwin's government to take many personal treasures with him upon abdication. Sometime in mid-1936 a detailed list was drawn up, separating personal items from assets that might be claimed by the crown. Included on Edward's side of the ledger were 185 hunting rifles, many of them rare and precious gifts given to him during his years in waiting as Prince of Wales. Representing some of the finest work of the great British manufacturers such as Holland and Holland and James Purdey, plus a selection of guns from foreign manufacturers, the collection included some very rare American Colt rifles.

At the start of World War II, when Edward was shipped to Bermuda, he asked that certain assets still in London – including the cache of hunting rifles – be loaded onto the British frigate which would transport him across the Atlantic. When he arrived in Bermuda, instead of off-loading his possessions, he asked that they be taken to New York, where he'd supposedly already made provisions for them to be stored in a bank vault.

He died in 1972.

Apparently no one remembered the rifles in New York, until an attorney acting for Wallis Simpson – who by this time had become a recluse – discovered papers referring to them and, with Mrs Simpson's permission, decided to sell them.

According to the story, she insisted they be sold privately, discreetly and as a collection. A Swiss buyer heard about them and offered £4 million. His offer was accepted. He took possession of the rifles, brought them to England and had them appraised at three times what he paid for them. They were now being offered to us at £8 million.

Under normal circumstances, this is exactly the kind of deal Peter and I drool over. Clement assured us that he would give us the money to buy them. And the prospect of making a fast £4 million took us to Scotland.

The Swiss collector had a hunting lodge there. Neither Peter nor I had any interest in hunting, but that didn't preclude sharing a few good meals and drinking some very fine vintage malt whisky. Knowing nothing at all about guns, they looked exceptionally good to us. Knowing a lot about buying and selling, we came back to London with a complete inventory and photographs.

First, we hit the auction houses. I went to Sotheby's and Phillips, Peter went to Christie's and Bonhams. We spoke with the experts and showed them what we had. All four were interested, confirming the fact that we were on to something good.

So now we began negotiating a deal. We agreed with the experts that, if we marketed this as the Duke of Windsor's personal gun collection, we should be looking at a premium over book value and that could bring

£10–16 million. We demanded a guarantee of £12 million, against a flat commission of 8%. We also insisted that they spend at least 1% of the total of the reserves on advertising and promotion of the sale.

Sotheby's and Christie's put too many conditions on their participation. I resented their arrogance, refused to budge from my position and they both backed out. Phillips agreed to a guarantee of £9 million, against 10%. Bonhams offered £10 million, but against 12.5%.

With Clement's money to pay for the stock, plus a guaranteed profit of at least £1 million for our trouble, I set off on the tedious task of checking out each and every gun against whatever records I could find for them.

Although the manufacturers were oddly reluctant to help, I was permitted to see some of the original entries in their records for some of the guns. Often included was the name of the man for whom each gun was made. And while the manufacturers did seem keen to impress me with the fact that they'd done custom work for the Maharaja Whoever or the Sultan of Somewhere, that's not what caught my eye.

Each gun in the collection was impressively chased. They each had plenty of fancy gold or silver engraving lining the sides of the handle or on the body of the rifle above the trigger mechanism. Yet there was very little mention of chasing in the original records. When I asked about this, I was assured that if the chasing was done at the time the gun was made, it would have been noted.

When I rang my new friend in Switzerland and explained to him what I'd learned, he seemed genuinely shocked. I don't think it was an act, although the better the con-man the more difficult it is to tell. I pointed out that we were still interested but that the anomalies would have to be cleared up before we concluded any deal. He promised to get back to us.

The very next day he rang to announce that he was withdrawing the guns from sale.

Ever apologetic, he told me what I believe to be a

true story. It seems that a man he'd known rather well had approached him to buy the collection and had provided him with all the documentary evidence he'd subsequently shown us. He forwarded those documents to his attorney who, being too lazy to check them out, merely reported back that they looked genuine. And, despite having had the good business sense to insist on seeing the guns, when our new Swiss friend was taken to a London bank vault, he never bothered to ask why they were in the UK, when the original version of the tale put them in New York.

Left alone in the vault to inspect the collection, he discovered there were six more than had been listed on the inventory. If he'd been half as smart as he thought he was, bells should have gone off, because mistakes like that don't happen. Those kinds of things are purposely built into the equation to play off someone's greed.

What's more, the man selling the guns had claimed they were worth £8 million wholesale and perhaps as much as twice that on the retail market. Our new friend had offered half the wholesale price and, after some less-than-heated negotiations, the seller had accepted.

That should have been another tip-off that something was amiss. No one in their right mind sells so much for so little – unless there isn't so much there to begin with.

It turned out that the chasing had all been recently added and that the paperwork had been forged. Because the Swiss gentleman hadn't invested a dime in shoe leather, he paid £4 million for a collection of rifles that probably weren't worth more than £500,000.

I don't have a clue what happened to the guns. For all I know, someone else might have bought them thinking they'd once belonged to the Duke of Windsor. But we didn't fall for it. And, needless to say, when I told Clement the story, he turned beet red.

His embarrassment was substantial.

He started taking us out for meals, insisting in restaurant after restaurant that he knew nothing about the scam. We believed him. But we didn't say so right away because we enjoyed watching his shame and guilt being transposed into bounteous appeals for absolution. Thanks entirely to Clement's humiliation, Peter and I ate in every great restaurant the United Kingdom had to offer.

A couple of months – and more than a dozen major meals – after the rifle sale fell apart, he came to us with a deal that he promised would instantly put him back in favour.

He'd discovered a small trucking company out of Glasgow that had overexpanded into car rentals at provincial airports. They also owned a motorcycle messenger delivery service in London, six auto parts stores in and around Birmingham and three Ford dealerships scattered across the north of England.

Their initial plan had been to buy trucks and cars through their own dealerships, through which they'd intended to furnish their trucking and rental businesses. But they'd paid too much for their airport sites, their trucking business had slowed and they'd not built enough margin into the auto dealerships to protect their downside. They'd gotten into a cash-flow muddle and had panicked.

Management had lost its way and, Clement was totally convinced, the operation was ripe for plucking.

The company's shares were trading in the 17–20p range. We estimated they had a break up value of 32–35p, so Peter and I raided the market.

Using BFCS's money, we picked up 40% of their shares, averaging under 20p, before they knew what hit them. We went to the board and offered 22p. Playing one disgruntled board member against the others, we were able to create such dissension that, within two days of our dawn raid, we controlled 54% of the company's shares. We then made an offer for the remaining shares at 24p. And it was accepted.

Over the next six weeks, with Clement's help, we

sold the motorcycle delivery firm to the guys running it in London and allowed the local management of the auto parts chain to buy us out. We unloaded the trucking company in Glasgow to its biggest competitor in Edinburgh and convinced Ford to buy back their own Yorkshire dealerships.

We were long since into profit the day that Peter and I were sitting around the office wondering what we were going to do with our car rental business, when Clement appeared – almost like a genie jumping out of a lamp – leading the chairman of Hertz Europe into our office by the hand.

Our average investment was just under 22p a share. Our net return was just over 34p a share.

It was at about this time Peter decided we really had to jump on the Thatcher bandwagon and take Pennstreet public. Suddenly everyone was doing it. There were long lines of companies wanting to float issues on the London Stock Exchange and the Unlisted Securities Market because it was an easy way to make a fortune. So we did it too. And to show Clement that we did, in fact, forgive him, our lead bank was BFCS.

In return for such a display of confidence, Clement now bombarded us with deals. He also, unabashedly, told the *Sunday Telegraph* that Peter and I were his best friends.

Before long, a certain Swiss Italian woman, whom he brought to London to run his Corporate Development office, became mine.

Chapter Nine

Francesca Guardi was born in Lugano, Switzerland, in 1952, the same year that Dylan Thomas published his *Collected Poems*, Samuel Becket wrote *Waiting for Godot*, Jean Anouilh staged *La Valse de Toréadors*, Truman Capote wrote *The Grass Harp* and Cesare Pavese wrote *Il Mestiere de Vivere*.

She was the only person I ever met who'd read them all in their original versions.

After getting a law degree in Lausanne, she was hired by the Swiss Volksbank in Geneva for their Mergers and Acquisitions Department. A year later, the Banco di Roma stole her away and sent her to Zurich to work in Corporate Finance. In 1982, Clement enticed her to London. Considering the fact that she was a 30-year-old female, and that Swiss merchant banks have never been known as champions of the women's movement, her arrival in the City was met with a flurry of press attention. I even phoned Clement to congratulate him on what I thought was a surprisingly refreshing attitude, only to be told, "Yes, even if I have to say so myself, it was a masterful publicity stunt."

"I thought you hired her because she was the best qualified person for the job."

He laughed. "She's good. In fact, she's very good. But if I wanted the best-qualified person for such a job I would have found a 45-year-old man with 25 years' experience. No, we'd grown too sleepy and I needed to wake us up. The minute I met her I knew she was what the bank needed. And I was right. Our phones haven't stopped ringing. It's magic. New business is banging down our front door. Now, when do you want to meet her?"

"Next you're going to tell me that for a banker she has terrific legs."

"My friend, I am going to tell you that for a woman she has terrific legs."

"Does your mother know you're a misogynist?"

"No, you're wrong. If I am any sort of 'ist', I'm an iconoclist."

I corrected him, "That's not 'ist' that's 'ast', and in this case the 't' is silent."

He didn't get it. "I shall be remembered in the City as the man who loved women enough to tear down traditional barriers."

"You and the guy who publishes *Hustler*."

"Trust me," he said, "this one you will like. So when do you want to have lunch with us?"

I couldn't bring myself to play his game. "I'll wait until you fix the front door."

Word around the City was that Clement had indeed pulled off a major coup, that this woman had single-handedly breathed new life into BFCS. If that was true, I believed, it was for all the wrong reasons. And my doubts were widely confirmed.

A foreign exchange dealer I occasionally bumped into told me he'd met Francesca Guardi and that she was as tough as nails. "But what a turn on." A senior partner in an accounting firm that specialized in receiverships and liquidations confided, "I have dreams about her because she's so beyond reach." He added, "The rumour is that she's got some high-powered married man on the hook in Geneva and spends every weekend there." A merchant banker we sometimes did business with assured me, "She's untouchable. I mean, she's so untouchable I'm certain that she must be a lesbian." Another banker

102

told me that behind her back they were calling her "Mademoiselle Zermatt", referring to Europe's most famous glacier.

I kept asking, but is she any good at her job? And not one of those men could give me a straight answer. The most revealing reply came from a guy I knew who ran a small chemical company who'd just negotiated a refinancing deal with BFCS. "She's hot stuff," he insisted. "Every bank in London is suddenly looking for Corporate Development departments who can fill a Dior dress the same way she does."

I finally got a chance to make up my own mind when one day, about six months after Clement first told me about her, Francesca Guardi rang me.

"Mr Radisson, we might have something for you." She spoke English with only the slightest trace of a foreign accent. "We've been engaged by two industrialists in Italy to help them find a British partner. It would require someone with imagination, the risk element is high but the profit potential is great. It's not something for the fainthearted. Which is why Monsieur Marc suggested it might be right for you."

I joked, "Doesn't Monsieur Marc know that I am genetically fainthearted?"

If she had a sense of humour, she wasn't particularly anxious to display it. "That's not the general opinion around this bank. Monsieur Marc has briefed me on some of your previous business dealings and fainthearted is not the word that comes to mind."

"Oh." That stopped me. "Okay, Ms Guardi, when and where?"

"Not yet. Before we get to that stage, I'd like you to look at something we've put together. Obviously this must be kept in the strictest of confidence, but the file explains in broad terms what this is all about. Once you read it, and if you then decide it's something that could interest you, at that point we can discuss when and where."

I said, "That would be fine," and we hung up. The dossier arrived by messenger an hour later. In it, Francesca outlined how two fellows in Venice wanted a London-based benefactor to help them take over and consolidate a network of small companies that developed and manufactured communications equipment. Although most of that market was then controlled by state-owned post offices, these two guys believed that the time was fast approaching when Europe's telephone industry would be privatized. By grouping 15–18 small companies – and the file included some stunningly detailed intelligence on their possible targets – they hoped to have a powerful multinational in place, poised to compete, as soon as the state monopolies broke up.

Francesca was right in saying that a deal like this required imagination. The Thatcher regime was forging full-speed ahead with the privatization of government-owned industries. But Britain was the only country doing it. Around the rest of Europe, full-scale privatization seemed a long way off.

So my initial impression was that the project was too fanciful. The Italians were gambling that if it proved successful in Britain, the trend could spread throughout Europe, and if that happened, the early bird would get the biggest share of some very juicy worms. However, it struck me that there were too many variables in their equation.

Nevertheless, I had to agree, if these guys got their numbers right and if they also got their timing right, the profit potential would be phenomenal. And because I believe in the "dartboard theory of life" – throw enough darts at the bull's eye and eventually you have to hit it – I told myself, fanciful or not, it was certainly worth the price of a dart to find out more.

"Okay," I phoned Francesca that same afternoon. "Let's meet." I nearly suggested we set up a quiet lunch somewhere.

Instead, she proposed, "How's 11 tomorrow? I'll come to you."

I said, "Fine." And at 11 sharp the next morning she and Clement walked into my office together.

Seeing her for the first time was a bit of a shock. She was taller than I'd imagined, with dark hair and very dark eyes. She had a big smile, wonderful teeth and a firm handshake. She was wearing very expensive clothes, but she wore them in the classic French under-stated way.

Frankly, for a woman who'd been the object of so many male fantasies, she was not an international beauty. On the other hand, for a woman who was not an international beauty, she was extremely attractive.

It's difficult to describe why. There was something about the way she walked and about the way she held her head. Most of all, I think, there was a certain look in her eyes. It was a sort of warning signal. It was the look of a woman who is superbly confident in herself – sexually confident – the look of a woman sending out the message, I set the ground rules.

And her self-confidence unnerved me.

As the three of us sat face to face, and she looked me straight in the eyes, I found it difficult to concentrate on the pitch she was making.

"Is that a problem for you?"

A sudden silence in the room brought me back to the moment. "What?"

She repeated the question. "Is that a problem for you?"

I didn't know what she was talking about, but I hoped she wasn't reading my mind. "A problem?"

"Yes. Would it pose a problem for you to front the operation in certain areas where it would be politically advantageous to have an American or a British national?"

"Ah . . . no." I responded before I even had a chance to give it any thought. "Although, I'd have to make those decisions on a case by case basis." That sounded like a good enough fudge to me.

It obviously wasn't good enough for her. "In other words, it worries you."

"Worries me?" I tried to think of something fast. "I'll tell you what does worry me. How I can trust their numbers?"

She answered right away, "You can't. They're Italian. Don't even try."

"So what am I buying?"

"If you're foolish enough to pay for promises in a business plan, well then, you'll wind up owning 50 pages of hot air."

I glanced at Clement who sat next to her grinning like the Cheshire Cat. "I don't get it."

He shrugged and acquiesced to Francesca.

She explained, "The numbers shouldn't be theirs and, in fact, won't be theirs. We'll insist that the numbers be ours. That will be a clearly stated condition. But at this stage we're not talking about bookkeeping, we're talking about personalities. In a very real sense, we're also talking about castles in the sky. These are two highly entrepreneurial men with an impressive track record. But they've only ever operated on a small scale. You've done well in Britain but you've never branched out into Europe. We see ourselves sort of like alchemists. We're hoping that we've found some base metals that can be turned into gold."

I raised my eyebrows. "I seem to recall that the alchemists failed."

"Hardly," she said. "Late medieval alchemists discovered nitric acid and sulphuric acid and hydrochloric acid and ethanol, which they called aqua vitae, the water of life."

I couldn't think of anything to better that. "Really?"

She stared right into my eyes. "Really."

I didn't want her to see how off-balance she made me

feel. Yet all I could muster was the slightly meek, "But they never came up with gold."

"You might not either." She let slip one of her big smiles. "But you'll have a few good meals."

I turned to Clement. "I could have guessed someone who works for you would have suggested that."

The three of us flew to Venice the following week.

Until we got onto the plane, she kept calling me Mr Radisson and I kept calling her Ms Guardi. Once we were safely strapped into our seats, I insisted that if she didn't call me Bay I'd pretend to be an American tourist and tell her, in a much-too-loud voice, more than she ever wanted to know about Baltimore. So she agreed to call me Bay and I offered to call her Francesca. But first names didn't seem to change anything. I reminded myself that there was skiing in Zermatt all summer long.

When we arrived in Venice, Clement had a private speedboat waiting to bring us from the airport to the Gritti Palace. As we checked in, he announced that we were just in time for lunch. Before I even had the chance to open the window in my room and admire the Grand Canal, he was whisking us off to a small restaurant called *Centi Piatti*, which means, one hundred dishes.

Without exaggeration, I think that's how many were delivered to our table.

Clement had insisted on ordering for me and I was foolish enough to let him do it. I'd eaten with him often enough to know better. And the moment I said, "Sure, go ahead," I kicked myself for making such a mistake.

Lunch went on for three hours.

He never stopped complaining, "You can't get a great meal in Venice." Yet he never stopped eating. I was bloated after the third pasta, only just fumbled my way through the *osso bucco* and had long since abandoned any hope for survival by the time he gestured loudly to the head waiter, "*Dolci, dolci*," and tried to gorge me with a sample of everything from a pair of overflowing dessert trolleys.

Francesca was smart enough to insist on ordering for herself and skilfully nursed a salad for the entire afternoon. Clement paid the bill, then came up with some grandiose excuse to get away – "My mother's maiden aunt winters here and she's been sickly lately" – and because it all sounded so contrived I suddenly thought to myself, the son of a bitch has lined up a hooker.

Dragging himself out of his chair, he wavered, mumbled to Francesca, "You are in charge," then staggered distendedly out of the restaurant.

Once he was gone, I wanted to know, "Where's he going?"

She answered flatly, "That's Clement."

Something told me my hunch was right. "Do you feel like a baby sitter?"

"No." She stood up. "I feel like an herbal tea."

"No more food," I begged.

"Trust me." She wound us through narrow streets to the Piazza San Marco and to a wonderful café called Florian. There was a vacant table outside, I pointed to it and the waiter motioned for us to take it, but she said no, "They're for the posers," and led me inside.

Dating back to the early 18th century, Florian is a maze of six small rooms. We crammed ourselves behind a table off to the side of the last room and she ordered linden and mint tea for two.

"*Tiglio e menta?*" A large, white-bearded man at the next table leaned over towards ours. He wore black jeans, a black open-neck silk shirt and a black Borsolino hat. His long white hair was tied into a tiny pony tail. "*Tiglio e menta,*" he repeated several times in a plaintive tone – linden and mint, Francesca whispered her translation to me – "*Ezio bevve tiglio e menta.*" Ezio drank linden and mint tea.

I asked Francesca, "Who's Ezio?"

So she asked the gentleman in black, "*Chi è Ezio?*" And he told her, "*Mia moglie. Mia sposa.*"

"His wife," she said to me.

"His wife's name is Ezio?"

"*Si. Mia sposa* . . ." The gentleman in black looked at me. "*Mia moglie. Ma . . . Ezio e morta.*"

"Yes, his wife," Francesca explained. "But Ezio is dead."

"Oh," I said to her. "Ah . . . please express my deepest sympathies."

She did.

That's when this man reached across the table and took my hand. "*Grazie, grazie. Lei è molto simpatica.*" Thank you, thank you, you're very kind.

Our teas arrived, giving me the chance to reclaim my hand.

The waiter looked at our new friend and asked if he wanted another drink. He gestured towards us while telling the waiter, "*Sciampagna per miei amici. Sciampagna per tutti.*"

"*Sciampagna?* Champagne?" I gasped, then told our bearded neighbour, "Thank you. *Grazie.* Thank you, anyway." Speaking loudly and slowly, the way you have to when you want a foreigner to understand English, I begged off. "No champagne. No *sciampagna.* Thank you. But that's very kind of you."

He began babbling away to Francesca. When he was finished she told me, "He says we have to drink with him because his wife Ezio just died and he doesn't have anyone to drink with. He would be very grateful if we'd toast the memory of his wife."

"We just had a meal that's left me in a stupor," I complained. "If I drink any alcohol now. . ."

Our new friend interrupted, took Francesca's hand and went into a long explanation that I feared might be his life story.

I was right.

As she related it to me, he called himself Giorgio Canaletto. And suddenly I thought to myself, how funny, to be sitting in Venice with Guardi and Canaletto. Except it turned out that his real name was Giorgio Martinelli. He was a local sculptor who told people he was related to the famous Venetian painter Canaletto, but then Canaletto's real name was also something else.

Anyway, Ezio was his agent, his dealer, his friend and his wife. Except that Ezio was also a very large man with a white beard. The two had lived together for nearly 40 years. Ezio had died the week before and his funeral was going to start in an hour. Giorgio was sitting at their table – where he and Ezio always sat – getting juiced up in preparation.

The champagne arrived.

To be polite, we toasted Giorgio's health. *Salute.* And toasted the memory of Ezio. *Salute.* And then our new friend Giorgio toasted us, saying he found us to be a lovely couple. *Alla vostra, amorosi.* Here's to the lovers.

By the time we finished the champagne – which didn't last long because Giorgio belted it back pretty well – our teas were cold. I thought getting some hot water might be a good idea, but before I could do anything Giorgio called the waiter, paid the bill, and dragged us out of Florian.

"Where are we going?" I asked.

All Giorgio would say was, "*Andiamo, andiamo.*" Come on, come on.

No sooner were we out of the piazza, than he led us to a shaky wooden dock where a gondola was waiting. He introduced us to the gondolier, sat himself down in between Francesca and me – the boat rocked so badly I thought for a moment we were all going to be tipped overboard – and Giorgio shouted, "*Avanti.*"

Off we went, paddling down the Grand Canal.

Now Giorgio linked his arms in ours and began singing a loud and melancholy song.

I leaned behind his back to ask Francesca, "Where are we going?"

She put her finger to her lips to tell me to be quiet.

By the time he finished the song, another gondola had joined the procession. But this one was draped in black with a coffin in the middle.

"Jesus Christ!" I shot a glance at Francesca. "This is Ezio's funeral."

Moved by the sight of a coffin, she held Giorgio's hands in hers.

And he broke out into another song.

Soon our gondolier joined in, as did the gondolier steering the boat with Ezio's body. I tried to catch Francesca's eye but noticed, over her shoulder, that two more gondolas were tagging along. One was empty. The other had four Japanese tourists taking pictures. I looked around and on my side there were three other gondolas shadowing ours, all of them filled with people. At first I thought they must be friends of Giorgio, but then I heard loud American voices. One of them actually called out, "Follow that gondola."

Our flotilla headed into the lagoon.

Two speedboats joined us, and so did a few more gondolas, and all this time Giorgio was singing.

I prayed he wouldn't slip into *Volare*.

We wound up, 35 minutes later, at a lonely wooden dock a long way from the Grand Canal, where there was a horse-drawn cart waiting. The tourists left us there, waving goodbye, telling us what a wonderful time they'd had.

Oblivious to them, a now-weeping Giorgio instructed the two gondoliers to bring Ezio ashore. When the coffin was loaded onto the back of the cart, he and Francesca – her eyes were also red – and I walked behind it as the horse pulled it slowly along a narrow dirt path, then up a steep incline to a tiny cemetery.

There, we laid Ezio to rest.

The grave diggers stepped aside and when Giorgio and Francesca bowed their heads, I bowed mine. Giorgio cried openly – only just managing to get through a very sad ballad – and by this time Francesca was crying too.

When his farewell song to Ezio was finished, Giorgio beckoned us to return to the gondolas. He left his mate of 40 years to a pair of men in brown overalls with shovels.

With Francesca again holding both of Giorgio's hands, we wound up right back where we started, those same two tables at Florian.

The waiter automatically brought champagne and as soon as the cork was popped Giorgio broke out into yet another song. Everyone in the café applauded. He forced a smile through his tearful eyes and slipped into an encore.

At last, it was *Volare* time.

And everyone in the café joined in.

We went through two bottles of champagne – more accurately, Giorgio went through one and a half of them – before he decided to switch to brandy. A bottle of that went the same way and, by now, I was half gone too.

Eventually, a very wobbly Giorgio made his way to his feet, kissed Francesca on both cheeks, then reached over to give me the same treatment. I reluctantly accepted. Although it turned out to be painless.

"*Miei amici.*" He took both our hands and held them tightly. "*Per Ezio . . . per me . . . andate godersi la vita. Andate fare l'amore.*"

And just like that, he was gone.

She watched him leave, as tears ran down her face.

"What did he say?" I asked.

Francesca turned to me and whispered, "He wants you to take me home."

It didn't dawn on me what she was talking about.

We left Florian, she moved close to me and it seemed perfectly normal that I should put my arm around her. We walked that way back to the Gritti. The concierge gave us two keys. Francesca took them both and, without a word being spoken, led me to her room.

We stepped inside, she locked the door, then buried her head in my chest and held me tightly. After a while

I kissed her. And then it was the most natural thing in the world to undress each other. I carried her to the bed and, as she wrapped her long legs over my back, she murmured, "*Godersi la vita.*"

To celebrate life.

Light pouring into the room woke me.

Lying flat on my stomach, I opened my eyes, only to see that her side of the bed was empty.

Oh shit, I thought, it's going to be another one of those first mornings. I hate them. I've always hated them. I've never been good at morning-after forced smiles and morning-after embarrassed chatter. How are you? All right. Did you sleep well? Yes, thank you. Ah, I guess I really have to be going now . . .

"*Prima colazione,*" Francesca announced in a loud, cheery voice.

I slowly turned onto my back.

She was standing at the foot of the bed, completely nude, with a waiter's towel over her arm while she balanced a huge breakfast tray on one hand. "Does *signor* take milk and sugar in his coffee?"

I stared at her, not sure what to think, while she posed, throwing her hip to the side and pouting. All I could say was, "God, you're gorgeous."

She put the tray on the floor and moved her hands slowly down the sides of her body. "And a croissant with jam?"

I couldn't take my eyes off her.

Then she touched herself. "Or perhaps *signor* would like something else for *prima colazione*?"

"Perhaps he would." I extended my hand.

She walked towards me, grabbed my wrists and began moving against my hand. "The coffee can wait."

And with the Grand Canal waking up to the morning just beyond her wide open windows – double windows large enough for everyone on the Canal to see us – she greedily used me to make love to herself.

*　　*　　*

113

Just before lunchtime, Clement phoned her room. She lied that I'd gone out somewhere to take care of something. He instructed her to make certain I was at the meeting by 4 o'clock. She promised to find me and get me there on time.

We soaked in the bath together for half an hour, then made love again. It required a second bath.

Somehow, the two cleanest people in Venice arrived at BFCS's local office ten minutes early.

Clement met us, with a pair of Italian gentlemen in tow – a tight-lipped guy named Guido and his jovial companion, Paolo. After introducing us and going through the usual round of small talk – yes, I love Venice and yes, isn't it sad that it's sinking – he escorted us into a beautifully decorated wood-panelled conference room. With the snap of his fingers a waiter appeared carrying a silver ice bucket with a magnum of Asti Spumante.

I played with my glass, not drinking, while they went through their spiel.

It was difficult to keep my eyes off Francesca. In fact, I felt as if I was slipping in and out of consciousness. I heard everything they were saying. Yet very little of it registered. I could still smell her and taste her and I wanted to reach out and touch her.

Guido and Paolo rambled on.

They were both in their mid-30s with black, blow-dried hair. I didn't mind their expensive silk suits or the gold chains that dangled from their wrists. But I couldn't understand why they wore big gold Rolex watches on top of their left shirt cuff. For an instant I wondered if they were both wearing pointed shoes, but I didn't know how to take a peek without making it seem obvious.

From out of the corner of my eyes I could see Francesca staring at me.

They sang their own praises like well-rehearsed vaude-villians. But even through the haze of a semi-trance, I could tell it was all a bit too pat. Their numbers ended in too many zeros. Everything was rounded up too high. I didn't like the way Guido never once looked me in the eye or how, whenever Paulo caught Francesca's eye, he'd wink at her and say that we were all going to be good friends.

The straw that broke the camel's back was when Guido told me they had some politicians in their pocket.

That brought me back to the moment. "Did you say you've got politicians in your pocket?"

He grinned, "Call them silent partners."

I confirmed, "We're talking about bribes!"

"*Benvenuto in Italia*." Paulo opened his arms majestically. "Welcome to Italy."

Guido tried to reassure me, "No one in this country does any business without taking care of the politicians first. *Vivo. Vivi. Vive*. I live. You live. He lives. In Italy, we all live. The rules are not complicated."

Paulo continued the lesson. "Think of it as a quaint local tradition. The ritual of *chiavi*, which means keys. In this case it is not dissimilar to the way you use the word when you speak of key money. Here we are not dealing with bribes, in the way that you might bribe a policeman when he wants to give you a speeding ticket. Here we are dealing with *chiavi* because you need keys to open doors."

"The problem is," Guido volunteered, "that Italy is a country with many closed doors."

I didn't know how to get out of this gracefully, but I was certain I wanted out. "What concerns me . . ."

Francesca must have been reading my mind because she suddenly switched gears and went from trying to sell me a deal to manoeuvring me away from one.

"What concerns both *Signor* Radisson, and me as well," she cut in, "is that neither he nor my bank can be seen to be participating in any activity, regardless of business culture, that might be construed as illegal. Making payments to interested parties is one thing. Buying off politicians is another. It is something that creates extremely dangerous situations, especially where both my bank and my client are concerned. Although this is not to say that we wouldn't pay proper fees where they are properly due."

Now Guido became a bit too tight lipped and Paulo became a bit too jovial. The meeting ended with all sorts of polite promises to think about what we'd discussed and eventually to be in touch.

Over dinner, Clement lectured me incessantly about how I was passing up the opportunity of a lifetime. "You're dealing in a different business environment. This is not England. This is not America. Things are done differently in Italy."

All I wanted to do was get out of the restaurant and take Francesca back to the hotel.

"Look at the way business is done in the Arab countries," he went on. "You would be required to have a local partner who would be entitled to a commission for his input. And what is his input? Nothing more than the fact that he's a local. In Italy. . ."

After two hours of suffering his increasingly unintelligible discourse on business in foreign cultures – Clement alone polished off three bottles of wine – Francesca finally put an end to the evening. She reminded her boss that she and I had an early plane to catch. He called for the bill and the three of us made our way back to the Gritti.

There was one brief awkward moment when the concierge handed us our keys and I reached for Francesca's.

Clement reached for it too.

He was too drunk to pick up on what had just happened, so I let him have it, and was quietly relieved when he handed it to her. I caught her glance, said thank you for dinner and wished them both goodnight. I left them in the lobby and went upstairs.

Ten minutes later she knocked on my door.

Without saying anything, she stepped into the room, went straight to the double French doors that looked onto the Grand Canal and opened them. Next, she turned on every light in the room and pushed a large armchair directly in front of the windows. When she had that where she wanted it, she stood at the window, her back to the Grand Canal, and inspected the place. She ordered me to snap off lights, one by one – first the overhead, then the stand lamp next to the couch, then the two bedside lamps. The last one – the desk lamp – now cast just enough light to silhouette anyone in the window.

"That's perfect," she said. "Take off all your clothes and sit here."

I did.

She faced me – staring into my eyes – while she very slowly slipped out of her clothes. It seemed like forever before she climbed up to me, balancing herself with one knee on each arm of the chair. I took her like that. Then she turned around and straddled me, and I took her that way, as she watched boats moving through the night along the Grand Canal.

As they watched us.

The next morning, when a newspaper arrived with breakfast, a front-page headline announced that the Venetian sculptor Giorgio Canaletto had been found dead in his studio.

Shocked, Francesca read the story to me.

It said that, after the funeral of his companion, he'd been drinking with friends at Florian, left them there, walked home and committed suicide. The note found next to his body explained, "I cannot live without Ezio."

On the editorial page, a local art critic wrote that Giorgio had never received the professional praise he was justly due. "He was an artist who bathed himself in the tradition of this city, an artist whose every breath was filled with the passion of life. His work," Francesca read on, with tears now filling up in her eyes, "was a celebration of that life."

We held each other for a while – she wept in my arms – until I gently reminded her that we had a plane to catch.

She said she wanted to stay.

I left her in Venice to bury Giorgio, convinced that I'd finally found a soulmate.

Chapter Ten

Pippa, the girls and I came home from Cannes at the end of the first week in January and I went straight back to work on the Howe Wharf project.

Sitting on my desk when I walked into the office was a small but heavy rectangular package. I asked Patty where it came from and instead of telling me that it was from Peter – I opened it myself to find a card reading "Combined Humbug & Birthday" – she answered, "Don't you know Cartier when you see it?"

Tearing through the wrapping, I uncovered a bar of gilded sterling silver, about the size of an audio cassette, standing on a plexiglass base. Inscribed across the front of it was the equation:

> "If A equals success,
> then the formula is A equals X plus Y,
> with X being work,
> Y being play
> and Z keeping your mouth shut."
> *Albert Einstein*

I put it in the centre of my desk, right next to the framed Snowdon photo of my daughters.

As Robert Maxwell's body lay a-smouldering in the grave, writers and journalists – and hordes of would-be writers and journalists, too – were engrossed in a frenzied race to tell the hitherto banned versions of his story. These weren't revisionist historians who had lately uncovered diaries, letters and previously silent witnesses to reveal a new view of Churchill, Stalin or Roosevelt. These were big shots, little shots and contenders all over the country banging on word processors, rushing to satisfy publishers who, suddenly unshackled from the bonds of libel, believed that the pot of gold at the end of a rainbow looked exactly like the public's insatiable appetite for lurid tales of Captain Bob.

For a brief few months, it was one of Great Britain's most animated cottage industries.

But Bob was no Elvis. The cult market dried up and the national attention span – at least where things prurient were concerned – swung quickly back to *Coronation Street*, *EastEnders* and the Royal Family.

At first, I didn't pay much attention to the vast amounts of ink that Maxwell was getting. But Pippa did and she spotted another reference to the Stock Exchange inquiry. Towards the bottom of a extensive article on the financial debris left in Maxwell's wake, the *Daily Mail* wrote – almost as a throw-away line – "There is more to the probe than Goldman Sachs."

When she showed it to me, I waved it off with my best nonchalant-indifferent expression. She accused me of being cavalier. I responded that I was merely putting this into the proper perspective.

Then she found a second mention of the probe, this one in *The Economist*. And a third reference to it, now in the *Guardian*. And a then fourth article, this one in the *Sunday Times*, where a spokesman for the Stock Exchange was quoted, "We do not comment on our investigations."

Wearing my best brave face, I tried to appear unmoved, reminding Pippa at every turn, "We did not trade on inside information." But her apprehension was contagious. The more I saw in the papers about Maxwell, the more slightly paranoid I became that someone would go into detail about the Stock Exchange probe, would find one of those unnamed inside sources, and mention my name.

I remembered a dream I used to have as a kid. I was about seven or eight and I'd hear voices – people standing on my lawn in the middle of the night, chanting my name. I'd lie there, terrified, staring at the ceiling, until I could muster up my nerve to race out of bed and make a dash for the bathroom. I instinctively knew that I was safe there, that the people calling out my name couldn't hurt me as long as I kept flushing the toilet. So I'd stand in the bathroom and flush, non-stop, willing them to go away. I have no idea what the dream meant. It's probably pretty weird. But I knew that as long as I flushed I was safe. Eventually, all that flushing would wake my mother. She'd gently reassure me that there was no one on the lawn, that there were no voices. I never believed her. Even when she'd coax me, hand in hand, to the window to prove it, I'd tell her that as soon as the toilet stopped flushing they knew she was coming to save me and so they all went to hide in the bushes.

Without admitting as much to Pippa, I found myself worrying about people hiding in the bushes.

I skimmed every book and every newspaper article and every magazine article I could find. I watched every television programme about him too. And when there wasn't anything more about the probe, when it seemed just to disappear – when I could hear my mother's voice saying, there is no one on the lawn – I started to feel queasy.

One side of my brain yelled, stop it, there is nothing to worry about, you've done nothing wrong. The other side asked, how come the papers have gone silent, how come no one is reporting it, how come the Stock Exchange refuses to comment?

Silence can be the worst torture of all.

That only summer I went away to camp, a whole

bunch of us "frenched" the counsellor's bed. We turned his inside sheet up, doubling it over so that he couldn't tell there was anything wrong until it was too late – until he got into bed and inadvertently pushed his feet through the inside sheet and ripped it. He was furious and he vowed to get even with us. As the ring leader, I was chosen to suffer last. One by one, the other guys found mint toothpaste squeezed into the bottom of their underpants – which makes your crotch tingle in a very annoying way – or they got their fingers doused in water while they slept, which caused them to pee in bed. However, a nastier fate awaited me. The counsellor swore that something terrible would happen in the middle of some night, but wouldn't tell me when. For the next two weeks I lay awake. Not knowing what he had in mind, or when it was coming, turned out to be sheer agony. Finally, at the end of those two weeks, he came to me in the middle of the night and said, "It is the silence. And you have suffered it long enough."

Now I was suffering it again. I heard a little voice inside me saying, it's not the people on the lawn screaming your name you must worry about, it is the silence in the bushes.

My dictionary defines insider trading as, "The buying and/or selling of shares by someone who has special knowledge of a company's affairs which other investors are not privy to."

It's a difficult crime to prove and, at least until 1980, was not an offence in the United Kingdom.

Generally speaking, what happens is that a company director trades on private information he's learned in the course of doing his job and trades on that information before it is made public, giving him a definite advantage over other shareholders. But just because someone hears a bid is coming down and manages to get into the game before anyone else hears of it, that doesn't mean he's necessarily committed a crime.

More to the point, company directors do it all the time. So do stockbrokers. So does everyone else who sees that there's money to be made this way. One of the reasons it's hard to prove is because it's hard to spot. If you have inside information – taking for granted the fact that you're not a total numskull – you don't ring your broker, happily announce that your company is the subject of a secret takeover bid and instruct him to buy a block of shares for you while the price is still low. You either pick up shares or options off-shore, or have your brother-in-law buy them for you in his maiden aunt's name. Or you hide your purchase inside a bunch of shell companies, tangled into a complex network that is virtually impossible to unravel.

Unless you're too greedy, chances are no one will ever spot the trades. The reason that guys like Michael Milken, Ivan Boesky and Dennis Levine got caught was because they were pigs. Rich wasn't good enough for them. They never believed the old adage, quit while you're ahead. They were out to prove they were the best ever – and to get mega-rich – and in turn they allowed their mega-egos to push them over the top.

However, for every Milken, Boesky and Levine who got found out in the '80s, there were a thousand or five thousand or ten thousand who quietly went about living their life, making a little here and a little there, until they could quietly turn it into a 350SL convertible, or a chalet in Aspen, or just meet the orthodontist's bill for their kids' braces.

If they could get away with it so easily in the United States, where they risked the wrath of the Securities and Exchange Commission, just imagine how easy it was in Britain, where markets have been traditionally self-regulated. Even when Parliament made insider dealing illegal – and gave the Stock Exchange the right to hand over the results of its investigations to the Department of Trade and Industry – the gentlemen who self-regulate themselves never seemed to have the stomach to dig too deeply into the affairs of other gentlemen.

It was generally only when unusual prices or trading volumes could not be logically explained that the DTI would ask to look at a jobber's books, might try to identify the brokers involved and perhaps then compel those brokers to reveal the name of their client. And yes, the Stock Exchange did establish the Insider Dealing Group, specifically to monitor suspicious trading. But, except for the most blatant cases, there was so much grey area that no one could actually say where good old-fashioned military intelligence ended and insider knowledge began.

For instance, sometime around 1985, Peter found himself inadvertently running around with a married woman. The way he tells the story, he and a date were supposed to have dinner one night with the woman and her husband, when his date rang to cancel because she had a cold and five minutes later the married woman phoned to say that her husband had to cancel. While Peter was typically gallant about it – remember this is his version – she confessed she was furious with her husband because these days he was always cancelling everything and she never got to go out. So Peter said that simply because her husband couldn't make it and his date couldn't make it, that was no reason why they shouldn't have a meal together.

Apparently the married woman was so touched by Peter's compassionate understanding of her problem, that she wound up in his bed.

Again, his use of the word "compassionate" should be taken with a large dose of salt.

Pillow talk being what it is – a strange phenomenon that has often changed the course of history – she told him the reason she felt abandoned was because her husband was working for a bunch of men who were trying to take over the Harvey Nichols department store. She told him the whole story – in minute detail – and, as

124

Harvey Nichols was owned by the Debenhams Group, the very next morning Peter and I put in an order for a large block of Debenhams' shares.

It was public knowledge that, earlier in the year, the designer Terence Conran – who'd built himself a small empire with his Habitat shops – was involved in merger talks with Debenhams. He'd been thinking their shops could merge together nicely with his, so he'd come up with a modest offer. But Debenhams' chairman had rejected it and, when it didn't look as though anything more could come from their talks, Conran had supposedly gone away.

It was not yet public knowledge, however, that Conran had been hanging out with Ralph Halpern, plotting to take over Debenhams together.

A thin, physically fit but overly nervous man with a receding hairline and a tacky penchant for girls younger than his own daughter, Halpern was then chairman of the Burton Group. Before he took over the clothing store chain in 1978, Burton's profits were running just under £7 million annually. Seven years later, he'd driven them eight times higher. And now Halpern too had ideas for Debenhams. He believed that by combining his retailing skills with Conran's design skills the world could be their oyster.

The two men agreed that the old-fashioned department store was a dinosaur and that the future of retailing lay in a much sexier shopping environment. They envisioned a variation on *La Galleria* in Milan, intending that the modern store should provide the walls, plenty of glass and lots of green plants, assure a general quality of merchandise and establish an overall shopping ambience. However, the merchandise offered for sale would come from trading partners. Call it, if you will, an accumulation of specialist boutiques pretending to be a hi-tech High Street.

According to what Peter's new friend told him in bed – and this information directly contributed to our decision to buy the shares – Debenhams attracted them for several reasons. First, they were an already established specialist retailing operation. Next, they also owned a shoe manu-facturer and a company called Welbeck Finance, which was a boomingly successful consumer credit operation. But the best part of the deal was the group's two major properties: a sensational Oxford Street location for their flagship store, and the upscale £40 million Harvey Nichols department store, immediately down the block from Harrods, in Knightsbridge.

Peter's new friend's husband had been called in to help them win the takeover, then split up the group. Unfortunately for Conran and Halpern, the management at Debenhams had their own ideas and these did not include outside, upstart partners.

It goes without saying that no one ever uttered the name Terence Conran in the same breath with any of the great takeover magicians of the 1980s – Hanson, White, Goldsmith, Murdoch or Pickens. He wasn't even close to being in their league. And while no one could doubt Ralph Halpern's retailing skills, he didn't have much of a track record in big-money takeovers either. In fact, just before this deal, he'd climbed into the ring with James Hanson and a tough north London street fighter named Gerald Ronson in a very rugged battle over the future of the UDS retailing chain. And Halpern came out a definite third.

But that wasn't going to stop them now.

A week after Peter and I purchased our first block of shares in Debenhams, Halpern's Burton Group did what we knew they were going to do – they launched an all out attack. True to form, the Debenhams' board dug in, the battle heated up and we bought some more.

Halpern now announced, for the first time, that Conran was with him. Although he wasn't bidding himself, Conran's role would be to revamp the group's 67 stores, take up 20% of the group's trading space and hold an option to buy a 20% stake in the redesigned

Debenhams. No sooner said, national newspaper ads appeared showing a smiling Halpern and a grinning Conran with the headline, "Either of them could turn Debenhams around. You are being offered both of them".

In response, the Debenhams' board fired their own public relations salvo, pooh-poohing the *Galleria* concept and outrightly rejecting Halpern's bid.

We bought a third block of shares.

Then Roland Smith, who'd been chairman of the House of Fraser, got in on the act. Together with the Al-Fayeds – the Egyptian businessmen who came to own the House of Fraser and Harrods – he picked up around 25% of Debenhams' shares. Smith's move looked as if it was aimed directly at foiling Halpern.

That's when Gerald Ronson showed up with Phil Harris in tow. Harris was chairman of Queensway, a carpet and floor covering retailer. Together they bought a 7% whack.

Halpern and Conran might have been thinking about *Gallerias*, but now the big kids were in the game. Caught in the middle of severe crossfire, Halpern had little choice but to find an ally somewhere. And all the time Peter's new friend told us what to expect. When she said that Halpern was going to turn to Ronson and Harris and offer to negotiate a truce with them, we unloaded our shares.

In the end, it was the 7% held by Ronson and Harris that swung the group to Halpern. The press called it one of the bitterest and most colourful takeover battles the city has seen.

And we walked away with a profit of nearly £2 million.

Was it insider trading? Difficult to say. Although, come to think of it, being told of a takeover while having sex with the wife of a man involved in that takeover is, perhaps, the purest kind of insider-something.

Chapter Eleven

Agreeing terms for Howe Wharf with VisionStar Ltd meant I was negotiating with myself, so I gave myself all the best options. I had 30 days to come up with £1 million to finalize the deal, plus an additional 90 days to fund the rest of it. Clement had committed the bank's participation, subject of course to the usual negotiations. And, even though there were still a few wrinkles to iron out, having come to understand Clement's intrinsic sense of greed I had no qualms about hiring a freelance design team to put together some development ideas.

Behind his back, I also shopped around for a better deal.

Clement was skiing at Crans Montana and wouldn't return to London for another two weeks, so I booked a few confidential meetings to see if I could barter more favourable terms with another bank. Putting a second deal in my pocket would make tying up loose ends with Clement that much easier.

One bank I've always liked is Hill Samuel, but when I spoke with my contact there – William David Romney was the corporate loan manager assigned to the Pennstreet PLC account – he said thanks anyway, because Hill Sam was trying to cut back on their exposure in that part of London. I tried Citicorp, only to get the same story from them. Banque Nationale de Paris was looking to place some money, but I wasn't comfortable when the fellow I knew there told me that everything we might agree in London would have to be okayed by some anonymous bureaucrat in France. A small private German bank that we occasionally used said they'd come in on the deal with us. But under their terms we'd have to raise a big whack of the capital with a bond issue on the back of Pennstreet's shares. I explained that, if I was going to finance the project myself, I didn't need them. My argument fell on deaf Teutonic ears.

In the end I got bored, decided to hell with this, and phoned Clement in Crans.

He said, "Get the final draft to me, I'm sure it will be fine, then come here on Tuesday."

I said, "You'll have it tomorrow, it is better than fine, and okay, I'll see you Tuesday."

When I mentioned my trip to Peter, he said he'd gotten a note from his old mate in Geneva, Etienne Pont – we'd long ago Anglicized his name and usually referred to him as Stevie Bridge – and wondered if I had time to see him too. I agreed to lunch on my way back.

So Tuesday morning I flew to Geneva where Clement had a car and driver waiting to bring me up to Crans. I walked into his place just after lunchtime and found him sitting on the living-room floor, dressed in a day-glo red, white and blue nylon track suit – it made him look like a US Air Force hot air balloon – tenaciously putting a dent into a huge bowl of pistachio nuts.

"Want some?" He popped shells into his mouth, cracked them loudly with his teeth, extracted the biggest pieces of broken shells with his fingers, spit the tiniest shell fragments into a brass mortar at his side and chewed the pistachio meat, all with amazing speed. "Take some."

"Thanks anyway."

"I loved the proposal," he cracked, picked, spit, chewed and reloaded. "I'm sure we'll do it."

I was thinking to myself, you'd better be sure, when Francesca stepped into the living-room with a towel around her head, drying her hair. "Why it's Monsieur Radisson."

It hadn't dawned on me that she might be there, least of all looking as though she'd just washed her hair at his place. "Hi."

"What brings you to the land of snow, watches and chocolate? Slumming, are we?"

The idea that the two of them might be shacked up together was too gruesome to contemplate. "Clement doing perms these days?"

"Just a wash and set." She fell into a big chair under the window, across from Clement and me.

He didn't miss a beat with his pistachio routine. "Was the room service waiter any better this morning?"

I didn't know if that was Clement's way of telling me that she wasn't staying with him, or, in fact, that he was now delivering breakfast to her in bed.

"He's improving," she answered. "This morning all he forgot was the coffee."

I had to know, "Where are you staying?"

"At the Golf."

With a mouthful of shells Clement managed to say, "The same hotel as you."

I looked at her. "Did Clement show you the proposals?"

"I've read them." She turned to stare out the window while she rubbed the towel through her hair. "Are you skiing?"

"No. I've just come down for the . . ." I nearly said night, but thought better of it and settled on, ". . . for today."

"Then perhaps we should discuss it today." She continued drying her hair.

"Oh, Francesca . . ." Clement was having trouble getting one piece of shell off the underside of his tongue. "I was hoping to ski this afternoon." He spit. "Please, can't we talk about it over dinner tonight?" He spit again, but the shell stayed where it was.

She waved him off. "I can't make dinner tonight and I'm skiing . . . I'm skiing with some friends tomorrow." She wasn't going to turn around. "Of course, if the two of you want to keep this just between boys . . ."

I suggested, "Clement's always considered you one of the boys."

"Now, now," Clement said, and spit twice more into the mortar. "We must maintain our civility." He kept spitting but the shell wouldn't come off his tongue. "Here . . . have some. . ." He motioned for me to have some pistachios. "Damn this one."

"Take it with your finger," I suggested.

"It's too slippery. You try it."

"I don't think so Clement." I moved to the window and sat down on the sill, cutting off her view. "Maybe a Kleenex. . ."

"Damn," he whimpered, incapable of getting at that piece of shell.

I asked Francesca, "What don't you like about the project?"

Now she had to look at me. "Who said there was something I didn't like?"

"I did."

"And what makes you think that?"

"Because you think there are things to discuss."

She yanked the towel away from her hair, draped it across the arm of the chair, stood up and moved to the other side of the room. "I guess there are."

"Tell me."

"All right." She rattled it off as if she'd been rehearsing. "Your gearing's too high, the market is going to hell and I think your figures are padded out too much."

"And I think you're wrong." I tried, "Who was it who said, when you're talking about property, there are only three things that count. Location. Location. And location."

"What's more," she cut in, "your location stinks."

"Docklands is hot."

"Docklands sucks," she said. "And you're not even in Docklands. You're on the way to Docklands. Second division."

"Long term."

"Bad deal."

"The City and Docklands have to meet somewhere and Howe Wharf is where things will be happening when it does."

"Howe Wharf will have changed hands ten times before that comes about."

"My people don't think so."

"My people do."

"I think the project is right."

"Ask the Reichmann brothers about Docklands."

"Ask me about Docklands."

She snapped, "Then finance it yourself."

I looked at Clement who was still fighting with the errant pistachio shell and reminded him, "I don't have to audition for either of you."

"Don't drag me into the middle," he said. "I'm very busy. People can probably die from this. You've got to sell the deal to her."

I took Francesca's towel from the chair, tossed it to him – it landed square in his lap – and got up to leave.

He shoved a corner of the towel into his mouth and a second later yelped triumphantly, "Got the bugger." Then he screamed, "Blech," made a terrible face and started spitting into the mortar. "Blech. Blech. Blech. The towel. It's full of your hair. Francesca . . . my mouth. . ."

"You've both made enough money on my back to afford a hair dryer," I said. "And better quality towels."

Clement was too concerned with the hair in his mouth. "Blech. . ."

I told Francesca, "I'm at the Golf until tomorrow. When he returns to the land of the living, let me know whether you're in or out." And with that I left.

132

The moment the door closed behind me, I knew I'd made a stupid move and mumbled, shit!

Furious that she could still get to me like that, I walked very slowly towards the elevator. I was hoping that one of them would come rushing out to call me back inside. I even stood there, facing the lift door, not pushing the button, until long past the time when anyone would have believed that I was still waiting for the elevator to arrive.

Back at the Golf, I went up to my room, fell on my bed, stared at the ceiling for a couple of minutes – "Goddammit, Francesca" – then got up and tried to make myself comfortable in a plastic chair on the tiny balcony that overlooked the cross-country run.

First I asked myself, why do you have to be so idiotic? Why do you let her do that to you? And, when I couldn't come up with any reasonable answer, I asked myself, now what?

It seemed to me that I had three options.

I could go over her head and pressure Clement into the deal. I'd get my financing, but I couldn't be sure of the ultimate costs. There was no doubt that my personal relationship with Francesca was strained beyond repair. But mishandling this – being my usual clumsy self – could put our professional relationship in the same hapless category.

Or, I could say to hell with BFCS, and keep shopping the deal. I'd find a bank. There wasn't any doubt in my mind about that. But again, at what cost? People talk. Word gets around. Deals start to look stale, worn out, over-shopped. One guy tells another he said no, and that guy tells a third and by the time you've pitched the deal to the seventh banker, he knows six guys before him have turned it down.

Confidence is infectious. So too is doubt. It's especially true with bankers. They are, as that hackneyed saying goes, quick to hand you an umbrella on a sunny day and even quicker to snatch it back the instant it starts to rain. So the first rule in dealing with bankers has got to be, never let them look at the sky.

That left option number three.

I could bail out, take my losses and forget the whole thing.

Sitting on the balcony at the Golf Hotel in Crans Montana, I assured myself options two and three were not options at all.

I stayed on the balcony, listening to cross-country skiers scraping their way along the icy path.

I promised myself, I can make this deal work.

I said, I refuse to let Francesca get in the way.

I stayed on the balcony until long after the sun went behind the trees and I started to get very cold.

If Clement was aware of the extent of my emotional involvement with Francesca, he never showed it. I'd never spoken to him about it and knowing her as well as I did – as well as I do – I was positive that she'd never spoken to him about us either. Finding her in Crans like that, at his apartment, bothered me. So did her professional chilliness to Howe Wharf. So did the fact that I'd permitted Clement to see that she still had an effect on me.

He rang my room just before dinner asking if I'd join him, and made a point of saying it would just be the two of us. I said fine. We met at a local place he particularly liked where they did a strange dish called seafood couscous.

Considering that it was a Swiss-French restaurant, not Moroccan, and that we were high in the mountains, in the middle of a landlocked state about as far away from the sea as you can get in Western Europe, I expected the meal to be a total failure. Clement assured me this was the best seafood couscous in Switzerland. And, essentially, we were both right. This, undoubtedly, was the best seafood couscous in Switzerland, but probably only because I can't imagine any other restaurant in the country being foolish enough to serve anything quite so atrocious.

Clement not only ate all of his, but finished mine too.

Frankly, I was grateful for such a disastrous meal because it meant we could spend the evening discussing the food instead of other things. He clearly didn't want to talk about business. And I definitely didn't want to talk about her.

When I finally got to bed, I tossed and turned all night. The next morning, early, I gave in to myself and rang her room. "Will you have breakfast with me?"

She answered, "I'm off skiing in about 20 minutes."

"Time for one cup of coffee."

There was a moment's pause. "All right. I'll meet you in the lobby in five minutes." She came down wearing a stunning pink and black nylon ski suit that highlighted the wonderful shape of her legs.

I said, "Hi," and she said, "Hello," and we walked onto the terrace at the back of the hotel where I ordered *café au lait* for two. She passed on a croissant. I settled for a *pain au chocolat*.

"Pure butter," she tsked. "All that cholesterol."

I smiled. "I hadn't expected to see you yesterday. . ."

She sipped her coffee, then said matter-of-factly, "I was only washing my hair at his flat because there was a problem with the sink in my bathroom here." She looked over the rim of her cup. "Just in case you were wondering about that."

I admitted, "I was."

She said, "I know."

Now I asked, "Are you here alone?"

"Does it matter?"

I shrugged. "I don't know."

She said, "I'm skiing with friends who will be picking me up very soon, so if you want to talk about Howe Wharf . . ."

"Okay . . . if you don't mind."

135

She wanted to know, "How much of it have you spun through the Caribbean?"

"Who said I've spun anything through the Caribbean?"

"I did."

"It's a legit deal, Francesca. The property is good. The prices are real."

She glared at me. "Perhaps you've forgotten that I know you very well."

There was no denying that. "Then you know if I tell you it's a legit deal . . ."

"No. Please don't lie to me."

"I have never lied to you."

"On a personal level," she said, "I know that's true. You are perhaps the only man in my life who has never lied to me. But you and I no longer operate on a personal level. This is strictly professional. And I don't know what I'd do . . . I mean, I don't know how I'd react if I ever found out that you were lying to me."

"Then I'll repeat what I just said. I have never lied to you."

"And I'll repeat what I just said. I don't know what I'd do if you did."

Someone called out, "Francesca?"

She stared at me for several seconds, before turning to the three people who'd appeared at the terrace door. She motioned to them – two men and one woman, dressed for a day on the slopes – and they approached our table.

When they got to us, the four of them exchanged kisses on the cheeks and then she made polite introductions. *Monsieur* Radisson, this is *Signor* and *Signora* Di Toscana. And this is *Signor* Guilivi. We shook hands, she took the last gulp of her coffee and said goodbye. I said, have a good day, and watched them leave.

I can't describe *Signor* and *Signora* Di Toscana because I didn't take any notice of them. But *Signor* Guilivi was in his mid-50s and extremely handsome. If he skied as well as he dressed then he was at least as good a skier as

Francesca. My instincts also told me he was extremely rich and recently divorced.

As they walked through the lobby and out of the hotel, I saw him put his arm around the small of her back.

I ordered a second coffee and asked myself, why the hell should I care? But then, I already knew the answer.

Chapter Twelve

Clement assured me that Francesca would approve the deal and promised to have a faxed final draft of the contract on my desk by Friday. I left him in his chalet and rode back down the mountain to Geneva for lunch with Etienne Pont.

A 65-year-old professional middleman – an ageing foot soldier in the army of freelance guys who stalk the periphery of the world's markets – Peter had befriended him in the late '60s when he first started playing at gold and silver futures. Pont would phone every now and then to say he thought there was going to be some action in bullion and, based on his advice, Peter would buy or sell. Over the years they'd made some money together. Not obscene amounts, but still enough to maintain their friendship. However, I always had my doubts about him, and most of the time, when his name came up I refused to stand on ceremony and preferred to back off. "Not my cup of tea."

Most of the time Peter would admit, "He's an acquired taste. Kind of like raw oysters."

I'd ask, "Ever hear of botulism?"

"It's your fault," Peter would say. "You're just a snob. If he was American you'd think he was a terrific chap."

I'd suggest, "If he was an American he'd be flogging used cars."

Peter would shrug. "He is."

And I would remind him, "It is written in the Bible, 'Thou shalt always suspect a man in a thousand-dollar suit, with blow-dried steel grey hair and perfect ivory white implants.'"

What worried me most about Pont was that he was either a terrible liar or he had a terrible memory. He once told Peter he was a Swiss national but he once told me he wasn't. He once told Peter that he was born Etienne Pont and liked it when his English-speaking clients called him Stevie Bridge, but he once told me he was born Steven Bridges and had his name legally changed to Etienne Pont. He once told Peter he had a castle just across the border in France, but he once told me he had a castle just across the border in Austria. He once told Peter he owned shares in the best restaurant in Zurich, but I always suspected there were times when he didn't know where his next meal was coming from.

In this case, I knew precisely where his next meal was coming from because he'd booked the table in my name.

"What can I tell you about the world that you don't already know?" He mused, "Gold is going nowhere fast and silver isn't in the least interesting. Times have changed, *mon vieux*. When that Yamani bloke did it to the world, quadrupling the price of oil in just a few months, even guys working out of telephone booths made fortunes. Today the fun is gone. Where is Yamani when we need him? Where is the havoc? That's what we need. Chaos. Mayhem. Or more guys like the Hunt brothers. God, how I loved the Hunt brothers."

Through the soup and into the pasta, he explained how in the early 1970s, just before the Arabs pulled the plug on oil, silver was gently riding along at around $2 an ounce. Knowing that silver is a primary component of both the electronics and photographic industries, Bunker and Herbert Hunt – a pair of good old rich boys from Texas – reckoned it would not only be amusing but also highly profitable if they could quietly corner the market.

Their father, the legendary H. L. Hunt, had been an oil speculator and gambler and almost certainly the model for Jock Ewing in the TV series *Dallas*. The main difference between H. L. and Jock was that H. L. was much richer than any Ewing ever got to be. Probably meaner too. He died in 1974, a free-range billionaire, at a time when there weren't a lot of them running loose.

Predicting that silver could one day be worth more than gold, Bunker and Herbert helped goose up the price from $2.90 an ounce in December 1973 to $6.70 an ounce a couple of months later. By that time they'd acquired 35 million ounces and thought they'd effortlessly managed their squeeze.

What they hadn't counted on was that, only a few miles south, the Mexican government was sitting on 50 million ounces.

From Mexico City, the world at $6.70 an ounce looked pretty rosy, all the more so because they'd bought their stake at under $2 per. So the Mexicans came into the market as sellers. And before the Hunt Brothers could say, "*Ay caramba*," the price tumbled back to about $4.

Now, with their appetites sufficiently whetted and their fingers slightly charcoaled, Bunker and Herbert spent the next four years buying up all the silver they could.

By the end of 1979, together with the royal family of Saudi Arabia, they owned or controlled several hundred million ounces – something like one-quarter of the world's silver shares on the New York Commodity Exchange and five out of every eight silver shares on the Chicago Board of Trade.

Consequently, prices went up.

When silver hit $19, the Hunts and their cronies had more than tripled their money. But that wasn't enough for them. Between February and March 1980, the Hunts borrowed a staggering $1.3 billion, to kick the price as high as $49.

Pont disclosed that, throughout the Hunts' buying sprees, the margin calls were as little as $1,000 per contract. Each silver contract represents 5,000 ounces. At $2 an ounce, $1,000 means you've put down 10%. But at $49 an ounce, the $1000 margin becomes a minuscule percentage. So the New York Commodity Exchange, in an attempt to bring some stability back to the market, decided to raise the margin requirements. The Board of Governors, by declaring an emergency, eventually got the margin requirement as high as $60,000. They then instituted a "liquidation only" rule, meaning that no new contracts could be taken up. The only business on the floor could be the closing out of contracts already held. And that effectively put the brakes on silver.

It also, effectively, put a squeeze on the Hunts.

Silver prices began falling. As prices slipped, cash calls came in. Because the Hunts had been buying silver with borrowed money, then using that silver to secure more borrowings, their collateral quickly diminished in value. Wise to this, the banks demanded more collateral.

On 25 March 1980, the New York investment house Bache Halsey Stuart Shields sent the brothers a call for $135 million.

They couldn't meet it.

And the floodgates opened.

Reserves poured into the market and prices disintegrated. The Hunts got caught short for $400 million. In the end it took a long-term $1 billion loan from the US government to keep both the Hunts and the world's silver market afloat.

"It was a dream come true," Pont boasted. "Sheer and utter havoc. I loved every minute of it."

I was interested in knowing, "How did you make out during all of this?"

"Terrific. I was running some of their contracts and when we hit $25 I wanted to sell. They'd given me discretionary power so I sold. I bought back at $28, sold again at $32, bought in again at $38 and sold for the final time at $41. When the market crashed, I cashed them out at $25 and they were glad to get that much."

"Oh." I looked at him. "What happened to the deals on the way up to $41?"

He gave me a wide-angle view of his over-priced dentures. "Let's just say . . ." He gestured to suggest I'd know exactly what he was talking about . . . "they were very glad to get out at $25."

I nodded and made a mental note to tell Peter we weren't ever again going to deal with Stevie Bridge.

"I love those guys," he went on. "I just love them. The pandemonium they created was beautiful. A real work of art. They bought me a Roller and a Jag and a new heating system for the pool. I'm telling you, I L-O-V-E them."

"I'll B-E-T you do." They'd probably paid for his teeth too.

"I could talk about them for hours," he said. "But the best story was the plane ride."

I knew there was no sense in asking what plane ride, because he was going to tell me. "The plane ride."

"Listen to this . . ." He leaned close so that I wouldn't miss a word of it. "Somewhere in the middle of their quest up the silver mountain, Bunker and Herbert got it into their heads that the US government was going to shut them down. They became convinced that your Uncle Sam was going to try to seize whatever silver they were actually holding. So they decided to move a lot of it to Europe. They loaded something like $100 million worth of silver on to a commercial flight to London. And then, just to be on the safe side – I mean, we're talking a hundred mill crated in the hold of that plane – they bought themselves a pair of tickets for the flight over. In economy!"

That did surprise me. "In economy?"

"Apex. You know, extra-cheap, bucket shop round trips where you have to stay a Saturday night, wear a green sweater and change your name to Gladys."

"They had $100 million in the plane and they came over in the back of the bus?"

"Wait, it gets better." He started laughing. "These blokes are not small men. And the seats are tiny. So they're already pretty cramped. Now, picture this. Bunker's on the aisle and Herbert's in the middle and just after take off the air hostess comes around asking if anyone wants a headset for the in-flight movie. Bunker refuses to pay. This is two dollars, right? But Herbert wants to see the film so he buys one. The movie comes on and now Bunker's staring at this silent screen, watching the opening credits. He figures maybe the movie isn't too bad, so he leans towards his brother, pulls one of those headset plugs out of Herbert's ear and sticks it in his own ear. You like that?"

I had to agree it was a fabulous tale. What I didn't tell Stevie was that I also had to wonder if any of it was true.

The waiter came by and delivered two portions of wild Scotch salmon – I didn't recall ordering it – but Stevie dug in before I could ask if it was a mistake, so I picked at mine.

"How about," he said with his mouth full, "you and Peter doing something with me in metals?"

I replied, "The Hunt Brothers are too hard an act to follow." And because I didn't want to sit through a sales pitch, I turned the conversation around to the weather.

We got through occluded fronts at the same time he finished his salmon, so I suggested dessert. He had the *tarte tatin*. I passed and settled on a coffee, then casually asked if the name Guilivi meant anything to him. He pondered that for a moment and wondered if I was talking about Gianni Guilivi who was a lawyer out of Milan. I described him and Stevie said that sounded like the guy but he couldn't be sure.

"What do you know about him?"

Stevie said immediately, "Significantly rich."

"What else?"

"What do you want me to find out? I've got plenty of the right contacts."

"Nothing."

In exchange for settling the bill – he didn't even put up the pretence of an argument about it – he offered to drive me to the airport. And, on the way, he repeated his question about Peter and me doing a little something with him in metals.

I tried to fob him off with the excuse, "That's Peter's department."

"I was sort of thinking . . ." He took his eyes off the road and looked at me . . . "I mean, how about maybe the two of you getting interested in something rather special . . . I mean . . . what would you say to a little fling with plutonium?"

"With what?"

"Plutonium," he repeated.

"What the hell would we do with plutonium?"

"What some people do with it is make bombs. What you do with it is make a fortune."

I couldn't believe it. "Bombs?"

"Yes, as in nuclear bombs."

"What in Christ's name are you talking about?"

He leaned closer to me while he steered through traffic. "Okay. This is just between us. But there happens to be a lot of plutonium being sold on the black markets in Eastern Europe at the moment. The prices are low and hard currency is king. There's nothing to worry about because you never take possession of the stuff. But the people who've offered it to me need a middleman in the West to broker it with buyers, mainly in the Middle East. Now, I've already got someone in place who's got all the right contacts. Qaddafi. Saddam. Even the Israelis. But someone has to pay for it before my guy can move it. We're looking for someone who's willing to come in with at least $5 million and perhaps as much as twice that. It's not a lot of money, considering that, you know, after brokers' fees, there should be an eight or ten times return on the initial investment."

"Jeezus."

"Please note that I said, after fees. This is net. I'm talking pure profit. Eight to ten times."

I was speechless.

He continued, "You're probably thinking to yourself, those are big numbers. But then this is the biggest game in the world right now. The break-up of Eastern Europe, especially of the Soviet Union, has dumped all sorts of weapons onto the black markets. Want to buy Kalashnikovs? I can get as many as you want, for under £5 each. Want rocket launchers? Hand held? Truck mounted? You tell me what you need, I can get it for you. All that stuff is easy. But weapons-grade plutonium is first prize."

I calculated outloud, "Eight times back on five . . ."

"And ten times back on ten?"

My mind wandered for a few seconds. With that kind of money snugly put to bed in a Swiss bank, I wouldn't need Clement or Francesca or anyone else to finance deals for the next several years. Or, maybe, ever.

"Interested?"

I came back to my senses. "No."

He seemed genuinely surprised. "No?"

"Absolutely not," I said. "No! We're not in that business. We have no interest in ever being in that business. As a matter of fact, let's forget we've even had this conversation."

"Are you sure?"

I snapped, "Yes!"

"Whatever you say." He took both hands off the wheel and raised them in the air. "It's forgotten."

I nodded, "Forgotten!"

Except that I thought about it on the plane all the way to London.

"Did you say $40-$100 million?" Peter asked, when I

rang him late that afternoon in Paris. "There's that kind of money involved with this stuff?"

"I told Stevie, no."

"I hope you did."

"Of course, I did. We'd be nuts to take those kinds of risks. We can get into enough trouble on our own without bringing Saddam Hussein into the game."

"Speaking of which. . ."

"Speaking of what?"

"Trouble. I had Roderick on the phone today. You'll probably hear from him tonight or first thing tomorrow. He's been contacted by the London Stock Exchange about his dealings in Maxwell shares."

"Shit. How the hell did they get to him?"

"Officially he bought the shares."

"So?"

"So one of the brokers talked."

"What did he tell them?"

"I guess he told him about Roderick."

"I mean, what did Roderick say?"

"What do you think he said? He said, in extremely polite Bahamian, fuck off man."

I hung up with Peter and immediately phoned Adrian O'Neil. His switchboard operator asked, "Who's calling?" I said it was personal.

A few seconds later Adrian got on the line. "Can I help you?"

One of the great benefits of having an American accent in Britain is that it stands out. So all I said was, "I think we should talk about a lot of things."

He recognized my voice and promised, "I'll ring you straight back."

He did, about 15 minutes later. "I'm not calling from the office. I'm on a pay phone but I don't have a lot of coins so we'd better talk fast. I tried to get you this morning but your secretary said you were out of town and I didn't want to leave any messages."

"What's going on?"

"We had a visit from two guys who work for the Insider Dealing Group at the Stock Exchange. They wanted to know about some short-selling of MCC just before Maxwell's death. I'm sorry, but all our trades are recorded. We had to tell them."

"What did you tell them?"

"I told them what you told me to tell them. I mean, what you told me. I told them that the trades were down to Roderick Hays-White at Tivoli Court Trading."

"And what did they say?"

"They said they wanted to get in touch with Roderick Hays-White so we gave them his number in Nassau. Bay, we don't have any choice. We're members of the Exchange. We have to cooperate."

"What else did they ask?"

"They asked me if I knew Mr Hays-White, if I've dealt on his behalf before, if I felt there was anything suspicious about his trading patterns."

"And what did you say?"

Adrian was getting annoyed. "I said yes, I knew him. I said yes, I'd dealt with him before. And I said no, I never felt there was anything suspicious about his trading patterns. What the hell would you expect me to say?"

"You're right," I apologized. "I'm sorry." Then the fact that he wasn't ringing from his office dawned on me. "Why are you calling from a pay phone?"

"Because it might look very odd if they knew I was telling this to you."

"Listen to me . . ." I needed him to understand. "We didn't do anything illegal. We didn't do any insider trading. We didn't break any laws. We didn't break any rules."

He said, "I certainly hope not."

"What do you mean, I certainly hope not. I didn't and neither did you."

"I'm just not used to having investigators coming around asking questions."

"If they come back, throw them out."

"I can't do that. We have to cooperate."

"Okay, so cooperate. Roderick Hays-White bought for Tivoli Court and that's the end of that."

"But what happens if . . ." He stopped for a few seconds, then blurted out, "What happens if they hear the tapes?"

"What tapes?"

"Don't you listen. All our calls are recorded. The tapes of our phone calls. Why in God's name do you think I'm ringing from a pay phone?"

I took a deep breath and tried to remember the exact wording of my conversations with Adrian on the day Maxwell died. I played our conversation back in my head as best as I could recall it, then finally decided, so what?

And that's what I told Adrian. "So what? So there's a tape of me saying the deals are down to Roderick Hays-White and Tivoli Court Trading. What does that prove?"

"Well . . . it proves . . ." He couldn't think of anything. "I guess it doesn't prove anything."

"I guess not," I said, just as the signal flashed to tell us his time was running out. "Are you still there?"

"I don't have enough coins."

"Okay. I'll speak with you tomorrow."

"Don't ring me in the office," he said.

I started to remind him, "We've done nothing . . ." when the line shut off. So I finished the sentence to myself . . . "wrong."

With the phone still to my ear, I'd just clicked onto another line to dial Roderick in Nassau when his call came in. "Great minds think alike."

"That should teach me to be more patient," he said in that beautiful, slow voice of his. "I prefer to see you spending your money than to be me spending mine."

"What's going on? Peter says you got a call."

"They asked me about the trades and I told them my

business was none of their business and that, unless they were prepared to come to the Bahamas to speak with me in person, I would never discuss my business with anyone over the phone."

"How did they take that?"

"As my good mother used to say, lying down."

I related to him my conversation with Adrian and reiterated that I didn't think there was anything to worry about because we'd not done anything wrong.

"But authorities get their jollies being authoritarian," he said. "That's by definition. If they take the time to look for something wrong and they can't find anything wrong, then they make up that there's something wrong."

I laughed. "Is that something else your good mother used to say?"

"No," he replied. "That's what Meyer Lansky used to say."

When I hung up with him, I rang Gerald to brief him on what was happening. His advice was, "Just wait it out. Let them come to you. Let them play their cards first."

"What happens if they do come to me?"

"Maybe they won't."

"Maybe they will."

"We'll cross that bridge when we come to it."

"How can you be so calm about this?"

"Because that's one of the things you pay me for. There's no reason to think that you're at all involved yet."

"Unless they listen to the tapes in Adrian's office."

"And what if they do? What does that prove?"

"I guess it proves I bought the shares."

He repeated his question, "And what does that prove?"

I didn't understand. "What do you mean?"

"Does it prove insider dealing?"

"No."

"So, what are you worried about?"

I hung up with him and phoned Peter again, to assure him that everything was otherwise under control.

"What about Francesca?" He asked.

"What about her?"

"Make certain they never ask her."

"Ask her what?"

"Ask her anything."

"Ask her anything about what?"

"Anything about anything."

"There's nothing to worry about."

"The hell there isn't." He insisted, "She knows too much."

I brushed him off. "There's nothing to worry about."

On Friday morning, as promised, Clement faxed me the final terms of our Howe Wharf deal. But he'd added two clauses that I'd never seen before.

Chapter Thirteen

For Clement, Howe Wharf was a *fait accompli*. His memo, marked "Highly Confidential", was unsigned and on regular non-headed A4 paper.

That was his way of saying, "I can always deny this."

He wrote that he was delighted to join us in the project and heartily looked forward to a fruitful partnership. But in the same upbeat tone, he pointed out that the two new stipulations were, unfortunately, non-negotiable.

To begin with, he wanted personal guarantees – from Peter and me – equivalent to one-half of the debt. I was shocked, because he'd never asked for anything even remotely similar before.

Then, he wanted Peter and me to indemnify his position at the bank. He said he was willing to go out on a limb for us, against Francesca's advice. But he insisted that, should the deal backfire and he get fired, we'd have to provide an escrow nest-egg of £1 million to hold him over until he was on his feet again.

At first I thought he'd gone insane. There was no way I could agree to any of this.

I faxed it to Peter, who said right away, "Tell him forget it and we'll move on to the next one."

And when I showed it to Gerald, he concurred that these terms were unacceptable. He also felt that Clement's £1 million safety-net jeopardized his own position at the bank. "It's very dodgy. His duty is to his employers and this appears to me to be a definite conflict of interest."

I reminded Gerald, "Clement's greed is his most attractive trait."

"I'm not immediately sure how it's illegal. My nose tells me it is but I'd have to look into it. However, even if it isn't, I have no doubt that it is immoral. My instinct is to say it is also, probably, unenforceable."

"Unenforceable?" That made me start thinking that this was something I should consider. "You mean, even if I agree to it, there's nothing he can do about it?"

"To enforce the agreement, he'd have to produce evidence in court that you'd agreed to this deal and, by producing the terms of the deal, he would be admitting that he'd deliberately violated his employer's trust."

"How very inspiring." It was a lesson straight out of the J. R. Ewing School of Ethics. In business, always have something on everyone. Lamentably, more often than not, it's easier said than done. Even if you find out that some major tycoon on the other side of a takeover battle likes to sleep with sheep, knowing that and using that are two different things. Yet here was Clement handing me something that he clearly wouldn't want his chairman in Zurich to know about. So, against Gerald's advice and Peter's better judgement, I met with him. Over the course of an afternoon – just the two of us locked behind the door of his office – we forged a deal.

In exchange for dropping the non-negotiable demand that Peter and I put up personal guarantees equalling 50% of the bank's position, I pledged to place a bouquet of assets worth £4 million – to be considered extraordinary collateral against the Howe Wharf debt – into a company, title to which would be held by solicitors mutually agreeable to the bank and Pennstreet. But those assets would not cede to BFCS unless Pennstreet PLC defaulted on three consecutive interest payments, or if the value of those assets should fall below £3 million.

Securing the loan was the price we had to pay to keep Francesca on our side.

The price I had to pay to keep Clement between me and Francesca was the secret escrow account – a non-negotiable £1 million, which I negotiated down to $1 million. He also agreed that the money would revert back to Peter and me once 50% of the debt on Howe Wharf was fully paid.

When Gerald heard about it, he shook his head. "I don't want to be a party to it."

"You said it was unenforceable. It's the perfect deal. We've got it, he thinks we've spent it, we've still got it."

"No," Gerald said. "It doesn't work like that. What you are really talking about is a bribe. So, right away, the answer is no. And even if I would be willing to get involved, which I'm not, this shouldn't be done onshore."

I ended our conversation then and there. If he had his reasons for not wanting to represent us in this one, that was fine with me. Anyway, when it came to finding a lawyer who was more than willing to do things that Gerald wasn't, Peter and I knew the best.

Roderick's cousin, L. James Morgan III, was now in his 70s and, for all intents and purposes, retired. He spent most of his days on a 65-foot sloop called "The Bar". But he kept an office in Nassau and came in a couple of days each week to handle the affairs of a few special clients. A man of enormous charm and class, he did not suffer from Gerald's vigorous sense of moral right and wrong. He was also, perhaps, the single best-dressed solicitor anywhere in the Caribbean. Tall and handsome, with soft chocolate skin and owl-like deep brown eyes, he always dressed entirely in white, including white shoes, a white shirt, a white tie and a wide-brimmed white hat.

When I got him on the phone and told him what I was doing, he promised to take care of everything. He and

Roderick set up a little company in St Kitts and Nevis called Jura Mercantile Trading – I thought the Swiss reference was appropriate – and I transferred title to a three-condo luxury apartment block in Freeport we'd bought five years earlier at a bankruptcy auction on Roderick's advice. When it was first built, the place was worth $3.6 million but we'd picked it up for just $850,000. And then we only had to put down 10%. We were financing it through a private bank in Nassau run by one of Roderick's school chums. Although the flats were rented and they generated a good income, for tax reasons we maintained our mortgage payment schedule with funds funnelled through a Bahamian shell company called Golden Shores.

Playing on Clement's infinite greed, I had no trouble convincing him that the condos had, by now, doubled in value. He therefore agreed to assign them a collateral value, based on the outstanding debt, of $680,000. I topped up the rest, bringing the combined asset value over the $1 million figure, with a block of shares in Golden Shores.

Admittedly, Clement had no idea that Peter and I owned Golden Shores. All he saw was a pile of certificates and a series of annual reports that Roderick supplied to him, which showed money flowing through the company and valued the shares at $334,000.

"No one must ever know about this," he insisted. "I'm serious, Bay. No one. And by that I mean, you know who."

"Who?"

"Her."

"Oh. Her. Well, I'm not going to be the one to tell her. She's the last one I'd think of mentioning this to."

"This is perfect," he kept nodding.

His secret was safe with me. There didn't seem to be any reason on earth why I should confess to Francesca that Clement was double-dealing behind the bank's back to get me the very deal she was trying to stop.

To keep it hidden, Clement stipulated that no paper-work should be sent to him. He asked if I knew someone in the islands who could represent him and I told him I'd heard about a fellow named L. James Morgan III. So he hired L. James to act on his behalf. The fact that our Bahamian attorney was also Clement's attorney – he never knew that – acting in a matter that might be defined as a bribe, didn't seem to bother anyone, least of all L. James.

Next, I took some small commercial holdings from the Pennstreet Properties portfolio, had them valued at just over £4 million, then assigned title in them to a Swiss company I formed called Pennstreet Properties of Great Britain Trust, SA. Shares in that company were held in escrow for Pennstreet PLC and BFCS by solicitors in Geneva. Mainly a pencil-whipping exercise, it meant that I could still maintain the properties on my books, while Clement had the comfort of believing that, should we default, BFCS was protected.

When I happened to mention to Gerald one evening over dinner that my deal with Clement was going ahead, he immediately told me to change the subject. "I don't want to know. Your friends in the islands are not exactly kosher."

"You should see how well they dress."

He refused to be impressed.

Once Clement received word from L. James that everything was in order, a bundle of contracts – minus the two supplemental clauses – arrived from BFCS. I sent it over to Gerald for his inspection.

At that point, Roderick phoned from Nassau to explain that, unless I was willing to commit additional company funds to Howe Wharf, any delay in getting the money for the project out of Clement would back up our repayment schedule with Long Beach and Britannica Consolidated.

I assured him the BFCS money was on the way.

He said he was merely reminding me that accruing

interest on those accounts would overextend us with our bankers there.

I reiterated that I wasn't going to tie up any more money on this and that he'd just have to find a way to keep our bankers in the Caribbean pacified until Clement processed the paperwork. I assured him, "We're only talking about a few more days."

Somehow I got the impression that Peter must have spoken to Roderick and that this was their way of ganging up against me. So now, intent on showing everyone that I knew what I was doing, I began looking around for a small deal to fill the coffers with fast cash. I scoured the press, went through hundreds of annual reports and spent a small fortune pulling information out of several computer databases, reading everything I could about any company that might somehow be vulnerable. It took the better part of two weeks before I narrowed my sights on a handful of likely victims.

There was a company in Yorkshire called Capital and Europe Timber, which I liked at first because they were cash rich, but ultimately rejected because their asset base was in Czechoslovakia and there was no way I was going to sink money into any country where the name of the ruling political party was unpronounceable.

There was a company in Birmingham called Carthage Medical Providers Mutual, which on the surface appeared to sell specialist insurance to firms on the periphery of the medical and health care industries. In reality what they did was to take a majority stake in those businesses – they currently owned two private ambulance firms, a supplier of gauze, a manufacturer of operating room spotlights and a distributor of dental equipment – then over-insure them. They'd write huge policies on the companies and their employees, spin profits by reinsuring everything through one of their own offshore subsidiaries in Panama, and eventually pawn off the coverage through the market at Lloyd's. Once the company was locked into more insurance than they could ever use, they'd help the employees finance a management buy-out. It was the weirdest scam I'd ever run across – a company whose profit base was entirely dependent on forced over-insurance. My gut feeling was that someone would eventually come along, break them up and make some money. But my head prevailed.

There was a company in Bradford called Royal Strand Latex, which caught my eye because they weren't in the latex business. Companies which promise to be in one industry and wind up in another create confusion, and I continue to believe, ardently, that there is profit in confusion. Royal Strand Latex had long ago diverted out of synthetics and plastics and expanded in several different directions, including holiday let flats, copper mining and a small chain of discount frozen food retailers. They'd gone so far off course that I felt obliged to take a very long second look at them. But while I was looking, the chairman and chief executive announced that he was splitting his own job in two – always a good sign – and hired a young hotshot to run the business on a day to day basis. The new CEO immediately sold off the holiday flat let business to concentrate on their other holdings. Beaten to the punch, I backed away from Royal Strand Latex.

Then there was a company in Slough called TJF Worldwide. I fancied them straight away because management there violated just about every rule of good business. To begin with, no one could tell me what TJF stood for. The tag Worldwide was equally intriguing because they'd never exported anything. My only conclusion was that, somewhere along the line, a wise-ass manager had hoped to make someone believe the company was bigger than it really was. I saw it instead as a company with no corporate past. That meant there was no corporate tradition. And a company with no corporate tradition is, to my mind, a company with no corporate soul.

They went straight to the top of my list.

Their annual report was filled with colour photos of everyone on the board and everyone in senior management. On its own, that's a sure sign of a lethal ego problem. But the report also contained colour photos of every property the company owned and every product the company produced. By my reckoning, if you have to spend so much trying to sell your product to your own shareholders, either something's radically wrong with your product or you've got a bunch of idiots running sales and marketing.

Then I discovered that one of the perks for senior management was use of company flats in Cyprus and Malta. If I'd been a shareholder, I would have raised holy hell. Why in God's name should a company maintain flats in foreign places where they don't do any business? It all gets down to arrogance. And arrogant management is always bad management.

I began to think I was falling in love with TJF Worldwide.

Just as promising, the company was exceedingly over-autoed.

Under UK tax laws, companies can provide cars for their staff and use fleet leasing as a deduction. Even though the employee then pays the tax man for the perk, a job with a new car every other year is one of the anomalies of British business. It allows poorly paid employees to feel better about their lot because they've got a bigger car than they might otherwise be able to afford. That's especially true when you get to the board of directors, who invariably take enormous pride in driving Silver Shadows at the shareholders' expense.

When Peter and I started hiring people we made the firm decision, no cars. We pay everyone a little extra and then wish them luck buying whatever wheels they want. I've got a small Mercedes and also a runabout 1960 bug-eyed Triumph that spends most of its time in the garage getting fixed. But I paid for my toys, my shareholders didn't. Peter keeps a Jag in France and an old Citroen DS–21 convertible in London, which is exactly the opposite of any sane person. But as long as he paid for them he should be able to do anything he wants with them. So whenever I spot a company like TJF Worldwide – where 350 employees accounted for 393 company cars, including two stretch limos – I know something is drastically wrong.

Frankly, it was hard to believe that they'd managed to survive as long as they had. Their debt was excruciatingly high and their cashflow was just about non-existent. They were screaming at the top of their lungs, "Ripe, ripe, ripe," and I came very close to going after them. I only stopped short at the last minute because I couldn't figure out what to do with them.

Their largest single product was a minuscule component for radar guidance systems and their largest single client was the Manchester-based electronics firm Ferranti. But Ferranti was in big trouble and their main competitor, GEC, already had a very sound radar guidance business. So the question in my mind was, if I broke up TJF Worldwide, who'd buy that component from me? I knew Ferranti couldn't and GEC wouldn't. The last thing I wanted was to get stuck holding a company that had too many eggs piled into one basket, especially in a market where spare baskets were in short order.

In other words, my downside risk was too high. And downside risk is something I always think about. If I can help it, I never consciously add up how much money I'm going to make on a deal should it all go right before looking with cold, clear eyes at how much I can lose should it all go wrong. So I took a deep breath – more like a sigh – let my better judgement prevail and backed away from TJF Worldwide.

In the end, I settled on a company in Leicester called Ohio G. Holdings.

Derived from the Japanese term meaning "good morning", their main business was orange and other citrus fruit flavourings for canned juices. But over the years –

under the direction of their California-born chairman, Tokyo Katayama – they'd diversified into all sorts of unrelated areas. They wholesaled wire and cork, imported Spanish marble and Dutch tomatoes and owned a foundry in Wales that made die cast tools for the coal industry. They had an exclusive distributorship through southwest England for an obscure Japanese brand of spark plugs, whose name translates to Soft Mist. And an 18% stake in a firm called Buffalo Ltd, the British arm of a loss-making Japanese manufacturer of light farm machinery. They also owned a 49% stake in a loss-making Lake District real estate agency, a commercial auction house near Gatwick, a stationers in Hove, a newsagents in Cardiff, a travel agency in Liverpool – specializing in tours to Japan – a cash-and-carry food store outside Stockton-on-Tees, a one-star hotel in Birkenhead and a six-boat, nearly-broke fishing fleet on the Isle of Man.

Simply put, Ohio G. was a company that didn't make any sense.

Except for the travel agency – which is, of course, an old trick to get free airline tickets – Katayama had long ago lost his way. That showed quite clearly in his company's accounts. Although the group had been in the black every year for the past two decades, profit had never exceeded 4% of turnover. And most of the time it was half that. With bank interest rates hovering around 10%, they could have done five times better simply by shutting off their lights, unplugging their phones and sticking their money in a building society.

The company was obviously a direct reflection of its 79-year-old chairman.

Katayama's father, Hideki, had been the black-sheep fifth son of a minor Japanese shipping magnate. At the turn of the century, after marrying a woman his parents considered to be below their station, Hideki migrated to California. Life there was good until World War II when the Katayamas were among thousands of Japanese

Americans who found themselves interned. Three years later, both Hideki and his wife were dead in the northern California prison camp.

Incensed at having been subjected to such indignity, within minutes of being released at the end of the war Tokyo Katayama insisted that his family cash out of the United States and sail for Europe. When their ship docked at Bristol, they checked a map, decided Leicester was as close to the centre of England as they could get and settled there.

Building the company from scratch, Katayama fervently maintained that it should be a family affair. His 74-year-old twin sisters were on the board, as was their 73-year-old cousin. The company secretary, a distant relative on his mother's side, was 68. The sixth member of the board was the chief executive, a comparative stripling of 55. But Clive Armour North – who signed his name on official documents as Puck – happened to be Tokyo Katayama's son-in-law. He'd fallen in love with Katayama's oldest daughter when they met in school and went to work for the company when he was 18. Never having had a job in what I'd call the real world, I had little doubt that Puck had earned his stripes intravenously.

What's more, Mrs Puck and all three of their half-Japanese little-Pucks were also on the payroll.

Shares in Ohio G. Holdings were so lightly traded that none of the major houses bothered covering the company. I couldn't locate a single analyst report on them since 1977 – when Puck had ascended to the board – and even then the recommendation was, "A poor hold, a better sell."

For the past three years, the shares had languished at 9p. Dividends had been declared but you needed a magnifying glass to see them. The company was a tangled mess of nepotism and general incompetence. And the more I studied it, the more convinced I became that, once I'd extracted it from beneath the wing of the

Katayama clan, I could sell off the parts for considerably more than the whole.

Based on my most pessimistic calculation, my downside risk was extremely low. After all, the company was a grab bag of assets. Based on my purposely conservative estimate, I believed the break-up value would be somewhere close to 30p a share.

The dossier I put together soon covered my conference table, with the spill taking up a couple of chairs. It seemed like a lot, so Patty and I piled everything in a single stack on the floor and measured it. Our old record was 58 inches. Ohio G. beat it by half a foot.

Having broken our own record – and also smashed the five-foot barrier, which I explained to Patty had the same mythical quality as the four-minute mile – I insisted we open a bottle of champagne. She suggested celebrations might be premature and thought we should wait until we secured the deal. I accused her of having inherited Peter's terminal sense of worry and popped the cork.

When the bottle was done, I bought a few million shares of Ohio G. Holdings and put them into one of our British companies, Truro Trading. At the same time, I had Roderick set up a series of purpose-built shells, ready-made offshore companies that we would secretly control while accumulating Ohio G. shares. One was in the Channel Islands and two were in the Caribbean.

I continued buying for Truro until I had a 4.9% stake, then stopped, because Stock Exchange rules require anyone holding 5% to make a declaration of intent, and I wasn't ready to do that. However, our phantom ready-mades were still buying.

Unfortunately, because so few of Ohio G. shares had been traded in the past several years, my interest in them did not go unnoticed. They quickly edged up to 13p. Except that, by that time, I already owned 28% of the company.

I now brought in a Dutch bank based in Curaçao and a French bank based in Martinique – without mentioning anything to Peter, I was also funnelling some of our own funds into the deal through a Hong Kong bank – and came back into the market as Truro Trading. I purchased a single block large enough to bring Truro's holdings to nearly 9% and that same morning declared my intention to take over the company.

Ohio G. Holdings' shares jumped to 19p.

My average purchase price, thanks largely to my offshore buying, was far below my estimated net asset value, so I did a little flow chart and determined that I could afford to go all the way up to 35p in a blitz for those shares that would get me past the 50.1% winning post. What's more, I could bring the shares I was holding off shore into my camp at 35p because I was going to pay for them with the banks' money and have a neat short-term cash injection to bolster Howe Wharf.

My fallback position was equally sound. The sharks swimming around the City loved a hostile takeover bid because it usually meant instant profits for them. Their greed was also their Achilles' heel. By playing up to their takeover frenzy, it would be easy to stuff them with it, to dump all my shares on them and walk away with a fast profit just before the market price sank like a stone.

What I hadn't counted on was how far off course the board had become. They'd been caught napping and had no real defence against a takeover.

To my utter glee, it was like Pearl Harbor in reverse.

The best the chairman could muster was a personal call to demand that I cease and desist. "This is a very dangerous thing you're doing, young man. People's livelihoods are at stake."

I said, "I understand that."

"I don't think you do." He insisted, "This isn't a game. What you're doing is despicable. You have no interest at all in running my company. You are going to pick it apart and leave nothing but bones. I will not permit you to do that."

With the shares riding now around 25p, I tried to explain in a gentle way, "Perhaps, Mr Katayama, you've got me wrong. There are several parts of your company that I believe will function better in a different environment. And no, this is not a game. This is about progress, about moving forward, about providing better profit potentials for the shareholders and better working conditions for the employees."

He barked, "This is very wrong."

I deliberately spoke softly so that he could see that his temper would not shake me. "As I'm sure you know by now, I have, today, purchased a rather large block of shares, and believe that I know where several other large blocks of shares are, which would effectively give me nearly 40% of the company. That's four times your own personal stake, which makes me the largest single shareholder."

"I'm not interested," he cut in. "Not interested . . ."

"Sir, I can easily afford to offer for the remaining 10–11%. You, on the other hand, cannot afford to take up the shares you would need to stop me. So it strikes me that the best deal you can get for your shareholders, and for yourself, would be to settle on a price and recommend the takeover to the board."

"Not even on my death bed," he promised. "I have seen you cowboys come and go. You build nothing. You ruin lives. You are no better than vultures."

I asked if he would meet with me.

He said he wouldn't.

I asked if there was any way that I could reassure him mine was the best course of action for his shareholders.

He said there was not.

So I played one of my big cards. "If I sold my holding right now, unloaded it, your share price would crash to below what it was when I first started buying. You would probably be lucky to get 3–5p. And if your share value fell to less than half of your net asset value, you would then be required to call an Extraordinary General

Meeting. Any loans you have secured with your shares would almost certainly be called in. At that same time, I can guarantee, your shareholders would mutiny."

"Scum. That's all you characters are. Utter scum." He slammed down the phone.

I now dictated a letter to him. "My Dear Mr Katayama: I am willing to offer 27p a share for all of the outstanding shares in your company. I must now insist, as the largest single shareholder of Ohio G. Holdings, that you present my offer to the board and recommend it. If you refuse, I will be forced to insist on an Extraordinary General Meeting, at which time I will demand your removal from the board. I await your answer in no more than 60 minutes. Sincerely yours, Bay Radisson."

Patty sent the fax and I sat back to wait.

With ten minutes to spare, a fax came in from Puck North saying that as chief executive and a member of the board, he would recommend my offer of 33p. "Are you now prepared to meet with the board to discuss your intentions for the company?"

It was a critical mistake. By picking a figure like that he was telling me two things. First, that there was a price at which they would be willing to sell. And second, that his price lay somewhere between 27p and 33p.

I answered, "Dear Mr North: Thank you for your fax. Considering the nature of this bid for Ohio G. Holdings, I must regretfully decline your invitation to meet with you and the board until your recommendation is made, accepted by the board and accepted by your shareholders, and you duly advise me that my offer at 27p is formally accepted. At that time, I would look forward to discussing our future cooperation."

It was the most polite way I knew to say, you don't have any choice, this is about war, and in this war we don't take prisoners.

Now Puck phoned me. In extremely formal tones – the way Westerners who work with the Japanese can often overdo it – he said he couldn't recommend a takeover at anything less than 33p. Even at that level, he said, he would be overriding his father-in-law's staunch objections to this bid. I held my ground, again threatening to sink the shares if my offer was not accepted. He now made his third mistake of the day and came down to 32p.

That's when I knew I'd won.

I told him I could not possibly consider it and said that, unless he had a better proposition, I would be issuing a press statement with a final and unconditional offer. He said he couldn't do any better than 32p and I wished him the best of luck. I then composed a news release, which ran in the papers the next morning, making public my conversation with Puck and raising my concluding offer to 29p.

Shares for sale at that price were plentiful and I easily acquired another 5%.

When Puck phoned, now in a furious temper, demanding to speak with me, I refused to take his call.

He'd been had and he knew it.

His faxed message came in a few minutes later, accusing me of having torpedoed our negotiations.

I answered, by fax, simply, "My 29p offer is final and unconditional."

Half an hour later a fax came back saying nothing more than, "The board will recommend your offer to their shareholders."

Winning the company was the hard part. Now came the fun part – breaking it up, selling off the pieces and putting the profits into Howe Wharf.

Chapter Fourteen

Summer in London that year was on a Tuesday afternoon in early June. The rest of the time it tried to rain.

The money to pay for Howe Wharf came in from BFCS, exactly as Clement had promised it would, and that pacified our bankers in the Caribbean, exactly as I promised Roderick it would.

In the meantime, Roderick hadn't heard anything more from the Stock Exchange. Neither had Adrian. The papers had gotten bored with Maxwell stories. And even Pippa stopped talking about it.

Every now and then Peter would wonder if I'd been arrested recently and I'd say, "I told you there was nothing to worry about."

He'd say, "It took them years to track down Bonnie and Clyde."

I'd say, "If only you were Faye Dunaway."

Then he'd say, "Speaking of Faye Dunaway. . ." and ramble on about some 20-year-old he'd just met who did unthinkable things with hot buttered popcorn.

I began to contemplate the possibility that I'd overreacted – that I'd flushed the toilet one too many times and had awakened the whole world – and that there really wasn't anything to fret about. Little by little I managed to push the words "insider dealing" to the far-reaches of my brain, to the dustiest corner where I file stuff like batting averages and how many letters there are in the Greek alphabet.

Pippa and the girls headed back to Cannes for a few months of sunshine, but I needed to be in town because interest rates were much too high, business around the country was drying up and we couldn't afford to let Howe Wharf become the dripping faucet of our cashflow. The Tories had gotten themselves re-elected on the promise that green shoots would soon be coming through the gloom. Instead, the only people doing any business were umbrella salesmen.

That's when Peter suddenly had an overwhelming urge to go skiing. He flew off to Chile, where he assured me it was winter and that sipping South American *gluhwein* in front of a roaring fire with the daughter of some Argentinian beef mogul – actually, she turned out to be the 23-year-old niece of the guy from Uruguay who'd bought our meat cleavers – was what every young healthy American male should be doing in June.

I reminded him, "You're not young, you're not American and as for healthy . . ."

He cut in, "I'm talking about you. Hop on a plane and join us."

"Yeah, right. And what happens to our business?"

"You must be getting old. Once upon a time you would have asked, what happens to my marriage."

"My marriage is fine. It's Howe Wharf that needs a kick in the ass."

"Listen to me, if it starts going sour, just bail out. Put it up for sale, we'll take our losses and move on."

"We're not going to just bail out. I'm committed to make it work."

"Terrific. Macho man and his electric overdraft."

"I said I'm going to make it work."

"No, you said you were committed to make it work. That's not the same thing."

"Okay, I'm committed to make it work. And I am going to make it work."

"What you really mean is that you're going to prove yourself to Francesca."

"That's not what I said. That's not what I mean."

"Bay, we can't afford too many Pyrrhic victories. Trust me, if it starts going wrong, get out."

"If I were you, I'd worry more about Ms Uruguay's father. You know those things the *gauchos* swing above their heads while riding through the *pampas*? The ones with the balls on the rope? Well, guys like you who mess around with their little girls . . . that's where they get the balls from."

"I love it when you go into your Jewish mother mode. But that's Argentina, not Uruguay."

"Tell me there's a difference when you're a contralto."

The beauty of the break-up of Ohio G. was that so many of the elements had natural homes.

I offered the orange and citrus fruit flavouring business to Cadbury Schweppes and they said they were interested. Eventually we struck a deal. I offered the wholesale wire and cork business to the employees and they began putting together a management buy-out. I found distributors for Spanish marble and Dutch tomatoes and melded them into a little company that Pennstreet owned called Euromarket92 Investments. I didn't know the first thing about Spanish marble or Dutch tomatoes, but that hardly mattered. I knew where to hire people who did.

Stonewall and I came up with an inflated valuation for the six-boat fishing fleet on the Isle of Man, then sold it to the fishermen in exchange for 35p on the pound and a generous tax loss.

Doing something with the foundry in Wales that made die-cast tools for the coal industry wasn't easy. Coal was out of favour under the Tories and, as that business wound down, so did all the ancillary industries that supported it. Our answer was to have Stonewall set up some new procedures and assure the workforce that we would try to make a go of the business, at least until I could figure out how to get rid of it.

I then put up for sale the five minor businesses we definitely didn't want. We found quick buyers for the auction house and the stationers and came out of both deals with a fair profit. The man who ran the hotel in Birkenhead made us an offer for it – much too low – and under normal circumstances I would have said no. But this wasn't the Savoy, I knew nothing about the hotel business, I didn't care to learn anything about the hotel business and I needed his cash. We haggled a little bit – just enough for me to keep face – and I gave in. Stonewall felt I could have gotten more if I'd shopped it around. I reminded him, I might also have wound up with nothing.

Inadvertently, I proved that point when I tried to flog the newsagents, plus the cash-and-carry operation. I set a fair price, rounded up all the usual buyers, did everything we could to get a little bidding war going, and never so much as got a nibble.

As I had no intention of keeping our 49% stake in the loss-making Lake District real estate agency, I offered our shares to the man who owned the controlling interest. His attitude was that he didn't have to pay me anything for it because he could get it for nothing simply by running the business into the ground, then buying it back from the liquidators. I told him, that sounded like a fine idea and that same day instructed Gerald to call in the liquidators. I caught the son of a bitch by surprise and bankrupted him.

If nothing else, I added another tax loss to our balance sheet.

I didn't want a Japanese spark plug distributorship or an 18% stake in some light farm machinery manufacturer, but after shopping them around it became evident that nobody else wanted them either. So it looked as if I was stuck with them, at least for the time being.

The one business I was glad to have was the travel

agency. I even took the day to go up to Liverpool to meet them – it was a store-front operation not far from Lime Street Station – and assured the half-dozen employees that we would stand behind them in their effort to make the business work. Stonewall came with me and gave them a lecture on our particular accounting procedures. The stout, young woman who ran the business mumbled something about how she and the other employees might be interested in acquiring it. I said we could certainly discuss that possibility, but before we did I wanted to make sure that the business was in sound financial health. I assured her, having contemplated the state of business in Britain, that was the best short-term strategy for all of us. I didn't say that, in the meantime, Peter and I were going to fly for free.

By the time Pippa and the girls came home from Cannes and Peter was back from South America, I'd managed to sell off five of the 15 businesses, three of them at a profit. I'd closed one and was waiting for a management buy-out to take another off my hands. I'd recouped nearly 60% of the purchase price of Ohio G. – which kept my cashflow steady – and also put three nice tax losses through my books.

But I was still running six businesses – which I felt was at least five too many – and getting a bit edgy about the final two, which felt as if they were hanging around my neck, while waiting to be sold.

I was also moving funds through the Caribbean to keep the Howe Wharf deal sweet. Roderick wasn't pleased about that and Peter wasn't pleased that Roderick seemed so concerned. I reminded them both that when you walk in on a pal in the middle of his plate-juggling act, that's not the moment to ask for a match.

Peter reminded me, "I don't smoke."

I pointed out, "Unless you're especially fond of broken porcelain, please do me a favour and, temporarily, bugger off."

He did. Except that he continued to ring me every day, as usual, to remind me he'd buggered off.

Then Clement showed up in Nassau.

That bothered me because nobody in their right mind goes to the Bahamas in the summer unless they have to. The last thing I needed was to have him looking into the way I'd manipulated the Howe Wharf purchase price. So I asked Roderick to find out what he was doing there. It turns out he'd gone to meet with L. James, to secure a private real estate purchase, leveraged with the assets in Jura Mercantile.

Considering the fact that he didn't actually own the assets in Jura Mercantile, it seemed fair to assume that good old Clement was being a bit audacious. It was, however, comforting to know that he always ran true to form.

The real surprise of the summer came when we got an offer for the cash-and-carry business. The manager of the place rang to say he'd put together a buy-out. I went there, spent the afternoon doing a month's worth of shopping at wholesale prices, then accepted his offer.

No sooner had I signed away that one, when I got an offer for the newsagents. Again, as I'd done with the hotel, I haggled just enough to keep face before giving in. I didn't get more than the storefronts themselves were worth, but in my mind I hadn't paid for the business anyway, and I was happy to take that much.

With eight of the 15 disposed of, I'd recouped 70%.

I now made the mistake of thinking that luck was on my side. I hadn't taken into account Murphy's Law – "Anything that can go wrong will go wrong" – and the interpretation of it that reads, "Murphy was an optimist."

The woman running the travel agency left – she just walked out one Friday afternoon and never came back – taking the entire staff with her. On Monday morning, she announced that she was setting up in her own agency. I closed mine, put the premises up for sale

172

and filed a lawsuit against her. So much for our free airplane rides.

Two weeks later, the management buyout at the wire and cork business fell through. They couldn't raise the money and I couldn't afford to finance them. I assured the employees that we'd try to keep the business open, but the creditors smelled trouble and started knocking on my door.

The obvious thing was to approach our competitors and offer the business to them. I was hoping there were at least two, because that's how many you need to get an auction going. It turned out that there was only one similar enterprise of any importance in the UK, a six-year-old Business Expansion Scheme success story in the West Country called BEStoftimes Wire. I did my homework and liked the figures they were reporting. It was run by a couple of public school kids with accounting degrees who obviously knew what they were doing. So I approached them with a straightforward deal. They promised to chew it over. And we agreed they could have two weeks to make a bid. The next thing I knew, they'd not only turned me down but, based on the documents I'd prepared for them, they'd made overtures to and had successfully stolen one of our major customers.

When I told Peter the story and asked what we should do about it, he paraphrased Bobby Kennedy. "Don't go nuts, go ballistic." Before I could stop him, he was in his "oblique approach" mode, personally plotting our takeover of BEStoftimes.

From the comfort of his pillow-propped bed – phones and fax machine at the ready – he snuck up on BEStoftimes, bought out a few of their small share-holders, got our toe in the door, then kicked the damn thing down. Later he said he fully expected the snotty brats who ran the company to fight back. Admittedly, so did I. The problem was, no one had told them they were supposed to and therefore they didn't.

"That only goes to prove one thing," he grimaced,

as his master plan fell apart at our feet. "The public schools of this country are responsible. Never trust anyone who got his driver's permit before his first pair of long trousers."

We now found ourselves owning not one but two wire and cork businesses, neither of which we wanted.

I dared, "Got any other brilliant ideas?"

"A million of them," he reassured me. "Maybe I should make a call to my new pal Escobar."

"Escobar?" My gasp was loud and clear. "Are you sure we want to be doing any sort of business with anyone named Escobar?"

"Not that Escobar. It's Jones in Spanish. My guy is Jorge Manuel Escobar and he's into better stuff than cocaine. He's into Chianti."

"George Manny Jones," I mused. "Sounds like your average Italian Chianti salesman."

"What makes you think all Chianti comes from Italy?"

"Silly of me to presume that."

"Jorge is the Chianti baron of South America."

"I should have known."

"You would have if you'd have come skiing with me. We met in Chile. I'm telling you, he's our bloke."

"Don't forget to write," I said. "And remember to put your cheque inside the envelope before you seal it."

According to Peter – who really does know a lot about this sort of stuff – more Chianti is produced worldwide than the Italians could ever manage. In other words, less than half the world's Italian Chianti actually comes from Italy. A good part of the world's stock derives from Argentina and Chile. That his pal Jorge was putting "*Vino d'Italia*" on his labels when he was putting South American grape juice inside the bottle, struck Peter as merely a minor detail.

He flew back to South America and convinced Jorge that the way to get his non-Italian Italian wine into Italy was – again, the oblique approach – to bottle it in England. It didn't make any sense to me but Jorge thought it was a terrific idea.

Within a month, J. M. Escobar Importacion SA of Buenos Aires had established its UK presence through a shell company we purchased on Jorge's behalf called Lime Street (Food and Beverage) Importers, Ltd. By sheer coincidence, its rented offices in Liverpool turned out to be a storefront where once was found a travel agency.

Jorge used Lime Street to buy our two wire and cork companies, which he believed came hand in hand with free entry into the Common Market. His plan was to ship his South American wine in barrels to England where he'd bottle it, using his own corks, and crate it, using his own wire, then sell his wine in Italy for less than the Italians could themselves.

He paid us 60% of the agreed price in cash for the two wire and cork companies, which was more than enough to get us square on our books. Peter accepted the remaining 40%, calculated on the wholesale price, in South American wine. But he agreed to take the plonk only after we'd found a wholesaler in Austria who said he had a market for it in Indonesia. How anyone was going to explain away South American Chianti with "Produce of Italy" and "Bottled in the UK" on the label was his problem. I only cared that the Austrian's cheque cleared. When it did, we wished him good luck. Then we wished Señor Escobar good luck. And then Peter and I promised each other never to get involved in anything quite as dubious ever again.

The PS to the story is that, not surprisingly, Señor Escobar didn't get very far. As soon as word reached Brussels that tankers loaded with ersatz Chianti were landing in Britain, the Italians screamed foul and the EEC slapped all sorts of restrictions on Jorge. By that time, however, he'd sold the wire and cork company to the Italian exporter whom he'd originally gone into business with in Argentina.

The next thing we knew, Escobar was sending us cases of vintage Crystal Champagne. It looked like the real thing and tasted like the real thing and Peter said, if this was Argentinian champagne, he wanted to own the company.

It turned out that Jorge had made himself a quick 300% profit on the sale.

Suitably chuffed, and rightly so, he arrived in England to thank me personally. He brought me a stunning green leather Louis Vuitton attaché case and brought Pippa six litre-sized bottles of Chanel No. 5, both of which turned out to have been made in Valparaiso by his brother-in-law. From London he travelled on to Paris to thank Peter personally, bringing him a dozen Hermès ties made by the same brother-in-law. Two days later Peter sold him our Spanish marble business.

We edged over into the profit column on Ohio G. That bolstered our cashflow. Anything we picked up with the four remaining assets meant we could reduce our debt by that much. Life looked very promising, all the more so when Lady Luck came back for a brief visit late that autumn.

The management at the Welsh die-cast tool factory approached us with a buy-out plan. Because I wasn't as desperate to sell now as I might have been six months before, I could afford to sit around until they upped their original offer three times. I accepted and we washed our hands of die-cast tools for the coalmining industry.

Next, I did a deal with Safeway and unloaded our Dutch tomato business. Although we haggled for a while, I finally accepted 68% of my original asking price in cash and took the additional 32% in the form of orders over the next 18 months placed with Schools Jams and Jellies.

Only the two Japanese firms were left sitting on the shelf. And I was absolutely determined to find someone to take them off my hands so that I could wind up the year on a high note.

That's when the Stock Exchange Surveillance Unit asked if I would help them with their inquiries.

Chapter Fifteen

The letter, on Stock Exchange stationery, was signed by someone called Alastair McCue, whose title was Head of the Surveillance Unit.

He said he was taking this opportunity to alert me to the fact that his office was making cursory inquiries into some specific share dealings involving Maxwell Communications Corporation in November 1991, and the fact that this letter was being sent to me should not be construed to imply that I was, in any way, involved or even believed to be involved with any of those share dealings. He noted this was strictly routine, asked that I consider this to be a confidential matter and closed by expressing the sincere desire that I might help his office clarify certain points.

On the surface, it was a simple request for a brief interview, in my office and at my convenience. McCue's tone was innocuous and never gave the impression of any urgency. Considering the fact that it came a year after the incident and nearly ten months after his office had first contacted Adrian and Roderick, and that none of us had heard from them since, it didn't appear as if speed was one of McCue's priorities.

Which is precisely what sent me into a near-panic. I wanted to know what the hell they'd been doing all this time in between.

I faxed a copy of it to Gerald and asked him to reply.

He phoned back to say it would be best, at this stage, to meet with McCue to see what he wanted.

"I know what he wants," I said. "My ass in a sling."

Intrinsically levelheaded, Gerald advised, "Just meet with him. Let him put whatever cards he's got on the table and we'll decide what to do from there."

"There was no insider trading."

"Doesn't sound like it to me. And it probably won't sound like it to him either."

"Maybe you should be here."

"As long as he doesn't bring his solicitor, you don't need one at this stage either. You've done nothing wrong so don't give him the impression that you have. Don't let him tape anything. Don't sign anything. Answer whatever questions he has in a unembellished, straight-forward manner. Don't offer any explanations if he doesn't ask for them. Don't volunteer any information. If you can get away with yes and no, that's best."

"Sounds like the Inquisition."

"You can start to worry if his middle name is Torquemada."

My head told me that Gerald was right. But my gut feeling was that McCue would turn out to be like a dentist – the sort of guy who shows you his perfect smile while his drill is whirring deep into your root canal. "Silence can be nerve wracking. What have they been doing for the past year? And how did they get to me?"

"They got to you," Gerald said, "because they must have checked the tapes at your broker's office. As for the past ten months, they've been sitting on their bottoms doing what functionaries always do, which is wasting time."

"Or," I suggested, "building some sort of case."

"Yes," he said. "You're probably right. They're building a rock-solid case against you for being a pain in the bum to your solicitor. I'd even testify."

"I don't like the fact that it's taken them all this time

to get around to me. It makes me think they've been busy with this thing."

"Did you trade on inside information?"

"No."

"Then it doesn't matter how long it's taken them. End of case."

I said thanks, hung up and dictated a letter to Patty, addressed to McCue, saying that I would be pleased to meet with him on the following Wednesday, at 4 o'clock.

She asked, "So soon?"

I grinned. "Date the letter Monday and mail it that night. Hopefully he won't get it until Wednesday and by then it will be too late for him to rearrange his week's appointments. When he can't make it, I'll be unavailable until next February. Or March. Or April."

Lamentably, for once, the Post Office worked the way it's supposed to. Someone phoned first thing on Tuesday morning to confirm the appointment. And two guys from the Stock Exchange arrived on Wednesday afternoon, a full 30 minutes early.

"We're terribly sorry," one of them explained to Patty, "Mr McCue was unavailable and asked us to speak with Mr Radisson on his behalf."

She stepped into my office, shut the door behind her and related their message to me. I was so annoyed at having outsmarted myself – I simply could have said I wasn't available until February or March or April – that I purposely kept them waiting until 4:25.

The first one moved brusquely past Patty, extended his hand to me like a robot and said nothing more than, "Fosdick."

I tried not to laugh because there had been a comic strip character in my youth named Fearless Fosdick. This guy was in his late 20s, tall and so thin that I worried his green suit might slip off his body and wind up around his ankles.

His sidekick was at least 30 years older, short and fat

and sporting a moustache that was too small for his round face. He bowed and introduced himself as "Brian P. Wynn. W-Y-N-N, Brian P."

I deliberately avoided any glance towards Patty because I knew that, if we locked eyes, both of us would break up. "Do either of you gentlemen care for coffee or tea?"

Fosdick put his attaché case on my conference table, claimed a chair and asked if he could have a cup of hot water. Wynn put his attaché case on the table, took a seat opposite Fosdick and wondered if there was any room temperature Diet Orangina.

Patty quickly closed the office door, promising to arrange everything.

"Rather than dally . . ." Fosdick was keen to get down to business, ". . .the purpose of our visit is to obtain your help with our inquiries. And yes, naturally, our discussion must be in the strictest of confidence."

I told him, "I was expecting Mr McCue."

"No, he's unavailable," Fosdick said. "Yes, he's a very busy man."

"I'm sure," I nodded.

"So, in Mr McCue's absence, we're here to obtain your help with our inquiries."

I said I would be happy to do just that, but first I needed to clear up a few things in my own mind. "Apparently you are both with the Stock Exchange?"

"Not apparently," Fosdick said. "Definitely. The London Stock Exchange, Surveillance Unit. And no, we work for that gentleman. Yes."

"Yes," I repeated.

Wynn reached into his shirt pocket and produced a small card which he handed to me. It announced that he was a Senior Inspector with the Surveillance Unit. Then Fosdick handed me his card, which showed that his full name was Stanley Ravenhill Fosdick but didn't list his job title. I assumed, therefore, that he worked for Wynn.

Thanking them for their cards, I took my own place at the head of the table, put their cards neatly in front of me and smiled politely.

The two stared back at me, as if they were waiting for me to say something. I tried, "The hot water and the Diet Orangina will be here shortly."

"And you?" Fosdick wondered.

"No, nothing."

"No, I mean, you do have a card, yes?"

"Ah . . ." I shook my head, too lazy to fetch one. "I'm afraid not."

Fosdick opened his attaché case, withdrew a teabag and a napkin, carefully laid the napkin on the table, placed the teabag on top of it, then reached for a large notebook. Turning to the first clean page, he took a cheap ballpoint pen and scribbled, "Radisson, Bayard, Mr Interview conducted at the offices of Pennstreet PLC. Wednesday, 16 November, 1992, 1625 hours. No business card."

I watched what he wrote, then pointed towards his last three words. "Is that important?"

"Yes. We never discount any fact," he explained. "No, not even the smallest thing."

"Yes," I conceded, mimicking him. "No, of course not."

He didn't get it. "Yes, of course not." And he wrote that down too. "Now, if I may begin. Have you at any time in the past had any contact, social or otherwise, with one Robert Maxwell?"

I told him, "We never ran in the same social circles."

"In other words," Fosdick pointed his pen at me, "you never met him."

"Like I said, we didn't run in the same social circles. He wasn't the sort of man I cared to hang out with."

"You're avoiding the question. Are you saying that you never met Robert Maxwell?"

I didn't like his tone of voice. "I'm saying . . . I'm saying that, if you're going to write down my answer to that question, you'd better write down the words, we didn't run in the same social circles."

"That's not good enough," Fosdick remarked.

"Well," I shrugged, "that's my answer." I stood up and walked to the door to ask Patty if she had the drinks for our guests, just as she appeared holding a tray. I took them for her and served them. Fosdick dunked his teabag in the hot water. Wynn put the can of Diet Orangina up to his face to make certain it was room temperature and only when he was sure, did he pour it into his glass.

I returned to my seat.

Fosdick squeezed the teabag between his fingers, took a Kleenex from his attaché case, wrapped the teabag in it and put them both back into his attaché case. Then he picked up exactly where he'd left off. "Yes, whether or not you've ever met Mr Robert Maxwell."

"I've answered that question."

"Not to my satisfaction, you haven't."

"Frankly sport," I leaned forward and said very quietly, "I don't give a rat-fuck about your satisfaction."

"We'll have none of that offensive behaviour. No." He said, "And, yes, I'll ask you please to watch your language. . ."

Wynn remained calm. "Now, this isn't doing any of us any good. Perhaps we'll just move on to the next question."

Fosdick was angry, "I'll decide which questions to ask . . ."

Wynn reminded him, "We're guests here so I think perhaps we should concede to Mr Radisson's wish that we move on to the next question."

I sat back and waited.

Fosdick now tried a different approach, "When was the last time you either saw or communicated in any way with Robert Maxwell?"

I didn't have any intention of going into details about that. "You don't give up, do you?"

"No. These are questions I've deemed to be important

and yes, your ability to answer them to my satisfaction . . ."

Now I asked, "Just what are you two guys doing here? Are you looking for answers or accusing me of insider trading?"

Wynn shook his head. "No one has said anything about insider trading."

"Yes, you run a public company," Fosdick cut in. "Yes, you are therefore bound by the rules and regulations of the Stock Exchange, and yes, also subject to the laws of Great Britain. After making a preliminary investigation we believe that there is some evidence to suggest that you. . ."

"Go ahead. Say it." I tried to control my temper. "Use the words 'insider trading'. Say it and watch me pick up this phone right here and ring my lawyer and order him to sue you for slander."

Wynn clearly didn't want that to happen. "There's no need to bring your solicitor into this. . ."

"Insider dealing is, I believe, a crime. So if you are about to accuse me of having committed a crime . . ."

"No one is accusing you of anything," he put his hand out to me, as if he was going to give me a reassuring pat.

This was the right tack, I decided. Stay on the offence. "Am I under investigation for insider dealing?"

Fosdick replied, "We are not prepared at this time. . ."

"Not prepared to do what at this time?"

"Yes, if you'd just allow me to finish," he said. "Mr Wynn and his associates have, for the past several months, been collecting evidence that suggests you might have possessed certain knowledge that was not yet public and with which you were successfully able to trade in certain shares. . ."

"Time out sport." I glared at him. "What do you mean, Mr Wynn and his associates?"

Wynn answered, "I have already introduced myself as a Senior Investigator for the Stock Exchange Surveillance

Unit. I will inform you that I am assigned to the Insider Dealing Group. . ."

I turned to Fosdick. "What about you?"

He nodded, "I am also with the Stock Exchange. And I also investigate matters such as insider dealing."

"With the Stock Exchange?"

"Yes, that's right."

"With the Insider Dealing Group?"

"I work with them, yes."

"But you don't work for them."

He paused, as if he was thinking of the correct answer, then told me, "Yes, I am assigned to the Surveillance Unit."

"Assigned to?"

"Yes," he said. "Now, may we get back to my questions? I'd like to know, in civilized tones, when was the last time you either saw or communicated in any way with Robert Maxwell?"

I stared at him for the longest time.

When he saw I wasn't about to answer, he repeated the question, "Would you tell us please, when was the last time you either saw or communicated in any way with Robert Maxwell?"

There was something about the way he phrased it. "I'm sorry, can you ask that again?"

He did. "Would you tell us please, when was the last time you either saw or communicated in any way with Robert Maxwell?"

That's when the penny dropped. "Ladies and gentlemen of the jury." I said straight to his face, "You're a schmuck if you think I'm answering any more of your questions. The interview is over."

"Arrogant and offensive," Fosdick cried, writing those two words on his pad. "This will go into my report."

I warned, "Don't put too much ink on the paper because it will get into your bloodstream when I shove that report up your ass."

185

Wynn tried to calm me down. "Mr Radisson, there is certainly no need for. . ."

I was furious. "You're an attorney, aren't you?"

Fosdick insisted, "I work for the Stock Exchange."

"But you're an attorney."

"I'm here in my capacity. . ."

"Bullshit," I screamed, "you're a solicitor or a barrister and you never properly identified yourself when you began this interview."

Wynn suggested, "Perhaps if we begin again, we might be able to . . ."

"You are an attorney," I persisted.

He stammered just a bit. "Yes, I did train as a solicitor but no, I'm here in my capacity as someone assigned to the Insider Dealing Group of the Surveillance Unit of the Stock Exchange."

"The fact is, you're a lawyer."

"It hardly matters what my background is . . ."

"Bullshit!" I reached for his pad, dragged it to me – he tried to stop me but I'd beaten him to it – took his pen and wrote in very big letters across the front of his notes, Gerald Chappell's name and phone number. "This is my solicitor." I shoved the pad towards Wynn. "Any further communication with your office or the Stock Exchange will be handled through him."

Standing up, I walked to the door, opened it, stepped to the side and warned them, "If you communicate to anyone or insinuate in any way that I have committed a crime, I will sue you both personally and sue the Stock Exchange as well for slander, libel or whatever happens to be the case. Furthermore, I will devote every cent I own to seeing both of you financially ruined. Now, get out."

They stared at me.

"Yes, I should advise you that, no, this is a very foolish attitude," Fosdick said.

Wynn stepped back into his good-cop role. "Mr Radisson, I'm sure that we can discuss this . . ."

"Tell it to my solicitor."

Fosdick came back with, "You would be well advised to heed . . ."

"Please," Wynn held up his hand to stop Fosdick. "Mr Radisson, if you would care to discuss this with me, perhaps Mr Fosdick wouldn't mind if . . ."

I wasn't buying their act. "The two of you yobbos have exactly six seconds to get out of my office, before I pick you both up by your throats and throw you out."

Wynn pleaded, "There's no need to be quite so insulting . . ."

I screamed, "Get the fuck out."

They slammed their briefcases shut and hurried for the door. "Yes, I can assure you," Fosdick said, "this will be reported."

On a foolish whim, I swung my shoe towards his rear end. He stepped out of the way and my foot crashed into the wall.

"He's a mad man," Fosdick yelped, and the two of them scurried out of the office.

Patty rushed in. "What in God's name . . ."

I moved away from her. "Get me Gerald right away."

She took the phone next to the conference table and dialled his number.

I paced the office floor, steaming, until he came on the speaker-phone. "Listen, I just threw two jerks from the Stock Exchange out of my office. One of them was a lawyer and he never properly identified himself. . ."

"Calm down," he said. "Just calm down. Tell me quietly, what happened?"

I related the whole story, especially the fact that Fosdick had tried to deceive me by not properly identifying himself as an attorney.

Gerald was more astonished by my footwork. "So you kicked him?"

"Bad luck, I missed."

187

"Very lucky, you missed."

"What now?"

"Now you refer them to me."

"I have."

"If they ring back, refuse to speak with them."

I said, "I don't think they'll ring back."

"Trust me," he warned, "they will."

Two hours later a fax came in from Gerald.

It was a copy of a letter he was sending to the chairman of the Stock Exchange, deploring the Surveillance Unit's Nazi-like tactics – his exact words – and warning that in the future, if a Stock Exchange attorney came to call on any of his clients and failed to identify himself properly, the way Mr Fosdick had clearly and improperly done, deliberately intending to deprive someone of representation by counsel, a formal letter of protest would be filed with the Law Society and the courts would be asked for an order preventing the Stock Exchange from further misrepresentation.

Furthermore, he continued, any communication by the Stock Exchange with people not otherwise directly involved in the normal course of an ongoing investigation conducted through an office such as the Surveillance Unit that insinuated, implied, suggested, presumed or accused his client of committing a crime would be considered libellous and dealt with to the full extent of the law.

It was strong and to the point.

Late the following morning, another fax came in from Gerald. It was a copy of a polite reply from the Stock Exchange's chief counsel, thanking Gerald for his fax to the Chairman and suggesting that perhaps his client had misunderstood when Mr Fosdick introduced himself.

I grabbed the fax, photocopied it myself, scribbled something on the bottom of it and faxed it straight back to the Stock Exchange's chief counsel.

My note to him read, "Fosdick is full if shit. And, obviously, so are you!"

The following Monday afternoon, Brian Fellowes – a journalist I knew on the *Financial Times* – called me to ask if I'd heard anything about a Stock Exchange investigation into Pennstreet.

I replied honestly, "I have never been contacted by anyone at the Stock Exchange, or any regulatory authority for that matter, about Pennstreet."

Then I asked him, strictly off the record, that if he heard anything I'd be grateful for the information. I assured him that in exchange for his information, if anything was happening, I'd see that he got the story first. He promised to check some of his sources and get back to me.

Next, someone from the *Telegraph* rang. I wouldn't take his call.

Then Clement phoned to say that Francesca had heard a nasty rumour.

"Which one?" I asked.

He had to know, "You mean there is more than just one?"

"I meant, what did she hear?"

"She heard that you are being investigated by the Department of Trade and Industry."

I assured him, "Clement, with my hand on my heart I can tell you that, as far as I know, there is absolutely no truth to that rumour at all."

"But she heard that they've even come to question you."

"Who came to question me?"

"The DTI."

"Clement," I repeated, "with my hand on my heart . . . no, with one hand on my heart and the other on my children's heads, I swear to you that I have never met with, or spoken to, or heard from any investigators from the DTI."

"Honestly?"

"Honestly."

He sighed, "That's good news. Because Francesca says, if you're being investigated, we have to pull out of the Howe Wharf."

Chapter Sixteen

I don't know where I was the day God passed out the gyroscopes, but I didn't get a very good one because even when I was old enough and, I thought, emotionally mature enough to protect myself – to barricade my heart behind a high wall of early-warning radar – I was still too easily knocked off course.

Elizabeth and I had grown up within five miles of each other and never knew the other existed, until the day before Winter Break of our sophomore year at Johns Hopkins. I had one last exam to finish – it was sociology – before taking a train with my college pal Jerry to New York where, he claimed, his girlfriend Susan had a sure thing lined up for me named Carolyn.

There was still half an hour left to the exam period when I spotted Jerry's face in the window of the classroom door. He was pointing to his watch, motioning for me to hurry up and kept his face framed in the tiny glass, showing me his watch every time I glanced up. So I rushed through the final essay – I didn't care much about New Guinea tribal customs anyway – and by the time I turned in my paper, Jerry seemed as if he was ready to have a fit.

"We have plenty of time," I said, stepping into the hallway.

"No we don't." He had both of our suitcases with him. "Come on, let's go."

We couldn't find a taxi and had to gamble on a bus.

At one point he told the driver, "We're going to miss our train," and the man took such pity on us that he ran a red light. We got to the platform with only seconds to spare, jumped on the train just as the doors shut and were still looking for seats when it pulled out.

Had Jerry not shown up to hurry me along, or had I written one more paragraph on my exam or had the driver not run that red light, we never would have made that particular train to New York.

Had I not been on that particular train to New York, my entire life would have been different.

That's where I met her.

She and two other girls were making their way down the aisle when I heard her say, "It should be one more."

I looked up.

And my heart stopped.

It was like seeing a vision.

I couldn't take my eyes off her as she walked away. Realizing that she was going to the dining car, I grabbed Jerry's arm and told him, "Come on."

We sat at the next table.

She caught me staring, looked away, then peeked back again. I smiled. She dropped her eyes.

Jerry understood what was happening and whispered, "How's this?" He took a pen and a piece of paper out of his pocket, and wrote her a note. "My dear, my associate finds you extremely attractive. May we have the pleasure of meeting you." He signalled for the waiter and discreetly asked him to deliver the note to the dark-haired lady at the next table. He did. She read it, looked up at me as if she didn't know what to do, then showed it to her friends.

I kept staring, waiting for her to respond. Finally I told Jerry, "She's not answering."

He said, "I'll solve that," leaned back and tossed his pen to her.

It landed directly in front of her.

Slightly taken aback, she used it to write a note, which she asked the waiter to hand to us. "Gentlemen, thank you for the compliment. But if you keep throwing your pen around like that, you're bound to lose it." It was signed, "Elizabeth Bolt."

Long before we stopped at Philadelphia, Jerry had gone back to our seats, her two friends had left too, and I was thoroughly besotted with her.

My four days with Jerry were the longest of my life. Carolyn turned out to be a splendid redhead. I wasn't in the least interested. All I wanted to do was rush back to Penn Station on the Sunday night, to meet Elizabeth as we'd planned.

I got there early. She arrived late. I was a nervous wreck. She seemed totally unperturbed by such an encounter.

That night, when I took her home, she kissed me.

A week later I made love to her for the first time.

I spent the rest of the year saying, "I love you."

She spent the rest of the year saying, "I want to tell you that I love you too."

In those days, I thought that meant the same thing.

If I made one crucial mistake in those first few months with Francesca, it was that I told her that story about Elizabeth. That I told her everything about Elizabeth – how I met her, how I loved her, how I walked out on her, how I still sometimes missed her.

I'm afraid now I told Francesca once too often that the day Elizabeth walked past me on the train was indelibly etched into my memory as the single day in my life that I would give anything to re-live one more time.

And yet I couldn't figure out why, six months after we first got together in Venice, Francesca was still refusing to live with me. Every time I broached the subject, she said no. She wouldn't explain it and, at that point, I wasn't capable of seeing it.

Most of the time I didn't force the issue because

Francesca was not the sort of person who could be coerced. She did what she wanted to do when she wanted to do it. In the back of my mind I figured she would just, one day, eventually, move in. The trick was to get her to think of it first. That mixture of Mediterranean blood and Swiss genes meant that, if it wasn't her idea, she could be remarkably stubborn.

I knew how obstinate she could be and yet, one night, as I watched her sleeping next to me, I told myself it was time to play all my chips on one spin of the wheel. I convinced myself it was now or never. So I put my arms around her and gently woke her. "You have to move in with me."

She turned away, whispering hoarsely, "No."

Thinking she wasn't fully awake, I pulled her closer. "You have to move in."

She shifted again. "No."

"Francesca . . ." I needed to be sure she was wide awake. "Francesca, listen to me. I can't live without you."

"The answer is no." She was wide awake. "Now, please, let me alone. I'm tired."

"For Chrissake, you sleep with me. Why won't you live with me?"

"Why do we have to have this discussion in the middle of the night?"

"Why don't you just say yes?"

She was annoyed.

I was too uncompromising to leave well enough alone.

After a few seconds, she reluctantly turned to face me. "Do you know the story of Charlemagne? When he was an old man he fell in love with a very young and very beautiful girl. He was so taken by her that he couldn't eat or sleep or think of anything unless she was by his side. His ministers were worried, but there was nothing they could do about it. And then one day, very suddenly, the girl died. His ministers thought the king would now be himself again. But Charlemagne needed her so much that he had her body brought to his bed chamber. The court physician suspected Charlemagne might be under a spell, so he snuck into the bed chamber one night while the king was asleep and examined the girl's body. Under her tongue he found a gold ring with a large precious stone. He took it. The next morning Charlemagne woke up, no longer in love with the girl. He had the body buried, then called for the court physician and announced that he was in love with him. In a panic, the court physician threw the ring into a lake. So Charlemagne went there and sat down along the shore, in love with the lake."

She stopped.

"So? Then what?"

"Don't you understand the point of the story?"

"No."

"It's the ring," she said. "First you have to set yourself free from its spell."

I challenged her. "What does that mean?"

She shook her head. "Never mind. Just go to sleep."

"Wait a minute. I have a right to know. . ."

"And I have a right to sleep."

"I don't know what that story was all about, but I do know that I love you and I want you to move in with me permanently." I reminded her, "You've been here every night this week. You were here every night last week. You've been here almost every night this month. Your own flat has turned into nothing more than a very expensive closet." I took her by the shoulders. "You live three blocks from here. It's not as if I'm asking you to do something important like change your resident's parking permit."

She slid out of my reach. "I'm warning you, go to sleep."

"Warning me?"

"Dammit," she screamed, tearing herself out of bed.

"Where are you going?"

She didn't answer.

I watched as she grabbed her clothes. "Okay, okay. Come back."

"No. I told you no." And she meant it.

I waited for a few minutes after she'd left, hoping she'd return, but knowing that she wouldn't. So I pulled myself out of bed, got dressed – cursed my own stupidity for having forced a confrontation – and drove to Draycott Avenue. I found a parking spot right outside her front door, put my car there and locked it, still expecting to spend the night with her. I walked up the front steps and rang her bell.

There was no answer.

I rang it again.

Still nothing.

I stepped back to look up at her living-room window but her apartment was dark. Then I checked the street, to see where she'd parked her car – a red BMW convertible with a white top – but it wasn't there.

This is crazy, I said out loud. She was coming right home. Where the hell is she? I waited for nearly half an hour but she never showed up. So I went back to my flat, thinking – hoping – she was there.

She wasn't.

The next morning I rang her private line at the bank. When she refused to take my call, I sent her a six word fax. "Where did you sleep last night?"

She phoned back two seconds later, in a rage, calling me names in three languages, yelling like a crazy woman, furious, swearing that we would never go to bed together again.

She kept her promise for five months.

I spent most of that time trying to figure out why my world had caved in on me.

One Saturday morning, several weeks after Francesca left, a package arrived from my sister. It was a shoe box wrapped in brown paper and tied in brown cord. Inside there was a handwritten note where she explained that after my mom and dad both died, when she cleaned out their house, she found 15 unmailed letters they'd written to me. She said when she found them she was still so angry with me for not coming home for their funerals that she decided not to send them. She put them away. Then she forgot about them.

"Last week," she wrote, "I came across them in a drawer and figured it was only right that you should have them. I'm sorry it's taken me all these years. Please forgive me for that." In a PS she added, "I haven't read them myself because I think your parents wanted to speak privately to you."

The letters were stuffed under crumbled pieces of newspaper.

Six of them were from my father, saying how disappointed he'd been in me. The rest were from my mother, saying that, deep down, she and my dad were proud of me and that if I'd left the country because I felt so strongly about the war, then having a son who'd been willing to live by the courage of his convictions was ample reason for their pride.

Seeing their handwriting and hearing their voices in my head saying the words on those pages was perhaps the most painful thing I've ever had to endure. So much guilt came flooding back to me. I was heartbroken that I'd hurt them. And I was grief struck to realize that they never intended to show me the letters while they were both alive.

The only consolation I found was one line in one letter where my mother wrote, "Did you know that Elizabeth is divorced? Her married name was Pepperdine."

My first instinct, when I saw that, was to phone her. Checking with Information, they had a listing for E. B. Pepperdine. I took that to mean she hadn't remarried. Except that it was much too early to call. So I persuaded myself to wait until 2 o'clock that afternoon, which would be 9 o'clock in Baltimore. And all that morning I sat around trying to plan what I was going to say to her.

By the time 2 o'clock came around, I couldn't go through with it.

Maybe if I'd had a good gyroscope.

Suddenly I was too frightened that the Elizabeth I'd find on the other end wasn't the Elizabeth I'd left there all those years ago. And I didn't know if I could cope with that.

For a brief time, there was a stewardess in my life, but she soon grew restless and flew away. There was a dancer too. But she didn't like the music I played in the morning and stopped spending the night with me. I found a blonde who said she just wanted to talk but after a time she accused me of never having learned how to listen. And then there was a brunette who swore she couldn't get enough of me, and yet one day she simply announced that she had.

They all went away. In their own way, they all knocked me off course. But none of them ever left the void that Francesca did.

And I tried to fill that void by remembering Elizabeth.

Peter and I continued to deal with the bank. There was no reason to end that association simply because I'd been having a major love affair with one of our two main contacts there. Although I personally cut down on my meetings at BFCS. Peter, who understands these things better than almost everyone else on earth, stepped in to handle as much of our business as he could directly with Clement.

Francesca was present on the odd occasion – sometimes there was simply no avoiding each other – and, even though I made an effort to be civil, she was as cold as ice.

Some guys get turned on by that.

I got angry.

It took several weeks for my anger to fade and, when it did, I began to admit that, without Francesca, I felt lost. So I went to Cannes and stayed there for two months, letting Peter run things. I thought about her. And I thought about Elizabeth too. And when I realized I was getting them mixed up in my mind – when I started getting confused about how they tasted and how they laughed – I returned to London.

Francesca still refused to take my calls.

I moped around the office. Peter suggested I either go back to Cannes or get another partner. I told him I was bored with London and bored with business. I told him I didn't know what I wanted to do but I needed to do something. I told him that maybe I needed to save my own life. I said I was thinking that, maybe, the time had come to go back to America.

"Are you crazy? Big brave Yank goes home to face the music?"

"If you're talking about amnesty, it's done."

"So is the legalization of marijuana. Explain that to the guys at the border when they arrest you."

"No one is going to arrest me."

He sneered, "I'll tell you what, mate. Instead of going back to Baltimore to take your medicine, I'll buy you some good old-fashioned British suppositories and hire a brass brand to play the Star Spangled Banner while you shove them up your bum."

I finally confessed, "I'm not talking about the Draft Board."

It took him a moment to figure it out. "Oh." He raised his eyebrows. "Oh yes. As if she's going to give you a warmer reception than the Draft Board."

"It's unfinished business."

"No it isn't. That business was finished a long time ago. And you're a bloody fool to think otherwise."

I vacillated throughout the winter, sometimes convinced that Peter was wrong, at other times wondering if he might be right.

Then, one day, totally out of the blue, Francesca phoned. All she said was, "Take me to Paris."

I told her, "I've missed you."

She answered, "I need you."

It never dawned on me that there was a difference. "I'll come and get you now."

Four hours later we checked into The Lancaster, off the Champs Elysées, and spent five days running up our room service bill. I did not mention Elizabeth. And this time when we came back to London, she rented her flat and moved everything she owned into mine. This time it was her idea.

She lived with me for two years.

If Elizabeth was indeed unfinished business, Francesca's love gently shoved her back into the shadows. We skied over Christmas at St Moritz — her brother had a chalet there — and spent two weeks in February in the Bahamas. The first year we stayed in a hotel. The next, Roderick Hays-White rented a wonderful house for us on the beach at Eleuthera.

One morning, very early, I took a picture of her on the deck of that house, with her hair blowing in a gentle wind and her face lit in the sunshine. She was laughing. I told her that if, ten minutes from now, a flying saucer filled with Martians came down to Earth and took her away from me, I would never forget the way she looked at that very moment.

I told her, "I love you."

She told me, "There aren't enough Martians in the galaxy to take me away from you."

I had the picture printed and put into a beautiful antique silver frame and it lived in the centre of my desk.

The Martians came that spring.

We'd been out to dinner around the corner, had gotten a little drunk and tried to find a place where we could make love outside. But it was too chilly, so we went home and undressed each other on the stairs. We were totally naked and so turned on by the time we finally got into the apartment that we wound up making love on the living-room floor.

When we were finished, I asked Francesca to marry me. I knew she'd say yes.

She said, "No."

"What do you mean, no?"

She repeated it. "No."

"Why not?"

"Because . . . no."

I stammered, "But . . . Francesca . . . I want to marry you."

"No. The answer is no." She got up and went to stare out the window. "No."

I followed her. "How can you tell me no and walk away from me like that?"

"Why do you always have to ruin everything?"

I was astounded. "What are you talking about?"

"Why do you always want to fix things that aren't broken?" She shook her head several times. "You can't ever leave well enough alone."

"What is going on here?"

She swung around and told me, "Alain rang me last week."

"Who's Alain?"

"He was Geneva."

"Geneva?" I said, "That's been over forever."

She said, "I thought so too."

"What do you mean, you thought so?" I took her by the shoulders. "What about you and me. I want to marry you. . ."

"Turnabout is fair play." She started to shake her head and then she walked away from me.

"Turnabout?" I followed her but she kept moving out of my reach.

"We all have our Elizabeths," she said. "He promised to marry me but he had a wife. So we'd meet on weekends. This went on for five years. Of course, his wife found out and he told her he was going to marry me. At least, he told me that's what he said to her. But she wouldn't give him a divorce and he obviously never pressed her for one. And all that time I just waited for him. It got to the point where we even started spending weekends at his house. How's that for a neat arrangement? He and I would sleep in the guest room while his wife slept upstairs in their bedroom. It was the only way she could keep him."

I cut in, "Francesca, I love you . . ."

She kept on talking. "So after five years I finally got smart and left and you know what happened then? He came running after me. He spent two years trying to get me back and when I finally gave in he promised to marry me again. I believed him. We lived together for a year. Then he started asking me if his wife could visit on weekends. . ."

"I don't care about him. I care about you and me . . ."

"I refused to sleep alone on weekends while he slept with his wife in our guest room so I walked out again. I thought I was free from him and almost made it for another couple of years before he came back into my life. This time he was divorced but now he had a very young girlfriend. A girl the same age as I was when I first fell in love with him. So he asked me to marry him, and I almost said yes. Except that I realized how, before long, she'd be sharing the guest room with him on weekends . . ." Now she faced me. "He called me last week to tell me his young girlfriend is gone."

I tried to think of something intelligent to say. All I could come up with was, "Right now. Come with me right now. We'll get on a plane for somewhere, the first plane out of Heathrow for anywhere and wherever we land we'll get married."

"No."

"The first plane to anywhere. Come with me." I reached for her. "I love you. Please. Wherever we land, we'll get married there."

"No."

I brought her down onto the couch and took her, more

forcefully than the first time. And I kept on telling her, "I love you."

We eventually fell asleep there, both of us exhausted. When I got up the next morning she was already awake. I moved close to her. And she whispered, "I have to go."

I told her, "I've never asked anyone to marry me. . ."

"I have to go."

I stayed where I was, on the couch, as she took a fast shower and, still slightly wet, stepped into her clothes. Then, just like that, she walked out the door.

I couldn't focus my mind on anything. I paced the floor like a caged animal. I kept trying to convince myself, it's not over. It's not finished.

The phone rang and I grabbed it, knowing it was her.

It was Peter.

Thoroughly annoyed with myself for expecting Francesca, I mumbled, "I'll call you later."

"Have a nice day, as you would say if you weren't feeling sorry for yourself, yet again." He hung up.

I held onto the phone, then slammed it down.

It's not over, I said out loud. And I kept saying that, louder each time, trying to make myself believe it.

Now Francesca's story about Charlemagne came back to me.

It's the ring.

But I didn't know which one of them had cast the spell.

So I took the phone again and called international directory inquiries – there was still a listing for E. B. Pepperdine – then dialled that number. It rang on the other end four times before a sleepy voice answered, "Hello?"

"What time is it?" My heart was racing.

She whispered, "Who is this?"

I almost couldn't get the words out. "It's . . . me . . .

Michael." My clock said it was 7:30 so it was only 2:30 in Baltimore. "I'm sorry to wake you."

She was staggered. "Michael?"

"I needed to speak to you."

"Michael? Where are you? Is something wrong?"

"No, nothing's wrong. I'm in London." I was trembling. "Where are you going to be at 3 o'clock this afternoon?"

"Tell me what's wrong?"

"Nothing's wrong. Where will you be this afternoon?"

Still mostly asleep, she said, "Here."

"Okay. I'll be there. Give me your address." She did. I said, "Go back to sleep. I'll see you at 3." Then I rang Peter and told him I was going to America.

He asked, "Have you thought this out?"

I answered truthfully, "Not a bit."

Chapter Seventeen

It was an odd sensation to land at Dulles Airport. I didn't know if I wanted to applaud or cry or both. I handed my passport to the Immigration Officer, who looked at it, checked my name on his list of undesirables, banged a stamp on it, handed it back to me and motioned that I could enter the United States of America.

I said to myself, I'm home.

And now my eyes got very red. I must have been quite a sight because some woman walked up to me while I was waiting for my luggage and asked if I was all right.

"Hay fever," I told her.

She forced a smile and walked away.

I thought about trying to sneeze, but I knew she didn't believe me. Anyway, it didn't matter.

My cab driver in from the airport wanted to know, "You live here?"

"I'm from here," I said.

"Oh yeah." He was a fat man with no neck and very broad shoulders, who wore a red Orioles cap backwards, the way the black street kids do now. "So, you're from here."

"Yeah, this is home. I'm from here. I mean, I grew up here. I don't live here . . ." I stopped. What the hell am I doing, I asked myself. "Yeah . . . home. . ."

He peered at me through the rearview mirror as if he was waiting for me to finish the sentence.

I said, "I'm just back to see an old friend."

"A girlfriend?"

"Ah. . ." I didn't want to explain my life story. "Something like that."

"I understand." He nodded and didn't say anything for nearly half an hour. When he finally spoke to me again, he said, "Time to check your palms."

"My what?"

"Your palms." He peered back at me and took one hand off the wheel to point. "Your palms. Check 'em out."

I opened my hands and looked at them. "What about them?"

"They sweaty yet?"

"Why should they be sweaty?"

He pulled up to the curb. "'Cause we're here."

I paid him, stepped out of the cab and pulled my bag onto my shoulder.

He leaned out the window. "Good luck, lover."

I admitted to him, "Yeah, they're sweaty."

Elizabeth lived in one of those buildings where the elevator brings you up to a catwalk and each apartment opens onto that. I rode up to the fifth floor, found a red door marked 52, took a deep breath and knocked.

Nothing happened.

I checked my watch. It was 3:10. I knocked again and waited for nearly a minute before I started to knock a third time.

That's when the door swung open and Elizabeth was standing there smiling. "You're ten minutes late."

Suddenly it was 1969 again. I reached out for her and she came into my arms. I held her tightly. We still fit together. I didn't let go for the longest time.

She looked up at me, saw that I was on the verge of crying and slipped right back into my arms. I couldn't stop myself. And she held me while I wept.

"I'm sorry," I kept saying. "I'm sorry."

"Michael . . ." She was crying too.

It took a while until we both regained some control. Then she led me inside and closed the door. She sat me down on her couch – two cats jumped up and she shooed them away – and took her place next to me.

She wasn't as thin as she used to be. And her face had lines I'd never seen before. But her eyes were the same. And her voice was the same. And she still wore her hair the same way – parted in the middle and falling into her face so that she could hide behind it.

I reached for her, kissed her forehead and whispered to her, "I have never stopped loving you."

She put her head on my chest and left it there for a while. When she finally spoke, she said, "I'm going to do something very English. I'm going to make tea."

I watched her walk into her tiny kitchen, wiped my eyes, took several deep breaths, then sat back and looked around. The flat was small, a couple of bedrooms, with a dining table at the far end of the living-room. There were some toys on the floor under the window and a school photo on the end table of a young boy.

And there were cats everywhere.

"How many of these things live here?" I asked.

"Six?"

"Aren't you sure?"

"It's only supposed to be six but we get out sometimes and we bring our friends home with us. And sometimes we get pregnant." She poked her head out from the kitchen and made a funny face. "Cats are just like people."

"Speaking of getting pregnant . . ."

She asked, "Are you offering already?"

I laughed. "No, I was wondering . . . I guess you have a kid, right?"

"Yes." The kettle whistled. "Wait a second." When the tea was ready, she brought out two mugs and a plate of chocolate chip cookies. "Yes. I happen to live with an extremely wonderful human being who is just 11. His name is Christopher. And by the time you finish your third cookie, you'll meet him." She sat down, clinked her mug with mine and said softly, "I hated you for leaving me like that."

I sipped my tea. "I've thought about you."

Now she asked, "Why are you here? Did someone throw you out?"

I didn't want to tell her about Francesca. "I needed to . . . I wanted to see you."

She shook her head. "You haven't learned to fib very well."

That's when the front door opened and a blond tyke in jeans, a Baltimore Colts sweatshirt and a bright scarlet ski parka stepped into the apartment. He dropped his school bag in the hallway, spotted me and stopped dead in his tracks.

I said, "Hi."

He said nothing.

Elizabeth held out her hands to him but he didn't move. "Darling, this is my very old friend Michael Bayard. He lives in London, England, and he's come to visit us for . . ." She looked at me.

"A few days," I said, extending my hand. "I'm very proud to meet you, Christopher."

He came into the room, hesitated, then shook my hand. "My name is Christopher Bolt Pepperdine. Bolt was my mother's name before she married . . ." He thought about that for an instant, then continued, "Before she married her husband."

"And my middle name is Radisson, which was my mother's name before she married her husband."

"Where does you mother live?"

"Well . . ." I wasn't sure what to tell him. "She used to live in Baltimore."

He asked right away, "Is she dead?"

"Ah . . . as a matter of fact. . ."

"What about your father?"

I shrugged, "Him too."

He also shrugged. "My daddy's not dead. My mommy

208

just divorced him. But it's sort of like he's dead because he doesn't come to see me. I don't think he likes us a lot."

I shot a glance at Elizabeth. "I'm sure he likes you."

"No, he doesn't," Elizabeth corrected. "He doesn't care for either one of us."

I didn't know how to get out of this conversation, so I said the first thing that came to mind, "Tell me something, Christopher Bolt Pepperdine. Do you know Joe Beamish?"

He shook his head, "No."

"Come here." I motioned to him and after he checked with his mother – she nodded it was all right – I whispered the routine in his ear. He didn't get it at first, but after I explained it a couple of more times, he decided it was pretty funny. "Let's try again." I asked, "Do you know Joe Beamish?"

Christopher said, "What's his name?"

I said, "Who?"

He said, "Joe Beamish." And the two of us fell about laughing.

Elizabeth didn't get it, so we did it again for her.

"Do you know Joe Beamish?"

"What's his name?"

"Who?"

"Joe Beamish."

She still didn't understand. Now I asked Christopher if he and I should take his mother to her favourite restaurant for dinner and he proclaimed that her favourite restaurant was The Texas Ranger – a high-class burger joint not far from the race track at Pimlico – which just happened to be his too. We went there and all through dinner Christopher and I kept asking each other, "Do you know Joe Beamish?" and Elizabeth never got the joke.

It was early when we got back to her flat, but it was a school night and Christopher had to go to sleep. We did our Joe Beamish routine one more time, then he said

209

goodnight. Elizabeth went into his room to read him a story. A few minutes later he came into the living-room – now wearing his pyjamas – to ask, "Where are you going to sleep tonight?"

I told him, "I'll probably find a hotel."

He nodded a few times, said goodnight again and went to his room.

When Elizabeth came back I wanted to know, "What was that all about?"

"He asked me and I told him the truth. I told him . . ." She paused, "I said to him, Michael can sleep anywhere Michael wants to sleep."

"Maybe a hotel is a good idea."

"If you're shy," she teased, "we can always turn out the lights first. But if memory serves . . ."

I grinned, trying not to feel any more awkward than I already did, because I didn't think I could handle the emotion of being with her after all these years. At least, not quite so soon. "Is the couch all right?"

"If the choice is between a hotel or the couch, then the couch is fine."

And that's where I slept.

I kept telling myself, there'll be plenty of time for other choices later.

Christopher came in the next morning, obviously to check if I was there. I pretended to be asleep, although I got up in time to see him off to school. Elizabeth and I had a quiet breakfast. Afterwards I suggested, "Let's take a drive." I don't know why I wanted to see my old house, but I did, so we got into her car and went there.

It was a lot smaller than it used to be.

She told me she'd heard about my parents. I shrugged it off. Then I asked about her marriage. She shrugged that off too.

I took her out for lunch and afterwards I emptied several shelves in her local supermarket, stocking her fridge for her. We whiled away the rest of the day, just sitting around, talking about old times, until Christopher came home. Then we went out for dinner again.

"How long are you going to stay here?" He asked.

"I don't know," I answered.

"Well," he said, "if you stay until after tomorrow, that's Saturday and I don't have any school and maybe we can go somewhere?"

"Like where?"

"How about if we go to see some dinosaurs?"

"It's a deal."

That night, once he went to bed, Elizabeth asked, "Are you going to sleep on the couch again tonight?"

I looked at her. "I feel like such a . . . I mean, it's been so long since you and I . . . and there have been people in between. . ." I almost started talking about Francesca, but caught myself in time and said, "Do you mind if I sleep on the couch again?"

"Are you really playing the virgin?" She stood in front of me with an odd look in her eyes. "Am I supposed to drag you into my bed?"

"No." This wasn't the way she used to be and it made me feel uneasy. "Really, the couch is fine."

She raised her eyebrows. "Cold feet? We could always wear our socks."

"Sort of," I said, and fell asleep thinking to myself, she never used to say things like that.

On Friday I asked if I could borrow her car for a few hours. She let me have it and I drove to the cemetery where my parents are buried. I bought some flowers at the gate. I don't know what I'd expected to find once I got inside but I put the flowers in front of their tombstones and stood there, staring down at their graves. I whispered, "I'm sorry," and left.

I picked up Elizabeth and we drove around Johns Hopkins, until I spotted a sandwich joint we used to go to. For old times' sake, I suggested we have lunch there. She refused to eat anything except the fruit salad, but I opted for nostalgia and ordered a submarine –

211

you know, a long loaf of Italian bread stuffed with luncheon meats and onions and cheese – and a large cream soda.

It was awful.

The wooden benches were more uncomfortable than I'd remembered and the music was louder than it used to be. The room was also very smoky, so much so that, at one point, Elizabeth started sneezing – tiny little sneezes one after the other – and I reminded her that she used to be able to sneeze ten times in a row. This time she only made it to eight.

We left our half-eaten lunch on the table and strolled around the campus, arm in arm, until it was time to go home.

"Do you know Joe Beamish?" Christopher said, walking in from school.

"What's his name?"

"Who?"

Elizabeth answered, "Why, Joe Beamish, of course."

Now the three of us started to laugh.

I announced, "I feel a deep-in-the-heart-of-Texas coming on," and, over her objections, took us all out for a Friday night hamburger.

Again that night, after Christopher went to bed, Elizabeth asked where I intended to sleep. "Really. This is kind of silly, isn't it? Of all people not to sleep in my bed."

I suggested, "How about if you give me another day or two to think about it?"

She demanded, "What's there to think about? I'm a grown woman offering to fuck you. As I recall, we used to be pretty good at that."

The only thing I could think of saying was, "As I recall we were kids then."

Now she wanted to know, "Who threw you out? I get the very distinct impression that I'm staring at some guy bouncing off the wall on the rebound."

"It's not that . . ."

"Not much." She shook her head and walked towards her bedroom. "If you change your mind, the door is open and . . ." She turned to say, coyly, ". . . my legs are too."

Much later that night, after I was sure that Elizabeth was asleep, I picked up the phone and dialled my sister.

"You're not calling because you need money," Sandy said right away. "But if you do need some money. . ."

"No. I'm calling to say hello. I'm in . . ." I didn't want to tell her where I was. "I'm in the States."

"Where?"

I lied, "Boston."

"Did you have any trouble coming back? Did they ask you any questions at the airport?"

"No."

"Are you coming out to Colorado?"

"I don't think so."

She reminded me, "You have a nephew and a niece you've never seen. Michael, they're all the family you've got. They're growing up so fast and you don't even know them."

"I have some things I have to do," I told her. "It's business stuff. . ."

Her husband picked up an extension somewhere in their house. "Is that you Michael? Listen, son, I'm willing to bury the hatchet if you are."

"Thanks very much, Hal. And I'm not your son. But I'll think about it."

"I'm sure you can afford a ticket. It's only $189 round trip if you get an Apex fair and stay a minimum of seven days which includes a Saturday night. Of course, you can bunk here with us. And if you can't pay for the ticket, I'll put up the money and you can pay me back whenever."

I sat there shaking my head. "Thanks very much, Hal. I'll think about it."

Sandy cut in, "You'll like our home. There's plenty of room. And you'll like our friends. You know, I'm very

213

active in local environmental issues. I'm vice president of one group and last year I was nominated to serve on a statewide committee. I even met John Denver. I actually spoke to him."

Her political conscience had finally come full circle. The girl who made up for not having been at Woodstock by smoking grass at sorority parties, got laid for the first time, stoned out of her mind, while listening to John Denver records. She wound up marrying a dentist and using her suddenly acquired affluence to get onto a committee so that she could meet John Denver and tell him, not about her first time, but about recyclable ice cream cartons.

"Did you say thank you?"

"Did I say thank you to who?"

"To John Denver."

"What for? His work on environmental issues?"

"Your first poke."

"Michael . . ."

Hal cut in. "What are you talking about?"

"Michael. . ."

I asked, "You mean he doesn't know?"

She said a third time, "Michael. . ."

"Of course, I know," Hal said. "What's he talking about, Sandra?"

"John Denver's influence on your wife," I assured him.

"She only spoke to him for a few minutes," he assured me, snidely. "You have a filthy mind."

I kept shaking my head. My sister may be sort of a jerk, but her husband is a major league idiot. He always encouraged her to do her own thing, not because he believed in what she was doing but because it kept her out of the way so that he could sexually harass his dumpy dental assistants. It never dawned on my sister why none of the women who worked for him ever lasted more than six minutes. Except the really stupid ones. As far as I was concerned, his only contribution to Western society —

except for bringing two kids into the world, both of whom were supposedly normal despite their parents – was a heavily footnoted article he wrote for a technical hygiene magazine on the merits of something asinine like non-waxed dental floss.

When Sandy started dating him, she dragged us – my parents and me – to his office where the article, in a heavy, gilt frame, hung as the centre piece of his waiting room.

"I'm glad that you're both well," I said, because it sounded like the right thing to say. "If my plans change, I'll let you know."

"Where are you staying?" My sister asked.

I didn't want to tell her. "It's not easy . . . I'm moving around."

"Have you called Elizabeth?"

I lied again, "No."

"You know she's divorced and she's got a child and maybe it's time the two of you got together . . ."

I stopped her. "I'll let you know."

"If you go to Baltimore, will you go to see the old house?"

"What for?"

"Just to see it."

"We used to live there. I know what it looks like."

"Well then, what about the cemetery?" She said softly, "Michael, they would like that if you visited them."

"They're dead, Sandy. They're not lying there with a periscope waiting to see who walks by."

Hal snapped, "Don't use that tone of voice with your only sister."

"Thanks very much, Hal. I'll think about it."

"Now, Michael, you listen to me . . ."

I started to say, "No, Hal, you listen to me . . ." but let it drop because it simply wasn't worth it. "I've got to go. Tell your kids if they ever run away from home, they can always come to me. And Sandy, next time you see John Denver, don't forget to tell him about you know what."

"Michael!"

"You know what, what?" Hal wanted to know.

"Nothing." Sandy changed the subject, "Are you sure you can't come for a visit?"

"Michael!" Hal's voice was firm, "I want you to know that I don't . . ."

I cut in, "Thanks very much, Hal. I'll think about it," and hung up.

Just as I did, a plate somewhere in the flat crashed to the floor.

It scared me.

A fraction of a second later, a cat raced out of the kitchen.

It took a moment before I realized what had happened. I got to my feet and walked into the kitchen. I put the pieces of the plate in the sink, then turned around, startled to find Elizabeth standing in the doorway.

"What time is it?"

I said, "It's late."

She was mostly asleep.

"What happened?"

"It was one of the cats."

"Oh. Leave it. I'll take care of it in the morning."

There was enough light behind her to see through her knee-length night shirt. She was wearing white panties. Her shoulders were bare and I could see the top of her breasts. She'd always been very small there. We used to joke about it when we were kids. And suddenly all of that came rushing back to me . . . how it had been to hold her and to sleep with her and to wake up with her and the taste of her mouth tight against mine. . .

"Goodnight." She rubbed her eyes and moved slowly back to her bedroom. I took a couple of steps, following her into the living-room and almost called out to her. I almost said, "I want you."

And, maybe if I had. . .

Or, maybe if she'd stopped and turned around. . .

But I didn't. And she didn't.

I stood there and watched as she walked away.

And just like that, the moment was gone.

The next morning I got up first, slipped into a pair of jeans and made tea for the two of us. Not bothering to put on my shirt, I brought it into her with toast and marmalade jam.

We'd nearly finished a quiet breakfast together – with her propped up against her pillows and me sitting near her on the edge of her bed – when Christopher appeared in her doorway.

"Hi." I said. "Sleep good?"

He stared at me, then looked at his mother, then rubbed his nose while he was working out what to say. "Where's your shirt?"

"My shirt?"

"Yeah," he said. "Where's your shirt?"

I shot a glance at Elizabeth. "My shirt's on the coffee table, in front of the couch where I slept."

He thought about that one too. "You should put it on before you catch a cold."

I said, "Okay. You get it for me and I'll put it on."

He nodded and went to find it.

I whispered, "I guess he doesn't like the idea of men on his mother's bed."

"Or in it. Or even near it," she said. "Kids do have a remarkable way of putting an end to miscellaneous fooling around outside school hours."

Christopher came in carrying my shirt, which was fine because I didn't want her to explain that last remark.

I asked him, "What do you say we all go out for breakfast?"

He looked at me suspiciously, "You just had breakfast."

"But you didn't."

He paused. "Do you like pancakes?"

"Me? Pancakes? I invented pancakes."

"No you didn't." Then he asked his mother, "Did he?"

He insisted we go to some really awful place for pancakes – one of those joints that puts 12 different kinds of syrup on your table and none of them pour. When breakfast was done, I announced that it was my turn, so we drove into Washington to have lunch at the Air and Space Museum. He said that was his favourite. He showed me Charles Lindbergh's plane and the model of Sputnik and told his mother and me all about the Bell X–15. Then we went to the Natural History Museum, where he explained to his mother and me everything we always wanted to know about dinosaurs. We finished up with ice cream at a soda fountain she and I used to like in Georgetown.

After Elizabeth made a quiet dinner and Christopher went to bed, she announced, "No couch tonight."

I gently laughed it off. "We've had a nice day. . ."

"No couch, Michael. I mean it. Why do you think you can just parade in here like this and take over my son? You waltz back into my life after the way you disappeared, after what you did to my life . . . what are you doing here?"

Her mood swing frightened me. "I came to see you. I wanted to see you. . ."

"It doesn't work that way."

I reached for her, but she stepped back.

"You're not going to do it to me again, Michael. All the pain . . . all the hurt . . . the divorce . . . the way you walked out on me . . ." Her voice grew harsher and louder. "You walked out on me. You disappeared. You didn't call me or tell me, you just walked away."

"I wrote to you . . . I wrote to you and you never answered. . ."

"Big fucking deal. You wrote two letters. Do you think that makes everything all right? Well . . ." She shouted, "Well, now it's too late."

I tried to calm her down. "Elizabeth, listen to me . . ."

"It's too late, Michael." She began moving from one

side of the living-room to the other. "It's too late." She never stopped shuffling back and forth. "You can't do that to me again, Michael."

I stood there, dumbfounded.

"It's my life and it's his life and I won't let you do that to us any more. Never again, Michael. . ."

Christopher appeared in the doorway. "Mommy . . . what's wrong?"

She ran to him and held him tightly. "Michael was just leaving, darling . . ." She looked at me. "Say goodbye to Michael, darling. Michael was just leaving."

Christopher seemed terrified. "Do you have to go?"

"Yes, darling, he has to go." Elizabeth kept clutching him as she started to march around the room again. "Don't you, Michael? Don't you have to go now?"

"Elizabeth, please listen to me . . ."

"No, Michael. You have to go now. I offered everything I have to you and you wouldn't take it." She said to Christopher, "Michael has to leave us alone now. Say goodbye, darling."

The boy began to cry. "Goodbye, Joe Beamish. Goodbye."

I packed — "Goodbye, Joe Beamish" — and walked out.

Elizabeth slammed the door behind me.

I came home to London, utterly shattered.

Peter said, "Go ahead and get it over with. Put yourself out of your misery, for bloody fucking sake. Ring Francesca."

I told him no, absolutely, no.

"She'll take you back," he said. "I wouldn't but she will. Call her."

"I categorically refuse."

Peter nodded, "Sure, you do!"

When he went out for lunch I phoned her. But she hung up on me. It took over a year before we got back together.

Chapter Eighteen

Yogi Berra was a philosopher.

I saw him play against the Baltimore Orioles when my father took me to my very first baseball game – he was the star catcher for the famous New York Yankee teams of the 1940s and 1950s – but his influence on me goes far beyond that singular childhood memory. It was something he said one morning on the *Today Show*, years after he'd retired. I must have been about 12 or 13 at the time and don't have the slightest idea what I was doing watching TV instead of being in school, but on the programme that morning Yogi mused, "In life, whenever you come to a fork in the road, take it."

I'd always intended that Pippa was to be the last one. I was willing to acknowledge that Elizabeth was, clearly, the most important one. But Francesca was, unequivocally, the most unsettling one.

I have measured out my life with forks.

One day in 1986, coming totally out of left field, Francesca rang to say she was lonely. So I took her back to Eleuthera, to that same rented house, where we spent two weeks pretending to make up for lost time.

But it didn't last long because, by then, we knew so well how to hurt each other.

She'd had a very good year at the bank, having grabbed the crest of the wave that looked as if it was about to wash over the City with the opening of the British investment industry. She'd waltzed through a series of major deals – with all the grace of a financial Fred and Ginger – netting herself £1.6 million through an incentive bonus plan with BFCS. Years before, knowing that one day she would score big, I'd convinced her to put all the necessary shelters and duck blinds in place so that she could keep whatever she might eventually earn away from the British tax man. I'd helped her set up a little secret shell in Vaduz, which I'd named "Zermatt International of Liechtenstein". She'd agreed it was funny because I'd abbreviated it, "Zilch". I'd somehow forgotten to explain the reference to Zermatt. I'd thought it was hilarious.

Her windfall, however, had not been without cost. The stress had taken its toll. Her temper was constantly on a hair trigger. She was annoyed by even the slightest things, made all the more irritable by the long hours and extensive travelling she needed to do to keep her balance on the crest of that wave.

I told her I still loved her and told her again that I wanted to marry her. She warned me not to say that. I told her I hated her for the way she'd turned my life inside out. She ran away again.

On the night she left – feeling emotionally battered and bruised and in a rage of my own for having yet again exposed myself to this – I got it into my head that it was high time I started taking life like a pot luck supper.

I grabbed a suitcase, intending to head for Heathrow and hop on the first thing smoking for anywhere. But, while trying to figure out which clothes to take, the thought dawned on me that the first plane to anywhere could be to Beirut or Baghdad. So I dialled British Airways to ask if they had a flight around 10:30 or 11, and if they did, where it was going.

It was just after 9 o'clock and all I got was a recording saying that the reservations office was closed.

My next idea was to jump in the car and drive

someplace. Paris was my first choice. Then I reminded myself that if I was going to France I might as well hide out where I hid out best and, in the end, I settled on the thoroughly unoriginal idea of going to my own flat in Cannes.

But Air France reservations in London was also closed.

Mumbling to myself that efficiency just wasn't a European strong-point, I called Air France reservations in New York. A woman there checked her computer, said their next flight to Nice was full but that there was room on BA. Determined to get the hell out of London, I booked my seat to Nice out of Heathrow with British Airways through Air France in New York.

The next morning, my taxi got caught in traffic along the Brompton Road and by the time we made it to the Chiswick Roundabout, I was sure I'd missed the plane.

What I hadn't counted on was the Irish Republican Army.

In those days, the plane that went to Nice came down from Belfast on the Northern Ireland run. Because the British are paranoid about security anyway – but get especially nuts whenever there is the possibility of an IRA connection – the police routinely went over the plane with a fine-toothed explosives detector.

Considering that my ass was about to get strapped into a seat 29,000 feet up in the air for 105 minutes, I was grateful. All the more so when I finally got to the check-in desk, knowing I'd missed the flight by 30 minutes, only to have a clerk tell me it had been delayed for security reasons. She said if I hurried I could still make it and told me to carry my suitcase with me, that someone would check it in for me at the gate. She even phoned the gate to say there was one more passenger on his way.

Suitcase in hand, I was stopped at security.

The rocket scientist manning the X-ray machine pointed out that I had two carry-ons. "I can't allow

222

you to pass because airport policy is only one carry-on per passenger."

I explained, "I don't have two carry-ons. One is an attaché case. That is a carry-on. This is a suitcase. It is not a carry-on. I'm going to check it in when I get to the gate."

"No," he said. "You must check in all suitcases at check-in."

I pointed out, "At check-in they told me to bring my suitcase with me because I'm late. So I'd be very grateful if you'd be kind enough, on this occasion, to please put both of these through the machine."

Before he'd do that, he demanded to see my ticket. I produced it and after great calculation, he deduced, "The flight has already left. It left half an hour ago."

I assured him, "It's been delayed. It's waiting for me." I gestured towards the queue of people behind me trying to get past security. "In fact, the whole airport is waiting for me."

He allowed my suitcase and my attaché case to go through the machine, then raced around to the other side and demanded to inspect them by hand. "I want to see what's inside for myself."

Getting into a discussion with these guys is pointless, so I opened both of them and stood there shaking my head while he rummaged around for what seemed like a very long time. Obviously my toe tapping didn't encourage him to move any faster.

When he finally looked up at me, he said, "I'll let you through this time. But only this time . . ."

I mumbled, "Thanks," and hurried to Immigration. When I handed a woman there my passport, she reminded me that I needed to fill out an embarkation card. It was required of all non-nationals leaving the UK. I once asked why this was necessary and the Immigration Officer told me, "So we know who's leaving." My next question was, "Why do you care who's leaving?" He said, "So that we know who's no longer in the country." I never felt I had the energy to continue the discussion.

Scribbling down my name, address and destination, I handed the card back to the woman. Without so much as reading a word of it, she stamped the card, stamped my passport, put the card on a small pile of similar cards, returned my passport to me and said, "Ta."

I assured myself, "If nothing else, futility keeps people employed," then ran as fast as I could to the gate.

Naturally, it was the last gate. It always is. I used to believe the airlines did that on purpose. Then I found out that the closer the gate, the more they have to pay for the slot. Now I *know* they do it on purpose.

When I got there I tossed my ticket on the desk and said, "Sorry I'm late." The BA clerk gave me an ornery glare – good old customer service – took my bag and, without saying a word, handed me a seat in smoking. I wondered, "Anything in non-smoking?"

She said, "We're full."

I suggested, "You could at least pretend to look at the seating chart."

"You're lucky the plane is even here," she commented, as if it was my fault.

I feigned resignation. "Anything in non-smoking would be most kind."

She took a deep breath, made a great display of inspecting a tiny piece of paper, then conceded, "I have one seat left in non-smoking."

I grinned, "We've made each other's day."

She revised my boarding pass and told me, with all the charm of a US Marine drill sergeant, "Wait in the lounge for boarding."

"*Semper fidelis*." I moved past her, glanced around for a seat in the lounge and found myself looking straight into the eyes of a young, dark-haired woman who was sitting in a chair against the far wall.

We stared at each other.

I half-smiled at her.

She half-smiled back, then dropped her eyes.

An odd feeling swept through me — almost, but not exactly, like that feeling I'd had, all those years ago, when Elizabeth walked by on the train.

There weren't any seats near her, so I positioned myself on the other side of the room.

She was obviously alone.

I pretended to study my ticket and my boarding pass.

She pretended to be reading a magazine.

We kept catching each other peeking.

I stayed where I was for another seven or eight minutes until they called the flight. With a huge collective sigh, everyone in the room stood up at the same time. I watched the woman with the short dark hair make her way to the rear of the line and I quickly stepped into place behind her. She was wearing designer jeans and a seersucker blazer. Shorter than Elizabeth and not as slim as Francesca, she smelled of Chanel.

I peered over her shoulder and saw that her magazine had something to do with horses. "I bet on a horse once," I whispered near her ear. "It went off at ten to one and came in at quarter after five."

She said, without turning around, "The old ones are the best."

"Old horses?"

"Old jokes."

"Oh." I thought for a moment. "How about, my horse was so slow that the photo-finish turned out to be an oil painting?"

"I take it back." She shook her head, still not looking at me. "The old ones aren't always the best."

The line was edging forward.

"You're not a jockey, are you?"

"Of sorts," she said.

"You're kidding?"

She finally turned towards me. And she was smiling.

"If you really must know, I show jump. At least I used to."

"Professionally?"

"It's an amateur sport."

I told her, "I'm very fond of amateur sports."

Making a face, she shook her head. "Tacky."

"You're right," I admitted. "Sorry."

By that time, we'd reached the BA clerk from check-in, who tore off the stub from my new friend's boarding pass and announced, "23C."

I handed mine to her, she looked up, noticed that the previous passenger seemed to be standing one step beyond as if she was waiting for me, and announced in a jovial way, "23C is a smoking seat, sir. 11C is non-smoking."

"And thank you for flying British Airways," I mumbled, retrieving my boarding pass, then joining my new friend on the line waiting to get onto the plane.

"What was that all about?" She asked.

"She's an Air France spy." I wanted to know, "Where are you going?"

"I'd naturally assumed we are all going to Nice."

"I meant from Nice."

"Villefranche."

"Oh."

The line moved forward.

She wondered, "You?"

"Cannes."

"Oh," she said.

"Vacation?"

"Mini-break. You?"

"Mini-break," I acknowledged.

We took several steps forward again.

"My name is Bay."

She thought about that. "As in harbour, inlet, cove, estuary and fiord?"

"Only in Oslo."

"Mine's Pippa."

"As in . . ." I gave her my best pained expression, "As in Pippa?"

"As in Philippa."

"Radisson," I added as we stepped inside the plane.

She presented her boarding pass to the stewardess who motioned towards the rear of the aircraft.

Pippa nodded, took a single step down the aisle, turned, said, "Woolcott," and went to her seat.

After finding my place – next to a couple from France who were babbling away about British hospitality – I craned my neck and tried to spot Pippa, but there were too many people still moving about in the cabin. So I waited until we took off before lowering the table in front of me and reaching into my attaché case for my pen and some paper.

"Dear Pippa, as in Philippa, Woolcott: Without wishing to sound tacky – again – may I ask, is that a) Miss Woolcott? b) Ms Woolcott? c) Mrs Woolcott? (Despite the fact that you're not wearing a wedding ring. I know because I checked.) d) About to be Mrs Someone-else who happens to be waiting in Villefranche? e) All of the above? Or f) none of the above?"

I folded it, addressed it to "The Young Woman in 23C", and asked the stewardess to deliver it. She did. Five minutes later the stewardess returned my note with the scribbled answer, "a) Miss Woolcott, pronounced Mizz."

Now I wrote, "Dear a) Miss Woolcott, pronounced Mizz: One of the more worrying things about the French is that they sometimes eat horses. Considering your sort-of-jockey status, I wonder, if I could find a restaurant somewhere along the coast that promised to serve nothing but Texas beef – or, even better, nothing but French bouillabaisse – is there any chance you might find an evening free for dinner?"

The answer came back, "Definitely no horse meat! Preferably no red meat at all. Not even Texas beef. Occasionally chicken and duck. As for bouillabaisse,

Mr Radisson, are we talking just anywhere or are we talking Chez Tetou?"

This was fun. I wrote, "CT, *bien sûr*. Will you be kind enough to confirm the evening in writing?"

Her next message read, "The last time I was in Villefranche, I was with someone who promised to take me to CT but he couldn't get reservations. The place was booked two weeks in advance. I'm going home one week from today. So if you can get us in on short notice, I'm yours . . . manner of speaking, *bien sûr*."

And I wrote to her, "I'm also going home one week from today. Have you ever heard of Yogi Berra?"

Getting off the plane in Nice, the stewardess suggested I wait just outside the door for 23C who was – she looked towards the rear of the plane – on her way.

Pippa and I walked down the gangplank together and onto the tarmac for the stroll into the airport. "Do you have a ride?"

"Actually," she said, "I'm meeting my parents in the airport. They're taking this flight home. They've got the car. Do you need a lift?"

She knew very well I was headed in the wrong direction. "Actually, I do. But Cannes is out of your way. Of course, I could always walk. It's not even 25 miles."

We got inside the airport and stood on line for passport control. Just as we stepped through it, she turned to me and said, "I'll think about it. We'll discuss it at the baggage claim area."

"Are you trying to get rid of me already?"

"My parents would never approve."

I let her go ahead to deal with them. But I lingered just long enough that I could walk right past the three of them standing in front of the Hertz counter. Her father was a pleasant-looking man, broad shouldered with a deep tan. Pippa resembled her mother. They were built the same way, had the same jaw bone structure and the same hips. And because I've always figured that a mother is a good indication of what a daughter will look like 30 years down the line, I made a mental note that Pippa would be all right when she reached that age.

My suitcase, which went on last, mistakenly came off first. I can only presume that British Airways didn't realize it was mine because they'd never managed that before, or since. I took it from the carousel and tossed it onto a trolley. Pippa showed up ten minutes later, grabbed her suitcase, put it on my trolley and jiggled her father's car keys. "I've thought about it and decided that Cannes is definitely the wrong way."

"Villefranche? Well, okay, if you really prefer . . ."

"My parents' flat?" She shook her head. "A little soon for that, don't you think? I'll get the car."

We walked through Customs together and I waited on the kerb while she went into the parking lot across the street. I had her pegged as a definite Peugeot type, when a dark red Rolls with Swiss plates pulled up and the trunk snapped open.

I only just managed to hide my surprise.

With our suitcases in the trunk, I climbed into the seat next to her. "If Cannes is the wrong direction for you, and Villefranche is the wrong direction for Chez Tetou, how about somewhere in the middle?"

"Such as?"

I dared, "The Negresco?"

She stared me straight in the face. "Are you pro-positioning me, Mr Radisson?"

I said, "I think I just have, Mizz Woolcott."

She put the car in gear and nothing more was said until we pulled up to the Negresco on the Promenade des Anglais.

As the doorman came to greet us Pippa warned, "If they know you at the front desk, the deal is off."

I grinned. "Same goes for you."

We got out together – the doorman in his handsome red uniform and plumed hat promised that our luggage would follow shortly — and strolled into the lobby. A young man behind the front desk welcomed us and asked our name. "Radisson," I said. "We don't have reservations, but if it helps, we'll pretend that we do."

He gave us both the once over, decided we were suitable and said he would see what he could do for us. After checking through a list of available rooms, he offered us, "A beautiful double with a seafront view."

I said that would be fine and handed him a credit card. He asked for our passports, didn't flinch when he saw that our last names were different — at those prices I would have been no-holds-barred indignant if he had so much as blinked — and wondered how many nights we'd be staying. I answered immediately, "Seven."

He said, "Certainly, sir," and rang the tiny bell on the desk for a porter. "Please show Monsieur and Madame Radisson to their room." He gave the porter our key and wished us a pleasant stay.

Pippa whispered to me in the lift, "Seven?"

I explained, "We're on a weekly rate."

The room was large, on the fourth floor, with a small balcony overlooking the sea. The porter went through the usual ritual of turning on half the lights and opening all the closet doors, until I tipped him and he left. Then someone knocked on the door — our suitcases had arrived — and that porter went through a similar ritual, turning on the rest of the lights and shutting the closet doors, until I tipped him.

When he left, Pippa asked coyly, "What now?"

I told her, "Now I get us into CT for dinner."

"You think you can do that?"

"Me? Probably not. But our new friend downstairs can. Watch." I rang the concierge and told him we wanted a table for two at 8. He said he would arrange it. I hung up and turned to her, "I do believe it's tea time."

"Tea time?"

I nodded, "Yes, tea time," and motioned towards the door.

She stared at me.

I knew what she was thinking. "There's no rush." I extended my hand. "Tea time." She took it and we left the room.

We found a suitable café on the Promenade, had tea, then walked around and stuck our faces into a few backstreet antique shops. She told me she collected antique hour glasses. Drawing a picture for a woman in one of the shops, we discovered the French word was *minuterie*. So we went in search of *minuteries*, but couldn't find any. By the time the shops closed, it was 6:30. Back at the Negresco, the concierge announced that Chez Tetou would indeed be holding a table for us at 8.

"I'm impressed," Pippa said.

"That's the easy part," I shrugged.

"So what's the difficult part?"

"Finding the world's greatest antique *minuterie*."

"You sound like a very determined man, Mr Radisson."

"Especially when I'm interested, Mizz Woolcott."

We unpacked together. I hung the few clothes I had in the closet next to hers, then offered to let her take the first shower before we dressed to go out.

She later told me that she couldn't believe any man would have been so gallant, especially as she'd been so obvious in offering herself. I later admitted that such uncommon gallantry had amazed me too.

Pippa showered and came out in a pale blue Negresco robe. I took my shower and came out in a similar robe, and by that time she was dressed. Now she went into the bathroom to make up while I dressed, then called for the car. She drove and I navigated, taking the route along the sea – the long way around Cap d'Antibes – to Chez Tetou. We arrived promptly at 8. I ordered champagne and bouillabaisse for two and we didn't get up from the table until 11:30. Then we walked along the beach, barefoot, and when she said it was getting chilly I put my arm around her and we kept walking.

I wondered, "How come you're here alone for a week?"

"I needed to get away," she said. "How come you're here alone for a week?"

I looked at her. "Probably for the same reason as you."

Still barefoot, we drove back to the Negresco and ambled through the lobby with our shoes in our hands. When we got to the room we found a small basket of fruit and a bottle of champagne with a note from the manager welcoming us to the hotel.

"What's this?" She made a face. "I thought you said they didn't know you here?"

"A case of mistaken identity," I assured her. "They think I'm Marcello Mastroianni." I popped the cork, poured two glasses and offered her one. "I assume that you see the resemblance, as well."

She took it and climbed into the centre of the bed. "You mean, they do this to you all the time?"

I asked, "Do you know the story about the couple arriving at the hotel on their honeymoon – they're still in their wedding clothes – and they get to the desk, just married, and the clerk says, hiya Brenda, usual room?"

She laughed, drank some champagne, hesitated, then motioned for me to join her. "This is always the most awkward part."

"It doesn't have to be."

"I hope not."

We clinked glasses and each took a sip. After a while I took her glass from her, put it on the night table and took her in my arms. She lay back and pulled me down on top of her. I kissed the side of her neck, moved my mouth along her shoulder and then up to her ear. She shifted her hips, bringing them against mine, hooking her right leg over the back of my left leg.

She whispered, "Please fuck me all week."

I did.

*　　*　　*

We stayed in bed for 39 hours.

We only got up to go to the bathroom or to slip into the tub together and drink champagne there. We didn't get dressed, except to wear our blue Negresco bathrobes when we received the succession of trays that we ordered from room service. In fact, the only reason we got out of bed at all on Monday was because she phoned her parents in London and after they complained that they hadn't been able to reach her at the flat – I've been running around antique shops, she lied – her father asked her to bring back his Rolex that he'd left in the bathroom and her mother said, if there's room in your suitcase, can you please bring me that yellow Hermès scarf.

So we drove to Villefranche, collected the watch and the scarf and then drove to Cannes, to my flat, so that I could pick up some clothes. As long as we were ambulatory, we headed into the hills, to St Paul, for lunch at the Colombe d'Or.

On Tuesday and Wednesday we got out of bed by lunchtime so that we could do the beach. On Thursday we drove to St Tropez for lunch. We forced ourselves to get up early on Friday for the outdoor market at Ventimiglia, just across the border in Italy, but were back at the Negresco by tea time. Armed with a magnum of champagne, we went straight to bed until mid-morning Saturday. We then checked out of the Negresco, brought the car back to the garage at her parents' flat and taxied from Villefranche to the airport.

This time, we sat together on the plane.

Just after take-off I handed her a small antique hour glass. "I hope you like it."

She stammered, "It's beautiful. But . . . but where did you get it? When did you get it? You were never out of my sight."

"If I tell you all my tricks Mizz Woolcott, the novelty will wear off."

"I've gotten to see a lot of your tricks, Mr Radisson

and I don't think the novelty could wear off for a very long time."

"I really do hope you like it."

"Your tricks or the hour glass?"

I smiled, "Both."

She held my hand for the entire flight.

When we landed in London she asked, "Now what?"

Feeling dizzy and light headed, almost as if I was drunk with her, I suggested, "Wanna get married?"

We did, three weeks later at Chelsea Town Hall.

Chapter Nineteen

Thanksgiving is the most traditional of all American holidays – the one day of the year when we Yanks eat better than the French.

I left the office early to supervise the turkey going into the oven. Pippa made candied sweet potatoes, commenting as she did every year that only Americans would eat anything like that. I reminded her, as I did every year, that for someone who thinks baked beans on toast is a real treat, she had her nerve criticizing melted marshmallows on yams.

There was chestnut stuffing, corn bread, plenty of cranberry jelly and several bottles of Beaujolais Nouveau, which is what the Pilgrims would have drunk had Pepsi Cola not already franchised Plymouth Rock.

We were six at the table – Gerald and his wife Viv, Pippa's parents, Pippa and me – paying our respects to more than three and a half centuries of giving thanks for the bounty we have received.

As we sat down, I asked Pippa's father to say Grace. He came up with, "Thank you Lord for the food we are about to receive and may we be forever grateful for thy blessings."

It sounded as good as any and served the purpose. I don't know if there is a set piece that God requires or if he'll accept whatever you make up, but Grace was always part of those long-gone Thanksgivings of my childhood and, for me, it is the only meal of the year when I would feel that something is missing if no one said it.

I carved, Pippa served and halfway through the meal the girls came in to say goodnight.

Their grandmother wondered why they were up so late. The girls responded by climbing into their grandfather's lap, at which time he announced it was all right to stay up tonight because it was Thanksgiving. Pippa remarked he'd always been a pushover when she was growing up. He said that wasn't true. Pippa's mother made a face and explained to Viv, "The original pushover."

He continued to protest, turning now to Gerald. "Counsel, I expect you to defend me."

Viv cut in. "Talk about pushovers."

Gerald protested, "I am not."

Viv said, "Not much, he's not," and Pippa said, "My dad makes Gerald look like a storm trooper," at which point my father-in-law looked at me. But I had no intention of being dragged into this. "What we have here is, obviously, a British cultural problem and as such, has nothing to do with immigrants."

"I am not a pushover," Gerald bellowed. "Nor was I ever a pushover."

"Nor me," Pippa's father maintained.

That's when the twins decided they wanted some of the wine.

Pippa said no.

But her father said, sure, why not, French people gave wine to their children – Gerald passed him the bottle – and, over the objections of his wife and daughter, my father-in-law let his granddaughters each take a sip from his glass.

When both girls decided they liked wine a lot, I told Malika it was time that they made their exit.

Pippa wanted to know why her father would give the twins wine after she'd specifically said they shouldn't have any and Pippa's mother also castigated him for interfering.

Mischievously, I reminded everyone, "It was Gerald who gave him the bottle," which set Viv off on a tirade about how he always did that sort of thing with their kids too.

With Pippa and her mother and Viv all talking at once, and Gerald and Pippa's father trying to muster their own defence, I decided to clear the air by announcing that, for dessert, Pippa had made her version of my mother's pumpkin pie. When that didn't work, I tapped my wine glass with a spoon, called for silence and launched into my rendition of the Thanksgiving story.

"The Pilgrims invited some Indians for a meal," I said, "because they'd just been given the vote and, as one of the founding fathers, the great Stan Freberg, once sang, 'Take an Indian to lunch this week' was sound political strategy."

Pippa's mother asked her, "What's he talking about?"

I tapped my wine glass again.

"But someone made the terrible mistake of putting the national bird, that is to say the turkey, into the oven when everyone was expecting nothing less than roast eagle. And thus, Pilgrim Freberg was right when he noted, this was a pivotal mistake which changed the course of history."

The five of them simply stared at me, too polite – or better put, too confused – to admit they didn't have a clue what I was referring to.

I grinned and sat back, thinking that it was just like those wonderful Thanksgivings I always remembered. A prayer, a family argument, enough minor social embarrassment and plenty of left-over sweet potatoes with melted marshmallows.

Before Gerald and Viv went home, I pulled him aside to say I hadn't heard anything from the Stock Exchange.

He patted me on the back with fond encouragement and mumbled, "Yet."

"That's just what I needed to hear."

"Then why did you bring it up?"

"Because I was hoping you'd say, forget it, they've gone away."

"People who get kicked in the bum have a nasty habit of coming back."

"I missed."

"Let's hope he does too."

I spent the next few weeks trying to unload the final remnants of Ohio G., but divesting myself of what I considered to be the dregs was proving easier said than done. No one in Britain wanted our spark plug business or our farm machinery company, so I slipped into one of my daydreaming trances and listed my options.

I could try to sell my interests in the businesses to the employees. Except it was obvious that they didn't want them either. Or I could throw them away, which would add to my tax losses. Except I already had enough of those for a while. Or I could hold on to them and hope that someone would ultimately come along to buy them. Except I couldn't afford to divert too much money in that direction, keeping them afloat on a punt, while I was so heavily committed to Howe Wharf. Or I could go to Tokyo and try to work out something with the parent companies there. Except that meant spending time in Japan.

When I finally decided that the only sensible thing was to flog the businesses back to the natives, I bit the bullet and booked myself a January trip to the Land of the Rising Yen.

Many Western businessmen believe they must romance our Oriental brothers because the Pacific Rim is where the money is and will be for the next 50 years. They head east, armed with the knowledge that there are two obvious and viable methods for doing business there. Either you study the culture and hire a tutor to help you pick up some of the language – after all, we wouldn't want to insult our honourable hosts – or you decide, what the hell, if the Japanese want to do business with me they've got to speak English because it's up to them make sure I'm the one who doesn't get insulted.

Both methods have their champions. But I take a different approach. For me there's still plenty of money left to be made in the West and I have always, purposely, tried to avoid the Japanese whenever I can.

I am ill at ease with bowing and ceremony, think that belching in public is a very unattractive national pastime, find all that traditional courtesy crap to be a pain in the ass and resent the way they make believe they invented baseball.

I also don't trust them.

As I see it, if we have problems with the Japanese today – and we most certainly do – the man to blame is Harry Truman. Instead of sending MacArthur to Tokyo, he should have let him march into Peking. China offers a bigger workforce, cheaper labour, more possibility for exporting our stuff into their economy, less arrogance and, indisputably, better food.

In other words, Truman backed the wrong horse.

He should have been a better student of history. The record shows that the Japanese are orthodox jingo-bullies, and have been that way since 1192, when Yoritomo Minamoto anticipated the invention of the TV mini-series by seizing power as the first Shogun.

They have constantly harassed their neighbours in the Pacific – ask the Chinese, Russians and Koreans how much they trust the Japanese – and now, thanks to jet travel, fax machines and electronic wire transfers, they're harassing us in the West.

From computers, cameras and cars all the way to international treaties on whaling, they are shameless in the way they flaunt their distinctive avarice.

What's more, there have been only two times I can think of in this century when they've let slip with the truth – that true grit is not part of the national character. The first was 1945 when the Enola Gay bombed the shit out of Hiroshima. The second was 1973 when the Arabs turned off their oil.

That initial A-bomb ended their reign of military terror – the attack on Nagasaki was merely the whipped cream, sprinkles and cherry on top of the sundae dessert – and the Arabs showed how Saudi light crude could, just as swiftly, put an end to their economic reign of terror.

The Emperor handed his sword to MacArthur because the original Big Mac refused to be intimidated, and 18 years later the very same Emperor went to the airport officially to greet Sheikh Yamani – until then emperors only ever greeted emperors, never common citizens – because, without Arab oil, the Japanese would have to turn off their Honda factories and go back to wading through rice paddies.

In 1989, their cherished Emperor – who'd led them, God-like, through 63 years of global belligerence – died at the age of 88, still on the throne. One wonders how come some of his cronies, notably Mussolini and that bunch from Berlin, weren't permitted to enjoy their pensions as well.

George Bush expressed American sentiment when, at a formal dinner in Tokyo, the President of the United States tossed his cookies. But symbolic gestures like that are much too subtle for the Japanese. They believed he'd actually taken ill.

When they first put quotas on our goods, closing their borders to us, we should have slammed our doors shut to them. That would have had the double-barrel effect of saying we won't stand for your protectionist strong-arm tactics, and also prevented millions of Western teenagers from going deaf while plugged in to a Sony Walkman.

Peter and I hit Tokyo the first time just after Pennstreet went public because we thought the exotic East was where we should be looking for opportunities. We lasted only until the second sushi dinner. It was much too crowded, much too noisy, much too foreign, much too overpriced and the beds were much too small.

I reminded him, "If nothing else, we can now add Japan to the list of places we never have to come back to."

He suggested, "As long as we're in the neighbourhood, let's go to Thailand."

I said, "I'm sure you'll find that the massage parlours are just as good in Hong Kong and, at least in Hong Kong, maybe I can do some business."

So we traded Tokyo Bay for the Fragrant Harbor, and that turned out to be a good trip because we befriended a young entrepreneur there named Lee Lee Woo with whom we've done a lot of business.

As much as I dislike Japan, that's how much I like Lee Lee. Not only is he a great pal, but we've made money in every deal we've ever done with him. And that includes the time his wife asked us to back her and her sister in a movie they wanted to make. Normally we wouldn't gamble on anything as risky as film production, but this was Lee Lee's family, so Peter and I each put up £25,000. We never saw a script, didn't have a clue what the storyline was, had no idea who was starring in it, and never thought to visit the set. We didn't even know what language they were shooting in. Lee Lee merely told us this film was all about saving his marriage, so we gave him the money. Just as quickly, we wrote it off as charity, expecting to lose it all.

Don't you know that it turned out to be a classic, the all-time bestselling soft porn contraband video on mainland China. We doubled our money in under a year and still get royalty cheques every six months. Once, when Pippa found a cheque in the mail from Lee Lee's wife and wondered what it was, instead of trying to explain it, I put a video into the machine and showed her. Ever since she's forbidden me from going to Hong Kong alone.

Tokyo is another matter.

To my own chagrin, I returned a few years after my first visit, only because Lee Lee wanted us to come in with him on a deal. We wound up with a minority interest in a Kyoto computer memory chip company that he ran for a couple of years, until we all sold out to some Silicon Valley operation, returning nearly six times our overall investment.

The third time I went, I insisted that Pippa join me. The best either of us can say about that visit was it lasted only six days. The highlight of the trip was a *fugu* restaurant where the speciality is the deadly poisonous blow fish. We refused to eat it, even though we were assured several times that the licensed chef had thoroughly removed any of the poison. But some American wise-ass at the next table did eat it and obviously the chef wasn't as good as he thought he was because the American's throat expanded to the point where everyone thought he was going to explode.

"Great experience," he gasped for breath as he came back to normal size. "Go for it, man. Go for it."

That trip was doubly memorable because we flew back to London via Moscow – stopped there for three days – and hated that too. In fact, we hated it so much that Pippa said, from now on, the only place she wanted to visit anywhere even vaguely east of London was Dover, and that was only to catch the ferry to France.

If the Stock Exchange was going to do anything, it wouldn't happen now until after the holidays. I assured myself it could wait. I pushed the Japanese out of my mind too, as life ground to a halt midway through December and caught that metaphorical ferry to France.

The twins got too many presents, Pippa and I had a few days on our own shacked up in various hotels, and Peter arrived to spend New Year's Eve with us, accompanied by his latest flame, a Dutch girl named Anika who used to dance at the Crazy Horse.

She was 12 feet tall and her legs went all the way up to the top. Even Pippa noticed.

Peter explained that, when Anika wasn't taking her clothes off in saloons, she was taking cooking lessons at the Cordon Bleu school, and cooking was, in his words, her second greatest talent. I knew enough not to ask what she did best.

Nicely enough, it turned out that this enormously tall, fabulously built, rather gorgeous redhead from Holland could cook anything. Just after midnight on New Year's Eve, when she heard it was my birthday, she marched into the kitchen and knocked off four apricot souffles, plus a pile of *crêpes Suzette*, without so much as blinking. The next morning she was up early, making croissants from scratch, which she, Peter, Pippa and the girls delivered to me in bed, along with a bunch of birthday gifts.

Before I opened my presents, I asked Peter if we could hire Anika and him as a live-in couple, so she could cook and he could do whatever it was he did.

He said, "I'll show you what I do best," grabbed his god-daughters, piled into bed next to me and proceeded – with the twins doubled up in laughter – to steal my breakfast.

I got a tie, two shirts, a sweater, two pairs of argyle socks and a piece of string.

"What's this?"

Peter whispered something into the girls' ears and they announced, "You have to follow it."

It was apparently attached to something in one of the other rooms, so I got out of bed and, with everyone dropping croissant crumbs along the way, just like Hansel and Gretel – Peter claimed, "This is so we can find the road back to bed" – I hunted for the end of the string. It took me from my bedroom, down the hallway, into the living-room and then around the corner and to the closed door of my study.

"Shut your eyes," the girls shouted.

243

I did and they opened the door.

When they said it was okay to open my eyes, I discovered that the end of the string was the world's largest baseball glove.

"It's a chair," they yelled and rushed to sit in it. "Happy birthday." Peter and Anika and Pippa joined them in singing "Happy birthday," and I joined the girls sitting in the middle of this large leather baseball mitt.

"Fabulous." I told them, "I love it."

Phoebe pointed to some writing on the side of the glove and Brenna asked, "What does this say?"

I read the signature, "Joe DiMaggio."

"Even I know who he is," Peter volunteered. "He married Marilyn Monroe."

"Is that who he is?" Anika seemed shocked. "I thought he was someone Simon and Garfunkel made up. You know . . ." She proceeded to sing . . . "Where have you gone Joe DiMaggio . . ."

I raised my eyes towards the ceiling. "Forgive them, Lord, for they know not who DiMaggio is," leaned back in my baseball glove chair, took my daughters in my arms and started the song all over again.

"Happy birthday to me."

Chapter Twenty

No, I am not a Japanophile.

The chip on my shoulder is hefty enough that, in mid-January, I nearly – and unashamedly – declared it at Customs. But I was selling, not buying, and when you're selling – especially in the over-mannerly world of Nippon – even an oaf knows he has to be polite. So I politely took my first meeting on my first morning in a freezing Tokyo with a wiry, 65-year-old bastard named Meiji Osuka, founder and chairman of Soft Mist Spark Plugs.

The Oriental gift for delicately named companies belies their no-nonsense approach. And Osuka personified that. He was rigidly formal and haughty. We met in his office, a bare room, with stark white walls and polished light wood floors, a black desk for him and two black chairs facing it. The only other person present was a surprisingly tall Japanese woman who introduced herself as his translator.

I thought to myself, sure, and I'm General Tojo.

My suspicions were reinforced when it immediately became obvious that Osuka understood every word I was saying. That particularly angered me because it meant the only reason she was there was to throw me off balance.

He began by expressing his sorrow that I'd taken over the interests of the Katayama family, for whom he had the greatest respect. I answered that the Katayamas would be very welcome to buy back this part of their business as my company was no longer interested in distributing spark plugs. He asked me if I'd brought with me the distributorship's accounts. I said yes, and handed them to him. Then he asked me where I was staying.

I told him, "Unfortunately, I'm very unoriginal. I've taken a room at the Imperial."

He understood. "There are better places."

"I'm only here for another four days."

"Do you think that will give us enough time to complete our business?"

I stood up. "It will certainly give you enough time to decide what you'd like to do about it. I felt it was only right to inform you first that we plan to divest ourselves of it."

"Have you any specific plans?"

I looked him straight in the eyes and hoped he would understand my vague threat when I repeated, "Unfortunately, I'm very unoriginal."

He nodded, stood up and motioned towards the door. "You will be hearing from someone."

With that I left. I needed him to believe that if he didn't take care of me I could cost him a lot of money in the UK. But I couldn't be sure that he got the message. The only thing I could read in his eyes was that he disliked having to deal with me as much as I disliked having to deal with him.

That afternoon I went to see Mr Inamura at Buffalo Corp. His offices were in a modern, black glass building that fit into the centre of Tokyo about as inconspicuously as a pagoda would fit into downtown Dubuque. I rode the lift up to the 9th floor – someone had taken the trouble of piping in Barry Manilow music – and after chimes rang, the door opened onto a huge reception area. In the middle of it, on a spotlighted podium, was a shiny red earth mover.

I told the receptionist – a young Japanese woman

dressed in French clothes – that I had an appointment with Mr Inamura.

She answered, in perfect English, "Which one? There are several. The chairman has four sons. And his brother has three sons. So, you have the choice of nine Mr Inamuras."

I confidently said, "Chairman Inamura will be fine."

She asked my name, I told her and she rang through. A few moments later another young Japanese woman dressed in French clothes came from behind a pair of large wooden doors to escort me into the conference room.

There was a long dark wood table, surrounded by straight-backed leather chairs – enough to seat 24 – and six well-framed Salvador Dali lithographs on the walls.

I thought to myself, at last, someone has finally wreaked revenge on the Japanese.

A smiling, overweight man of about 30 stepped into the room, extended his hand and said with a near-American accent, "Hi, I'm Akio Inamura, but please call me Sam."

I said, "Okay, Sam, I'm Bay."

He motioned for me to take a seat. "My dad will be in straight away. Is this your first trip to Tokyo?"

"Fourth," I answered. "Where did you pick up your English?"

"Stanford, class of '83. Dad wanted us all to have Western educations. He sent his boys to Stanford and his girls to Cambridge. Don't ask why. Reasoning is mysterious in the East."

"How many daughters has he got?"

"Four."

"Four sons and four daughters? Eight kids?"

"We Japanese are worse than Catholics."

Just then his father walked in. Heisei Inamura was a man in his early 60s, impeccably dressed in Western clothes, with about as much charm as Mr Osuka.

We shook hands and he said to me, in well-practised English, "You are my British company's minority shareholder."

I said, "I am."

He said, "I liked Katayama."

I answered, "Many people speak highly of him."

"I'm sorry that you have forced him out."

"It was strictly a business matter."

"Of course," he said. "I should now like to force you out. It is strictly a business matter. Will you sell your holding?"

Without hesitation, I told him, "Yes. That is, of course, dependent on the price."

He said, "You will be offered a fair price."

I informed him, "When shall we meet again?"

He pointed to Sam. "My son will present you with our offer tomorrow morning. If you accept, he will see that the paperwork is ready for you to take back to your board in London by the time you leave."

Extending my hand to him, I said, "I'll look forward to hearing from you."

He shook my hand, ordered his son, "Please see that our guest is catered to," and left.

Sam wondered, "Is there anything you want to do while you are here?"

I told him, "Just a hot bath."

He thought I was referring to a Japanese bath. "I can take you to one of the best bath houses in Tokyo."

"No, no," I said. "Not that kind of bath."

"This one has beautiful girls. . ."

I shook my head. "Thanks anyway. I'll wait to hear from you in the morning."

Back at the hotel I filled the tub – at least in the Imperial they've got Western-size tubs – and soaked for a while, trying to thaw out my bones. I thought about going out for dinner but wound up instead with room service. I fell asleep around 8.

And I was up again by 3:30.

That's another thing I dislike about Japan. Their clock and my clock never match.

The only generous thing I have to say about the nine hour time difference is that I could still call the office and also speak with the twins at home before they went to bed. Patty assured me no one even knew I was out of town. Pippa assured me that the twins did, and missed me.

Then she said, "Listen . . . maybe I should wait until you get back but . . . Bay, there was something in *Private Eye* yesterday."

"What did it say?"

She read it to me. "Here's one for Hotspurs. American-born, British-based Bay Radisson, who's known in City circles as a baseball fan, has been practising his football skills. It seems that City investigators, looking into allegations that Radisson scored a big point just before the referee-in-the-sky handed a red card to Captain Bob, were shown his best striker's form recently when he booted one of them out of his office. Sounds to us like an own goal."

All I could say was, "Dumb shits."

"I didn't know if Patty faxed it to you, or if you saw it."

"Get a copy to Gerald."

"I did. I rang him this afternoon."

"What did he say?"

"He said not to worry. He said he'd speak with you about it when you got back."

I hung up with her and rang Gerald at home. "Can we sue *Private Eye*?"

"Sure."

"Can we win?"

"Win what?"

"Just to shut them up."

"Have they libelled you?"

That stopped me. "Bastards."

"Don't be silly. It means you've arrived. Being made

fun of by *Private Eye* puts you in the same league as Jimmy Goldsmith."

"What can I do about it?"

Gerald was forever amiable. "Have it framed for your downstairs bathroom. When they write nasty about you, it means you're in."

I spent the rest of the night fighting to get back to sleep.

I'd only just managed it, sometime around 8, when Sam Inamura phoned to ask if I'd had breakfast yet. I agreed to meet him downstairs in an hour. We wound up in a dark corner in one of the hotel's 13 restaurants. He had the full American meal. I stayed with muesli, coffee and toast.

"What have you got lined up for today?" He asked.

I said nothing more than, "Other appointments."

"Maybe you want to go to the baths today? Or maybe, tonight, a geisha place?"

"No thanks."

He offered, "Girls are on us."

I waved him off. "Really, no thanks."

"Just trying to play the good host," he said.

"Let's stick to business."

"My dad will be very disappointed that you've turned down our hospitality."

"He'll be much more disappointed when I sell the company to your biggest competitor."

"Okay," he shrugged. "Strictly business."

I reminded him, "Your old man said you'd have an offer."

He nodded, "I do," reached into his jacket pocket, fumbled with something, then pulled out an envelope. Inside was a letter to me making a formal request for my 18% share of Buffalo Ltd. Attached to it was a banker's draft made out to Pennstreet PLC for £175,000.

I looked at it, mumbled, "Nice try," handed it back to

him and stood up. "When you're ready to talk seriously, let me know."

His face dropped.

"Breakfast is on me." I motioned to the waitress and gave her my room number.

"Just a minute," Sam said. "You're being too hasty. Please sit down. We will entertain any counter-offers."

I stared at the envelope for a while, recalling the way Peter and I used to stuff our pockets with cashiers' cheques, like when we did that deal for the meat cleavers. So, on a whim, I dared, "Tell you what we'll do. You put all the other envelopes on the table, I'll choose one and you choose one. I'll halve mine, you double yours and you've got a deal for whichever figure is the highest."

"What?" This clearly wasn't what he had in mind. "You want to do what?"

I repeated the rules of the game.

"Other envelopes?"

"Yeah," I pointed. "The other envelopes with the other banker's drafts."

"What makes you think. . ."

I stood up again. "Like I said, call me . . ."

Now he reached out, grabbed my hand and urged me to sit down again. "You're being much too American."

I shrugged, "What you see is what you get, sport," patted him on the shoulder and walked away.

Fifteen minutes later his father rang my room. "If you will meet with me, I will make you my final offer."

I replied, "If you'll fax me your best offer, I will consider it and then perhaps be willing to meet with you."

"There is little you can do besides sell the company to me."

"Or," I suggested, "someone like Caterpillar. What do you think a giant like that would do to your market share in Britain?"

"If this is a threat. . ."

I didn't respond.

Now he said, "I would not want anyone at the hotel

to read the fax, unless you have a fax machine in your room. No, it is best if I send a messenger to you with my final offer . . ."

"Your best offer," I corrected.

"There is no difference," he said.

I acknowledged, "Hopefully that is right. I look forward to hearing from you."

With that, I hung up, grabbed my coat and left the hotel.

It was still very cold, but the sky was bright blue and clear. I spent the morning fighting my way through the mass of humanity in the Ginza district. I had lunch out – Chinese hot and sour soup was specifically designed for days like this – and generally made myself unavailable until late afternoon.

I tried to find something to buy for Pippa but these days just about everything you can buy in Japan you can find at 10% off along Tottenham Court Road in London and at half the price on 23rd Street in New York. The only thing I saw for the kids was a huge toy mechanical Shar-Pei – one of those extremely ugly, wrinkly, Chinese dogs – that realistically wagged its head, walked, barked, sat up rolled over and, I suspect, peed on the carpet. It was as big as the twins.

I nearly bought one. But then I decided I probably should buy one for each of them. I got as far as trying to carry two of them, before I talked myself out of the whole idea because getting a pair of those things home would be too much trouble.

When I returned to the hotel, frozen, there was an envelope from Heisei Inamura and a pile of messages waiting for me. There were two calls from Meiji Osuka, one from Patty, one from Peter – I knew it was him because no one else would leave a message saying, "Your custom-made inflatable doll is now ready, please come to pick it up" – and two from Puck North asking that I ring him straight away.

I don't believe in coincidence.

There was no way in the world that North was phoning me in Tokyo, out of the blue, to enquire about my health. I couldn't be certain if he'd been in touch with Osuka or Inamura or both, but based solely on the urgency of his messages, I decided he'd have to wait.

Keeping the insecure insecure is usually a profitable strategy.

The envelope from Inamura contained his offer. He said he would pay me £250,000 for my part of Buffalo Ltd. He enclosed the main corporation's latest published accounts, which showed they'd taken a $6.3 million loss last year and, although they were expecting better results this year, he warned that the final figures would still be in the red. "All things considered, I believe this is a fair and equitable value for your holding."

But I didn't.

Even if the main company was losing a lot of money, the British side was losing proportionately less. In my head, I was looking for half a million pounds, would be thrilled with £450,000 and would gladly settle for £400,000 if it was fast. I based my figure on the belief that any of the other farm machinery companies in the UK would come up with nearly as much just to kill off the competition. Although selling to a competitor brought with it inherent risks, such as a long delay, while the sale was studied by the Office of Fair Trading.

No, I told myself, Mr Inamura was not yet in the ballpark.

Checking my watch, I calculated that it was just 8:30 in the morning in London. So I phoned Pippa and spoke to the twins, who were having a fight about some plastic monster at the bottom of a box of cereal. They wanted me to solve it for them. Naturally, I did what any sensible father would do. I told them their mother would settle it.

Next, I rang Osuka. He simply said, "I need to see you."

253

I presumed, "You're prepared to make me an offer."

He answered, "I am prepared to make you a proposition. Will you come to my office tomorrow at 11:30."

I said I would be there.

It was too early to ring Peter — he was never up before 10 — so I decided to call Patty. That's when my line rang. I picked it up and found Puck North at the other end. "You get my messages?"

"I just got in. What can I do for you?"

"Perhaps it's what I can do for you. How much do you want for Buffalo?"

"How much are you offering?"

"Will you take £300,000?"

"Nope."

"That's a fair and equitable offer."

I had to smile. North and Inamura had obviously worked this out. "Thanks anyway, but . . ." I lied, "someone new has now come into the game and the price has gone up."

"Who?"

"Come on, Puck, you know I can't say anything."

"Someone in Japan? Someone in England?" He stopped, then said, "I know who it is. Well, I can tell you that I am prepared to top any offer he makes."

I tried to hide my own surprise. "You'll have to come up with a lot more if you want to stay in the game."

"How much more?"

Thinking fast, I said, "Just a minute," cupped the phone, said, "Come in," paused, said, "Hello, hi, I'll be right with you. Just a moment, please," then came back on the line with North. "My guests are here. I must go. I'll have to get back to you on this."

"Make me one promise," he said. "Before you speak to my father-in-law, you'll call me."

I said, "I will," and hung up, trying to figure out what the hell was going on.

My phone rang again. This time it was Patty to tell me a fax had just come in from Katayama saying that he was willing to pay us £285,000 to buy back his interest in Buffalo.

The whole thing was quite bizarre. It struck me that Inamura might have put a figure on the table just so that Katayama could top it. In fact, I couldn't help but think that it smelled a lot like the Oriental variation on a technique used by cheap furniture dealers called "The Pass". One salesman tells you the price of the living-room set, then gets called away to the phone. A second salesman wanders by and just happens to quote a lower price for more furniture – "Of course, that also includes the ottoman" – hoping you'll think he's made a mistake and jump on the deal before the first guy gets back.

Or, maybe their idea was to pretend to bid each other up to the actual price, at which time two of them would drop out, causing me to panic and unload quickly to my one remaining prospect. Or, it was just possible, the first two didn't know they were a party of three. Perhaps North overheard a conversation between Inamura and Katayama, and because Puck had ambition, he was willing to outbid his own father-in-law.

My bet, though, was that all three had cooked this up together. So I instructed Patty, "Get the private fax numbers for Katayama, North and Inamura. In a separate letter to each of them say, I have considered your offer and must respectfully decline. As I already have a suitable offer on the table, I am willing to give you one final chance to top it. I will accept a bid of no less than ... blank ... but it must be made, conditional to the usual contracts, within one hour's time. I'm sorry that I will not be able to discuss it with you or, in any way, negotiate a lower price. I look forward to hearing from you. Yours sincerely, Bay Radisson."

She copied it down, then admitted, "I don't understand."

"Simple. Fill in the blank with £425,000 in the

fax to Inamura, £450,000 to North and £475,000 to Katayama."

"I still don't get it."

"If they're in cahoots, two of them should drop out."

"And if all three drop out?"

"Then you'll have to learn how to drive a tractor."

She phoned me back 20 minutes later to say the faxes had been sent.

North rang immediately. "What the hell kind of stunt is this?"

"That's the price," I said, "in or out?"

He grumbled, "Four hundred grand is my best offer."

"Sorry, Puck, but we're no longer entertaining offers. Read the fax. I've got to run. You've still got 55 minutes left."

I hung up and waited.

Thank God for CNN.

It's not just that they're keeping the world informed, they're also saving guys like me, stuck in foreign hotel rooms, from dying of boredom while turning the channels looking for game shows that are even less stupid than what you find in the States.

It's amazing how people always criticize American television. In England they do it all the time. They think British television is the best in the world. Except that the only things worth watching on British TV are American. And anybody who argues the opposite need only consider the fact that on American TV, people make fools of themselves for $3 million. On British TV, they do it for a plastic cheque book cover and a cheap ballpoint pen.

I watched the CNN headlines and sat through a feature on how some scientist in the Baltic had accomplished something incomprehensible with low temperature physics. There was an interview with Madonna and a slew of sports scores from around the world. Then they announced a financial feature. It was all about insider trading scandals on Wall Street.

I told myself, I'm not interested.

I turned it off.

I told myself, I did not trade on inside information.

Just as the hour was up, Patty phoned to say that Katayama had faxed back, "Decline."

Her call was followed by one from Inamura. "You have a deal at £425,000." I asked him to prepare the suitable paperwork and he said he would do that.

I never heard again from Puck North.

Sam Inamura showed up the next morning for breakfast, paperwork in hand.

"Strictly business," I reminded him.

He started to laugh. "What else is there? You think you win. I think I win. In the end we all win. You see, the difference between my generation of Japanese and, say, my generation of German, is that we don't feel guilty about the war. We didn't fry any Jews or gypsies, and yet we got nuked. The way we see it, we got the short end of the stick."

I stared at him. "You mean business is Act II."

He grinned, "It's our way of getting even. Young Germans are basically so ashamed of what their fathers and grandfathers did that they've allowed the Americans to turn Germany into the 51st state."

I told him, "That's Canada."

"Okay, the 52nd state."

I corrected him, "That's England."

He tried, "53rd state?"

"That sounds about right."

"My point is, because we don't feel guilty, when you guys tried to take-over Japan, we stood our ground. Sure we wear jeans, and sure there are fast-food joints on every street corner, but we don't eat as many cheeseburgers as you drive Mitsubishis. So who's doing what to who?"

I left him after breakfast to see Mr Osuka.

We met again in his stark office with his tall translator. "I am willing to make you a trade," he said.

"To trade what?"

"Caviar. Black Russian. Top quality."

"Spark plugs for fish eggs?"

"Exactly. I have been offered a shipment with a Japan retail value of $2.7 million. But I would not wish to unload it here because, at the moment, the market is saturated. Trade agreements have loosened considerably between Japan and Russia and caviar is one of the few things they have that's worth trading. I estimate the wholesale price of the caviar to be worth somewhere around $1.35 million. I estimate the distributorship to be worth less than $1 million. The difference would be your profit for taking the shipment off my hands."

My guess was that £600,000–650,000 for the distributorship was about right. The money on top made it worth considering. I told him, "I would want to see all the appropriate paperwork. Where is the cargo now?"

"Of course," he answered. "The cargo left Vladivostok this morning for Yokohama. It will be unloaded there within three days. At that point, it could be air freighted to anywhere in the world."

Before I would agree to anything like this I had to have some homework. "I will let you know at this time tomorrow."

He said, "That will be fine."

"If I go for it, can you recommend a shipping agent?"

"You are welcome to use the same agents we use."

I thought for a moment, "I may want to put something with it."

"Other purchases?"

I told him about the toy Shar-Pei. "I have twin daughters and I thought I might buy one for each of them."

He nodded. "Our shipping agent will be honoured to accommodate you." He asked his secretary to supply me with the agent's name, then promised to send the documents for the caviar to my hotel within the hour. We agreed to meet in the morning.

Once I had the paperwork, it took me most of the afternoon to locate the only guy I could think of who was a genuine expert in these sorts of weird deals – Stevie Bridge. When I explained it to him, he said that, before he could give his pronouncement, he had to have the paperwork. So I faxed it to him. That night he rang back to say he could unload it in Switzerland, net to me $1.1 million.

Many people who get involved with guys like Bridge make the mistake of worrying that they might be getting much more for the goods than they're willing to pay for them. I couldn't have cared less if Stevie was reselling them for a million or two or three. I told him, "You've got a deal at $1.1 million net to Pennstreet. You take the cargo, f.o.b. Yokohama. Eventually you can send one case to me and send one case to Peter as a late Christmas present."

He said, "Done."

I phoned Stonewall to have him make all the necessary arrangements – bills of lading, banker's drafts and contracts for the sale of the distributorship. And the next morning I returned to tell Osuka, "It's done." We exchanged letters of agreement and shook hands.

Now he motioned for his translator to leave. When she was gone he said to me in very fine English, "Will you be staying in Tokyo another few days?"

I told him, "Actually I'm going to try to get a flight back to London tonight."

He summoned his secretary and said something to her in Japanese. Then he turned to me. "I would be honoured if you would allow me to have my car and driver take you to the airport."

I replied, "That's very kind of you but unnecessary."

"It might be unnecessary, but it would be my honour. Now, please come with me."

Not knowing what he wanted, I followed him out of his office and into his conference room. He bowed and said, "I hope you will come back to Japan."

I stood there with my mouth open.

I will never understand the Japanese.

Sitting on his conference table were two of those huge mechanical dogs.

Chapter Twenty-one

We never discovered the exact process, how the decision was made or who took it, but at some point, the Stock Exchange Surveillance Unit elected to turn over their file on me to the Department of Trade and Industry. After not-so-lengthy consultations there – presumably with nameless and faceless bureaucrats, because nobody could ever tell us who'd acted on the file – the dossier was forwarded to the City of London Police Fraud Squad. They claim jurisdiction over matters arising at the Stock Exchange and, we suspected they were the ones who subsequently leaked word of the investigation to the press.

It all seemed very arbitrary and at no point did anyone ever bother to advise me that any of this was happening. Later, Gerald questioned these tactics in a very strong letter to the Secretary of State for Trade and Industry.

I'd urged him to say, "The case against my client is sheer and utter bullshit."

He wouldn't.

I'd urged him to say, "You couldn't possibly have based your case on anything more than a six-minute confrontation in my office with two clowns straight from Central Casting, a brief answer to one question and a missed kick in the ass."

He wouldn't.

I'd urged him to say, "This is, first and foremost, a glaring violation of my client's civil rights."

And he'd reminded me, "This is Britain. There is no such thing as civil rights."

Couched in British *politesse*, he spelled out our mutual indignation. "By taking the extreme measure you have, that of sending the case forward to the City of London Police Fraud Squad without first confronting my client with any evidence whatsoever, you are wrongly implying that the case against my client is of such a serious nature as to prejudice his otherwise fine and untarnished reputation and to impede his further business dealings. We see this as highly irresponsible behaviour and respectfully request an urgent meeting with you."

The Secretary of State for Trade and Industry acknowledged receipt of Gerald's letter, but did nothing more than forward it to his departmental lawyers for reply. The DTI's lawyers responded that, as long as the case now lay with the police, they could not otherwise comment on any aspect of it.

Such was the extent of the government's concern for my civil rights. The rest of the time, there must have been very long lines at lavatory basins throughout Whitehall, because everyone else we subsequently contacted was busy washing their hands.

Although the tiny City of London Police often operates in the shadow of the very large Metropolitan Police at Scotland Yard, the two are independent. But the culture is the same, especially when it comes to dealing with the media.

Until the end of the 1980s, the police and the press in Britain maintained a nauseatingly polite relationship. Scotland Yard and the City of London Police never commented and after a while Fleet Street stopped trying to break down the barriers. However, as prosecutions became more complex and the various fraud squads went into general retreat – giving way to the formation of the Serious Fraud Office, a government agency under the supervision of the Attorney-General – a strange alliance was forged. Someone high up in the business of policing financial crime argued, if you can't beat 'em in the courts then you can at least beat 'em up on the front pages. Official policy remained, no comment. But in practice, when their case stalled, the fraud cops knew how to jump-start it again – knock back a few pints with a tame reporter from the City pages.

It was an obvious ploy. As obvious as the fact that the police tended to do it only when they didn't have much of a case. But we took little comfort in knowing that when someone at the City of London Police leaked word of their investigation into my affairs to the *Sunday Telegraph*.

A young reporter, whose name I can't remember, rang one afternoon in early March 1993 – Patty took the call – to say he was going to run a story claiming that an inquiry was proceeding. He said he had it from a highly reliable source inside the police department and that I might therefore want to speak with him before the fraud squad arrived at our offices.

At Patty's insistence I got on the line.

"I know for a fact that they're trying to make a case against you," he said.

"Who is?"

"The City Fraud Squad." –

I asked, "What for?"

He said, "Insider dealing."

I told him, "It's bullshit. And you can quote me."

"They're looking into your purchase of MCC shares just before Robert Maxwell's death was announced."

"Let me say that at no point did we have any insider knowledge of Robert Maxwell's death."

"That's a pretty guarded response."

"That's an unequivocal denial of insider dealing."

"Has anyone ever contacted you about these allegations?"

I explained, "The Stock Exchange Surveillance Unit contacted me late last year. They asked one question. The entire meeting took less than five minutes." I wondered if I should say anything more about that, but decided it might be best if I didn't. So I assured him, "We did not deal in MCC shares on any insider knowledge and there has never been any evidence whatsoever to the contrary. I told the Stock Exchange exactly what I'm telling you. We do not and did not deal on inside information. I believe this is nothing more than a witch hunt. And you are welcome to quote me as saying, if it turns out to be that, I'm going to ram lawsuits up their asses. End of statement."

It was Sunday morning, 14 March. I was still asleep when Gerald rang. Pippa answered the phone and woke me.

"Room service," I said innocently enough, with my eyes still closed, "two eggs over easy, crisp bacon and a couple of bagels . . ."

He barked, "Have you gone mad?"

"All right," I said, not having any idea why he'd call this early. "When you're right, you're right. Too much cholesterol. Hold the eggs. We'll have the continental breakfast instead, with sunflower margarine and decaffeinated . . ."

"If you'd have seen the papers this morning you wouldn't be such a wisenheimer."

"Wisenheimer? Good God, it rubs off. You're starting to talk like an American."

"No, I'm talking about an American. Get the papers."

"What papers?"

"Start with the *Sunday Telegraph*." He read the unsigned article. " . . . ram law suits up their arses."

"They have their nerve," I said. "It's not arses, it's asses!"

"There's also a blurb in the *Sunday Express*, in the gossip column."

"I made the gossip columns?"

"Listen to me," he ordered. "From now on, keep your mouth shut. Do not make any more comments to anyone. I'll see you first thing tomorrow morning, in your office." Then he added, as if I needed to be reminded, "Bay, this is serious."

Just then, Peter called on another line. Pippa took it and handed it to me. "You're bonkers. Why did you talk to the papers? Get Gerald on the phone and keep your mouth shut."

"I didn't talk to them and I am talking to him."

"Did you really say this?"

"No. I said asses. Only Brits call them arses."

"Well, it's just about the stupidest thing you could have said. You can't start threatening to sue people. You live in Britain. You can't sue the Crown. And even if you could, you'd lose."

"The Stock Exchange isn't the Crown."

He hesitated. "Well . . . they have the Queen's picture up in the lobby so you probably can't sue them either. Just keep quiet and let Gerald handle this."

"Why is everyone so worried?"

"Because if they nail you for insider trading. . ."

"I'm not the one who's bonkers." I tried to jog his memory, "We did not do any insider trading. We put down a bet on a hunch. Maxwell was dead. We had no special knowledge of that. We knew nothing more than any waiter at the local café where you were hustling some bimbo. His boat was parked down the block. In public. We did nothing wrong."

He bellowed, "If they think we did, then they'll make a case. So why didn't you just tell them what happened?"

I bellowed back, "Because it's none of their god-damned business. We are innocent until they prove us guilty."

"Bay, you're a bloody fucking idiot. You are not innocent until proven guilty. This is Britain."

I told him, "Stop worrying about it. We're taking care of it," and hung up. Then I got back on the line with Gerald and said, "It was a wrong number. Sorry. I'll see you tomorrow."

No sooner had I hung up with him when Clement rang. "What's this all about?"

"Doesn't anybody in this town sleep late on Sunday mornings?"

"Are you really in trouble?"

"No. It's a tabloid gossip column. You can't believe anything you read in tabloid gossip columns. You have to wait until you see it in a broadsheet gossip column."

"The *Sunday Telegraph* is a broadsheet."

"Oh, sorry, I forgot there are people who buy papers that don't have pictures to colour in."

"How can you be so flippant about this?"

"Clement, what would you like me to do about it?"

"And what happens when Francesca sees it?"

I sighed, "I can't wait."

Next it was Pippa's parents. Her father asked, "Are you in trouble?"

I answered, "It's a case of mistaken identity."

Her mother wanted to know, "Bay darling, what have the neighbours said?"

"They've all moved out." I handed the phone to Pippa and let her deal with them.

Following that, a call came in from a reporter at the Mirror Group wondering if I was prepared to go on the record with a comment about the present government's total failure to combat white collar crime. I told him I wasn't prepared to say that and couldn't otherwise speak but suggested that he ring me in the office towards the middle of the week, and I'd see him.

Then a woman phoned from the *Guardian*. She wanted to know if she could get an interview. I told her too, try me on Wednesday.

Brian Fellowes from the *FT* also rang. I asked him where I could reach him the next morning. He gave me his home number and said he'd be there until 10.

Before anyone else called, I switched on my answering machine.

It stayed busy all day.

For a guy with unlisted phone numbers, I was starting to wonder if there was anyone left in England who didn't know them.

Among the many arguments Peter and I have had over the years is the one about how to deal with the media. He takes the position that the best thing to do is to avoid them, claiming he who lives by self-publicity shall die by self-publicity. But then he's British. He doesn't understand that the media aren't necessarily the enemy. My feeling is that a working relationship with a handful of specialist reporters is sound business strategy.

I accept that being a self-publicizer is a bad idea. However, when the press rings you, it's too late to start thinking about a relationship. What's more, hiding from the press when a story breaks is the worst thing you can do. The bigger your bunker, the bigger the prize you become for the first person who can bulldoze it down.

Sometime around 1985, I proved that point to him. We were contacted by an American guy writing a book about risk-takers. He wanted to include a chapter on us. Peter felt we should avoid him, believing that anonymity is its own reward. But I likened investigative journalism to big game hunting and said there was no reason to turn ourselves into prize elephants. I took the writer to lunch, bored him to tears about Pennstreet, and then explained to him that our egos – Peter's and mine – didn't work the same way that other businessmen's egos did.

"Fame and glory aren't part of our equation." I even quoted to him another American ex-pat, a fellow named Gerald Murphy, who lived in France in the 1920s. "Living well is the best revenge."

"Is it?" The writer asked.

"It sure is."

"What about the game?"

"Yeah, that's fun."

"And the money?"

"Money is just the means of keeping score."

The writer liked the quote and wrote it down. In the end, it was our only input to his book. And it went uncredited, at that.

Keeping our names out of the papers takes more skill than getting it in. By the same token, the thing that Peter doesn't seem to believe is that, figuratively speaking, journalists are no less gluttonous than the average bear. When you hand them something to munch on that costs them nothing and also tastes good, it's a rare journalist who'll say no thanks, I've just eaten. I have, therefore, made myself reasonably accessible to journalists so that they, in turn, will be reasonably accessible to me. One never knows when one might come across a good story. And my definition of a good story is one that suits my purposes.

That's why, on Monday morning, before Gerald showed up, I made two calls.

The first was to Anthony Carpenter, one of the old hands on the business section at the *Sunday Times*. I found him at home, still asleep. "You didn't hear this from me, but this whole thing started because I insulted two jerks from the Stock Exchange. One's name is Wynn. He's with the Surveillance Unit. The other one's name is Fosdick. Fearless Fosdick. A schmuck. A lawyer. I threw them both out because he hadn't properly identified himself. He was there in his capacity as an attorney and he deliberately hid that fact from me so that I would not be suitably represented."

Carpenter mumbled, "Sounds typical. Which one did you kick?"

"Don't believe everything you read in *Private Eye*."

"It's one of the few places where you probably can believe everything you read."

I let that remark slip by. "Now you know the background. They were insulted. They're getting even."

My second call was to Brian Fellowes. "You might enjoy making friends with the reservations clerk at El

268

Castillo in Las Palmas. It's a pretty fancy joint and it won't be easy, but if you had their guest list for the day Maxwell drowned, you might recognize a name and put two and two together a lot better than the Stock Exchange."

That was all I'd say to him.

Gerald arrived shortly after 9 in a fiery mood. "I thought I told you not to speak to anyone from the press."

I had no idea how he could possibly know about those two calls, and nearly confessed to them, when he tossed me a copy of the *Daily Mirror*.

"I'm sure you only buy it for the crossword puzzle and never look at the Page Three girls."

"Try the business pages."

A small story under the headline "City Yank Investigated" carried the gist of the *Sunday Telegraph* piece but noted, "Radisson refuses to comment on the charges but has made no attempt to deny the undeniable, that the Tory government had totally failed in policing the City."

I handed it back to him. "Not guilty, your honour. When they phoned yesterday, I said nothing more than, call me again later in the week."

"From now on," he said, "your answer is, no comment. If they pester you, have them ring me."

"That's a terrific idea. My solicitor says I can't speak to you but if you get aggressive enough he'll issue a statement. Sounds precisely what you'd expect from an innocent man."

"No. It sounds precisely what you'd expect from a prudent man who doesn't want to make this thing any worse than it already is."

"It's hot air."

"Hot air gets balloons across the Alps."

"Yeah, and Hannibal was in love with his elephants. What does any of this have to do with me?"

"I want you to go to the police and tell them everything you know about this before they come to you and start poking their noses into areas where you wouldn't want someone's nose."

"I have done nothing wrong and I categorically refuse to start acting as if I had."

"It's time for a meeting with Peter," he said.

"Why bring him into this?"

"Because he's already in this. And maybe he can drum some sense into your head."

I wondered, "Why don't we just handle this thing the American way? Issue a few writs against those shitheads at the Stock Exchange. Sue everybody in sight. Put the entire world on the defensive."

"Because this isn't America."

"How very reassuring," I said.

It was always something of an event whenever Peter showed up at the office. He'd arrive with a gift for Patty, presents for the twins, something for Pippa and usually a case of wine for me.

He'd do his royal walkabout, make a pilgrimage downstairs to chat with the accounting staff and at some point bring Stonewall into our office for a private meeting. Just the three of us. That always put a glow in Stonewall's cheeks. Then Peter would send out for a large smorgasbord lunch, his treat to the entire office. If he wasn't intending to have dinner with Pippa and me, he'd be on his way back to Paris by tea time.

This time he showed up empty handed.

When Gerald got there, I told Patty, "No calls," shut the door and said to Gerald, "Can you fill Peter in on the law about insider trading, in case there's anything I've missed."

Peter said, "We can skip the formalities, Gerald and I have already spoken."

"When?"

"This morning from the airport."

I looked at Gerald and he nodded. "A little over-anxious, no?"

"A lot concerned," Peter said.

"Rightfully so," Gerald added. "Fraud Squad cops are always looking to score points, so they go for the easiest goals."

Peter agreed, "I told Gerald that I think we need to circle our wagons."

Gerald said, "We decided that was the single most important point that we needed to get through your head."

"First you gang up on me . . ." I fell into a chair at the conference table and threw my legs onto the chair next to mine. "Now you try to bury me with metaphors. Soccer goals. Cowboys and Indians and their wagon trains. When do we start using terms like bailiwick and the whole five foot shelf of books. . ."

Peter snapped, "Fuck you, Bay. If those sons of bitches start looking into our affairs . . ."

"Why should they?"

"Jeezus H. Christ! Why shouldn't they?"

"Because as soon as they see we didn't do any insider trading. . ."

"Then why the bloody fucking hell haven't you told them that?"

"I'm going to. I mean, I have. But I'm doing it my way."

"You always bloody fucking have to do it your way. . ."

Gerald cut in, "What do you mean, your way?"

"I'm handling it."

Gerald asked, "What does that mean?"

I didn't want to explain that I'd phoned Carpenter and Fellowes, so I raised my hands in defeat and answered, "It means, okay, we'll do it any way you want to."

Gerald said, "That's good."

But Peter knew me better than that. "He's full of shit."

I assured them, "We'll do it any way you say."

"Don't give me that crap," Peter said. "What have you done so far?"

"So far? I've listened to you guys insult me. Just tell me what you want me to do, and I'll do it."

Peter apprised Gerald, "He's jerking us around."

"I said, I surrender. This is an unconditional surrender. I repeat, I will do it your way. Tell me what you want me to do."

Gerald obviously wanted to get us back on to the subject. "Peter's right about circling the wagons. The way I see it, they'll come at you from two fronts. The first is the insider trading allegation."

I reminded both of them, "We did not do any insider trading . . ."

Peter scolded, "Bay, shut up and let him talk."

Gerald continued, "They'll work on trying to catch you out for insider trading until they see there's nothing. They'll make a nuisance out of themselves. However, because insider trading is so difficult to prove, there's little they can do besides become a nuisance."

"Especially when you're innocent," I chimed in.

"Okay," Gerald conceded, "you're innocent. We know that. But they don't. And it's their job to prove you're not. While they're going about that, and you'd better be prepared for this, they're going to upset a lot of apple carts."

"Soccer, Indians and apple carts," I mumbled.

Peter shook his head. "You never give up, do you."

"Why do I have to prove that I'm innocent?"

"Because this is Britain."

Gerald added, "And that's only for openers."

"What's only for openers?" I asked.

"The insider trading claim."

My private-private line rang.

"Yeah, yeah, yeah." I grabbed the phone, knowing it was Pippa. "Hi. Can I call you back in a little while?"

She asked, "Did Peter arrive yet?"

"He did, and he's being even more of a pain in the ass than usual. I'll ring you back. . ."

"Did he tell you that he rang me this morning?"

I glanced at Peter who was staring at me. "No, as a matter of fact, he did not tell me he rang you this morning."

Peter nodded. "From the airport."

"From the airport," she said.

"Stereo," I mumbled.

She went on, "He's very upset about this. He knows how immovable you can be and he wanted me to remind you that we're all on your side."

I asked him, "Who else did you phone from the airport?"

"Just these two."

"Bay?" Pippa said, "I think he's right that this could be more serious than you believe it is."

I said to Peter, "Why would you talk to Pippa behind my back?"

He pointed to the phone, "Ask her."

"No, I'm asking you."

"Bay . . ." Pippa cut in, "Bay, for God's sake, stop arguing with Peter and hear him out. He's got some very good ideas and I agree with him."

"I just don't understand why you would phone my wife without telling me. . ."

She admitted, "He was returning my call."

I bellowed, "What the fuck is going on around here? What else is going on behind my back?"

"Good one," Peter said shaking his head. "Revert to your natural tacky self."

"I rang him," Pippa explained, "because I'm worried about all of this. I wanted him to know that. He's concerned too, and for all the right reasons. Sometimes you're so damned pigheaded. If you'll hear him out, maybe you'll agree with him as well."

I asked her, "Whatever happened with agreeing with your husband?"

She tried, "Whatever happened to listening to the people who love you? Whatever happened to. . ."

"Just stay out of it, Pippa." I hung up on her and

turned back to Gerald. "What do you mean, for openers?"

"They'll go for the easiest goal," he indicated. "They're under a lot of political pressure. If they can nail you for anything, the insider trading allegation will become secondary."

Peter moved to the window and stared down at Covent Garden. "What an arsehole you are."

My private-private line rang again. I took it and said to Pippa, "Can we settle this when I get home tonight?"

She demanded, "How dare you hang up on me like that?"

I looked at Gerald, "Nail me for what?"

Peter cut in. "We've got to restructure the Bahamas."

Pippa said, "You're acting like a total shit and I don't have to stand for that. . ."

I asked Peter, "What for?"

Pippa called out, "I'm warning you . . . Bay, are you listening to me?"

And just as Peter said, "Because that's where they can crucify us," I hung up on her again.

Chapter Twenty-two

By the end of our meeting, I'd calmed down enough to compromise. Gerald said he'd like to bring in some outside counsel to advise us and I conceded that was a good idea. Gerald left, promising to ring me with some suggestions.

I turned to Peter. "Lunch?"

"Can't," he said. "I'm heading straight back to Paris. But first I need to stop at the nearest video store and at Harrods."

"What do you buy in London that you can't get in Paris?"

"The video store is because I've recently come to the conclusion that *Lawrence of Arabia* is one of the three best films ever made. I saw it on television the other night and figure it's probably even better in English. There's something disconcerting about listening to Peter O'Toole greeting Arabs with, "*Bonjour, mes amis.*"

I wondered, "What about the other two?"

"Alec Guinness and Anthony Quinn shouldn't speak French either."

"I meant, the other two best films ever made."

"No contest," he said confidently, "*Birth of a Nation* and *Debbie Does Dallas.*"

"Dare I ask what you're going to buy at Harrods?"

"British marmalade for my French croissants which I eat every morning with Dutch butter, Greek yogurt,

Spanish prunes and Italian coffee. I'm trying to be the perfect European."

"Spanish prunes?"

He shrugged, "Marmalade, croissants, butter, yogurt and coffee do it to me. Prunes are the antidote. And, speaking of antidote, you've got the Bahamas to restructure."

When he left, I dialled Pippa but there was no answer. I knew she'd probably gone to her mother's because that's where she always went whenever we had a fight. I started to call her there, then I decided no, not yet, I'll let her brood.

It was too early to phone Roderick in Nassau. Anyway, I wasn't sure how I wanted to proceed. Most of our personal assets – Peter's and mine – were deliberately isolated from our corporate structure. But some were well enmeshed within it.

For instance, I owned, in my name, 5% of Pennstreet PLC's common shares. Peter, on the other hand, kept his 5% hidden inside a Jersey registered company called OnPar Investments. For tax purposes, his name did not appear on our shareholder register.

Forty percent of the Pennstreet's shares were traded on the London Exchange. A further 20% represented Preferred Shares, which were 45% owned by the public, with the rest split between Peter and me.

The remaining 30% of our common stock was in three equal parts, one of them held by Tivoli Court Trading in the Bahamas, which was jointly owned by Peter and me; one of them held by a Caymans Island registered company called Brittanica Consolidated Trust, which was 80% owned by Peter, 10% owned by me and 10% owned by the Blues Foundation, a secret trust held for Peter in Switzerland; and another company called Long Beach properties which was 80% owned by me, 10% owned by Peter and 10% owned by Roth Anstalt, a secret trust held for me in Liechtenstein.

What it all boiled down to was that Peter and

I, through our various holdings, controlled 55% of Pennstreet while being exposed to only around 10% of the tax liability.

By design, my private holdings were even more complicated.

I owned a Luxembourg company called Bayard Investments. Inside that was a private stock fund – into which I put my personal share dealings – and 80% ownership of Long Beach Properties. In turn, LBP owned Atlantic Beach Assets which had 50% of a company called Golden Shores Trust. Peter secretly owned the other half. LBP also owned a Honk Kong company called Lido Beach Investments and buried inside that was a company called Future Assets Inc. of St Kitts and Nevis.

It was this company that held the key to Roth Anstalt, and Roth Anstalt was one of the companies I needed to protect because it owned half the shares of a company registered in the British Virgin Islands called Snowman.

At the same time, Tivoli Court Trading, which I owned jointly with Peter, had two main arms. One was called Boardwalk, registered in Turks and Caicos. The other was called Broadway, registered in Barbados. Each of them controlled two companies. Boardwalk's were Park Place, registered in Panama, and White Sands, registered in Jersey. Broadway's were 42nd Street, registered in Panama, and Neon Lights, registered in Guernsey.

White Sands and Neon Lights were two more companies I needed to protect because, between them, they controlled the other half of Snowman. And the reason I needed to safeguard Snowman was because that was my private slush fund.

Inside Snowman I'd bedded down several million dollars' worth of hard-earned profits that I simply had no intention of sharing with the tax man. It was money I'd legitimately acquired outside the UK and had not, technically, repatriated.

In my opinion, the folks at Inland Revenue shouldn't

be entitled to any of this. Except, of course, they would claim I controlled the use of those funds from Britain.

Also, as an American, I'm liable to pay US taxes on my worldwide income. In this case, my argument is that these are corporate funds – albeit earned by companies owned by me – that have nothing to do with the United States. Except, of course, the IRS would argue that the funds have been made available for my personal use.

Given half a chance, tax inspectors in England and in the States would demand their share and more. The way to prevent that from happening was, simply, never to let them find the money.

As this private asset octopus of mine evolved, Roderick had built all sorts of roadblocks into the system so that, if the uninitiated ever tried to follow the money trail, they'd never make it past the first hurdle. And even if someone who knew what they were doing – like various tax inspectors – could somehow get inside one of those first few companies, all they'd find is a reference to another company. When they tried to get inside the second one, the trail would go cold at the front door of an office covered in brass plaques. They could always ask, who owns this company? But the only answer they'd ever get is, whoever physically has the shares in their pocket.

Peter uses a similar system, also designed by Roderick.

For me now to protect our assets properly it was obvious that I'd have to cut off several of the octopus's arms. Managing that, I knew, would be costly and time consuming. And the more I thought of it, the more I wondered if it was really necessary. The last thing I wanted to do was also kill the beast.

Additionally, there was the general health of Pennstreet to consider and the ramifications of any actions on our shareholders' assets. Scandals have a way of sinking share prices and, although ours was remaining steady in the 61–65p range, I felt I was right to worry about the consequences of a direct hit amidships.

The way we were geared – held together with bank

borrowing – meant that we were all right as long as our share price stayed in this range. If it dropped below 40p we'd probably have some nervous banks on our hands. If it dropped below 30p – bringing the corporate worth to half what it was now – we'd have to call an Extraordinary General Meeting of our shareholders. That would further worry the banks and, based on their congenital cowardice, the company could go under.

So, instead of making the Bahamas my first priority, I decided the best way to save our assets was to start selling some of them to reduce our burden of debt.

The way we'd structured Pennstreet, there were five separate, wholly owned entities within the company. The main ones were Truro Trading and Pennstreet Properties, both UK companies. Next in size was Euromarket92, a Bahamian company that held what few investments we maintained in Europe. Then came Pippawool Holdings, a general stock fund registered in Jersey. And finally there was Phonna Investments, registered in the United States as a Delaware Corporation.

I decided to go liquid with the last two.

Divesting myself of the shares in Pippawool should have been dead easy. I listed the assets, held back a few that were due to declare dividends – every penny helps – and picked up the phone, intending to parcel out the sale to four different brokers. But when I got Adrian O'Neil on the line he told me he could no longer handle our business.

"Why the hell not?"

He said he'd have to ring back. Ten minutes later, he called from a pay phone. "We've had too many people around the office asking too many questions."

"Who?"

"Policemen. Listen, if they ever find out I'm speaking to you now. . ."

"What were they looking for?"

"Our dealings with you, Roderick, Peter, everybody.

They've taken away tapes of our phone calls going back for as long as we've got them, which is about three years. They've also instructed us not to speak to anyone about this. Especially you. I've got to go. Please, don't get me involved in this . . ." Just like that, he hung up.

I sold those shares with other brokers and although the market was generally depressed – we took more than a few losses – I turned them into £1.67 million cash. Flogging the minor American assets held in Phonna Investments netted another $2.3 million, although we took some losses there as well.

Feeling better about our cash position, I put the money on deposit for future use.

Then I decided, what the hell, I'd do the same thing with Euromarket92. Our annual report put those assets at £7.9 million. But when I looked into getting rid of them – mainly shares in large European companies that I'd considered to be recovery stocks – I was rudely awakened to the fact that European recovery was still a long way off. At market prices, the best I could hope for was £4 million. As those assets were leveraged at 75%, it meant that any sort of fire sale here would wipe out my cash reserves in Pippawool and Phonna. I either had to hold on to them until Europe recovered or, somehow, goose up the share prices and bail out fast before anyone realized I was pulling strings.

Frankly, that last option appealed to me. All I had to do was somehow hype the market into thinking there were a few takeovers in the offing.

In an amusing way, it felt like going back to our roots.

Sorting through Euromarket92's assets, I was looking for a smallish company traded in a shallow market that might be vulnerable to an international takeover. I had Patty pull up everything on our database and spent the afternoon going over faxes that came in from Europe-based brokers.

We had a small holding in a swimsuit manufacturer

in Milan — Peter liked it because, he said, it gave him the excuse to go to fashion shows every year, as if he needed any excuse — but I couldn't see myself pretending to be Silvio Berlusconi launching a dawn raid on a bikini factory.

There was no one else whose name I could use in Italy and I couldn't think of anyone in the UK.

Where was Jimmy Goldsmith when we needed him?

I ruled out Germany, because the market wasn't shallow enough. And the only guy I could think of in France was that Socialist politician in Marseilles, Bernard Tapie. Except that he was having troubles of his own. Then again, that's what he gets for being a champagne socialist.

I thought about our fruit-based joint venture in Spain but, ever since Asil Nadir and Polly Peck were shot down by the Serious Fraud Office, foreign fruit-based holdings were decidedly out of favour.

The one prospect that might have appealed — although it was a real stretch — was our 10% stake in a Dutch electronics business that supplied some minor components to Philips for their CD players. They were small enough that the Pippawool and Phonna cash would amount to a serious stake. The Amsterdam stock exchange was also compact enough that a blitzkrieg buying spree would attract attention. My only problem was putting a name to the greenmail rumour. I couldn't think of a single Dutch entrepreneur who might strike terror into a company board, or any other entrepreneur, anywhere in the world, who would bother playing a game like this in Holland.

No, if it was going to work, I convinced myself, it was going to work only in Britain or the States. And my better judgement kept telling me that I had no choice but to leave Euromarket92 in tact.

When I got home that night, Pippa wasn't there. I rang her parents, and they seemed genuinely surprised that I was calling to ask for her. The only other place she could possibly be was France. So I called her there and, when Pippa answered, I said, "It's me."

She slammed down the phone.

Reassured that she and the twins were all right, I told myself, she'll come home when she's ready to come home. And I fell asleep, thinking that was fine with me, because I had plenty of other things to worry about.

On Tuesday I got a call from William David Romney at Hill Samuel. "We had a meeting late yesterday afternoon because we're concerned with that press report Sunday."

I told him, "You're too long in the tooth to believe everything you read in the papers."

He said, "There are some things we always look into, whether we believe the story or not."

"No reason to worry," I assured him. "We've got the situation in hand. There are a few stories about to break which will set the record straight and put an end to the malicious rumours."

"That's always good to know. But I think it would be prudent if we, nevertheless, met to speak about reassessing my bank's exposure." He added, "We are, after all, holding about £18 million worth of your paper, you know."

I tried joking, "I'll buy it back at ten cents on the dollar."

But he didn't like that. "Is that all it's worth?"

"No, no, no," I hastened to make clear, "it's just my sense of humour." I should have reminded myself that bankers never laugh at anything that's not within an arm's length of their crotch. "No, don't start worrying. Honestly, there's no reason to be concerned. However, if it makes you feel better and you want to meet, I'll be happy to do that."

He asked, "This week?"

I told him, "Next week would be easier for me."

"As soon as possible," he said. "Monday morning?"

I didn't have any choice but to say, "Sure, fine," and make it sound as if I'd be happy to see him.

On Wednesday I tried Pippa again. Malika answered, called Madame, told her who it was, then came back on the line to say, "She do not take your phone."

There was no point in arguing with Malika. Anyway, that's when Peter called to announce that he'd just gotten a message from the manager at El Castillo in Las Palmas to say that a British reporter had been on to them about his stay there.

"It's all right," I assured him. "I'm behind this."

"What for?"

"I'm fighting back."

"Remember the Alamo? Just get the Bahamas restructured before you start trying to manipulate Fleet Street."

On Thursday, Clement rang saying he needed to see me.

"Busy week, my friend." I asked, "Want to do lunch one day next week?"

"No. Lunch is not a good idea."

That was an odd thing for him to say, and I told him so. "You, of the four-hour snack?"

"It's not the four-hour snack that I mind. But I'm not sure I want to flaunt the fact that I'm speaking with you like this."

"What does that mean?"

"It means I am going to do you a favour and tell you that your former friend is getting very nervous. I can only exercise so much control. You'd better know that she wants to pull the plug."

"Pull the plug? On Howe Wharf?"

"On you."

"I'll ring you back," I said.

He warned, "Don't call her . . ."

But I had no intention of listening to him. I rang Francesca, told her secretary who it was and, a bit to my surprise, Francesca took the call. "What can I do for you?"

"How about starting with, hello Bay, what's new?"

She was in one of her more acerbic moods. "I know what's new. What I don't know is if I'm inclined to listen to you tell me what I should do about it."

"Why do you want to pull the plug?"

"I see that Clement did ring you after he said he wouldn't."

I admitted, "And asked me specifically not to call you. But you and I . . ."

"Let's not speak about you and I," she said flatly. "If we have anything to say to each other, it's about BFCS and you, and Pennstreet and you."

"We're meeting our payments. Everything is on schedule. We're developing Howe Wharf. We're doing everything we're supposed to be doing. What's your problem with that?"

"Confidence."

"Our share price is, for the most part, unmoved."

"It's down to 55p this morning. Last week it was as high as 63p. That sounds to me as if I'm not the only one who's losing confidence."

"Or that the market is just generally down." I flicked on my screen and saw that the FTSE–100 was up eight points. "You're letting your personal feelings cloud your business judgement."

"I simply reported to Clement that, in my opinion, we should get out at the earliest possible moment."

I took a chance, "And Clement told you that he was staying in."

She paused for a brief second, just long enough to lead me to believe that I'd guessed right. "If the share price keeps dropping, he won't have any choice. I will personally go over his head and put my case to Zurich."

I tried, "Shall we meet?"

She said, "No."

"Okay." There was nothing else I could say except, "Have a nice day, Francesca."

284

She said, "Goodbye, Bay," and hung up.

If I'd had any doubts before who the enemy was, I didn't have any now. All these years later, Francesca was finally getting even.

Hell hath no fury. . .

I stood up and walked to the window.

A tramp trying to get across Long Acre caught my eye. He was pushing a shopping cart, his worldly possessions stuffed into black garbage bags. I stood there, watching him as he boldly stepped into the street, stopped in the middle, held up both his hands to halt the oncoming traffic, then proceeded to the other side. He took up his place on the corner, standing flush against the building there, with his shopping cart snugly tucked under his right elbow while his left hand was extended in front of him, palm up, hoping to collect coins from passing strangers.

No one gave him anything.

From top to bottom and back again, I said to him, it's a fend for yourself kind of world.

Just then, one of those brown United Parcel Service vans pulled up to the corner.

My first thought was, the bum's got an overnight express letter.

That made me laugh.

I watched as the driver climbed out of his van, carrying a large UPS envelope and walked up to the bum. My mouth opened in sheer astonishment as I waited for the driver to hand him the envelope. Instead, he put a coin in the bum's hand and the bum leaned forward to pat the driver on the back.

The UPS delivery went next door.

I strolled over to my chair, fell into it, threw my feet up on my desk, closed my eyes and tried to slip into one of my daydreaming trances.

Behind my eyelids, like a CinemaScope screen in those wonderful old movie houses where they always had double features with plenty of cartoons on a Saturday morning, I played the scene with the UPS delivery to the bum over again and again.

Each time, it struck me as funnier than the time before.

Then, suddenly, the film stopped and I sat up, knowing exactly what I wanted to do.

I said out loud, I'll deliver it to myself.

Chapter Twenty-three

Nothing appeared that week in the *FT*. Nor was there anything in the *Sunday Times*. I couldn't be sure if Brian Fellowes and Anthony Carpenter were still working on the story or had moved onto something else. I was tempted to ring them but I knew better. I didn't want them to think I was overly concerned with what was going on around me. And anyway, when Americans push even a little, the British mistake it for pushing a lot.

The way we push is just one of the many cultural differences Americans must get used to if they're going to live in the United Kingdom. Because, in fact, it is not true that we are two nations separated by a common language.

Instead, we are more like a common language separated by two nations.

I have always maintained that, for Americans, at first glance, England is Europe without the pain. Sort of, downtown Kansas City with a funny accent. Here is a country where the plumbing works – it is entirely thanks to the British that a toilet in the States is referred to as a "crapper" – and where the food is generally familiar. Bangers and mash, bubble and squeak – or the even more remarkably named spotted dick – may not be *l'haute cuisine française*, but a hot dog is a hot dog is a hot dog. The same goes for a double Whopper, barbecue ribs, the Colonel's secret ingredients and Chinese take-out.

Americans tend to find the British hospitable, honest, and almost always with a cousin living somewhere odd, like Oregon. Every cab driver in London has been to the States at least once – who else goes to Orlando in July? – and, as it so often seems, is planning to leave for California in a few weeks on a ten-day driving holiday which will include Las Vegas, Miami and one night at Niagara Falls.

On my only visit to the Tower of London, a Beefeater confided to me how sorry he was that the Colonies broke away from the Crown back in '76. I wondered why. He answered, with a perfectly straight face, "Had you stayed with us, today you would be one of Britain's finest Dominions."

It's a fair bet that every Brit over a certain age has served with Yanks – it was, they proudly acknowledge, way back in double-you-double-you-two, the big one – and customarily likes Yanks. It's an equally good bet that most Brits under that certain age own at least one American college sweatshirt and/or a baseball hat, have seen two consecutive episodes of *The Cosby Show*, can tell you which state Graceland is in and know the difference between a quarterback and defensive tackle.

Because so much in Britain is so familiar, we come in droves and have, since Ben Franklin's day, visited and lived and generally felt right at home here. We may be dubious about cricket, and rightly so, because it is unfathomable that any game should go on for five days, religiously break for tea and end with no one winning. But we generally admire all things British, including the Royal Family – at least those members old enough to have a pensioner's bus pass.

We are especially in awe of a civilization that is so rich in history and tradition. Trust me, standing on top of Geoffrey Chaucer in Poets' Corner more than rivals Hollywood's pavement hand prints of Bette Davis, Lon Chaney and Clara Bow, all put together.

We have differences of opinion when it comes to the

subtleties of politics and economics. There are Brits who wish they'd never heard of Pizza Hut, rap music or Cruise missiles. And there are Brits who honestly believe that, as a group, Americans are loud, demanding, rude and forever wearing checked slacks with striped shirts. Individually, we may be any or all of those things. But there's no denying that, as a group, Americans are England's biggest fans.

The so-called "special relationship" works fine. That is, as long as we don't have to live together 24 hours a day. Break that rule and it all goes wrong. Because we speak the same language, we expect the other to think like we do.

And we can't.

In the States, everything happens fast. Decisions are made right away. Time is money. If you've got the right deal, you can get anybody you want on the telephone and make your proposition. The class system is defined by money, not blood or the stripes on a regimental tie. The customer is always right. No parking, no business. And banks will take real risks. This is not to say America is better. It's just different.

One very noticeable contrast is the legal system.

We put cameras in courtrooms because we believe a courtroom is the public's business. The British put wigs on their judges to emphasize that it isn't.

To American eyes, British jurisprudence is needlessly clumsy because it's based on the concept that solicitors do what they do best and barristers do what they do best and never the twain shall meet. You wind up having to deal with solicitors to handle the preliminaries and paperwork involved with your case and barristers to plead for you in court. What's more, if you're involved with a criminal action, you can't hire a barrister directly – you've got to go through your solicitor – and then you aren't allowed to spend too much time with your barrister. His instructions must come from your solicitor. That's so you can't feed him a line of bull and get him to lie for you in court.

Perish the thought!

Because there is this wall between you and your mouthpiece, making him believe unequivocally in your innocence is probably a non-starter. And that can be a nasty handicap when it's his turn to make the jury believe it.

Just as worrying, because he comes into the game fairly late, it always struck me, he couldn't possibly have any sort of natural feel for the case. After all, the quality of his argument must depend almost entirely on how well your solicitor communicates, at the very last moment, the essence of the matter to him.

Yet another drawback is that lawyers in Britain cannot take cases on a contingency basis. If you go out looking to sue someone, you can't get anyone to accept the case on a punt. In the States, attorneys take a third of the profits for winning and nothing but a thanks-anyway for losing. True, it clogs up the courts with superfluous cases but it also means that the little guy can afford to take on the big guy. Although no one in Britain bothers to say as much, I'm convinced that contingencies don't exist here because the very structure of British society has always been about protecting the big guy at the expense of the little guy. Big guys can afford to hire barristers to fight their case. Little guys must hope they can find a solicitor to work out a settlement.

I liked Gerald's idea of bringing in outside counsel but I wanted someone big and ballsy on our side. However, when I told him that, Gerald cautioned against it. He said there were dangers in bringing in one of the major firms at this early stage. After all, no one had charged me with anything and he didn't believe there was any reason to react as if someone had. "We don't want you to look guilty."

"If I try to defend myself, I'm guilty?"

"If you try to defend yourself before anyone has

formally accused you of a crime, there are some people who would construe that to appear suspicious."

"The Marquess of Queensberry's Rules, no doubt."

"This is Britain." His suggestion was to meet with a guy he'd been to law school with, who had a low profile. "Consulting him won't look suspicious. It will seem perfectly normal."

"You mean," I chided him, "it would be cricket."

"Now you're beginning to understand."

His name was Henry Thistlewaite and the moment I saw him I knew he was the wrong guy. Although he was Gerald's age, early 50s, he looked much older. Tiny, almost effeminate, his thinning hair was parted in the middle. It made him appear very bookish, sort of like an assistant librarian at a minor Midwestern university. But the thing about him that I'll remember forever was his shirt garters. He is the only man I ever saw who had garters on his sleeves to keep his cuffs from spilling too far forward over his hands. Most of us find it simpler to buy shirts that fit.

"If you have anything to hide," he said to me in a soft, one-octave-too-high-voice, "I suggest that we work out a compromise with the police. It's not the same as you North Americans would call a plea bargain, but . . ."

I found myself being uncharacteristically gentle with this little man. "Except that I haven't done anything wrong."

"That's not necessarily the point. You are a target because, after the euphoria of the Thatcher years, the entrepreneur population has grown too unruly. This isn't about your guilt or your innocence. It's about the nation's guilt for having had a decade like the 1980s. This is a cull."

He talked sense. But advising me to roll over and play dead was not what I wanted to hear, not what I was going to continue paying money to hear and nothing that I intended to do. So I thanked Mr Thistlewaite for his time, and when we left his office I said to Gerald, "Now we'll try it my way."

"What does that mean?"

"It means we're going to get someone big and brassy and kick butt at the City of London Police Fraud Squad before the City of London Police Fraud Squad has a chance to kick mine."

He raised his eyebrows. "What I like about you, Bay, is how the only lessons that matter are the ones you learn yourself."

I told Peter about having met a fellow with shirt garters – he'd never seen that either – although he agreed with Gerald that big and brassy was wrong. "No, what you want is someone well connected. Big and brassy is suspicious. It's the old boy network that's worth paying for."

"How old boy?"

"Very old boy. Preferably someone whose great grandfather slept with Queen Victoria and every important Tory frontbencher since."

"Like who?"

"Any of those very proper old farts who secretly wears ladies' underwear."

The only man I knew who might be able to put a name to someone like that was Pippa's father. He'd been a staunch Tory all his life. I explained, "I want very old boy," and he said, without any hesitation, Lord Neville-Bolt. I rang Peter back to try the name out on him. "Hyphens are good. That's the one."

Phoning the firm of A. J. T. Neville-Bolt the following morning, and asking for the noble lord, my call was passed along to an efficient-sounding woman who answered, "This is Mrs Chatham."

I gave her my name and wondered if I could get an appointment sometime in the next few days. She wanted to know if I'd been referred. I admitted, no. Then she wanted to know what this was all about. I said, "I'd truthfully prefer not to discuss anything on the phone."

She said, "Certainly sir, if I might just check his Lordship's diary." She put me on hold for a few moments then came back to say that Lord Neville-Bolt could see me the next afternoon at 4:30. I promised to be there.

Anxious to crow at having so easily gotten an appointment, I rang Gerald. "Tomorrow at 4:30 we're seeing old boy Neville-Bolt."

He was taken back. "Neville-Bolt? You mean, Lord Neville-Bolt? What on earth for?"

"I'm going to hire him."

He started to laugh. "Are you firing me?"

"Don't be ridiculous. I just decided we needed a major heavyweight. This guy is supposed to be the best connected lawyer in the country."

Gerald agreed. "I suspect he is the best-connected lawyer in the country. But why do you think he'll take your case?"

"Because that's what lawyers do for money."

"Bay, this is, or at least could be, a criminal matter."

"So?"

"So A. J. T. Neville-Bolt wouldn't touch it with a barge pole."

"What's he got against my money?"

"This is Britain."

"So?"

"So . . . okay," he said. "Enjoy yourself and let me know how you get on."

"Aren't you coming with me? This whole thing was your idea."

"First of all, it was your idea. I already introduced you to the counsel I'd prefer to use. Second of all, you want me . . ." There was a healthy pause before he said, "Bay, I don't think you could even begin to understand how embarrassing it would be for me to come with you and have someone like Lord Neville-Bolt wonder what on earth I'd recommended him for."

"Terrific," I said. "It will be a pleasure watching you blush. I'll meet you there tomorrow at 4:25."

Neville-Bolt's offices were on Lincoln's Inn Fields, a beautiful Georgian square with a manicured lawn, not far from the Law Courts, off High Holborn. True friend that he is, Gerald was standing on the pavement in front of the building as I turned the corner and came into the courtyard.

"You ready?" I asked.

He nodded. "I've thought about this. I'm not the one who made the appointment. I'm not the one who should be embarrassed. And because I know exactly what's about to happen, I've decided I'm going to sit back and enjoy every minute of it."

"Money talks," I reminded him.

"I hope you've got some that speaks British," was all he'd say.

We stepped inside and, instead of walking into a well-decorated lobby, we found ourselves in a dimly lit hallway with a sign that said A. J. T. Neville-Bolt, Fourth Floor.

"Where's the elevator?" I asked.

"It's called a lift," Gerald corrected, "and there ain't none."

We started climbing the stairs.

"How come," I wanted to know, "such a well-established guy has a suite of offices on the fourth floor of an old walk-up? This place isn't F. Lee Bailey, it's Sam Spade."

"It happens to be very fancy real estate."

"Compared with lawyers on Park Avenue, it's a slum."

"This isn't America, this is Britain."

We plodded up another flight and I pointed to a light fixture. "I've often wondered who buys 40-watt bulbs."

"Think of this as the ultimate in British reverse snobbery."

"I like my lawyers and my doctors to look like they make a lot of money. Big offices. Big cars. Fancy wives. Lawyers who lose cases and doctors who lose patients can't afford expensive toys."

"You called him, I didn't."

"I'm here because he's supposed to be the best."

"In many ways, he is," Gerald assured me. "This firm is very old-fashioned, very quiet and very effective. Mention the name Neville-Bolt to any Tory in the land and you'll witness extreme reverence."

I waited for him to continue and when he didn't I asked, "But?"

"But he's not going to take your case."

We went up the last flight. "Even Eskimos eat ice cream, my friend. Just watch."

"With pleasure."

"All we need is to get his noble Lordship to hit a few of the right buttons, and this whole business with the fraud squad disappears."

Now Gerald took a very firm tone. "It isn't done that way. Listen to me, Bay. Don't expect, or even dare to suggest, that he ring anyone on our behalf."

I wasn't so sure. "Connections aren't worth a damn if you can't use them."

"There is no question of his direct intervention."

"How about if I ask and we see what he says?"

"This is Britain."

"How come you keep telling me that?"

"Because you obviously have to be reminded of it often."

The reception was a small, cluttered room with old furniture. And it smelled of stale sherry. There were two dark and dreary portraits on the wall. I decided one was Neville-Bolt's grandfather, the other Neville-Bolt's old man. I also decided that neither of them seemed terribly likeable.

"I'm Bay Radisson. This is Gerald Chappell."

"Mrs Chatham," retorted a barrel-chested woman in

a dark suit. "I believe we've spoken on the phone." With a wave of her hand, she directed us into His Lordship's office.

Antony J. T. Neville-Bolt III was a tall, thin man in his early 80s, with a head of thick white hair, who wore a musty old three-piece pinstripe suit. He forced himself out of his chair and came round his desk to shake our hands. Mrs Chatham introduced us. He then asked her to please send in some port, his son and his son-in-law.

When he invited us to take a seat, Gerald opted for the well-worn leather couch. I walked to the window, stared for a moment at the courtyard below – for the lack of anything better to say I mumbled, "What a lovely view" – then chose the only spot on the windowsill that wasn't covered in files.

Making his way slowly back to his desk, Neville-Bolt fell into his leather swivel chair, turned to face me, and wondered, "What can I do for you, young man?"

I told him, "I'm having a few problems and thought you might be able to advise me on how best to solve them."

He nodded several times towards Gerald.

Gerald nodded politely, in return.

"I'm grateful that you could take the time to see me." I inspected the silver-framed photos on a small shelf against the wall, just behind his desk. There was the obligatory shot of him bowing to the Queen, then pictures of him with Margaret Thatcher, with Edward Heath, with the Duke of Edinburgh, with Prince Charles and Princess Diana and with a man I guessed was Anthony Eden. There was also a good assortment of family photos – His Lordship with a woman I supposed must be Her Ladyship, His Lordship and his children, His Lordship with his grandchildren. I was very tempted to ask, where's the one with Robert Maxwell, but I knew he wouldn't get the joke.

"I've always got along well with Americans," he said,

this time pointing to a silver frame that sat square in the middle of his desk. "So did he."

I leaned over to see a much younger Sir Antony in deep conversation with Harold Macmillan. Behind them, slightly out of focus, was a smiling Dwight Eisenhower. "When was that taken?"

"Washington," he said. "Mac and I were there together."

"While he was Prime Minister?"

Neville-Bolt stared at Gerald. "Did you know Macmillan?"

Gerald apologized that he'd never had the pleasure.

I tried again. "Was he Prime Minister at the time?"

His Lordship looked up at me. "Washington ... Washington DC ... of course, you know it ... it's the capital."

Just then the office door opened and two men walked in, both of them, I imagined, in their late 50s. They were dressed the same, in dark, three-piece pinstripes. The son – Sir Harold Neville-Bolt – resembled his old man, and even shared his good crop of white hair. The son-in-law – Sir John James – was smaller, his hair was thinner and he sported a very tiny, perfectly trimmed white moustache.

We shook hands and were about to slip into the minor pleasantry stage when Mrs Chatham returned carrying a silver tray with two bottles of port and five glasses. "Excuse me."

All conversation stopped while she went through her routine.

First she placed the tray on the coffee table in front of the couch. Then she took one glass and one bottle and placed it in front of His Lordship. Then she returned to the second bottle and half filled the four remaining glasses. She left them on the tray while she went to His Lordship's desk and filled his glass from his bottle. She handed the glass to him, went back to the coffee table and handed one glass each to the rest of us, starting with Gerald, then me, then Son, then Son-in-Law. When that was done, she mumbled "Excuse me" again and left the room, closing the door behind her.

His Lordship raised his full glass and said, "To the Americans."

Son and Son-in-Law repeated, "To the Americans," and so did Gerald. And we all drank from our half-filled glasses.

It tasted awful.

I put mine on the windowsill, next to me, and never touched it again.

Son, Son-in-Law and Gerald somehow managed to finish theirs and, when they were done, they put their empty glasses on the silver tray. His Lordship nursed his, staring into it, engrossed with the colour and taste and aroma.

I sat and waited.

Eventually, Sir Harold asked, "How can we help you?"

I told them who I was and explained a little bit about what I do. I mentioned, in general terms, my dealings in the Maxwell shares and how I'd subsequently had a run-in with the Stock Exchange. I said that the dossier was now sitting with the City of London Police Fraud Squad and that Gerald and I both felt we needed outside counsel.

Suddenly all eyes turned to Gerald.

He responded instantly. "Mr Radisson has taken it upon himself to ring you directly. I trust you will appreciate the fact that I was informed about this only after the appointment was made. I also trust you will appreciate that some of our American cousins have particularly headstrong tendencies."

I turned to Neville-Bolt, senior. "Sir, I want the best attorneys in the country. I have not traded illegally. And I refuse to be treated shabbily by a bunch of functionaries. If I've upset some people at the Stock Exchange and the

DTI, it's because I suffer fools badly. I'm here because I need your help."

His Lordship piped up, "A criminal matter? No, no, my dear boy, no."

I looked at Son and Son-in-Law. "It's not yet a criminal matter. I mean, no one's charged me with anything."

"I understand," Sir Harold answered for his father. "But you must understand, that we could best serve you by simply directing you towards another, more qualified firm in this area."

"You mean, you don't want to take my money?"

"I'm afraid that it would be quite wrong of us to accept any money from you as we could not possibly act on your behalf in this matter."

I glanced at the three of them, then at Gerald. He was wearing his "I told you so" face.

There wasn't anything left for me to do but lean across the desk to shake His Lordship's hand. "Thank you, sir, anyway. It's been very nice meeting you." Out of the corner of my eye I noticed that the label on his port bottle said Cockburns 1953. Then I went to shake hands with Sir Harold and Sir John. The port sitting on the silver tray was straight off Marks and Spencer's shelf.

Gerald and I made our exit.

He was gracious enough not to gloat, at least not until we were downstairs on the street. "Is it my turn again?"

I raised my hands in defeat. "Okay."

"Henry Thistlewaite was the right chap at this stage."

"No, I want young lions."

"All right, I'll find you young lions."

Feeling like an utter fool, I walked back to my office and told Patty West, "Get a good case of port and send it to His Lordship Antony J. T. Neville-Bolt. Then send the same thing to Gerald. The note should say, to both of them, thank you."

Two hours later Gerald rang to say, "Apologies accepted."

"That's not an apology," I insisted, "that's a bribe. I want young lions. No, even better, I want gunslingers. I want guys who earn a living being nasty. Guys who aren't afraid to draw first blood."

"Trust me."

I reminded him, "Gerald, I do."

The next morning he brought two of them to my office.

Gareth Evans was in his late 30s. He dressed conservatively and spoke softly. But he was burly, with big hands and heavy forearms. He told me he was born in Wales – his father had been a coalminer – and that he was the first in his family ever to go to university. He said he had studied at Cardiff, but that he'd taken a master's degree at the University of Wisconsin. "I went out there for a year to do US law. And, as you would say, I froze my butt."

Gerald brought him in because he knew I'd appreciate the American connection.

"What did you learn in the States?"

He laughed, "Among other things, I learned that a half-decent Welsh rugby player is no match for an average American university line backer. I was looking to waltz my way into the spotlight. I couldn't wait to score touchdowns. Instead, I spent that whole winter getting the shit kicked out of me."

Andy Maloney was a year or two younger, much smaller, had longer hair and dressed more modern. He was born in Belfast and studied law there, before making his way to London to work in the legal department at the Home Office. After three years of pushing papers, he moved to the Department of Public Prosecutions. "I did another three there. That's where I made all my best social connections. Rapists, fraudsters, murderers, bank robbers, prostitutes, street bums, you name it. I also got on a first name basis with every skeleton in every cupboard at the DPP. I know what they do well and I know what they're useless at."

Gerald and Evans called Maloney because of those three years with the DPP.

I asked, "What do they do well?"

Maloney said, "Bully people."

"And what is it they're useless at?"

He said, "Standing up to someone who refuses to be bullied."

I wanted to know, "Do you have elevators in your offices?"

They both nodded yes.

"Do you drink port?"

Maloney answered, "Come on, I'm from Belfast."

Evans said, "Give me Coors Beer anytime."

I told Gerald, "They're hired."

Chapter Twenty-four

I phoned Pippa several times over the weekend – she was still refusing to talk to me – but Malika put the girls on so I could speak with them. I spent the rest of the weekend going over the Pennstreet accounts, trying to find every spare penny.

Bright and early Monday morning, William David Romney showed up. I'd forgotten about his appointment until Patty announced that he was there. I checked my calendar and noted that he was precisely on time. There was nothing else I could do but see him, although I planned to make short shrift of him and get back to more important things.

He stepped into my office with a nervous grin and a wet-fish handshake. He was wearing his best banker's brown suit, a starched white shirt, black brogans and a beige tie with a handkerchief that didn't match. I immediately assumed he got the tie and handkerchief set as a gift during the January sales because no one in their right mind would have paid full price for such a thing.

Pushing 40, but looking 50, he had a nervous tick in his left shoulder and was constantly thumping the fingers of his right hand on the inside of his thighs. He once told me that his idea of heaven was a lifetime pass to Arsenal games with a never-ending supply of Websters Yorkshire on draught, served to him by a busty Page Three girl "with titties like ear muffs".

Sadly, this guy was walking proof that corporate banking should be sold only to young men with a health warning attached.

"Rumours are no good for business," he began. "They rattle a banker's confidence."

"I would have thought it depends on the rumour."

"Rumours drive markets."

"No," I corrected. "Good and bad business decisions drive markets. Rumours misdirect them."

"Whatever," he said, his shoulder noticeably starting to tick. "In this case the rumours are that you're in trouble."

"Before you take any hasty decisions," I suggested, "it might pay to find out whether or not there's any truth behind the rumours."

"Is there?"

"No," I said firmly.

He took a deep breath. "The bank is queasy. What can you do to settle our stomachs?"

"Maalox helps."

"I'm serious, Bay. My neck is on the line here too. I signed off on all your loans."

"I'm serious too, William. But you're asking me, when did I stop beating my wife."

"You beat your wife?"

"No, I don't beat my wife. But . . ." Sometimes I had to wonder if any of these guys truly understood that there was more to life on this planet than merchant banking and soccer. "What you're asking me is, how can I get out of trouble and save your ass? Well, the only answer is, I'm not in trouble."

"What about those rumours?"

"Did you ever hear the one about Catherine the Great and the horse?"

He looked at me as if I were crazy. "What horse?"

"I guess you never heard that one." I thought for a moment, "How about the one that goes, Tina Turner is really a man with a sex change?"

"She is?"

"No. I mean, I don't know. It was just a rumour. It doesn't mean that it's true." I thought of a third example, "How about Mark Twain? You've heard of Mark Twain."

"Of course. Huckleberry Finn and Tom Sawyer and the girl with the white picket fence ... what's her name?"

"Thatcher. It was a famous *ménage à trois.*"

"Margaret?"

"Becky," I said. "But that's not the point. Mark Twain came to London and while he was here a newspaper editor in New York heard that he died. So he sent ..."

"Mark Twain died in London?"

"No. Mark Twain died in. .." I decided, "Connecticut." It sounded right to me so I said it a second time with great assurance. "He died in Connecticut."

"The Mississippi River doesn't run through Connecticut, does it?"

"Only through the black neighbourhoods of Hartford," I sighed. "Just listen to the story."

"I'm listening."

"Okay. So the newspaper editor in New York hears that Twain is dead in London, and he wires his correspondent asking him to write a 1000 word obituary. The correspondent goes to where Twain was staying, only to find that Twain is very much alive. He shows Twain the wire and Twain sends one back to the editor in New York saying, something like, 'Reports of my death are greatly exaggerated.'"

Romney stared at me.

I peered back at him. "You do get the point?"

"That he wasn't dead."

"That's right," I said. "And neither am I."

"But the rumours?"

"Reports of my death are greatly exaggerated."

"I can't tell my boss that. I need something more. I need to see that everything is business as usual."

"It is business as usual, except on mornings like this when I have to keep insisting that I don't beat my wife."

"If we could only have a little extra assurance . . ."

"Don't even think about renegotiating your position."

"It's not . . ." His fingers were thumping his thigh at full speed and his nervous shoulder was now in third gear. "Well, if, perhaps, we could have just a little extra assurance . . ."

"That's called renegotiating your position."

"But, you see, if there is a fraud squad investigation . . ."

"Who said there was?"

"The rumours. The rumours. I keep telling you. I keep hearing all these rumours . . ."

"William . . ." I stood up. "Why don't you find out if they're true before you start wasting your time and my money." I went to the door and opened it. "You'll have to forgive me but I have a business to run."

It was several seconds before he took my not-so-subtle hint and moved to the door. "I'll have to report back to my boss . . ."

I patted him on the ticking shoulder. "You can tell him that I have never seen, never heard from, never spoken with anyone at the City of London Police. Please quote me, word for word. I have never been in touch with any fraud squad, nor has any fraud squad ever been in touch with me. In fact, the only time in the past few years that I have even had two words with any law enforcement official, of any flavour whatsoever, was when a meter maid threatened to ticket me for thinking about parking on a double yellow line." I took his wet-fish hand and shook it. "Tell your boss, quote, it's business as usual."

The moment he left I rang Peter to inform him that Hill Sam was about to bail out.

*   *   *

The only spare money I had to play with was sitting in the Pippawool and Phonna accounts. I hesitated using them – my gut told me that, especially in light of Romney's visit, I shouldn't be walking a tightrope like this without a safety-net – but, as long as everything went the way I knew it should, I'd have more than enough cash to put back in the bank within a few days.

There was nothing more I could do until Roderick opened his office in Nassau, so I walked to Piccadilly Circus, to rummage through a bunch of those crappy souvenir shops that have sprouted up over the years. When I found what I wanted, I marched over to Regent Street, to Hamleys toy store, and bought the second thing I wanted.

Back at the office, Patty watched me superglue the two little toys onto a base of plexiglass – for some obscure reason they call it Perspex in England – then glide the plexiglass base all over my desk until I decided that the proper place for it was in between the Snowdon photo of the twins and the framed quote from Albert Einstein.

"You've finally gone mad," she declared. "What is that?"

"A fetish," I said.

"An obsession?"

"A fetish. A charm."

"Charming," she nodded.

"A talisman," I said.

"That explains everything."

I waved her off. "You wouldn't understand."

She reached for the plexiglass base.

I pretended to slap her hand away. "Don't touch. It's perfect just like this."

She shook her head. "A ceramic bag-person and a Match Box toy UPS delivery truck?"

I mumbled, "Now that I've built it, he will come."

"I think you should be living somewhere quiet with padded walls."

"Bye," I waved.

She went away, shaking her head.

At 3 p.m. London time, I got Roderick on the phone and asked him to set up a small web of shell companies that couldn't ever be traced back to Pennstreet, him or me. He wondered what I was doing. I told him that I was launching one of my old counterfeit takeovers.

He asked, "Who's the target?"

I answered, "Me."

My intention was to make the markets believe that someone was out there, lurking behind a computer screen ready to pounce on Pennstreet. By supporting my own share price for a while, with the unwitting help of those vultures who always get into potential takeovers looking to make a fast buck, I figured I could stave off the banks while Gareth Evans and Andy Maloney settled my account with the cops. At the same time, I planned to use the publicity that a takeover bid generated to sell a few minor assets – it's come to be known as the poison pill defence – which would bring in enough cash to replace the money I'd committed to my share support scheme.

Unlike my previous adventures in greenmail, I didn't need to find a suitable corporate raider. All I had to do was claim that I knew the masked man's true identity. The market pundits could play their own guessing game and fill in the blanks themselves.

Over the next few days, Roderick and I put together a phantom conglomerate, using several intermediate agents to wind up with a Luxembourg shell company called Crusader Venture Capital. I moved the $2.3 million out of the Phonna account – disguised as a real estate deal in Hong Kong – laundered it with a series of transactions through the Caribbean so that no one could follow the funds back to me, and plunked it down in a Crusader Venture Capital account I set up in Geneva.

Several times during the week, Peter asked me what I was doing. All I'd answer was, "Taking care of business." He also kept asking if I'd spoken to Pippa.

"She won't get on the phone."

He beseeched me, "How can you stay angry with her like that?"

"I'm not angry at her. She's angry at me."

"You want me to ring her?"

"That's what started this whole thing."

"So you got angry with Pippa because I rang her, which is why she's angry with you. How come you're not angry with me?"

"Because I'm not married to you."

"If you don't do something soon," he cautioned, "you're not going to be married to her either."

"If you're so concerned about my marriage, you shouldn't have interfered in the first place."

"I thought you weren't angry with me."

"I'm not. But when it comes to marriage counselling . . ."

"I give up," he said.

"You never even got off the starting blocks."

"Do me a favour. Get the Bahamas restructured, then get your marriage restructured. She's not waiting for a phone call. She's waiting for you."

Everything was in place by Friday afternoon. So I told Roderick to push the button.

We set off a chain reaction – a series of instructions through the succession of intermediate agents – ending in an agent acting for Crusader Venture Capital coming into the London market just after it closed to purchase £1.4 million worth of Pennstreet shares.

By that time, I was already at Heathrow getting on a flight to the south of France.

The twins were thrilled to find me at the front door. I couldn't honestly say that Pippa was quite as happy.

"It took you two weeks," she said.

I scooped up the girls and kissed them.

"What did you bring us?" They asked in unison.

I handed them some chocolates I'd bought at the airport.

"It's no good for them," Pippa remarked, then told them, "Only one small piece before bedtime. And brush your teeth."

After the girls went to bed, when Pippa and I were finally alone, we sat for a while on the balcony.

"I deserve better treatment," she said.

"I agree."

"If Peter rang me, it was because . . ."

"I know." I didn't have the inclination or the energy to argue with her. "Can we please forget the whole thing? I'd like to put it behind us. I'm sorry I reacted the way I did. But I'm under a lot of pressure . . ."

"You need to get your priorities right."

"I think my priorities are right."

She faced me. "What comes first?"

"What do you mean?"

"It's a simple question. In your list of priorities, what's first?"

"If you're looking for me to say, you and the twins . . ."

She cut in, "It's not what I'm looking for you to say that matters. It's what actually appears on the top of your list."

I told her, "Okay. You and the girls."

"Why don't I believe you?"

"I'm telling you, my first priority is you and the girls."

"But I don't think we come first. At least, not all the time."

"Well, you do," I insisted. "Pippa . . . I didn't come down here to fight with you. Can we change the subject?"

"What do you want to talk about?"

"I'd like to tell you how Roderick and I . . ."

"See?" She stood up. "See what I mean?"

"About what?"

"Your priorities," she said. "Goodnight." She left me on the terrace.

Later that night, when I crawled into bed next to her and took her in my arms, she responded to me quickly. But it had nothing to do with me. It was all about her. And when I started talking to her, she wouldn't answer.

Predictably, on Saturday, there was a small blurb about the share purchase in the *FT*, although there was still nothing from Brian Fellowes.

Peter phoned to ask, "Are you sure you know what you're doing?"

"How do you know I'm doing anything?"

"You forget. I'm the guy who taught you how to do it."

"I know exactly what I'm doing," I assured him. "I had a good teacher."

He merely said, "I hope so."

None of the Sunday papers picked up on the story.

That afternoon, Pippa announced that she wanted to stay in Cannes a little while longer. I told her it was probably a good idea, as I really wanted to concentrate on getting everything straightened out in London. I said that I'd try to come back the following weekend.

I returned to London on the first flight Monday morning and walked into the office at lunchtime. I went straight to my screen to check the Pennstreet share movement.

We were unchanged from the Friday closing at 55–57.

"Shit!" I'd been hoping for around 20 points. I'd have settled for 10. But unchanged meant that I'd just blown almost a million and a half pounds and gotten nothing back for my money.

Careful not to appear as if I was pushing, I phoned Brian Fellowes and asked him what he'd managed to find out. He said he'd received confirmation from El Castillo in Las Palmas that Peter had been registered there.

"Now you know how we found out about Maxwell."

"I put two and two together right away."

"So?"

"So, now we wait."

"Wait for what?"

"What do you want me to do with the information?"

It was obvious what I wanted him to do with it. "I thought you were looking for a story? Now you know the punchline."

"Except a punchline isn't a story. The Fraud Squad won't confirm any investigation into you and we stay away from rumours, at least we try to, as much as we can. Until they do something like arrest you or charge you, the fact that your partner was in the same place as Maxwell's boat when he drowned isn't news."

"Well . . ." I tried to hide my frustration. "At least now you know how we found out."

"If anything comes of the story, I'll get back to you."

"Anytime." I hung up with him and rang Andrew Carpenter at home. "You ever get anything from the Stock Exchange?"

"I spoke to that fellow Wynn but all he did was pass me on to the press office. I got nowhere."

"Wynn didn't say anything?"

"Not allowed to."

"And the press office?"

"Not inclined to."

"What about the cops?"

"Not likely to. Unless it's in their interest to be forthcoming, they hide behind *sub judice*. It's the best smokescreen ever invented for preventing the truth from being told."

"You see the blurb in the *FT* Saturday about someone buying a block of Pennstreet shares?"

"Yes, I did."

I tried, "If you hear any rumours about who's behind it, will you give me a call?"

"Sure," he said.

And that was the end of my conversation with him.

Monday, Pennstreet closed down a penny.

I phoned Roderick late that night and told him to come back into the market first thing Tuesday morning.

"Are you sure about this?" He asked.

"I'm sure." I needed to turn up the heat one more notch. The £1.67 million that had been sitting in Pippawool was already in place in Switzerland. I told Roderick, "Use it all."

Tuesday morning, just before the London market officially opened, an agent acting for Crusader Venture Capital bought another large block of shares.

Pennstreet nudged three points higher.

Crusader had surpassed the magical 5% threshold and, accordingly, announced its intention of launching a bid to take over Pennstreet.

The share price now jumped eight, reaching a mid-point at 67p.

I immediately issued a statement saying that the board of Pennstreet PLC would vigorously defend any attempt to takeover the company. That prompted another rally, bringing the shares to 73–75p range. That also prompted Andrew Carpenter to ring back, saying the *Sunday Times* wanted to do a profile on me.

I tried not to sound over-anxious by accepting.

We met Thursday morning in my office.

"Nice place," he said walking around, admiring the view of Covent Garden.

"There was a time when nobody wanted to be here."

He nodded, then looked at the telephone next to my desk. He seemed to be counting the lines.

"Six," I said.

He pointed to the phone next to the couch. "And six more over there?"

"Same six."

Then he spotted the phone next to the conference table. "And six more there?"

"Same six again," I said. "It's one of the rare examples in arithmetic when six times three still equals six."

"What do you do with them all?"

"Call journalists," I joked. "And order room service. Coffee? Tea? Stronger?"

He wanted a beer. I said, no problem, and went to the door to ask Patty if she would bring one in. That's when Gareth Evans phoned to say that he and Andy Maloney wanted to meet with Gerald and me immediately. "You're probably going to be arrested."

I asked, "What for?"

He said, "We don't know yet."

"I'll have to phone you back." I hung up and put on a brave face for Carpenter, "See? Sometimes people even call me."

His questions seemed benign enough, except I had trouble keeping my mind on them. Isn't the day of the asset stripper over? And, why don't you build things? And, how have the '80s changed you? And, how do you view the '90s?

I don't see us as asset strippers. And, we do build things, just look at our jams and jellies business. And, for many people, when the '80s ended, so did the easy money. And, the '90s is all about getting back to basics.

We spoke about the takeover bid and I emphasized my determination to maintain the management of my own company.

He asked, "How does it feel to be on the other side?"

I quoted John Paul Jones. "I have not yet begun to fight."

"How about some advice for the next generation of risk-takers?"

I thought for a moment. "Never invest in a company where the chairman's office is more comfortable than his home. It's one thing to live well. But when the chairman is living well at the shareholders' expense, the shareholders aren't getting everything they deserve."

He checked his watch and mentioned that his photographer should be waiting outside and I agreed to a photo. The fellow came in, took a few shots of me sitting on the edge of my desk. Then we shook hands – it was all very amiable – and they left.

As soon as they were gone I got Gerald, Evans and Maloney on a conference call.

Andy said he still hadn't managed to come up with any more details about the fraud squad's intention, and Gareth advised me that, if this was indeed about to happen, I should not try to resist in anyway. Gerald said the same thing, that I should make myself completely available to the cops. They agreed that I should not speak to anyone there without having at least one of my lawyers present. They also insisted that I avoid any contact with the press. I told them about my meeting with the *Sunday Times*. Gerald wondered if there was any way of killing the story, or at least postponing it. I said I didn't think so. Anyway, I assured them, it will be favourable.

Thursday night Pennstreet closed down four and Friday morning it dropped another four.

I told Peter I might be arrested. His advice was, "Do whatever you have to do."

I also told Pippa what was happening. She said she'd come right back to London, and walked into the office Friday afternoon just as I took a call from Clement.

"I can't hold her off any longer," he said.

I blew a kiss to Pippa and motioned to her to sit down. I asked Clement, "What's going on?"

"Francesca is calling in your loans."

"What on earth for?"

"Your share price is heading down too fast, there's a problem with Pennstreet Trust, and my head office is worried."

"Let me tell you something, my friend," I tried to rein

314

in my temper. "I am not in breach of any covenants. I'm meeting my payments. I'm still in business. So you can warn Little Miss Muffett for me that, if she thinks she's going to pull the plug, I'll have the bank and you and her in court in breach of contract. And I think she knows me well enough to know that I mean what I say."

I slammed down the phone.

Pippa wanted to know, "Who's Little Miss Muffett?"

"Francesca Guardi."

She glared at me. "There's a name I haven't heard for some time."

"She's one of my bankers," I reminded her.

"Is that all?"

My phone rang. Patty said William David Romney was on the line. I mumbled, "When it rains it pours," and took the call. "How are you?"

"Not so good," he said. "I'm afraid we're going to have to do some serious talking."

I didn't have much choice. "When shall we meet?"

"Monday? First thing?"

I needed to put him off for as long as I could. "I'm in the middle of a takeover battle. Can this wait for a couple of weeks?"

"I'll see what I can do." He paused, then obviously felt the need to explain, "Bay, this isn't me. This is coming from way over my head."

I took a deep breath. "I understand. Give me a few weeks. As long as you can."

He said, "Bay . . . I mean, I'd like to but . . . I can try to put it off for a while but they're worried. It's not me. I tried to explain to them about Mark Twain . . ."

There was nothing for me to say except, "I understand. I'll see you whenever. Thanks." I hung up and told Pippa, "Hill Sam is bailing out too. I knew they would. And this is just the beginning." Now I dialled Gerald.

But she cut in with, "You still haven't answered my question."

"What question?"

"Is that all?"

"Is what all?"

"Francesca Guardi?"

Gerald's secretary answered. "Mr Chappell's office."

"What about her?"

The secretary said again, "Mr Chappell's office?"

I said into the phone, "Hi, it's Bay. Ah . . . hold on just a second please . . ." Then I demanded of Pippa, "What are you talking about?"

"I'm talking about Francesca Guardi."

"What about her?"

"You tell me."

"She's one of my bankers. That's who she is. That's what I said. That's all."

"And I said, that had better be all. Then I asked, is it?"

I snapped, "Yes it is. That's all." Now I went back to Gerald's secretary. "Is he there?"

"Just a sec," she said. "I'm putting you through now."

"Because if it's not . . ." Pippa started to say.

I challenged her. "If it's not . . . then what?"

Gerald got on the line. "Hi."

She stood up. "Because if it's not, this time I really am filing for a divorce."

Chapter Twenty-five

Pippa and I had been down this road before.

She woke me early on New Year's Day 1988 by pouring baby oil all over me, whispering, "Just lie there and think of England," then having her way with me. At one point she panted, "Happy birthday". A moment later, she breathlessly confessed, "I've stopped taking the pill."

I fell asleep again, wondering if I was ready for this. All I knew about babies was that they cried a lot and generally smelled bad. I couldn't recall ever having held a baby in my arms.

A few hours later she woke me for the second time, the same way. Under the circumstances I was willing to concede that God must be an okay guy because he invented this particular method to ensure the continuation of the human race.

We wound up spending three days in bed, after which Pippa felt we had every right in the world to expect positive results. But nothing happened.

Secretly, I was relieved. Although I couldn't tell her that. Instead, I kept reassuring her that we'd figure it out. To bolster her confidence – and, in a real sense, to commit myself to the idea of fatherhood – I insisted that we start looking for a bigger place. The market was just beginning to overheat and, although prices were high, we bought a three-bedroom flat with a large double living-room on the top two floors of a house in Eaton Square, facing the tennis courts.

We finished that winter building bookshelves, painting the kitchen and giving procreation our best shot.

In March, Pippa came across an article in *Cosmo* that demonstrated, step by step, how a woman could tell when it was the perfect time to get "preggers" – which is what Yuppie Brits say, because "getting knocked up" means having someone pounding on your front door. We took her temperature every few hours and made love to order. When that didn't work, we gave up on quality and returned to sheer unbridled quantity. Except now we mixed in some fantasies. First, we pretended we were newlyweds. Then, even better, we pretended we were perfect strangers.

We also invented games.

I suggested Strip Scrabble. But that's the sort of thing that should be reserved for people who have met only an hour before, because the thrill of putting down a word like "xylocopid" – which ought to be worth at least three items of clothing – is overshadowed by the fact that, when it's your own wife who's taking off her bra, you know she'd take it off anyway if you just said please.

Next, Pippa thought, instead of taking off clothes we might try putting them on. But I refused to wear her underwear and, when she showed up one night in a school gym slip, it did absolutely nothing for me. When I was a kid, girls didn't wear stuff like that, so the reference was lost. She asked, what about a policewoman's outfit? I said, not really, although I might be able to go for a nurse. She vetoed that because in her mind the idea of sexy nurses was a male allegory contrived by chauvinists to keep women with authority in their place. I agreed with her, but she still wouldn't go for it.

Then I told her about one very wild, long weekend at college with Elizabeth where we spent three entire days naked and stoned, getting it on every other hour or so, and wondered what she thought about us having a naked and stoned weekend.

Pippa's response was, "That's how we brought in your birthday."

"Not exactly." I pointed out, "We only brought it in naked. Why don't I try to score a little grass . . ." Except I didn't have a clue any more how to go about that.

It didn't matter because she said, "Absolutely not," categorically refusing to get involved with any drugs whatsoever, even soft ones. "Out of the question."

"Okay, then let's get a little drunk and watch porn videos."

She pondered that for all of one-tenth of a second. "Sure."

Much too embarrassed to ask Gerald, Stonewall or Patty if they had any, I went to Soho and snuck into the first sex shop I spotted. I didn't know enough to request a specific star or title, and wound up confirming the old adage, you can't tell an X-rated video by the cover. The two I bought were so stupid that the best of our foreplay was fast forwarding.

Eventually, we got back to the idea of fantasies. I claimed that my sexiest daydream involved a pair of 19-year-old Austrian girls in *lederhosen* who can yodel.

She said, "Tough luck, mate," and told me about hers.

It came as a shock to hear my wife say that she sometimes thought about getting picked up in a sleazy bar by a low-life stranger. "With tattoos."

"Sorry," I said. "If I can't have my yodelling Austrians, then your ex-convict with 'LOVE' across his knuckles is out of the question. Come to think of it, even if I can have my nubile yodellers, you're going to have to keep your fantasies in the family."

"That's not fair. But I'm willing to compromise." She said, "You're low life enough, so let's get on a train and go somewhere, like Manchester. No one knows us there. We'll take separate rooms in some really awful hotel.

Then I'll dress up like a tart and hang out in the bar. When you come down, we'll pretend we don't know each other. I'll chat up a few blokes and you're free to chat up a few girls, and then we'll connect with each other."

"You want to pretend we're total strangers who go to bed together within an hour of meeting?" I stared at her. "Isn't that what happened when we met?"

"No good. You bought me dinner first. And by the time we got to bed it was six or seven hours later. I was thinking more like half a pint and 12 minutes."

When I confided in Peter that Pippa and I were in the middle of this little dilemma, he wondered if we'd ever tried toys. I said I didn't know if Pippa would go for that and anyway, after buying those videos, I had no intention of walking into another sex shop. He offered to send us one – "Something fancy, with four-speed stick shift and reverse" – if we'd name the kid after him. I broached the subject with Pippa, but she refused, stating that plastic things could never replace real things.

I argued, "A good battery can outlast a good man. And during the day we could always use it to mix cocktails."

But she held her ground. "No drugs. No toys. No food. No bondage. No other men. No other women. Nothing with four legs."

"I guess that means a sheep bearing handcuffs and a can of whipped cream is out of the question?"

A slow grin crossed her face. "Well, what I really meant was, no sheep and no handcuffs."

That night, I showed up with whipped cream.

She inspected the can, mumbled, "Too bad. I only use the low calorie sort," and promptly emptied it in my face.

When we finally ran out of ideas, I wondered if maybe she should see her gynaecologist.

Robert Lefever was a salty old guy – he'd delivered Pippa and her sister – now semi-retired. He saw only a few patients a week – as he put it, "Just to keep my hand in" – and devoted the rest of his time to breeding Siamese cats and growing prize-winning radishes. He greeted us at the front door of his old rambling house in Swiss Cottage, with his uncut white hair falling into his soft brown eyes, and led us into the sitting-room, where four cats glared at us suspiciously. "Tea?"

Pippa said no, and then I said no.

"How about a cat?"

This time we said no in unison.

"Radishes?"

"Perhaps later," Pippa said. "Yes. That would be nice."

He proposed, "Stirrups?"

"Not for me," I answered. "But Pippa will have two."

"What's the problem?"

"Babies," she told him.

"Oh good," he rubbed his hands together. "Miss the second one?"

She shook her head. "Can't even miss the first one."

"Ah. In that case, you'll probably have to come back. But if you do, I'll give you more radishes."

"I have to come back?"

He nodded. "I need a blood sample and it must be taken on the 21st day of your menstrual cycle. That's to make sure you're ovulating properly." Together they calculated the day for her appointment. "And, no sex for four days before the test." He turned to me. "What about you?"

"Thanks anyway. But if she's not having sex for those four days, then I won't either."

"I meant, do you fire blanks?"

"I don't know."

"Well, that's where we should start. It will make things easier on her if we can blame it on you." He went to his desk and scribbled a doctor's name, address and phone number on a piece of paper. "Call him tomorrow for an appointment and we'll find out."

I had to know, "How are we going to find out?"

Robert described the process.

I said right away, "I don't think so."

Pippa made eyes at me. "Sounds like fun. Can I come along?"

"Sounds like embarrassing," I said.

"You wouldn't be too embarrassed, would you, if this doctor had a nurse who looks like Kelly McGillis? Just in case you need a hand, dear."

"Enough with the jokes."

"Call him tomorrow." Robert patted me on the head and went to fetch some radishes.

I made an appointment with that doctor. And I was right. Being told to fill a little plastic jar, then having to deliver it to his nurse – who looked as much like Kelly McGillis as Jack Nicholson does – was one of the most awkward things I've ever had to do.

A week after our initial visit, Pippa returned for her blood test. Robert examined her and also took a urine sample, "Just for good measure." A few days later he rang to say that, at first glance, her plumbing seemed fine, that the urine sample showed absolutely nothing, that I'd passed my test – "You must have studied" – and that, as far as he could tell, everyone appeared to be playing with a full deck.

Pippa asked, what next, and he said, an ultrasound test. She wanted to know if it would hurt and he promised it wouldn't. I asked what it would show and he told us, "Masses."

"What does that mean?" Pippa looked at me, then at Robert. "Masses?"

"Any sort of blockage," he said. "For instance, ovarian cysts."

"Do you think there's something . . ."

"No, I don't. But we have to find out for certain."

She spent the next two days imagining the worst. "What happens if they find something?"

I tried to comfort her. "They're not going to find anything because there is nothing."

"Then why does he want me to have this test?"

"Because ... I don't know ... because that's the procedure."

"The procedure to find something. It happens to women my age all the time. Did you ever see *Love Story*?"

Pippa had never been sick a day in her life and the only time she'd ever been in a hospital was when she badly sprained her wrist at the age of 15 falling off a horse. I assured her, "It's going to be fine," but her apprehensions got to me too and I began wondering if there was something Robert wasn't telling us. At a clinic on Harley Street, I held her hand and watched a little screen while an ultrasound technician moved the scanner across her abdomen and showed me her insides.

Pippa kept asking, "Are there any masses?"

The technician didn't do much for her nerves by responding, "Your consultant will explain everything to you when he sees the results."

That night she was a wreck. The next morning, first thing, she was on the phone to Robert. He didn't have the results yet but promised to ring as soon as he saw them. I stayed home for her sake, although I wish I hadn't because she'd worked herself into such an awful state.

"Everything is going to be fine," I said.

"How do you know?"

"Because I know."

"Because you don't!"

When Robert called, around noon, she grabbed the phone and held it so tightly that her hand shook. "Is there anything?"

"No," he said. "Absolutely nothing. From what I can see, you've got gorgeous Fallopian tubes. Museum quality."

She subjected the poor guy to the third degree. "Are you sure? No masses? No cysts? No blockages? I mean, it's nothing like . . ." she had trouble saying it . . . "like c-a-n-c-e-r or anything?"

"Nothing of the kind."

"If you find anything . . . if there is anything, will you tell me?"

"If there was something wrong, of course I would tell you. But there isn't anything wrong."

"So why can't I get pregnant?"

"I don't know. But just so that you don't feel singled out, one couple in four faces some sort of problem in this area."

Pippa fell back onto the couch, emotionally frazzled, and tossed the phone to me. Robert repeated what he'd said to her. "Museum quality Fallopian tubes."

"So where do we go from here? And please don't say, the Tate."

"We keep looking for whatever is causing the problem. What I'd like to do is take a salpingogram X-ray."

"You want to do what?"

"Which one?" Pippa demanded. "What's he saying? Let me speak to him." She grabbed the phone. "What's wrong?"

He told her, "I want you to have a salpingogram X-ray."

"What is it? Why? Is it going to hurt?"

He said it wouldn't hurt and it didn't. In fact, it turned out to be nothing more than an ordinary X-ray, except that they filled her up with some fluid first.

When he saw the results he admitted, "I can't find anything wrong."

Next he ordered a laparoscopy. And this time when she asked, "Will it hurt," he answered, "You will be very comfortable."

That procedure is a wonder of medical science – a direct look at a woman's insides without all the hassle of exploratory surgery. An incision is made through the belly button and a kind of monocular is inserted so that a doctor can see whether or not something is getting in the way of fertilization.

Hearing Robert describe it, Pippa was terrorized. Making matters worse, she had two weeks to think about it before checking into the London Clinic.

They gave her something to drink to calm her down – she really needed it – then they knocked her out. That was the part I hated, seeing her fall asleep, scared like that, knowing that she was thinking there was always the possibility she'd never wake up.

The laparoscopy showed nothing either.

Because he couldn't find any physical impediment, Robert phoned me in the office to propose that the problem might be stress related. "Creating a life is a highly complex procedure and a lot of things have to be right for it to happen. The truth of the matter is that there are many aspects of it we don't understand. Didn't you ever hear stories about women who couldn't get pregnant no matter what they did, so they went out and adopted a child and then immediately they got pregnant? That's stress related. At least we think it is."

I had to accept, "This hasn't been easy on her nerves. Or mine."

He asked, "How do you think she'll take to the idea of artificial insemination?"

"I don't know."

"You'd be the donor, so it would still be your child. That's one option. But there are plenty of others. I'll sit down with the two of you and go over all of them whenever you want."

Afraid that she might think of artificial insemination as an admission of failure, I decided the best thing to do was invite Robert around for dinner, so that we could talk about our options in an atmosphere more congenial than his cat-laden office. Because I didn't want him to think we were looking for a way out of paying his fee, I said, consider it a house call. He reminded

325

me, gynaecologists don't do house calls. "Unless they're still in medical school and trying to make out with their neighbour's wife."

When I mentioned to Pippa that I'd spoken to Robert, she was anything but pleased. "Why? What's wrong?"

"Nothing's wrong. I just thought it would be nice if we had a meal with him."

"You're not telling me something."

"There's nothing to tell."

"Does he want to see me?"

"No, he wants to eat dinner."

"How did you invite him? Did you ring him or did he ring you?"

"I phoned him."

"Why?"

"To invite him for a meal."

"Why?"

"Pippa . . . if you don't want him to come to dinner, just say so."

"I don't want him to come to dinner."

Greatly embarrassed, I phoned Robert to explain the situation. But he was very understanding. "It's nothing to worry about. I'm afraid being slightly irrational is part of the syndrome."

I wanted to know, "How does it end?"

"Sometimes they get pregnant. Sometimes they have a nervous breakdown."

"What am I supposed to do in the meantime?"

"Get her pregnant before she cracks up."

That summer, for the first time since the day I met her, Pippa refused to have sex with me. "It doesn't work. I can't get pregnant."

"Unless we keep trying, or look towards professional help, you're only going to get more uptight about this. There's no way I can mail it in, so in that sense, we don't have a lot of choice."

"I'm not the one who's getting uptight."

"Robert wants us to go to a clinic . . ."

"What for? To be treated like a prize-winning cow? So that you can play the grinning bull while some doctor shoves all those little Bays up inside of me with a plunger?"

I thought maybe I could reason with her. "Robert and I are both on your side."

"Robert, Robert, Robert. That's all you ever talk about any more. You and Robert. So why don't the two of you get pregnant?"

"Okay . . ." I changed the subject. "Maybe we should go to Cannes for a few weeks. We'll sit on the beach . . ."

"We've already done that and it didn't work."

"Then we'll go any place you want. You name it. How about Rio?"

"Why?" She asked, "Do you think you can get me pregnant in South America?"

Two nights later I walked into the flat and found Pippa on the couch, crying. "Why won't you give me a baby?"

I went to hold her. "There are still lots of options . . ."

But she moved away. "That's all you ever talk about. Options. Well I have an option too." She took a deep breath. "I'm leaving you."

She went to her parents that night and stayed there for six days. No matter what I said or did, she wouldn't come home. She wouldn't listen to me or to her mother or to her father. They were just as concerned as I was and, when they tried to reason with her, she left and went to Cannes. I decided, she'll get over this if I just let her alone. So I sent her a note saying, "Take whatever time you need. I'm here." And ten days later she wrote back, "I want a divorce."

At first, I told myself she doesn't mean it. But every time I got her on the phone, she repeated it. She said she wanted to speak with a solicitor. I waited a week, hoping she'd change her mind. Then a second week. Then a third week. Then I went to Cannes, to speak to her face to face, but the moment I walked into the apartment she flew off the handle. All she wanted to do was fight with me. I finally lost my temper and returned to London. I resigned myself to the fact that this was what she intended to do. I asked Gerald to handle everything for her. He agreed to take the case as a personal favour to us. It was, he pointed out, his first divorce. I reminded him, mine too.

Even though, intellectually, I was willing to accept that my marriage was over, I was heartbroken.

Gerald advised that I hire someone to represent me, but I refused. I said I would not contest the divorce, that I would give Pippa anything she wanted.

I didn't go out of my way to mention to anyone that Pippa had left me. But I didn't keep it a secret either and whenever someone asked how she was, I answered, she's living in France for a while.

My life revolved around the office and our apartment. And because the apartment seemed so empty, the office got the larger share of my time. I didn't want to go out. I didn't want to see anyone. I spent as much time as I could in the office and, when weekends rolled around, I spent as much time as I could at home, asleep.

I hadn't felt so lonely since I first came to Britain.

Everything changed, suddenly, one Saturday morning, a couple of months after Pippa left. The phone rang and a familiar voice said, "I heard that you're living alone."

It took several seconds before I could respond, "I am."

There was a long pause. "Would you like some company?"

It took several more seconds before I could say, "Yes."

Half an hour later, Francesca stepped back into my life.

She kissed me on the cheek and nearly drowned me

under a wave of *déjà vu*. We made small talk for a few minutes. I felt off balance. She asked if I had mint tea. I apologized that I didn't. She said, "I've missed you."

I said, "I hated you for leaving me like that."

She said, "I've thought about you."

Suddenly I flashed back to the time I went to see Elizabeth. We were having the same conversation.

"Why are you here? Did someone throw you out?"

"I needed to . . ." There was a strange look in her eye, a look I'd seen before. "I wanted to see you."

We stared at each other for several seconds and then, without saying anything more, I took her in my arms. And now it all came rushing back to me. Her smell. Her taste. The feel of her hips against mine.

We tore at each other's clothes.

Two months later she told me she was pregnant.

My life was already in a tailspin.

Gerald and Viv had gone to see Pippa – without saying anything to me – had stayed at the apartment with her over a weekend, and had managed to convince her that, before she filed for a divorce, it would be best if she agreed to a trial separation.

He came back to London with a deal already worked out.

Title to the flat in Cannes would be transferred into Pippa's name during a six-month cooling-off period, to do with as she chose. She could keep it, sell it, rent it, or paint it orange. I would also provide her with £5,000 a month for personal expenses, above and beyond the expenses I normally incurred on that flat, such as the mortgage, insurance and taxes. At the end of the six months, I would consent to "a reasonable" settlement, which would be negotiated at that time.

In turn, Pippa would meet me in London for three sessions of marriage counselling and attend at least one meeting with specialists at a fertility clinic, as recommended by Robert Lefever. There was no obligation on either of us to continue the marriage or to conceive a child. But she would, at least, have to go through the motions of taking professional advice designed to get us back together.

Gerald was ever so proud of himself. "It's a way to save your marriage."

I had to tell him, "I don't know if I want to save it."

He was shocked. "Why?"

I gave him the first excuse that came into my head. "It may not be worth saving."

He didn't believe it.

I tried, "She won't come back, even if I do agree to this."

He said, "She will. Ring her. Ask her. You'll see."

So I did. I asked her, "If I sign this agreement, when do you want to come to London?"

Pippa answered, "I don't know if I really want to. I have to think about it. I'll let you know."

I now had the perfect cop-out. I told Gerald, "When she calls and says she's ready to come here for counselling, then I'll think about signing the agreement."

There was no more talk about a trial separation.

But that didn't make things any easier.

I didn't want Francesca staying at my place because it felt somehow as if I was violating Pippa. And I was uncomfortable sleeping at Francesca's, because I kept thinking to myself, if Pippa calls in the middle of the night and doesn't find me home, she'll know what's going on and that would hurt her. Love is all too often a no-win situation. So Francesca and I would go to supper and wind up in bed together, only to see one of us eventually get up to go home.

Confusion filled my head like a thick fog, as the irony of her pregnancy consumed me. "What do you want to do about it?"

Typically, Francesca threw the question straight back at me. "What do you want to do about it?"

I told her the truth. "I don't know."

It obviously wasn't what she wanted to hear. "There was a time when you would have begged me to carry your child."

There was nothing I could say.

Francesca stared at me, obviously waiting for me to tell her that I wanted her to have my child. And when I didn't say it, she rubbed the side of my face, then pulled herself out of bed. As the sheets fell away from her, she turned and stood in front of me, putting both hands on her still flat belly. "Do you recall that when we first became lovers?" Her voice was just above a whisper. "It was all about someone's death."

I knew she wanted me to reach out to her.

"How curious . . ." she said.

But I was afraid that if she came to me now I would lose Pippa forever.

". . . that all these years later it should end because of someone's birth."

Her foetus was aborted in a clinic in Switzerland. When she phoned to tell me, all I could say was, "I'm sorry."

All she would say is, "It's one hell of a way to find the ring."

I have never stopped wondering what might have been. Would our son have had his mother's eyes. Would our daughter have had her mother's smile. I have never stopped wondering what life would have been like had I not hesitated so long to take that fork in the road.

A week before Christmas, Pippa rang from France and asked me if I would come to Cannes. I didn't want to say, "I don't know," because I didn't know how to tell her how mixed up I was. So I took the coward's way out and said, "Yeah, sure."

I brought a couple of gifts for her. She said she was embarrassed that she hadn't bought anything for me. I told her it didn't matter. She asked what I'd been up to. I pretended not to know what she meant.

So she came right out with it. "Have you slept with anybody?"

A lie wasn't going to save my marriage but, I knew, the truth would end it. I told her, "No."

She said, "Me neither."

We didn't go to bed together that night, or the following night, or the night after that. I didn't mention it and she didn't either. I slept on the couch because it seemed as if that's what she wanted. Then came Christmas Eve and, when I asked her if she'd like to go out, she said no, she'd like to go to bed with me. So we did. Later that night she told me she'd missed me and when she said that I cried in her arms.

Pippa and I returned to London together just after New Year's and, without saying anything to me, she made an appointment for us at the fertility clinic. But we never got there. All by herself, she missed her period. A month after that, she went to see Robert.

I was pacing the floor of his sitting-room when I heard him whoop, "Break out the radishes!"

Chapter Twenty-six

Andrew Carpenter's article ran in the *Sunday Times*. But instead of a profile of me, he'd written a rambling treatise headlined "Abundant in the '80s – A Cropper in the '90s", and served me up as his sacrificial lamb.

The three column colour photo of me was not particularly bad – except that it made me look a bit heavy – but the caption under it was a really cheap shot.

It read, "Chairman Radisson in his extremely plush, 18-telephone-line office advising, 'Never invest in a company where the chairman's office is more comfortable than his home.'"

He knew damn well I didn't have 18 lines and he knew damn well my office was not extremely plush. What's more, the son of a bitch had never been in my home, so what the hell right did he have to make such a judgement?

Still, I could have lived with that. Where he put my head on a platter was further into the article, when he explained that many high flyers from the '80s had run up against the law in the '90s. It wasn't enough to detail Gerald Ronson and the Guinness Scandal or Asil Nadir and the demise of Polly Peck. He had to add, "According to well-placed sources at the Department of Trade and Industry, Radisson is currently being investigated by Fraud Squad officers from the City of London Police on insider dealing allegations surrounding the movement of shares in Maxwell Communications Corporation on the day Robert Maxwell died."

That was the killer.

He was publishing an unsubstantiated rumour in a quality newspaper, citing an unnamed source, which seriously undermined my position.

And there was virtually no way I could effectively defend myself against it.

Of course, I immediately dialled Carpenter's home number. His answering machine was on so I left the message that I'd like to speak to him. But the cowardly bastard never called back.

Friends rang me at home all day Sunday. Most of them thought I'd gotten a rough deal from Carpenter. A few added, it's your own fault for giving the guy an interview.

Professional acquaintances rang me in the office all day Monday. Patty fielded the calls, assuring everyone that it was business as usual. Although I suspect most of those people didn't believe her.

Conspicuous by his absence was Clement.

I worried that he hadn't called and my anxiety was confirmed when I received his faxed letter formally notifying me that BFCS's auditors in Switzerland had reassessed the assets held by Pennstreet Properties of Great Britain Trust, SA, and valued them at £2.28 million. As this was below the agreed £3 million threshold, he regretted to inform me that the bank was asking for full title to those assets. He also wanted me to make up the shortfall. In other words, I was supposed to turn those assets over to BFCS and settle the £4 million outstanding debt by coming up with £1.72 million cash. He gave me 15 days to manage it and pointed out, "Your inability to meet the payment of these monies now due will put you in breach of your agreement on the financing of Howe Wharf."

So Clement had at last surrendered to Francesca.

I cursed her, then I cursed the fact that I no longer

had that money in the Phonna and Pippawool accounts. If I sacrificed any assets now, the banks holding paper on them would also demand payment. The same thing would happen if word got around that BFCS was on my case. Lemmings that they are, every banker in town would call in his debts and wipe me out.

At any other time I could easily raise a couple of million quid by selling some Pennstreet shares, but to do that now risked triggering a downward spiral of my own share price. The last thing I could afford was to have it head so far south that it tripped off a massive computerized selling spree.

We had operating cash in the bank, but I hesitated touching that. I could always do a Maxwell, except our pension fund was minuscule compared to his. Anyway, I didn't have a yacht to jump off of. I'd either have to roll over and play dead, or fight back. And, because I'm not very good at playing dead, I figured I didn't have a lot of choice. I faxed Clement's letter to Gerald, then phoned to ask him, "How long can we tie them up?"

Gerald said he was looking at the fax now. "I'll have to get back to you."

"Ballpark figure. How long?"

"I don't know."

"Please, tell me something. Anything."

"Okay," he said. "How about a week or two?"

"A week or two? I want a year or two."

"For God's sake, Bay, let me work on it and I'll do the best I can."

I hung up and faxed Clement's letter to Peter. I added a handwritten page that simply said, "Francesca's revenge."

When Gerald rang back that afternoon, I thought he had an answer for me. Instead he asked, "What are you doing on Wednesday?"

"Why?"

"I heard from Gareth Evans. He and Maloney have been onto the cops. They want to speak with you."

335

"Who?"

"Aren't you listening? The cops. Evans said it doesn't now appear as if they are going to arrest you. The proper term is, you're going to help the police with their inquiries."

"When?"

"8:30 a.m. Wednesday at Wood Street Police Station."

"What do I do in the meantime?"

"Rehearse."

Gerald, Gareth, Andy and I met in my office the following morning at 10. We spent most of the day going over every question the cops might ask, then drawing up suitable answers to them. I felt sort of like the President or the Prime Minister being briefed for a press conference.

Did you have any insider knowledge of Robert Maxwell's death?

I did not.

How did you hear about Maxwell's death before it was announced by the media?

My partner Peter Goddard phoned me from Las Palmas.

Why did you sell two blocks of shares in the hours before Maxwell's death was announced?

It was like going to the bookmakers. I was betting that when the news was announced, the shares would drop in value.

Why didn't you tell this to the Stock Exchange when they asked you about it?

I felt it was none of their business.

But it is clearly their business.

Yes, I know that now. I made a mistake. However, I did not, at any time, have any inside knowledge nor did I, at any time, trade on inside information.

We went over it again and again, making sure that my answers were succinct, making sure that my answers were to the point, making sure that my answers only filled in the blanks left by their questions, making sure I did not hand them any superfluous information.

By the time Gareth and Andy left, just after lunch, the stress of all this had brought on a horrible, throbbing headache. I took a couple of aspirin, then asked Gerald, "What about BFCS?"

He said, "Maybe we can hold Clement off for a month or two. But he's put the knife in. I'm afraid this is only the beginning."

I went to my teletext screen to check the Pennstreet share price. We were down another couple of pennies. "I guess I've got to raise some cash."

"Are your own assets safe?"

"Sort of."

"Maybe you should do that first."

Strolling to the window and staring down towards the street, I noticed the bum was no longer there. "Even he's moved on."

"Who?"

"No one." I went back to my desk. "It's not Clement who's put the knife in, it's Francesca."

"Does it matter?"

"I feel betrayed."

"How do you think she feels?"

I didn't answer him. "What do we do about Clement?"

"We opt for benign obfuscation." He pulled a pad out of his attaché case and together we drafted a response. We will continue to meet our contractual obligations to you but at the same time will vigorously defend our position. We would have to see your auditors' valuations. We would want auditors of our own choosing to make a report. So on, so on, and so forth.

When we had the letter worded the way he wanted it, Gerald left for his office. As soon as he did, I phoned Roderick in Nassau and announced, "It's time to amputate the octopus."

He said, "Absolutely sure?"

I said, "Positive. I just hope it's not too late."

The next morning I left my flat at exactly 7:30. I found a cab right away and, as there was no traffic, I arrived at the Wood Street Police Station by 7:55.

Facing a slim, buttressed pure-Gothic tower built by Christopher Wren in 1696 – he didn't purposely stick it in the middle of the street but that's where it is today – the front half of the police station is a four-storey abomination, slapped together in 1965 out of some dirty white stone that is supposed to look like Wren's stone. The back half is a 13- or 14-storey office block – also in dirty white stone – with a forest of large, oddly shaped antennas perched on the roof.

Astonished that the City fathers could ever have permitted someone to build something so awful, I then realized that just on the other side of the tower – diagonally across the street – was the modern, faceless, highrise, equally unattractive headquarters of Hill Samuel.

And suddenly it dawned on me that Chris Wren and I shared a common plight – trapped between the cops and the bank.

It also occurred to me that, of the two, he was the survivor. His epitaph lives despite the bad taste that all too often surrounds it. I was fearing mine might read, "Here lies Bay Radisson, killed during the massacre at Wood Street."

A uniformed police officer at the front desk asked if I had an appointment. I said yes and told him my name. He looked through a log book, found it and nodded, "Right. Just a minute, please." He took his phone, dialled an extension, announced that I was here, hung up and asked me to please wait for a minute.

Eventually a large man with close-cropped dark hair wearing a decently tailored grey suit appeared to say,

"Mr Radisson? Thank you for coming here this morning. My name is Detective Inspector Nigel Salt."

We shook hands and he motioned to me to follow him. He led me into a room where he explained to me that the Custody Sergeant – the officer sitting behind the high desk – needed to record my visit. Then he said in a loud, clear voice, "This is Mr Bay Radisson. He has come here this morning of his own volition to help me with certain inquiries."

Looking at me, he continued in the same tone of voice. "It is my duty to inform you that you are not under arrest and that you may leave at any time. You are entitled to have a solicitor present with you. But it is also my duty to inform you that anything you say to me during these inquiries may be taken down to be used in evidence."

I stared back. "What does that mean?"

The Custody Sergeant, a skinny, sharp-faced man in his early 50s answered, "In America you call it the Miranda Act. On television and in films the police always say, you've been read your rights."

"I can leave at any time?"

"That's right." The Custody Sergeant motioned towards the door. "You've come here of your own volition. You can leave here of your own volition. Fair enough?"

I looked at Salt. "And as soon as I step outside, you'll arrest me, is that it?"

He said, "Not necessarily. This way please."

His ninth-floor office was a narrow room that seemed to run half the length of the building. There were ten desks scattered around – some facing others, some looking out at the windows – and three men already there. The rest of the space was taken up with straight-backed armless chairs, filing cabinets and cardboard boxes filled with documents.

Salt motioned for me to have a seat next to his desk at the very end of the room and asked if I'd like coffee or tea. I told him coffee would be fine.

Another cop arrived – he was short, balding and

with a thick neck – who introduced himself as Detective
Sergeant Booton. Instead of offering to shake hands, he
merely handed me a Styrofoam cup of coffee diluted in
too much milk. "You did say white, didn't you?"

I put it on a desk and left it there.

Salt threw himself into his chair. "We'll go into the
other room as soon as everyone gets here."

I said okay. "I'm in no hurry."

"We'd like to get this over with as soon as possible."

"So that you can charge me with something I haven't
done?"

"So that we can resolve the matter to everyone's
satisfaction."

I was seriously disadvantaged and both of us knew it.
This was an away game where the home team brought
the ball, made up the rules and had the referee in their
pocket. "When do you bring out the rubber hose?"

He shook his head. "Mr Radisson . . . I don't know
if you've ever had any dealings with the police before,
either here or in the United States, but I assure you that
for the time we spend together, I will be as courteous
to you as you are to me. I have a job to do. I have
to determine whether or not any crimes have been
committed. I hold no personal animosity towards you.
I hope, in fact, that when this is over I will be able to
say, thank you for your cooperation and I'm sorry to
have troubled you. I hope that when our inquiries are
over, you will be able to go about your life and I will be
able to go about mine, without either of us harbouring
any ill will."

I stared at him. "For a cop, you speak well."

He almost smiled. "I think I know what you're trying
to say. So, thank you."

Gareth Evans arrived. He and Salt had met before.
Then Gerald appeared. Booton fetched two more cups
of coffee. That's when Andy Maloney showed up. "Why
if it isn't Mr Salt."

They shook hands. "How are you, Andy?"

340

"Just earning a crust," he replied. "Why don't you spring my client right now. I guarantee we'll make fools of you if this ever comes to court."

Salt looked at me. "You've hired a good guy." Then he motioned, "Gentlemen, if you'll all come this way."

Booton delivered the coffees, then shook Maloney's hand too. "How you keeping Andy?"

He looked at me. "Have you met the Boot?"

I nodded.

Maloney winked and when Booton's back was turned Andy mouthed the word, "Stupid."

We followed Salt into a tiny office where a metal desk had been cleared to be used as a conference table. I sat on one side of it, crammed in between Gerald and Andy. Evans sat at the end. Salt, Booton and a third man in his late 20s – he was introduced to us as Mr Crane – sat on the other side. They brought with them several large pale blue folders, filled with paperwork. Salt then asked a young woman to come in, introduced her as Miss Billings, and said she would take notes.

Salt opened the meeting by reintroducing everyone present – for the sake of Miss Billings' minutes – stating the date and time, and mentioning that Mr Crane, who was an accountant assigned to the Serious Fraud Office, was present to help them all understand some of the more complicated financial aspects of the case.

Immediately, Maloney pointed to Crane. "I don't want him here."

"Why?" Salt asked.

"Firstly, because this is not being handled by the SFO. Unless they are assuming responsibility for the case, I see no reason why I should permit my client to have any dealings with anyone from the SFO. Secondly, because my client is not an accountant and cannot be expected to answer any questions about his company accounts. Mr Crane will have to leave."

That delayed things for nearly an hour, while Salt

consulted with his boss and Crane made a hasty set of notes so that Salt could ask the questions instead.

When we were ready to begin again, Salt showed his displeasure at having lost Crane from his side of the table. "May I remind you that I want to make this as easy on all of us as we can. If you gentlemen are here to help, that's fine. If you are here merely to encumber . . ."

Maloney cut in. "Mr Radisson has volunteered to come here. He has not been charged with any crime."

So the interview started a second time.

Now it was Salt and Booton against the four of us, with Miss Billings tagging along for good measure.

Salt began by officially informing us that he was investigating the charges of insider dealing, fraud and conspiracy to commit fraud. He listed several violations of the Companies Act. He also said that an investigation might be pending concerning my tax status and my immigration status. He said this meeting, and the information he was able to obtain from me during it, was intended to clear up several points and repeated that anything said in this meeting could and might be put down in evidence should the case ever come to trial.

The first area he wanted to discuss was my background. He wanted to know about my real name and how I obtained a passport.

Evans stopped him. "My client will only answer questions relating to matters within your jurisdiction. If there is an immigration case or a tax case to answer, that will have to be done separately."

Salt claimed he was well within his jurisdiction to bring up these issues. Evans insisted he was not. They argued about it for nearly 20 minutes when Salt conceded, "We'll put it to one side for the time being," and moved on. He asked me about Pennstreet and our related companies.

Maloney held up his hand to stop me, and suggested Salt consult our annual report. "It's a public company. Everything you need to know is there."

342

Salt checked that one off his list and tried, "How about Robert Maxwell? Let's discuss your share dealings on the day he died."

No one stopped me, so I told him the truth, precisely as we'd rehearsed it. I explained how Peter had phoned me and all I did was place a bet with my broker. "It was no different than ringing a bookie."

"But you did not deal in your own name?"

Maloney cut in. "Who said so?"

Salt answered, "The broker."

Maloney demanded, "And so what?"

Salt said, "If Mr Radisson didn't deal in his own name, I'd like to know why?"

"I seem to think that's probably considered common practice." Maloney wondered, "Why would he be obliged to buy or sell shares in his own name and how is that related to the insider dealing charge?"

"It may be related to a fraud charge."

"Who did he defraud?"

"That's what we're trying to establish."

Maloney barked, "Go fishing on your own time."

The morning wore on like that, painfully slow, with Salt asking questions and my counsel letting me answer only the ones we'd rehearsed, which turned out to be about one in every five or six. I could see that it was frustrating for Salt, but that was his problem. Gerald and Gareth and Andy were there to make sure that I wasn't going to hand them any presents.

By lunchtime I was exhausted. It didn't seem as if we'd gotten very far and, judging by the pile of notes Salt had in front of him, we still had a long way to go. Gareth suggested we take a break. Salt asked us to please come back by 2:15.

The four of us found a pub around the corner and had some bad sandwiches. While the lawyers munched on theirs and drank warm beer, I stared at the sandwich on my plate, wondering where the bread ended and the turkey began.

"So far so good," Gerald said.

I pushed my meal away.

He said, "Doesn't look like they've got much of a case."

"We're scoring and they're not," Maloney added. "So far they've missed every corner."

Evans corrected him. "Bay only understands American football metaphors."

"Go ahead," Andy said. "Be my guest."

"Okay," Evans poked my arm. "Here's an American football metaphor. It's first and goal and we're on the one-yard line."

Gerald asked, "What does that mean?"

"It means," Andy explained, "they don't have shit."

I looked at the three of them and mumbled quietly, "Salt hasn't even started."

Before we left the pub, I rang Pippa and told her everything was fine and that I fully intended to be home for dinner.

She said, "If they arrest you, will you ring me right away?"

I tried joking, "They only allow one phone call and I thought instead of ringing you I'd call room service for my last cigarette. You know, before the firing squad."

"That's not funny."

"Of course I'll call you," I said. "But only if they arrest me. If they let me go, I'll come home and pretend to be a just released ex-convict with tattoos so I can jump on your bones."

She didn't find that very funny, either.

Back at Salt's office, the questions continued.

We stayed there all afternoon, stopping only twice. Once when my head was pounding so badly that I needed some water to take two aspirins. And later when Salt announced it was tea time. Booton produced seven cups of hot water and three tea bags. I passed.

Now Salt took a new tack. "Tell me about Roderick Hays-White."

I shrugged, as if to say, there's nothing to tell.

Salt probed, "You know him, don't you?"

"Of course, I do." I tried to figure out where he would have found Roderick's name. My first thought was Francesca. "I've known him for many years."

"What's your relationship with Mr Hays-White?"

I sort of explained it. I said he was a company formation agent and that we'd done business with him over the years.

"Now, tell me about a company called ..." Salt fumbled with some papers ... "Here it is. A British Virgin Islands company called Long Beach Properties."

I sat back and rubbed my eyes, pretending that my headache had not yet gone away, trying to think of what I could say. "If memory serves ... let's see, Long Beach Properties ..." I settled on, "Yeah, they owned, at one point, a tract of land along the Thames that we eventually bought." I tried not to make it seem as if I was unduly concerned. But deep down, I realized, if they got this from Francesca, then it was just the tip of the iceberg. "I seem to remember that Long Beach owned it immediately before the people we bought it from."

He asked right away. "And a Cayman Islands company called Britannica Consolidated Trust?"

I decided to take my chances. "Never heard of it."

"Are you sure?"

"Doesn't ring any bells."

"How about a UK company called VisionStar?"

"Those are the people I bought that property from. It's called Howe Wharf." This had to be Francesca. No one else would have known these names.

"And who is VisionStar?"

"Property speculators."

"Who owns it? Who runs it?"

"It doesn't work that way."

"It doesn't?" He wanted to know, "How does it work?"

345

I described how we'd dealt through lawyers and never had to meet any of the owners.

"And what does Roderick Hays-White have to do with Long Beach Properties, or Britannica Consolidated Trust or VisionStar?"

I looked him straight in the eyes and said, "You'd have to ask him."

He snapped, "I'm asking you."

I repeated, "You'd have to ask him."

With that, Salt and Booton excused themselves and left the room. Miss Billings left also. Now Gerald nodded to me. "Well done."

"You did good." Maloney agreed. "They're about to punt. It's another American football metaphor. They don't have a case."

I looked at Gareth. "What do you think?"

He was up-beat too. "I think our friend Mr Salt knows the charade is over."

Ten minutes later, when Salt stepped back into the room, he announced, "Mr Radisson, you are free to leave."

Maloney challenged him. "Does this mean the investigation is concluded?"

Salt said, "No."

"Will you be charging Mr Radisson?"

"Not for the time being."

Evans demanded, "What areas are still being investigated?"

Salt said, "All of them."

Maloney stood up. "No more cooperation. You guys don't have anything and you know it. This is a fishing expedition. Either arrest him now or announce that the whole thing is done."

But Salt said, "Sorry, no."

When the four of us stepped outside, there was a reporter and a photographer waiting to speak to us. "Have you been charged?"

Evans answered, "No, Mr Radisson has not been

charged. Nor have we seen any evidence that a crime has been committed. Mr Radisson denies any wrong doing and is more than prepared to take whatever action is necessary in order to defend himself. He particularly resents whatever aspersions have been cast on his good character. That's all we have to say."

I kept half of my promise to Pippa and was home for dinner. I couldn't manage the rest.

By the time we got into bed my head was killing me. I took a couple of pills and started to fall asleep. I remember telling myself that lying to the police was bad for my health. But then, I also remember reassuring myself that telling the truth would have been even worse.

Chapter Twenty-seven

The Irish have a neat word, which is "begrudgers." It refers to those people who, all too obviously, take enormous joy in condemning success.

I heard the expression for the first time on a trip to Dublin, when I went over there to look at a small woollens business that I thought we might be interested in acquiring. Although the deal didn't work out, the guy who owned the company – his name was Joseph O'Flynn but everyone called him Joe O. – took me out for a meal. By the time we got to dessert, he was already three courses into the difference between the British and the Americans.

The waiter had just delivered dainty cups of Guinness sorbet – I remember thinking at the time, this is a dish worthy of Clement's palate – when Joe O. asked me, "Do you know the story of the chap driving down the street in his big, shiny Rolls-Royce?"

I said I didn't.

"Well, he passes this British bloke who scowls, 'Look at that flash bastard in his fancy motor.' And then he passes this American bloke who says, 'Gee, I'll bet if I work hard I could have a car like that too.' You see, the British are begrudgers."

I never forgot the Guinness sorbet. But, until now, I hadn't realized how many begrudgers I knew. Wherever I looked, there seemed to be long lines of folk ready, willing and anxious to hurl me to the lions, exactly as they'd already done with Robert Maxwell and Asil Nadir. Begrudge them perhaps. Begrudge me not. I was screaming, there is a difference. But most of them didn't care to know.

In the wake of Andrew Carpenter's article, we got bills at the office from suppliers who normally extended credit from 30 to 60 days — I paid them and cancelled our accounts — and bills at home, including one from our dentist who said that, in the light of our current battle against bankruptcy, he would have to demand immediate payment. I sent him a cheque and vowed to take my teeth elsewhere.

While I'm sure that I misread the milkman's look when I passed him on the street one morning, Pippa did overhear the woman who lives downstairs from us saying to a lady who lives next door, "I always suspected he was one of them." Pippa had no doubt the two old bags were speaking about me because, as soon as they spotted her, they shut up. She said she was tempted to ask, "Was one of them whats?" But at the last minute she decided it was probably so ungrammatical that they would think she was one of them too.

The begrudgers also sent letters about me to the *Sunday Times*, who published two of them. The first, from some guy in London whom I'd never heard of, said, "I've known Radisson for years and he's only getting what he deserves." The second, from a woman in Leicester, read, "The world would be a better place if people weren't so greedy."

Frankly, I didn't understand the point of either letter, but Peter claimed it was obvious and began singing, "They all laughed at Christopher Columbus, when he said the world was round."

"I don't think so."

"Aren't the old songs the best? The Rolling Stones might still be around today if they could sing Hoagy Carmichael."

"Hoagy Carmichael?" I shook my head. "Peter, I can

honestly say that Hoagy Carmichael is the last person on my mind these days."

"How about Robert Fulton?"

"Another terrific composer. And the second to last person on my mind."

"You don't even know who he is, do you?"

"Who, Fulton? He invented the steamboat. It was called the *Clermont*."

"No," he corrected, "Robert Fulton invented the steam engine and the way he proved that it worked was to put it on a boat called the *Clermont*."

"Whatever. Thanks for the history lesson. But if I don't get off the phone, we're going to be history too."

"I know for a fact that you don't know the story about Robert Fulton and the steam engine. And you know that I know. But that's okay. Because I'm going to tell it to you, anyway."

"I never had any doubts." I sat back and let him have his way.

"So Robert Fulton, who invented the steam engine, decided to take it down to the river one day and hook it up to his boat, which was, yes, called the *Clermont*. Of course, a crowd soon gathered to watch. When he tried to start the engine and it wouldn't turn over, the crowd began chanting, 'It will never work. It will never work.' Well, suddenly, the engine started, it did work, and the *Clermont* began moving up stream. And now the crowd chanted, 'It will never stop. It will never stop.'"

I asked, "What does that have to do with Hoagy Carmichael?"

"It's the letters in the *Sunday Times*."

"Okay. I get the point. But don't worry about those letters. I haven't given them a second thought. The world is filled with begrudgers."

"Begrudgers?" He was genuinely surprised. "How do you know the word begrudgers? Say, did you ever hear that one about the difference between the British and the French . . ."

350

I only managed to get off the phone with him because Patty came in to say that Clement was waiting on another line.

"Long time no hear, stranger."

"Bay, you wouldn't believe what it's been like here." He sounded especially jovial. "It has been crazy. You know, I'd planned on being away this week but I couldn't even consider a trip, that's how crazy things have been here."

I said sternly, "I guess it hasn't been so crazy around there that you didn't have time to call in my loan."

"Ah that . . ." He said softly, "I have to speak to you about that. It is not what it seems on the surface. I should have rung you earlier, because I need to speak to you about that, but it's been so crazy . . ."

I interrupted, "Let's meet right now."

"Now? No. No," he said. "No. I don't think right now would be a good idea. But tonight, if you like."

"Tonight? You mean, after dark? When nobody can see us meeting?"

He forced a laugh. "That's what I have always loved about you. Your sense of humour."

I wasn't laughing. "Where and when?"

"I know the best place." He offered, "Come to my apartment for dinner. Come alone. I am sure your wife won't mind. Perhaps I should send her flowers to apologize. Yes, I will arrange that. Please be there around 7:30. Do you mind eating early? I will personally cook for you."

By the time I got home, a large bouquet of flowers had arrived for Pippa. Clement's note said, "Thank you for letting him have a boys' night out."

"Why is he sending me flowers?" She demanded, "Who else is going to be there?"

I said right away, "No one."

"That had better be the case."

"It is."

And she repeated, "It had better be."

*   *   *

Clement lived at the Barbican, which when the complex was built on the edge of the City of London – combining apartments, offices and a centre for the arts – was hailed as one of Britain's major architectural achievements. But that was before anyone tried to find anything there.

The first time I went to the Barbican – it was for theatre with Francesca – we couldn't find the entrance. The next time was a couple of years later to visit Clement – he'd just moved into Cromwell Tower – and I couldn't find him either. I did somehow locate the main entrance to the theatre – two years too late – and when I asked for Cromwell Tower, people there politely directed me to Shakespeare Tower. After I found Shakespeare Tower, and asked for Cromwell Tower, people there politely directed me back to the theatre.

Ever since that night, wandering around the Barbican for over an hour – seething with frustration – I have proclaimed my eagerness to make a hefty donation to any movement capable of lobbying a bill through Parliament that would hold architects criminally responsible for their designs.

Clement had the duplex-penthouse, a beautiful four-bedroomed flat on the 39th and 40th floors, with some sensational views. His Filipino maid, Tita, greeted me at the door and showed me into the kitchen. I was relieved to find Clement alone, busy at the stove.

"Where's your chef's hat?"

Tied into a red and white striped apron – with the words, "*Banquier Extraordinaire*" in bold letters across the front – he swung around, sporting a wooden spoon in one hand and a glass of champagne in the other. "Vintage Krug is God's way of telling us he loves us." Pointing with the spoon to the bottle sitting in an ice bucket on a large butcher block, he said, "There's a glass just there. As you can see, I am much too busy to play the perfect host." Then he moved back to the stove and stirred something, before saying over his shoulder, "Tonight I am serving you duck with my special three-mustard sauce, on a bed of wild rice, and *fraises au poivre*."

"What's that?"

"Strawberries in pepper."

I suggested, "It sounds better in French."

"It is delicious in any language."

"Strawberries in pepper with wild rice?"

"Yes," he answered right away, before realizing that's not what he meant. "No. Of course not. No, the wild rice goes with the duck and three mustard sauce. The strawberries in pepper is for dessert."

"Oh." I poured myself a glass of champagne.

"If only you understood how hard I have worked to make you a memorable meal."

"Clement, I can say without hesitation that some of the most memorable meals I've ever had have been with you."

He mistook that for a compliment. "I am flattered."

Now I wanted to know, "How come you sicked your auditors on us?"

He stirred his sauce ... "Auditors?" ... took a sip of champagne and motioned for me to smell his sauce. "Must we discuss them at the same time we are discussing food?"

"Yes." His three-mustard sauce smelled exactly like mustard.

Dipping his wooden spoon in the pan, he stuck it in his mouth, let his eyes roll in ecstasy, then offered the rest to me. "You know I can't control the bank's auditors."

I declined the lick. "And of course it was just routine that they started looking into my business with the bank."

"They look into everyone's business with the bank." He pushed the spoon closer to me. "Come on, don't be shy."

I thought of saying, it's not the sauce that bothers me, it's where the spoon has been, but I didn't have the heart. So I crooked my pinky, stuck it into the spoon and put some sauce on the end of my tongue. It had a distinctive flavour and was, to my surprise, very good. But I couldn't let him know that. "Doesn't taste anything like strawberries."

"It's not supposed to taste like strawberries. This is the three-mustard sauce for the duck."

I nodded. "Tell me about your auditors."

He moved to his oven and brought out a dish with the duck pieces already sliced and cooked pink. "They're a law unto themselves."

"Of course," I said sarcastically, "and your hands are tied."

"I told you it's not necessarily what it seems." He put the duck pieces on a serving platter, took a pan that was filled with wild rice, spread the rice around the duck and then added his sauce. "First you must believe me when I say they are not merely accountants, they are also Swiss nationals. Combine the two and it is truly the worst of all worlds." He asked Tita to bring everything in, grabbed the bottle of Krug, said, "Follow me," and led into the conservatory.

"Why isn't it necessarily what it seems?"

In a room filled with plants and sweeping views across London, a handsome English mahogany table was set for two. Clement motioned for me to sit down. Still tied into his apron, he took the place opposite me and directed Tita as she served the meal. "A bigger piece for our guest . . . and more sauce . . . and put some sauce on his rice . . ."

"You haven't yet answered my question."

"That it's not necessarily what it seems? But it is obvious why."

I stared at him. "Why?"

He held up his hands, as if in defeat. "Your friend Francesca."

354

"What about my friend Francesca?"

"She is very angry at you."

"Is she?"

"You mean you have doubts?"

"Why is she suddenly so angry with me?"

"Suddenly? It is not as sudden as you think." He motioned, "Now please eat."

I didn't move. "Clement, what's going on? What are you talking about?"

He took his first bite. "Isn't this wonderful?"

"Dammit, Clement . . ."

He held his fork halfway up to his mouth. "How do I say this to you . . . I want to be empathetic and, you know, discreet, but I found out about . . . I mean, I've not said anything to anyone else. . ."

"Found out about what?"

"About . . . you and Francesca and . . ." He leaned across the table to pat my arm. "I always knew that the two of you would get along and I was always very happy when you seemed to be getting along. But after the . . . well, when she went to Switzerland to that clinic . . ." He stopped and looked at me. "I am sorry. No one else knows. But this is what it is all about. I wanted you to know that."

I reached for my glass and took a mouthful of champagne. I have no idea how he found out about her abortion. I didn't think anyone else knew. I couldn't for the life of me imagine that she told him, but even if she did, I decided, that was her business. And, after all these years, I didn't intend to let it get in the way of my business. I put him on notice, "I'm not going to allow the bank to call in the money."

"Eat slowly." He motioned towards my plate. "It is hot, so be careful."

I needed to make him understand, "There is no way I'm going to let you put me in default on Howe Wharf."

"Did Tita give you enough rice? Do you need more

355

sauce?" He ate for a few minutes. "You see, this is really all about you and . . ." he shrugged to apologize . . . "you know, your friend."

I ate silently, finishing the rest of my duck and my rice – it was probably the best meal I'd ever had with him – and when he offered another helping, I accepted. He took seconds, and then thirds. I stopped short of that, although I didn't say no when he opened a second bottle of Krug.

"You eat too fast," he said.

"I want more time."

"Yes." He continued eating. "That might be a good idea."

"I'm not talking about more time to eat, I'm talking about business. I want more time. So she tipped off the auditors and they reported to the bank, but you can stop her from pulling the plug. You can find a way to get me more time."

"Of course."

"Does that mean yes?"

"You should have more time with both. Please, one more little piece of duck."

"Jeezus, Clement, I'm talking about your demand for payment."

"Sure," he waved. "Isn't this sauce wonderful? You know, most people don't realize how many sorts of mustard there are in the world. Take Americans, for instance. You put mustard on hot dogs and think that's what mustard is for."

"How much longer?"

He looked at me. "How much longer do you need?"

"A year."

"Impossible."

"Six months."

"Perhaps. Yes, that might be feasible." He sipped his champagne, offered me another glass – I said no – poured one for himself and continued with his treatise on mustard. "The English think that mustard is their invention, and so do the French. But actually, mustard pre-dates the Romans . . ."

I warned, "I won't let Howe Wharf go under. You and I have made too much money together."

He put on a sympathetic face. "She is an angry woman."

"But you run the bank."

"Yes," he nodded several times, "I am the boss."

"I want more time."

He called for Tita to clear the table and bring all the ingredients out so that he could make the dessert there in front of me. "That's right," he said. "I am the boss."

To give the devil his due, Clement's dessert was a wonderful surprise. First he sprinkled a hefty amount of freshly ground pepper across a small mound of strawberries.

At that point I grimaced. "Are you sure you want to ruin perfectly good strawberries like that?"

Then he added an equal amount of fine brown sugar, two shots of Pernod, one shot of Armagnac and one shot of Cointreau. Finally, he tossed it all with a heavy helping of double cream.

I was convinced I would hate it.

I wound up having two large portions and insisting on a copy of the recipe.

"I don't know what I'm going to do about Francesca," I told him at the door. "But Howe Wharf isn't the price I'm going to pay."

Still wearing his apron, Clement reached for my arm and squeezed it. "I'm glad we can meet as friends."

"Thanks for dinner." I patted him on the shoulder. "Six months. Right?"

"You can count on me to do everything I can." He handed me a small bowl covered in foil. "This is for Pippa. So that she knows how the recipe is supposed to taste."

I thanked him and headed home.

As I played the evening's conversation over again in

my head, I was bothered that he knew about Francesca's pregnancy. But it wasn't until the cab pulled up to my own flat that I realized, each time I'd asked him for extra time, Clement had never once come right out and said yes.

Chapter Twenty-eight

Somewhere around Hoagy Carmichael and Robert Fulton, Peter had heedlessly slipped into his guru mode – it happened every few years – and now he phoned to declare, "I've been thinking about you, me and the meaning of life."

"It's not a moment too soon."

"This might be too Zen for your New World mindset, but did you ever see that movie with James Cagney?"

"Which movie with James Cagney?"

"The one where he's in the Navy and the ship sinks."

"James Cagney in the Navy and the ship sinks?" It didn't ring a bell.

"Wait a minute." He thought about it, then decided, "Maybe it was William Bendix."

"William Bendix? How can anyone confuse James Cagney with William Bendix?"

"I knew this would be too Zen for you. Anyway, they're on this ship and they get hit by a torpedo and the ship starts to take on water and the captain orders all the compartments sealed to keep the rest of the ship dry and afloat."

"So the ship doesn't sink."

"Ah . . ." He stopped. "No, it wasn't James Cagney, it *was* William Bendix. I remember now. It was called *Lifeboat*."

"So the ship does sink."

"That's right. William Bendix and Tallulah Bankhead."

"Peter, what's the point?"

"The point is, damage limitation. It's all about keeping your feet dry. If you can't save the ship by closing off the water tight compartments, leap into the nearest lifeboat."

"If you're telling me it's time for us to jump overboard . . ."

"That's exactly what I'm telling you. See, you do understand."

". . . then the answer is no."

"Damage limitation," he repeated.

"How come you're so easily defeated?"

"How come you're so stubborn?"

"We built this thing up from nothing. Doesn't it mean anything to you?"

He said right away, "Absolutely not. Living means something to me. Having a good time means something to me. Pennstreet was just a means to an end. It was never supposed to be the end. I'll prove it to you. Life is fun. Come and live in Paris."

I reminded him, "I've got a wife and kids."

He reminded me, "You let this thing get the best of you and, trust me, you won't have them for long."

"I'm not jumping overboard."

"Before the water gets up to your gonads, ask yourself, what have you got to win? Even if you beat the Stock Exchange and even if don't wind up in Wormwood Scrubs and even if you save Pennstreet, then what?"

"Then we're still in business."

"And then what?"

"You don't understand."

"Bay," the tone of his voice softened. "If you want to stay in business, I'll stay in business with you. But if you want to call it quits, that's fine too. I just want you to know where my priorities are."

"I'm not going to let them beat me."

"Make sure the cost of winning isn't too high."

"I am going to win. That's all there is to it. I refuse to let the bastards beat me."

"I know," he said. "You always were a jerk."

Hanging up, I mumbled out loud, water-tight compartments. Sure, why not. Damage limitation. Good idea. Great idea. Now what? I couldn't recall if William Bendix died in the end. But I was determined that it wasn't going to happen to me.

On the spur of the moment I rang Charles Patterson at Schools Jams and Jellies. "Get on to your bankers immediately. This morning. Don't waste any time. I'm selling the company to you. Get a management buy-out together right away. You're going to have to pay top dollar for it, no discounts, but if you don't do what I'm telling you to this very minute, you may wind up with nothing."

He wanted to know, "What's going on?"

"I told you, it's an instant management buy-out. Just do it."

Then I phoned Roger Griffith-Jones at Norwalk Lamps and Fixtures and told him the same thing.

He asked, "Is this legal?"

I confessed, "I don't know. But we can worry about that tomorrow. Buy the company today."

Before the week was out, both of them had made formal offers for their companies and, after calling an extraordinary meeting of the board of Pennstreet PLC, their offers were accepted.

Gerald warned, "This will never work."

"Why not?"

"Because no one is going to believe a management buy-out deal like this can be done in three days. You've got shareholders who aren't going to stand for it."

I pointed out, "We need the money and the management of these two companies is paying us a terrific price. This is no fire sale. If Pennstreet goes under, the shareholders might get 5p. This way they're getting a full pound for their pound. I stand to make absolutely nothing, so no one can claim that there's any conflict of interest. The press release I'm sending out explains that this is all about corporate restructuring. It's good for the banks. It's good for the shareholders. It's good for the company. So I guess that means it's perfectly legal."

"Except, nothing you've said is perfectly logical. I'll have to look into that. What I do know is, it's too fast."

"Any slower," I said, "and there may not be anything left."

That afternoon Pennstreet's share price dropped to 36p.

No sooner had the two management buy-outs been announced when the main ITN news programme at 10 o'clock broke the story that I'd been a draft dodger and had entered Britain with a forged passport under an assumed name. Two days later, Channel 4 announced that a team of investigative reporters was putting together a programme on me.

It was scheduled to run on the following Wednesday night.

I tried to find out what information they had. Besides the fact that I'd run away from the Vietnam War, there wasn't much to tell about my background. But they categorically refused to speak with me. They wouldn't even accept my offer to trade an interview on camera for a copy of their shooting script. So when BBC2 *Newsnight* rang and asked me if I was available, I told them, "Yes." And just to beat Channel 4 to the punch, I added, "But only on Tuesday."

That morning I rehearsed with Gerald and Andy, both of whom were totally against my doing the interview. I went to the BBC's studios in West London and we taped a long interview that afternoon. The story ran that evening.

Although they too pointed out that I'd left the States to avoid the draft, and mentioned my real name, for the most part they concentrated on how Peter and I had built up a business in Britain. They asked me about my dealings in the Maxwell shares. I said, as long as I was not under any obligation by the police or the courts to refrain from speaking about the matter, that I'd be happy to tell them the story. And I did, emphasizing that, by selling the shares before Maxwell's death was announced, it was exactly as if I'd been placing a bet on a horse before the race began.

They challenged me. "Did you know about Maxwell's death before it was officially announced?"

I answered truthfully, "No. But I knew that he was missing and guessed that he might be dead. However, that was public knowledge. It was like watching the horse galloping up to the starting gate and realizing he has a broken leg. I bet on him to lose. I did not learn for certain that Maxwell was dead until the rest of the world did, until after the Stock Exchange suspended trading on Maxwell Communications Corp shares."

Pippa said I came across very well. Even Gerald liked it.

Both of them agreed that the best part of it was near the end, when the reporter said, "According to records located in Baltimore Maryland, Bay Radisson was born Michael Radisson Bayard. There is no evidence to suggest that he legally changed his name before entering the UK with a passport issued to Bayard Radisson in Baltimore." He then asked me to comment. The camera came in close as I shrugged, "Self-made men often have self-made names."

The story closed with the reporter saying that the City of London Police had been invited to participate in the programme but had refused. Also, the Serious Fraud Office was believed to be studying the case, as was the Home Office, under whose auspices the Immigration Office fell. But it was unclear whether or not any formal action was called for.

I went to bed that night hoping Andy Warhol was

right. If one day everybody would be famous for 15 minutes, I reckoned that my time was up.

The next morning Brian Fellowes ran his story in the *FT* confirming that Peter had indeed been in Las Palmas on the day Maxwell died and that anyone there that day would have known that Maxwell was missing.

The Pennstreet share price rose a few pennies, then appeared to stabilize at around 39p.

Two days later we received notice that BFCS – a shareholder in Pennstreet PLC – had filed an action in court to stop the management buy-outs of Schools Jams and Jellies and Norwalk Lamps and Fixtures.

Evidently, Francesca intended to take us on at every turn.

I'd just hung up with Gerald – telling him that we were going to fight the action and proceed at full speed with the management buy-outs – when Patty's voice came over the intercom, "I think you should take the call on two."

"Who is it?"

"Trust me," she said.

"Journalist?"

"No. Just take it."

So I picked up the phone. "Hello?"

A young man asked, "Do you know Joe Beamish?"

A shock rippled through my entire body and it took several seconds before I could say anything. "What's his name?"

"Who?" He asked.

"Joe Beamish," I answered, then demanded, "Where the hell are you?"

"I'm in London."

I had to know, "Is your mother here with you?"

"No. She's home. But she gave me your number and said I should call."

I was slightly relieved. "Where are you right now?"

"In a phone booth."

"Wise ass, where's the phone booth?"

"Around the corner from your office."

I said, "Come on up," and, five minutes later, Christopher Pepperdine walked in.

He'd turned into a tall, handsome, athletic 21-year-old, with longish hair, too-tight jeans, a one-size-too-small Johns Hopkins sweatshirt and a broad smile.

He had his mother's mouth.

"I haven't seen you since . . ." I didn't know whether to hug him or just stand there gaping at him. So first I extended my hand and, when he shook it, I swung my arm over his shoulder to give him half a hug. He wasn't nearly as awkward about this as I was and he hugged me back.

"Tell me everything." I sat him down on the couch, instructed Patty, "No calls," and pulled a chair up to face him. "Absolutely everything."

"I just graduated and the trip to London was a present from my mother."

"How is she?"

He shrugged. "She's okay. You know, her health and everything is okay."

There was something odd about his answer. "But?"

"But . . . nothing much." He hesitated, then told me, "Her second marriage busted up. Other than that, I guess, she's fine. Really."

"Does she still sneeze ten times in a row?"

He laughed. "How do you know that?"

I smiled. "I used to know a lot about her."

"Yeah, she still does that. But when she split up with Sam . . . that was her second husband . . . well, she tried suing him for a lot of money and she lost. It got pretty messy. She got kinda messed up in her head."

I didn't know anything about that. "Is there anyone else in her life?"

"No," he said quickly. "Well, I mean, no one serious." He stopped and looked at me. "She dated a friend of mine for about a week. I didn't like that."

"I can understand."

"He was only a year older than me."

I changed the subject. "Where are you staying?"

"I don't have a place yet. I just got in this morning."

"You'll stay with us," I offered. "That is, if you'd like to. My wife is British and we have twin daughters. They're very young. But there's plenty of room."

"Gee, I don't know . . ." He hesitated, "I mean, I don't want to impose."

He didn't take much convincing, so I rang Pippa and told her we had a house guest. She asked, who? I explained, Elizabeth's son. She wondered, with or without his mother? I said, without. And she said, "In that case, okay."

There were all sorts of things I needed to do that morning. But it struck me that Christopher was a kind of missing link with the world I'd left behind. And even if I had nothing to do any more with his mother – except I thought about her sometimes – getting to know him made me feel better.

I ran him over to the flat. He shook Pippa's hand and politely called her Mrs Radisson. The girls appeared, played shy for all of about 30 seconds, then started flirting with him. Pippa announced she had to go out. Malika took the girls. I asked him if there was anything he particularly wanted to do while he was in London and he asked if anyone would mind if he went to sleep. I left him to settle into the guest room and returned to the office.

That afternoon Gerald and I met with a room full of people at Hill Samuel. We walked in expecting the worst. We walked out in total bewilderment. Against all the odds, William David Romney and his boss both agreed that restructuring Pennstreet was a sound idea. Everyone approved of our selling Schools and Norwalk. And the bank announced they would stand by us. They wouldn't be putting any more money into Pennstreet, but at least they weren't taking any out.

As Gerald and I left Hill Sam and walked up towards London Wall, I found myself filled with renewed faith. First I waved at the Wood Street Police Station, then I put my arm over his shoulder and told him, "Yes, Virginia, there is a Santa Claus."

Christopher and I didn't get much of a chance to spend time together that week because I was so busy. I apologized to him on a daily basis, but he said it wasn't a problem because he was getting to know London. I promised there'd be more time over the weekend.

Gerald swiftly managed to get the BFCS action lifted by arguing that the courts were not a suitable place for such a move. The judge agreed that company law provided several courses of action for dissatisfied shareholders to take, long before coming to court. He ruled that it was inappropriate at this time for BFCS to bring the matter to him, as they had not yet exhausted those other courses of action.

I thought about asking Francesca to meet with us, but decided against that – anyway, I knew she'd refuse – so I invited Clement to a meeting. A response came back from his office that a meeting would be arranged, as soon as possible, but unfortunately, Monsieur Marc would not be able to attend for the time being.

I didn't understand his answer and replied that we would make ourselves available at the bank's convenience. However, in the meantime, the sale of those two assets would be completed as approved by the Pennstreet board.

No sooner was the letter faxed to Clement than I decided, what the hell, and rang Francesca. I intended to tell her that I wasn't going to be pushed around. Not by BFCS. Not by her. Not by anyone. I intended to tell her, if she was looking for a fight, she'd get it.

But she wouldn't take my call.

Christopher went to a club on Friday night and didn't come back to the flat until very late. When he got up, around noon, he seemed a little edgy. I asked him if everything was all right. He said he was thinking it might be time to move on. I apologized, yet again, for having been so busy and wondered if there was anything in particular he'd like to do. "How about if Pippa and I take you to the theatre?"

He shrugged, "Thanks anyway. I did the Tate Gallery and Westminster Abbey, Madame Tussauds, Piccadilly Circus and I rode on a double-decker bus. I kind of think that's about it."

It was nearly 1 o'clock so I suggested, "How about dim sum?" He said he liked that. The two of us went to the New World off Cambridge Circus and ate our way through several trolleys of Chinese delicacies. We talked about Baltimore and we talked about Johns Hopkins. He told me that when he went back to the States he wanted to go to California and try to get a job in the movies.

"Can you act?"

"I don't know."

"But you want to be an actor?"

"Maybe. Or just any job in the movie business."

"This is because you like the movies? Or because you like ladies who like the movies?"

"I took some film courses."

"What does your mother say about this?"

"She says, no. She says she didn't send me to college all these years so I could go to Hollywood and became a waiter. She says I have to get a job in Baltimore."

"You mean, like a waiter?"

He laughed, then dropped his eyes and moved his chopsticks around for a few seconds, as if he was getting up his nerve. "Can I ask you something?"

"Sure."

"Did you sleep with my mother?"

I stared at him. "Why do you want to know?"

He made a face. "I just . . . I mean, you were her boyfriend when she was my age and . . ." He stopped. "Were you her first?"

I didn't know how to answer that because I didn't know what he wanted to hear. So I told him, "It's funny how times change. I could never imagine that my parents did it."

"She did it with one of my friends."

I got off that subject. "Have you ever been in love?"

He nodded.

"What happened?"

"She hurt me."

I said quietly, "That's what first loves do. Sometimes second loves and third loves, too." I smiled. "Your mother and I . . . she was my first love. And no matter what has happened to our lives since, she will always be my first love. That means she will always have a very special place in my heart. And even if your first love hurt you, don't be surprised if you always think of her with the same tenderness and affection that I will forever have for your mother."

He blurted out, "She wants money."

I said, "What?"

"She wants money."

"Who?"

"My mother."

I looked at him. "What are you talking about?"

"She told me . . ." He fumbled with his plate. "She sent me here to ask you for money. She said that you're rich now and that . . . she said you owed her."

I sat back and stared at him.

He pushed his plate aside and played nervously with his paper napkin. "I'm sorry. I didn't want to do this."

After a while I said, "I'm sorry too, Christopher." Then I told him, "The answer is no."

He admitted, "I knew it would be."

I needed him to understand, "I'm not saying no to be mean. I'm not doing it because I don't want to help her. I'm doing it because . . ." I told him the truth. "Because this has nothing to do with whatever she and I shared 25 years ago. The woman who still has that place in my

369

heart may look like your mother. And she has the same name. And she has some of the same memories. And she sneezes ten times in a row. But that's all."

His eyes got very red. "I'm sorry. Can we go back to the apartment? I want to get my stuff. I think I should go home."

"Go home?"

"Yeah. Back to Baltimore."

I tried to lighten up the atmosphere. "You didn't come all this way just to ride on a double-decker bus and have a Chinese meal. No good. You can't leave. I'd like you to stay with us for as long as you want. And then I think you should go to Paris. It just so happens that I know someone in Paris who specializes in girls your age."

He forced a smile. "Thanks anyway."

"Don't argue with me, I'm old enough to be your mother."

Back at the flat, I told Pippa we were all going to the theatre that night. He wasn't really in the mood but I insisted. We took him to see *Me and My Girl* because I wanted to cheer him up. He liked the song about the Lambeth Walk.

On Sunday, I took Pippa, Christopher and the twins for a meal at the Waterside Inn in Bray. He liked that as well. Over lunch, I told him that if he was going to Paris he'd have to dress the part, so on Monday Pippa took him to Harrods and bought him another pair of jeans and a blue blazer. I didn't know it but, when he saw something for Elizabeth, Pippa bought it for her. Except he had to promise not to tell me, or his mother.

The two of them strutted into the office that afternoon, to show off his new clothes.

That's when I handed him an envelope. "This is between you, me, Pippa and the lamp post that the guy was leaning against at the show on Saturday night. Open it."

370

Inside was a Eurail Pass plus a wallet of traveller's cheques, in his name, for $2,500.

"Here's the deal," I said. "That ticket's good for the next two months on any train in Europe. All you do is show it to the conductor. You can go anywhere you want to. Because I'd like you to have a good time, I'll change your ticket home to Baltimore so that you can stay in Europe until you're ready to leave. No fixed date. As for those traveller's cheques . . . when you get home, you let me know how much you've got left. Whatever you say, and I'll take your word for it, I'll send you a cheque for the same amount. In other words, whatever you don't spend in the next two months, I'll match. That should feed you for a while in Hollywood."

Then I tossed him an open, round-trip airline ticket between Baltimore and Los Angeles.

"And this will get you there."

He was speechless.

"The only condition is, in your acceptance speech when you win your first Oscar, you say thanks Pippa and Bay."

His eyes reddened again. He hugged Pippa and he hugged me. And I hugged him back. I told myself, it was the least I could do for Elizabeth.

On Tuesday, Christopher went to Hamleys and, without saying anything to me, bought a present for each of the twins. He left on the boat train Wednesday night for Paris where Peter promised to introduce him to the ways of European women.

The next morning, I was arrested.

Chapter Twenty-nine

Salt, Booton and another plain-clothes officer arrived at my front door at 6:45. Salt said he wanted me to accompany them to Wood Street. I asked if I had a choice.

Booton gave me a sarcastic grin. "No."

Indignant, I answered, "Then I'm not coming."

"All right," Booton said with noticeable pleasure. "Mr Radisson, I'm placing you under arrest, as I have reasonable suspicion that an offence has been committed."

I turned towards Salt. "In other words, if I don't come willingly, you'll arrest me."

He answered, "I'm afraid you have just been arrested."

Pippa began to cry.

I took a deep breath and asked Salt if they could please wait while I shaved and showered.

He said they could wait for a few minutes but asked me to hurry.

I took my time.

The twins woke up and, when they saw their mother crying, they both started to cry.

I came downstairs in a suit and tie and wondered if I should take any spare clothes with me.

Ever polite, Salt indicated that almost certainly wouldn't be necessary. "You will want to notify your solicitors and I suspect they will make suitable arrangements to have you home this evening."

Picking up the phone, I woke Gerald. "I've just been arrested." He promised to meet me at Wood Street.

Through her tears, Pippa insisted on coming along and asked Salt to wait a few minutes longer while she dressed.

He apologized, "That isn't possible just now," and handed her his card. "When you're ready, sometime later this morning, please ring me and I'll tell you what the situation is. I'm sure, if you'll just give us a few hours, it would be perfectly all right to come to the office later."

I took Pippa in my arms. "Stay here. I'll call you as soon as I can. Don't worry. I'll be fine." I pointed at Booton, "He probably won't get out the rubber hose until after lunch."

No one laughed.

I asked Salt, "Handcuffs?"

He replied, "This isn't the United States."

I kissed Pippa and kissed the twins and walked outside.

Much to my surprise, a television camera crew, a few photographers and a handful of reporters were standing on the kerb.

Someone called out, "Mr Radisson, are you being arrested?"

Startled at finding them there, I answered, "Apparently I am."

Someone else asked, "What are you being charged with?"

"Parking on a double yellow line." I stopped to speak with them.

Out of the corner of his mouth, Booton said to me, "There'll be time for this later."

But I wouldn't budge. "Actually, as far as I know I have not yet been charged with anything." And, with the cameras rolling, I quizzed Salt, "What are the specific charges?"

He didn't hide his annoyance with me for doing this. "We will make an announcement later today."

The mob fired off more questions. "Will Mr Radisson be charged with insider dealing?" And, "Are other City executives involved?" And, "Does this case relate to any of your other cases now in progress?" And, "When can we expect a statement?"

Booton tried to move me along.

Defiantly – because he really pissed me off – I stood my ground. "There's nothing much more I can say because I don't know what this is all about. Although my friend D.I. Salt assures me that they won't be bringing the rubber hoses out until after lunch."

That's when Salt stepped forward, putting himself in between me and the cameras. He asked the reporters, "If you would be kind enough to hold your questions for a few hours . . ."

Booton took me by the elbow and, with a very firm grip, moved me towards their car.

I glared at him. "You son of a bitch."

The third officer – a young guy who was never introduced – opened the rear door and reached for my other arm. He too clamped down on me.

This was too rough for my taste. "What the fuck . . ." I couldn't pull loose from them, so I let out a shriek – "Ahhhhh!" – and sank like a stone to the ground. The cops were completely taken by surprise. The young one jumped away. Booton nearly lost his own balance.

One of the reporters shouted, "They hit him," and the press gang moved in on us, cameras rolling.

Salt came to my rescue and helped me up.

Booton tried to keep the reporters back. "It's all right. He's all right. Give him some air."

Seeing my moment of glory, I scowled at Booton, "You miserable son of a bitch. That was totally unnecessary."

The reporters shouted more questions. "Why did you hit him?" And, "Mr Radisson, will you be filing charges?"

Salt hustled me into the car and climbed in next to me.

The young cop got in the driver's seat while a bewildered Booton raced around the rear of the car and joined us in the back seat. Salt yelled, "Go." The car pulled away from the kerb as photographers rammed their cameras flush against the windows and fired their flashguns in our eyes.

As we sped away, I could see a few of the photographers running for their cars to follow us. When we finally turned out of Eaton Square, I glanced at Salt. "Kind of heavy-handed for white-collar crime."

He was furious. "That was a very foolish stunt."

Booton warned, "You tripped and you're going to sign a statement to that effect."

I told him, "You should live so long."

Salt advised me not to say anything more until we got back to the office. "We'll discuss the matter with your lawyers."

I leaned close and whispered, "I am not some overbred polite City type who went to all the right public schools. When someone tries to bugger me, I get nasty."

That was the end of any conversation until we arrived at their office.

This time when he took me in front of the Custody Sergeant to record my visit, Salt explained that I'd been arrested on reasonable suspicion that an offence had been committed. He asked that the Custody Sergeant allow them sufficient time to interview me before coming back, either to lodge specific charges against me or to inform him that no charges would be forthcoming.

I didn't understand how they could arrest me without charging me, but I knew there would be time to discuss that with my lawyers.

Upstairs, I sat in the same chair, next to Salt's desk, although this time when Booton offered me a cup of coffee I said no. Salt took off his jacket and sat down. "We'll begin as soon as your lawyers arrive."

I pretended to flick street dirt off my slacks. "Why did you call the media?"

He said, "I didn't."

"So who did?"

He shook his head, "I don't know." And for some reason I believed him. "I was no more pleased to see them this morning than you were. But that stunt you pulled was stupid and your threat to me in the car wasn't very intelligent either."

I shrugged, "Write it off to cultural disparity."

"All right. It's forgotten."

I was tempted to say, you better not conveniently remember it when you see the television version, but the little voice inside my head told me that by antagonizing him, I was taking on more than I ought to.

Anyway, that's when Gerald walked into the room. He asked Salt if he could have a few minutes with me and Salt said, of course.

"Sorry to wake you," I whispered when we were alone.

"You've been arrested on suspicion."

"That's what they said. But what the hell kind of a crime is suspicion? How can they arrest somebody without charging him?"

"I don't know if it works this way in the States, but yes, here, they can arrest you on suspicion. However, they can't hold you indefinitely. After a reasonable amount of time, they either have to charge you or let you go. This is going way back to law school for me, but as I recall it's often the case that, when they arrest on suspicion, it means they simply don't have anything to charge their suspect with. But we'll have to wait for Evans and Maloney to decide what to do about that. This is their area. In the meantime, you haven't said anything, have you?"

"Said anything?" I made a face. "Ah . . . no, not exactly."

He glared. "Bay, what have you done?"

376

I told him about my prat fall.

He nearly choked. "You did what? And the cameras caught it? You made it look like one of the officers hit you on camera?"

I grinned, more out of nervousness than pride. "Where I come from it's called police brutality. You see it in the movies all the time."

He shook his head back and forth, mumbling, "I should have known. I should have known." He said, "You're a menace to society. Even worse, you're a menace to yourself."

"They were starting to get rough. It seemed like a good idea at the time."

"Trust me, it was a pretty stupid idea. This isn't America."

"Gee, you haven't said that to me in at least 12 hours! But don't worry, other people have."

He didn't find it funny. "I tried getting in touch with Evans but he wasn't at home. I left a message on his answering machine at the office and asked him to join us here. I found Andy Maloney, however, and he's on his way."

Salt asked Gerald, "Will you need much longer? I'd like to start as soon as we can as there's a lot to go over."

Gerald told him, "We're just waiting for additional counsel."

Salt said, "That's fine," and there we waited.

Maloney showed up about 20 minutes later. He came rushing into the room, apologized for being late, shook my hand, shook Gerald's hand and wondered, "They arrest you?"

"Yeah."

"What's the charge?"

Before I could answer, Gerald pulled him aside and whispered something into his ear. Maloney shot a glance at me, and the two continued whispering to each other for quite a while. Then Maloney told Salt that he and

Gerald wanted to speak with me in private. They let us use the office where we'd met the last time.

Andy shut the door and wanted to know, "Tell me exactly what happened when they arrested you. About taking a fall."

I explained what I'd done. "It's even on tape. Maybe we'll make the 10 o'clock news."

Gerald volunteered, "A very stupid move."

But Andy disagreed. "Maybe not. Those two blokes will worry about it. Nigel Salt is an ambitious man. Booton always was a hot-head and a fool. He's going nowhere. But Salt has a future. The last thing he wants is any hint of a blunder."

"There is no way," Gerald argued, "that anyone is going to believe a circus act like that."

Maloney said. "But if Salt believes that someone might believe it . . ."

Gerald shook his head. "An absolute non-starter. If it looks on the tape as if Bay faked it, which it probably will, then it's not just a losing card, it's a dangerous card to have in the game because they'll play it."

"We'll have to see the tape." Maloney looked at me. "But if it looks even vaguely like police brutality, these guys will get queasy."

"Police brutality on Eaton Square?" Gerald forced a laugh. "Roughing up a wealthy, white man suspected of financial crime and doing it in front of television cameras and newspaper photographers? Who on earth is going to believe that the police could be that stupid?"

"But if the tape shows . . ."

Gerald stressed, "It will show Bay to be the bad actor that he is. It will make him look as idiotic as the stunt he pulled."

"And what if the tape is inconclusive?" Maloney paused for a second, then raised his finger to make a point. "All we want to do is worry Salt. To make him think twice."

There was a knock on the door and Gareth Evans

came in. Andy and Gerald told him about my exploit in front of the cameras and he agreed with Gerald that it was a pretty dumb thing to do. Then Maloney called for Salt and demanded to know, "Just what are you guys up to?"

Salt said, "If you're ready, we'll start."

Booton followed him into the room.

Maloney was relentless. "You've arrested my client, called out the cameras, made a public spectacle of the arrest . . ."

"In the course of our investigation," Salt revealed, "it came to our attention that Mr Radisson has had dealings with various offshore companies, which we believe have included fraudulent transactions. We also believe that there is evidence to support these allegations on the premises of Mr Radisson's office. We have therefore arrested him this morning, and intend holding him, while a team of officers, with a search warrant, go to those offices . . ."

I cut in. "You're raiding my offices?"

"That's right."

"Why didn't you just ask?"

Maloney warned, "Keep quiet, Bay."

Evans requested to see the search warrant.

Booton handed it to him.

"Hey, guys . . ." I reached into my pocket, took out my office keys and tossed them to Salt. "This is so you don't have to break down the door."

He was as shocked as Gerald and Gareth and Maloney were. "I think you should speak to your lawyers before you . . ."

"I have nothing to hide."

"Take the keys back," Evans said.

Gerald chided me, "Bay, don't be so stupid."

"It's all right." I waved them off. "Go ahead. Here are the keys. Have a good time."

My lawyers went crazy and tried to talk me out of it, but I knew there wasn't anything in the office for

Salt to find. If he was looking for my private company papers, documentation of my own offshore stuff, or anything that might incriminate Peter, he was in the wrong hemisphere. Roderick and L. James had all our private stuff locked up in the Bahamas.

"It's all right," I kept saying.

When the lawyers couldn't talk me out of it, Salt tossed the keys to Booton. "Get moving." Then he looked at me and nodded, "Thank you for your cooperation."

"Now that I've cooperated, what do I do?"

"You stay here," Salt said. "This will take several hours. Until we're satisfied that we've located everything we need, you will have to remain in police custody."

Maloney cut in, "No cells."

"No cells," Salt agreed. "But no contact."

Gerald said, "And he's free to wander around."

Salt said sure, but I had to stay on that floor. I couldn't make any phone calls, nor could I discuss my case with anyone.

"Discuss it with who?" I reminded Salt, "Everyone on this floor is on your side."

He said, if I needed anything, Miss Billings would see that I got it. Coffee. Tea. Water. Newspapers. Whatever.

"The only thing I need right now is to ring my wife."

But Salt said, "Not yet."

Gerald volunteered, "I'll do it."

"No mention of the raid on the office," Salt warned.

"Pippa will be a wreck," I said. "Just tell her everything is all right and that I'll be home tonight."

He went to a phone and spoke with her. When he came back he nodded, "Yes, she is a wreck."

As Salt and Booton made ready to leave for my office, the three lawyers ganged up on me, berating me for what they said was my second mistake of the day.

I tried to point out, "The guy has a search warrant.

He's going to my office anyway." But that's not the way the lawyers saw it.

"We're here to protect you," Gerald explained, "not only from them, but in your case, from yourself."

They couldn't convince me that I'd done something wrong. And I didn't think it was a good idea to elaborate on why there was no need for them to worry about it. In the end, the only thing we could all agree on was that, as long as I didn't need them to babysit me through the morning, they could go back to work. Salt consented that one of them could come to have lunch with me, on the condition that as long as I was out of the office, I was considered released into the custody of my attorney who would guarantee that I did not communicate with anyone and that I would return.

Booton, who until this point hadn't said a word, started wagging his finger. "No. No. He stays here."

Salt overrode him. "It's all right."

So the three lawyers left and Salt and Booton did too – they joined the officers who had already gone to my offices – and I sat down at Salt's desk to do the *Times* crossword puzzle.

I didn't get very far.

Miss Billings kept coming by to ask if I wanted anything and after a while I wondered if I could have a few more newspapers. She said she'd take care of it. I gave her the money and told her, "The *FT*, the *Telegraph*, the *Mail*, the *Express* and the *Independent*."

I killed the rest of the morning reading them all, page by page. I was so bored, I even read two stories about cricket.

None of the cops were back by the time Andy Maloney showed up at 12:45, so he and I just walked out the front door and went to the pub around the corner. This time I avoided the turkey sandwich and settled on roast beef. I forgot to tell the woman behind the counter not to put butter, mayonnaise and horseradish on it – a terrible combination – and got only one bite out of it before

I muttered to Andy that the English make the worst sandwiches in the world.

"I'm Irish," he said. "Fuck 'em."

We were back at Salt's office by 2. I told Andy I'd be all right, that if he wanted to leave, it wasn't a problem. But he said, no, he'd stay because he expected the cops to return soon and, at that point, it would be best if I had someone with me.

"What do they look for when they raid a place?"

"Anything they can find," he said. "Files. Computer disks. Papers. Letters. Everything. They'll take every-thing . . ."

"Take everything?" I hadn't realized they'd be doing that. "They're going to take stuff out of my office?"

"They're going to empty it. They'll bring everything back here . . ."

"Shit."

"You mean, you didn't know that when you volun-teered your keys?"

"I thought they were just going for a look."

"Next time you won't be so cavalier. Next time you'll listen to your lawyers."

I rationalized, "We couldn't have stopped them even if we'd wanted to."

"No one said you had to make it so easy for them."

I hesitated for a second, then quietly admitted, "There's nothing in the office."

He said just as quietly, "Are you sure?"

I nodded. "I'm sure."

Half an hour later, Salt, Booton and a whole bunch of other cops showed up carrying a couple of dozen black plastic garbage bags filled with files, and a couple of dozen cartons filled with papers. They even took the computer off my desk.

"Jeezus," I gasped. "Did you leave the carpets?"

Salt told Andy, "This took longer than we expected. I want to hold him overnight."

"No," Andy said. "Absolutely not."

Salt threatened, "I'll charge him. I'll take him down to the Custody Sergeant right now. He'll deny police bail. You won't get to the Magistrates this afternoon so he'll be held over. That means a cell."

Andy stood his ground. "You have nothing to charge him with. And if you try that insider trading bullshit, I will pull every string I can to see that bail is set today. What's more, I will personally post his bail."

I cut in, "What's going on?"

Motioning for me to keep me quiet, Andy told Salt, "He goes home."

Salt said no.

I tried, "Would someone please clue me in?"

Again Maloney held me back. "I want to call Chappell and Evans." Salt pointed towards a phone. Maloney said to me, "Just sit down a minute. Don't worry. Keep your mouth shut. Trust me." So I sat down while he made his call. He was on the line with both of them, one after the other, for nearly 20 minutes. He kept nodding, saying, "Okay," and when he hung up he told Salt, "I need to speak to my client."

We moved into a corner of the room and Maloney said, "Here's what's happening. Salt has nothing. But he figures he can cook up a charge, like insider trading, to get you bound over for the night while he goes rummaging through all that stuff. I don't know what they're looking for, but my gut instinct is that they're looking for something specific. Obviously they didn't find it when they went to your office. They're hoping they've got it now. For some reason, they want you incommunicado. Can you think of anyone they wouldn't want you to speak to?"

I couldn't. "Except, maybe, Peter."

"But they know where he is."

"Of course they do. He isn't hiding from anyone. And he answers his own phone."

Andy took a deep breath. "They can take you down to the Custody Sergeant now, either ask that you be held on suspicion or charge you with something and, in both instances, he'll refuse bail. I'll argue that you're not a dangerous criminal and there's no way he can deny you bail. But that won't work. He's on their side. That pushes us into Magistrates Court. If we can get there tonight, it's 99% sure that bail will be set."

"So let's go there."

"Unfortunately, there are no guarantees. If we don't get the case heard tonight, you're a guest of Her Majesty. And even if we do get into Court tonight, if Salt or his boss can make the magistrates believe that they need you out of the way for 24 hours, the Court will err on the side of caution. There are all sorts of games they can play to hold you. Many magistrates know enough not to fall for the tricks. But there's always one who will. If you get unlucky, if they can sell a bill of goods to the Court, you spend the night in a cell."

"What the hell for?"

"Because you landed the wrong magistrate, the one who bought their story. Also on the downside, you've been charged with a crime. So far, you've only been arrested on suspicion. True, that makes the papers. But getting charged with a crime makes for bigger headlines. Also, it never goes away. You'll always be the bloke who was once charged with, whatever. It's a gamble and the odds might even be in your favour, but you have to know there's a chance you'll lose."

"That's it? No options?"

"If I can work out a deal, will you spend the night here?"

I looked around. "In this office?"

"It's better than jail."

"At least in jail they've got beds."

"Do you want to deal or not?"

At that point, Booton came running up to Salt with a copy of the *Evening Standard*. The front page had a photo of me, on the pavement, with Booton hovering over me, looking very angry. The headline above the story was "Yank Financier Arrested". The caption under the photo read, "Has Police Brutality Come to the City?"

Salt handed it to Andy. "This is the stunt that Mr Radisson pulled this morning. At no time did anyone in my command act in an illegal manner."

I looked at it. "Not a very flattering pose."

Maloney studied the photo, then asked Salt, "How come the press was there?"

Salt said, "I don't know."

He said, "If improprieties have taken place, we will see them properly noted."

"Radisson tripped," Booton yelled. "He did it on purpose."

Salt motioned for Booton to keep quiet. "There will be an inquiry into the matter of the press being present this morning."

I said to Andy, "There must have been eight, maybe ten people there this morning. Including a TV news crew. Not only are there witnesses, but what happened is on tape. With sound. And in living colour."

"He faked it," Booton slammed his hand down on the table.

"That's enough," Salt demanded.

"Okay," Andy said. "Here's the deal. My client volunteers to stay. But he is not to be charged. No cells. He goes to a hotel."

Salt looked at me. "Are you willing to foot the bill for a double room at a hotel?"

"Why a double?"

"Someone from my office will have to stay with you."

"Sure. But why . . ."

"Because I don't want you making any phone calls. You can't meet with anyone. You can't leave the room."

"Who are you keeping me away from?"

He wouldn't answer.

"I get to pick the hotel?"

He agreed. "You're paying for it."

"I'll need to ring my wife."

"All right. You'll have to do that from here while we listen."

I glanced at Booton. "One more thing."

Salt asked, "What?"

"A room-mate who's more pleasant than him."

Chapter Thirty

I shared a double room at the Inn on the Park with a young cop named Paul. We had dinner in the room, then sat and watched television. The videotape of my arrest did not make the BBC *Nine O'Clock News*. Nor did it make the ITN *News at Ten*. Even *Sky News* seemed to have passed on it.

Frankly, I was just as glad.

Paul wanted to watch a movie on the hotel's pay-per-view system, so I said be my guest, go ahead. Anyway, by then I was falling asleep. I got into bed and mumbled, "Goodnight."

Laying on top of his bed, Paul wondered, "Can I ask you a question? How much does a room like this cost?"

I said I wasn't sure. "A couple of hundred quid, I suppose."

"A couple of hundred quid for one night?" He sighed. "It must be nice."

I snapped off the light. "Nothing personal, but I'm not going to be good company tonight."

We had a room service breakfast, then I showered and tried shaving with the plastic razor from the hospitality pack that the hotel puts in every bathroom. It had been years since I'd used a blade and I didn't do a very good job of it. When both of us were dressed, we went downstairs and waited there until someone from the Fraud Squad picked us up.

The papers were filled with stories about how I'd been arrested, held and would definitely be charged. The picture of me on the ground at Booton's feet ran in the tabloids but not in the broadsheets. They didn't fall for it.

By the time we got to Wood Street, Gerald, Andy and Gareth were already there. Salt and Booton looked terrible. Andy confided, "They've been there all night. They've been going through your stuff, and from the look on their faces, they're pretty frustrated."

"Serves them right," I mumbled.

Now a third officer joined them.

He was in his 40s, heavy set and balding. He was introduced to us as D.I. Cunningham. I thought nothing of it. Nor did I think anything of the fact that, after Cunningham was introduced to us, Maloney excused himself, saying that he had to phone his office. When he returned, Salt, Booton and Cunningham sat on their side of the table, with my lawyers and me on our side. The faithful Miss Billings sat near the door taking notes.

Salt started the meeting in the usual manner – date, time, place, participants – then turned to me. "Let's put our cards on the table, shall we? I need some assistance here and, if you'll cooperate, I'll cooperate. We can save each other a lot of time and a lot of trouble." He asked, "What's Doublebrook?"

I said, "What's what?"

"I want you to talk to me about a company called Doublebrook."

I answered, truthfully, "I've never heard of it."

Salt pressed me, "Are you sure?"

"Positive."

"Doesn't mean anything to you? Doublebrook?"

"Not a thing."

He stared at me. "Never had any dealings with that company?"

"I told you, no."

"In England? In Switzerland, perhaps? Ever deal with a company called Doublebrook in Switzerland?"

"My answer is still no."

"Well," he said, "we have reason to believe you have, in fact, dealt with that company in the past."

I insisted, "Not me."

"What about your mate, Peter Goddard?"

"You'll have to ask him. But I have never heard of the company. And I don't think he's ever heard of it either. Certainly he never mentioned it. And there isn't a lot I don't know about him."

"Such as?"

"Such as . . . such as what I don't know about him?" I tried to figure out how to answer such a question. "You want me to tell you what I don't know about Peter?"

"Tell me instead about any business you do in Switzerland."

"Yes, we do business in Switzerland."

"With who?"

"With who? With lots of people."

"For instance?"

"I wouldn't know where to begin. But you've got all my files. Everything is in there."

He shot a glance at Cunningham, then asked me, "Do you know the name Etienne Pont?"

I might have hesitated just a fraction of a second too long before I admitted, "Yes."

"Have you ever done business with Mr Pont?"

"Yes."

"Like what?"

I explained about the caviar I'd traded in Japan. "That's the sort of thing Pont does."

Salt tried again. "And you never heard of a company he runs called Doublebrook?"

It suddenly dawned on me that Stevie had a Swiss operation called *Doppelbrücke* – double bridges – and that maybe Salt was just pronouncing it wrong. But I couldn't let on to that now. "Nope. Never."

"At no point in your dealings with Pont did you ever hear or see the company name Doublebrook?"

"No."

Ever persistent, Salt enquired, "What company did Pont use when you did that caviar deal with him?"

"As far as I know, he didn't use a company. He was just the middleman who sold the stuff on for us."

"Is that what he does?"

"Yes. Except it's not always caviar. He flogs futures. I guess, silver has always been his main thing."

There was a long pause as Salt stared at me. "Have you ever dealt in arms?"

I answered right away, "Nope," then tried to make a joke. "However, I once owned a lot of meat cleavers."

He didn't smile. "Any weapons of any kind?"

"Just those meat cleavers."

"Explosives?"

"Nope."

"What about Pont?"

Again, I probably hesitated a bit too long. "What about him?"

"Do you know if he's ever dealt in arms or explosives?"

"No, I don't. But from what I've read in *Time* and *Newsweek* about the arms business, it's a pretty small world and not easily accessible to just any old caviar middleman."

"What do you know about plutonium or plutonium nitrate?"

"Nothing at all."

"Have you at any time ever discussed weapons or arms or explosives with Etienne Pont?"

I tried not to fidget and hoped I didn't appear to be as uncomfortable as I felt. "I told you, fish eggs. That's what I discussed with Pont. Listen, I don't even like the guy. Oh, once I talked to him about the Hunt Brothers. They used Pont when they were trying to put a corner on the world's silver market." I paused, then lied, "But that's all. He's not someone I've ever spent a lot of time with. Nothing else."

Salt turned to Cunningham who stared at me without saying a word.

I stared at him for a moment and then, to cover my ill ease, looked at Gerald. "What time is lunch?"

Cunningham stood up and Salt did too. They excused themselves and left the room. Booton sat where he was for a few minutes until he realized that his presence was stifling our conversation. He got up, and when he left, so did Miss Billings.

Evans leaned forward and asked me quietly, "What's that all about?"

I answered, "Peter's friend Etienne Pont."

Gerald insisted, "If you've ever had any dealings with him, you'd better say so right now."

"No dealings like that."

"What about Peter?"

"No. Nothing. They used to play at commodities. Silver. Coffee. I seem to recall something about frozen pork bellies. They go way back, but that's all."

"Because if they think they can nab you on illegal arms dealing . . ."

"Trust me," I said. "We never got into anything like it."

Maloney started to chuckle. "Guess what folks, that's exactly what this is all about. Cunningham is at the Yard, on the International Crime Squad. I didn't know him, so I made that call to find out who he is. It now looks to me like this has nothing to do with Bay, that it's really all about this bloke Pont."

I wondered, "Shouldn't Salt have properly introduced him?"

"He did," Andy said. "But then, cops are typically too clever by half. They don't know that we know. And I don't think we should let on. It's best if we just let them play their little game. Obviously, though, they've got nothing on Bay."

Gerald concurred. "I haven't heard anything that sounds like a crime."

And Gareth agreed. "They've definitely switched from Bay to Pont."

Knowing what I knew about Stevie Bridge, I mumbled, "Rightly so."

Maloney leaned back and stretched. "All right, so we can cross off insider trading. It's finished. There's no way they can go with that. The passport business and your immigration into the UK isn't theirs to worry about, although we may have to face up to that one day. I suspect, just to be pricks, they've already passed stuff along to Inland Revenue and Immigration. But again, we can deal with that when and if. The question is, what do they do now? And I'll bet they do nothing."

"I agree," Evans said. "As long as there's no way to tie Bay to Pont, and accepting the fact that Pont is the one they're really after, they have no choice but to cut bait."

Maloney nodded. "There's always the possibility that they could come back with some sort of trumped up conspiracy to defraud."

I had to know, "Where? On what? Defraud who?"

"They make it up as they go along. It's just a way to keep you on a leash. I suspect that's what they're trying to figure out right now."

The door opened and Salt came back into the room. Booton and Cunningham were nowhere to be seen. "You're free to leave."

Gerald asked, "No charges?"

Salt said, "No charges."

Maloney said, "No police bail? No restrictions? Keeps his passport? Free to travel? Case closed?"

"No police bail. No restrictions. Keeps his passport. Free to travel. But the case stays open."

"Put up or shut up," Maloney challenged him. "If you're not charging him, it's because you've got nothing to charge him with."

"We may still bring charges."

"Your office or Mr Cunningham's office?"

He answered, "Either. Or both. I don't know yet."

Gareth said, "Tell us what you have got."

He thought about it. "I'm sorry, no." Then he turned to me. "I will try to get your office files and all the materials we've taken back to you as soon as possible."

"So the insider trading thing is total crap," Maloney interjected. "There was no insider trading. The rest of it is garbage too. Don't forget, I used to be on the team. I know a losing gambit when I see one."

Now I asked Salt, "It's not about me, is it? It's about Pont."

He paused before admitting, "I still believe that you've had dealings with Doublebrook and Pont."

"No." I shook my head. "I have never heard of a company called Doublebrook and I can document all of my past dealings with Etienne Pont. There haven't been that many. I'd tell you that you're welcome to whatever there is in the files on Pont, except you've already got the files."

"We'll go through them and I'll keep in touch."

"Can I go home now?"

He said I could, then extended his hand to me. "Good luck."

I shook it. "Thanks."

The Custody Sergeant duly noted that I'd been released and would not be charged.

A few reporters were waiting for us downstairs, anxious to know what was going on. Gerald told them no charges had been lodged, but asked that they kindly wait until tomorrow when we would be issuing a statement.

They weren't happy about that, so I told them, "Before you hear our side of it, see what they have to say. You might be amused to find the Fraud Squad office filled with some extremely red faces."

Gerald whisked me away before I could say anything else.

Instead of going directly home, I stopped at the office to see the mess they'd made.

The place was a shambles.

Everyone there was pretty upset, especially Patty, so I sent out for some champagne and tried to lighten the mood. Gerald, Andy and Gareth had a glass with us, and we arranged to meet the next morning.

Just before they left, a phone call came in for Andy. He took it in my office, at first talking quietly with his back turned to the rest of us, then finishing his conversation loudly, laughing, facing us. "All right," he announced when he hung up, "a fiver says no one can guess who tipped the press."

I didn't understand.

"The camera crew," he said. "The blokes who recorded your circus fall for posterity. I've got a fiver to prove you can't tell me who tipped them off."

I thought about it for a moment, then reached in my pocket for a five pound note. "You're on."

He asked, "Anyone else? I'll cover all bets."

Gerald declined, so did Patty and Stonewall. But Gareth said, "Salt's too obvious, so I'll go for Booton."

"Five on the Boot." Andy pointed at him. "Done." He looked at me. "Who?"

"Yeah, Booton. He's cretin enough to do something like that."

Andy extended his hands, palms up towards both of us. "You lose. Thanks, fellas." We handed over our money. "That was an old chum who now works at the SFO. He's named the culprit."

"Who?"

Grinning in triumph, Andy stated, "Him."

I had to ask, "Your friend at the SFO?"

"That's all right, I would have bet on Booton too."

"He tipped the press?" I couldn't figure out why. "They weren't even involved with the case. What's in it for them?"

Andy dangled his newly acquired gains from the tips of his fingers. "Try jealousy."

He described how the Serious Fraud Office was formed in 1988 as a result of massive police failure to win prosecutions in several complex cases that had been coming out of the City of London. At the time, he said, the government had accepted the simple truth that, no matter how well intentioned the police were, the average cop wasn't equipped to deal with the ever-increasing sophistication of financial fraud. So they stocked the SFO with dedicated accountants who couldn't necessarily make full partnership in private firms and underpaid lawyers – like his pal there – who weren't sufficiently ambitious to become high paid mouthpieces with City firms.

Amidst great publicity and a renewed sense of hope, the SFO waded in, hunting for the so-called "big boys". But they turned out to be pretty dismal marksmen. They blew some pretty big cases.

Faced with what can only be considered to be their own impotence, they called for laws which would deny financial fraudsters the right to a jury trial. In other words, Andy asserted, because the good guys weren't good enough to beat the bad guys, the good guys wanted the goal posts moved. When wisdom and common sense prevailed – the jury system remains intact – the SFO looked for a secret weapon and settled on misuse of the media. Unfortunately, some of the British media were willing to play along.

"It's now unofficial SFO policy," Andy went on, "to make the various fraud squads look even more incompetent than the SFO. That gives the SFO the chance to say, the case should have come to us because we've got the experience to deal with it. And, oh, by the way, as long as we're dealing with these big cases, how about increasing our budget?"

Once upon a time I might have been astonished by such a revelation – and horrified at the way I'd been used as a pawn in the battle for increased funding – but the older I get the more cynical I become when it comes to governments, functionaries, bureaucrats and politicians of all persuasions.

"Look on the bright side," I exclaimed. "If it wasn't for the SFO, I'd have never gotten my picture on the front page of a major metropolitan newspaper."

"You and Lee Harvey Oswald." Andy headed for the door. I shook his hand. He held it, then whispered in my ear, "They'll have tapped your phones. So don't even think about getting in touch with Pont. That's what they're hoping you will do."

I assured him, "I have nothing to do with the guy. Honestly, they're barking up the wrong tree."

When he slapped me on the back and walked away, I thanked my lucky stars that somewhere along the way Salt had made such a serious wrong turn. He'd come down the street looking for me, and was now, somehow, in a whole different part of town.

He couldn't charge me with insider trading. And he wasn't going to charge me with fraud either. I could deal with the immigration matter. But no one was going to throw me out of England as long as I had a British wife and half-British kids. They may do that to Indians, Pakistanis, Asians, Jamaicans and blacks in general, they don't do that to white Anglo-Saxon Protestant Americans.

As for the Inland Revenue, when and if they come knocking on the door, there would be a simple way to deal with them. Just pay up.

I left my office and went home to Pippa and the girls. When I got there, she asked, "Now what?"

I didn't say anything, because the only answer was, get even with Francesca.

Chapter Thirty-one

I couldn't sleep and I didn't want to eat. For the next several days, all I did was pace around the living-room. I refused to go to the office. I began to feel like I was on those cheap uppers we used to take at college to stay awake all night. The problem was I didn't know how to come down. It used to be that all you had to do was chugalug some beer, ram your index finger down your throat and throw up. But that wasn't going to work now.

When Peter called, and I told him – in a very cold and calculated way – I am going to ruin Francesca, he said, forget it. When I told Gerald, he warned me, be careful. When I told Pippa, she begged, please stop. But I wasn't interested in anyone's advice, I was searching for one golden moment of self-satisfying vindictiveness.

Wired as I was, I began to imagine myself as Adolf Hitler, striding across my Wolf's Lair retreat in East Prussia – constantly pacing back and forth — planning the invasion of the Low Countries, planning to rain hell on London, planning to dominate the world.

Next time, Eva, no more Mr Nice Guy.

It was ten days before the cops returned everything they'd taken from my office. That same day they issued a press release, which ran, word for word, in the next morning's *Financial Times*.

"The City of London Police has called off its investigation into Pennstreet PLC and its chairman, the American-born Bayard Radisson. Allegations had been made that Radisson had violated insider trading regulations when he dealt in two large blocks of shares in Maxwell Communications Corporation in November 1991, immediately before the death of MCC's chairman Robert Maxwell was announced. Fraud Squad investigators are satisfied that those allegations are false, that no violations have taken place, and indicate that no charges will be brought."

That was followed, over the course of the next few days, by editorials in several papers — two of them even used the same headline, "Another Fish That Got Away" — criticizing the police for their inability to bring cases to court. While no one dared come out and say that I was guilty, or that the cops should have prosecuted me, the papers did point out the undeniable fact that their batting average was pretty lousy.

The *Express* claimed, "One is hard pressed to find a single, momentous victory since Big Bang."

The *Observer* picked up on that, printed a list of so-called celebrity cases and showed how few convictions they'd managed. They added, "Radisson is merely the latest in a long line of the high-profile investigations that will not be brought to trial."

It seems I was running overtime on the Andy Warhol prophesy.

A journalist from the *Mail* rang to ask if I'd cooperate with him as he was writing a book about financial fraud. I politely refused on the grounds that I didn't know anything about the subject. He said, "Can I quote you?" I said, "Sure. Just don't forget to mention that I wasn't charged." He promised he'd get back in touch with me. I never heard from him again.

There were also two calls from television production companies who wanted me to speak on camera about the British police and crime in the City. Again, I declined.

I received letters from people whom I hadn't seen in years. Among them was a postcard from Peter's old girlfriend Phyllis – the one I shacked up with for a few days in the Lake District – who just wanted to say hello.

And I received letters from total strangers. Some of them wished me well. Two, in particular, spewed forth venom, which upset me.

The first was unsigned. The writer threatened that, if I didn't leave Britain immediately, "Someone will take revenge on you. Someone must take revenge on people like you for the evil you cause. Philistines. Capitalists. Money-grabbing Jews. Death to your twin daughters."

I didn't know what to do about it – besides not let Pippa see it – so I phoned the only person I could think of who might, D.I. Nigel Salt. He displayed some genuine concern and put me in touch with a friend of his at Scotland Yard. I met with that officer and showed him the letter. He assured me it was very rare that anything ever came of such threats and that, in fact, I probably had nothing to worry about. Nevertheless, he gave me a special phone number to ring if I felt uneasy about something, or spotted someone hanging around the neighbourhood, or received any more letters. At the same time, he said he would send the letter for processing, to see if it matched any of the tens of thousands of similar letters they keep on file. I continued to worry about it, until he rang me to say that the letter had been traced to a man in the West Country who'd been visited by officers from his local constabulary. The man admitted writing to me. The police gave him an official warning and were now satisfied that I would never hear from him again. So far, I haven't.

The second letter did not contain any threats but was just as troubling. It was written by a retired school teacher who not only signed his name but included his return address. He told me that he'd followed my case quite closely and wasn't in the least surprised that I'd gotten into trouble because, "They set out to trap you."

According to him, the "they" in question were the ruling Jewish classes who see the City as their personal fiefdom. He described how Jews owned the British media – Conrad Black's real name was Schwartz, Lord Beaverbrook had been Brookstein and Lord Rothermere was Rothstein – but really hit the jackpot when he maintained that Rupert Murdoch was not Australian, but rather a Polish Jew called Meyerson. "His accent is phony. He learned to speak English in the concentration camps." The fact that Murdoch is a born-again Christian and that no one in their right mind would deliberately speak with that accent, didn't seem to matter to this clown.

Anyway, he wrote that he had irrefutable proof that the Jewish media barons secretly conspired with Jewish bankers and Jewish businessmen and those very highly placed Jews on the Metropolitan Police to keep us God-fearing Christians – presumably that meant him and me – away from money and power.

He ended by avowing, "Mosley was right."

Even if I didn't have a clue who his pal Mosley was, I knew that schmucks like this should never be ignored. I had a Jewish friend at college who once told me, "Racism thrives in the dark." And I've never forgotten that. So after I read this, instead of chucking it in the garbage, I phoned around until someone mentioned to me there is a newspaper in London called the *Jewish Chronicle*. I told them about the letter and they said they would love to publish it. They did. The shithead who wrote it – they published his name and address – got so upset that he sent me a second letter, citing the *Jewish Chronicle* as proof that Jews were so high up in the post office that they even intercept my mail. I forwarded that letter to the *Jewish Chronicle* too, and they published it as well. He must have ultimately gotten the hint because I never heard from him again.

In addition to calls and letters, I also got some presents. An American lawyer in London whom I slightly knew sent me a t-shirt that read "Free the Radisson One". An accountant sent me a box of cake-mix and a file. And some fellow on the Isle of Man – who explained that he was one of the guys who bought the small fishing fleet I'd inherited with Ohio G. – sent me a case of canned sardines. I don't know why he sent me a case of sardines. I don't even like canned sardines. But the gesture was appreciated.

So was the gift I got from someone on the *Evening Standard* – a poster size colour print of the photo they'd run.

Pippa refused to let me frame it.

But that photo triggered a thought and I decided I'd also like to have a copy of the video that the TV crew shot that morning. I phoned around until I discovered that it was an ITN news team and found a friendly lady in their library who was kind enough to make a copy of it for me. I put it on the VCR one night for Pippa and her parents. They were horrified. I also played it for Gerald and Viv. They didn't like it either. I don't know who else to show it to, but I've kept it, just in case. After all, one never knows when one is going to need an audition tape.

Andy Maloney and Gareth Evans stopped by, and when I mentioned the *Evening Standard* poster and the ITN video, they asked if I wanted to pursue my police brutality case against Booton. They admitted that they didn't hold out much hope, which was fine with me because I'd long since lost interest. I said, "He's an asshole. Forget it. I've got other things on my mind."

There was still Francesca to deal with.

Now I made a critical mistake.

Instead of staying focused on her, I allowed myself to get distracted. I returned to work a few weeks after the Fraud Squad went away because Peter, Stonewall and Gerald convinced me that I needed to present a restructuring scheme to our bankers.

William David Romney was our most avid cheerleader. He helped to rally the others to our cause. The only one who wouldn't go along with what we wanted to do was some guy I didn't know who flew in from Switzerland just for this meeting to represent BFCS. He said his bank wouldn't join the others and, because he was such a morose son of a bitch, he successfully put a damper on everyone's enthusiasm.

But I refused to let that stop me. The two management buy-outs were successfully completed and the money from them went towards lowering our overall debt. We'd been much too highly leveraged – I was willing to concede that – yet I felt we could now see the light at the end of the tunnel.

Unfortunately – as they used to say every time someone used that expression to signal the end of the Vietnam War – the light at the end of the tunnel turned out to be a locomotive and it was bearing right down on us.

Francesca's timing was perfect.

Just when I thought we'd managed to hold off BFCS, they sued us in a Swiss court for the full value of the assets retained by Pennstreet Properties of Great Britain Trust, SA.

Concurrently, they hit us in Britain.

Based entirely on the home-town Swiss decision – we never had a chance to defend it properly – they claimed we were in violation of our original loan agreement on Howe Wharf and started foreclosure procedures. The papers carried that story. Our share price now slipped below 35p. A few of our smaller creditors got nervous and tried to call in their debts. Hill Samuel stood with us but even having them on our side wasn't enough to maintain the market's confidence.

Then BFCS struck a third time.

They went into the Caribbean and sued Long Beach

Properties. They got their hands on one of our bank accounts, which wreaked havoc with our cashflow.

Our share price kept slipping.

Late on a Friday afternoon, an order came into the market – we didn't know the seller – to unload a single block of 25 million Pennstreet shares. I guessed it was BFCS's salvo, because none of our shareholders had that amount. I alerted the Stock Exchange that speculators were trying to sabotage the company and asked that the shares be suspended pending an investigation. The Stock Exchange refused. I couldn't support the share price – my cash was all tied up – so Pennstreet now dipped below 30p. That set off what I'd dreaded most – a deadly spree of computerized selling.

The Stock Exchange finally acted, by suspending the shares on Monday morning, at 19p.

By then it was far too late.

As was their right, BFCS insisted on an Extraordinary General Meeting of the shareholders of Pennstreet PLC, announcing at the same time that they would petition the board of directors to call in the liquidators.

The strain was excruciating. Nothing could make it go away – not pills, not booze, not sex. And yet, just as the stress was about to split me wide open, I found myself slipping through some sort of weird threshhold.

Coming out the other side, I was totally re-focused on Francesca.

But now, the more obsessed I became with revenge, the more Pippa and I quarrelled. I promised her that as soon as I got this out of the way, as soon as I figured out how to even the score, everything would be all right. Except that now, whenever I spoke to Pippa, she snapped at me. She yelled at Malika. She was short-tempered with the girls. One night her parents came for dinner – she said her father wanted to speak with me alone – but I was too preoccupied and refused to sit down with them. When he said, "Bay, you need help," I threw them out.

Pippa flew into a rage. "How dare you?"

I blamed her for inviting them and told her she was more than welcome to follow them back to their place. She woke the girls and that's exactly what she did.

The next day I convinced her to come home, and tried to make her understand what was going on inside my head. I wanted her to know why I was haunted by this and how the demons wouldn't go away until I exorcised them myself.

When I found her on the phone, ringing Peter and asking him to come to see me, I exploded again.

That night she gave me an ultimatum. "Either you get help, like from a psychiatrist, or I'm taking the girls and we're out of here forever."

She slammed the bedroom door shut in my face.

I bunked down on the couch because I didn't want to argue with her. But I couldn't sleep. For the millionth time, I was going over my relationship with Francesca. I was playing it on the insides of my eyelids like a full-length feature film. I was watching every scene, re-running every minute I'd spent with her. I was trying to recollect everything anyone ever said about her.

I heard voices in the back of my head.

But what a turn on . . . I have dreams about her because she's so beyond reach . . . The rumour is that she's got some high-powered married man on the hook in Geneva and spends every weekend there . . . She's untouchable. I mean, she's so untouchable I'm certain that she must be a lesbian . . . Mademoiselle Zermatt . . .

My eyes opened.

And an amazing calm swept across me.

It felt like the blood pressure strap the doctor ties onto your arm and slowly blows up, tensing your arm, and then he lets out the air and your whole arm deflates.

Just like that, the demons were gone.

I got up and walked into the bedroom and gently woke Pippa. "I don't need a shrink. I've figured it out."

She moved away from me. "Bay . . . please . . ."

"Listen to me." I reached for her and rubbed the side of her chest. "I've got it." I started to smile. "I figured it out. It's over."

"No." She moved away and I could tell that my total composure unsettled her. "Bay . . . please . . . we're all right. We're fine. We can put our life back together. We're lucky. We've gotten out alive. Just leave her alone. I wish you wouldn't . . ."

"I know what you wish. And as soon as I do this, I'll grant you every wish. I'll be your genie popping out of the bottle, I promise. But I've figured it out."

She kept saying, "We're lucky. We've gotten out alive. Just leave her alone."

I didn't hear her. "Years ago, when she first came to London, someone told me she was as cold as ice, and he said around the City they called her Mademoiselle Zermatt. You know, the glacier. So when Francesca made big bucks, she set up a shell company to keep it away from the tax man. We sat around trying to figure out a name for the company and I convinced her to use the word Zermatt."

Pippa stared at me. "Bay, really, this is . . ."

I was triumphant. "I remembered where her money is."

She repeated, "Bay, this has got to stop . . ."

"It will," I said. "I promise you it will." I went to my closet and stepped into some clothes.

"Where are you going?"

"Now that I know . . . It's all right. I'll be back."

Pippa suddenly realized. "Don't go there, please."

"I've got to see her. Now that I know how to do it, I need to see her, just once more, and then I promise, it's over."

"Please don't." She grabbed for my arm. "Bay . . . don't . . ."

I walked out without saying another word.

There was a lot of traffic around Sloane Square

because the pubs were still open. It was the first time I'd been outside in two days. Crossing the square, I headed along the King's Road. I walked slowly, taking deep breaths, saying over and over again to myself, just once more and it's over.

A few blocks later I turned right and went straight to Francesca's front door.

Her car was parked just there. I stared at it for a moment, then rang the bell.

It was now 12:45.

I rang the bell again.

Just as I was about to step back to see if there were any lights on in her flat, her voice came over the intercom. "Who is it?"

I answered, "Me . . . it's Bay."

"Bay?" She paused. "What do you want?"

"I know it's late, but I need to speak to you."

The front door buzzed. I pushed it open, said, "Okay," and went inside.

By the time I got to the top of the stairs, she was standing in her doorway, wrapped in a silk kimono, her hair hanging straight down.

"I hope I didn't wake you."

She answered coolly, "What you really mean is, I hope you're alone."

"You wouldn't take my calls . . ."

"I didn't know that we had anything to discuss."

"We do."

She hesitated, then finally stepped back and said, "Come in." I moved past her. She closed the door, looked at me for a moment and – almost as if she didn't know what else to say – asked if I wanted a cup of tea.

I wondered, "Do you have any *tiglio e menta*?"

She almost smiled. "Why don't I make two?" She disappeared into her kitchen. I went into the living-room and sat down. She'd fixed up the place very nicely. It looked a lot more like a home than it did in the days when I kept referring to it as the most expensive closet in London. "You were right not to sell this flat."

She called back. "Does your wife know you're here?"

I told her the truth. "Yes."

She asked, "And why are you here?"

"Because I had to talk to you. To listen to you. I had to hear it from you first."

She came out of the kitchen carrying a tray with two cups. "If you want sugar . . ."

I said no.

She handed me one, took the other for herself, then sat down on a chair opposite me.

There was a long silence – we both covered it by sipping our teas – until she asked, "Had to hear what from me?"

"I wanted you to tell me, why?"

"Why what?"

There was another long pause before I blurted out, "I loved you."

She looked over her cup at me. "Bay, what is this all about? What are you doing here? What do you want from me?"

This wasn't as easy as I'd thought it would be. "I want to hear you tell me why. I think I know. I'm sure I know. But I need to hear you say it. I need to hear you tell me why you did it to me."

"Did what to you?"

"Ruined Pennstreet."

"Oh Bay . . ." She stared at me. "I don't think you ever truly believed that I loved you too."

"You kept running away."

"You kept pushing me away."

"It's funny how the human memory edits out the inconvenient parts."

She forced a smile. "You were never inconvenient."

I said again, "I need to hear you tell me why."

There was another long silence before she said, "Poor Bay . . . do you honestly think I did?"

407

"I think you have been very angry with me. Very angry at me. It's taken me a long time before I could be this calm about you and me. But tonight I finally solved that problem."

"Angry with you? Angry at you? Oh yes. And rightfully so. I deserved to be treated better."

I confessed, "You're probably right."

She shook her head, "Except, it wasn't me."

"Please don't lie to me." I was going to get even

"I never did." She raised her eyebrows. "But you can't say the same."

"Lie to you? I never. . ."

"Howe Wharf," she cut in. "You lied to me about the financing of Howe Wharf. And I knew you were lying. And I was very hurt." She took a deep breath. "Although I think that was probably the only time you did lie to me. I mean, I don't think you ever lied to me when we were together. But you lied to me about Howe Wharf."

I didn't say anything.

"So would you like to know what I did about it?" She held up her hands. "Nothing. I did nothing. I could have stopped the deal . . . and I didn't. I just backed away."

"Then why did you pull the plug?"

Francesca shook her head. "Poor Bay . . . foolish Bay . . . I'm not the one."

"Please don't try to make me believe . . ."

She looked at me. "You really don't know, do you."

"Know what?"

"That it wasn't me."

"If it wasn't you . . ."

She said, "Try your pal Clement."

That stopped me. "Clement? He had no reason . . ."

"He had every reason in the world."

"Clement?" I tried to think of a single reason why he would . . . "My God." My mouth opened wide. "Do you mean that he was in love with you too?"

"Clement?" She started to laugh. "Clement Marc?

Don't be ridiculous. Clement is only in love with himself. He's not capable of loving anyone else." She found that idea very funny, and after a while I smiled too. "No . . . Bay . . . it's because you gave him the key. Remember that Italian word, *chiave*? Once he had the key, all he had to do was open the door."

"What key? What door?"

"That company. Jura Mercantile Trading."

"How do you know about that?"

"I know about everything that goes on in my bank."

"He specifically told me that you must never find out, that you were not to know."

She grinned. "It seems as if he misjudged me almost as badly as you misjudged him."

I leaned back and thought about that. Now I wanted to know, "Did you tell him that . . . you know, you'd once been pregnant?"

She answered softly, "No."

"He knows. He told me . . . he said that was why you were trying to pull the plug."

"He found out about it because he saw the bill on my desk. He never asked what it was for or who . . . but the clinic is well known and I suppose he made a lucky guess that it was you."

"I had dinner with him," I told her. "He cooked. I sat there asking him for more time and he sat there trying to make me believe that you were a loose cannon."

"More time?"

"To restructure. To put off foreclosure of Howe Wharf."

"Did he give you more time?"

"I kept asking and he kept beating around the bush, except I didn't realize until I got home that night that he never said yes."

"Time was the one thing he couldn't give you." She explained, "His situation at the bank has been shaky for nearly a year. No one in London knew it, but there was talk in Switzerland that he'd be brought home and moved sideways. If that happened, he'd never get his seat on the main board, and that's what Clement has always wanted. So time isn't something he had to offer."

"What does that have to do with shutting me down?"

"You came along with Howe Wharf. I knew you'd spun the figures. But I never said that to Clement. Yes, I tried to convince him that we shouldn't get into it. And yes, once he got us into it, I tried to convince him that we should get out of it. I did that because that's what the bank pays me to do. But I never spelled out my reasons and he probably knew better than to ask. At least, he didn't worry about it until he realized that his seat on the main board was in jeopardy. That's when he did exactly what you'd expect Clement to do. He ran absolutely true to form. He started thinking of his own future. To hell with you and to hell with me and to hell with the bank. There was Jura Mercantile. All he had to do was pull the plug on you and blame it on me. His future was worth whatever Jura Mercantile was worth."

I was dumbfounded. "The son of a bitch."

"You handed it to him all by yourself. *La chiave*. You gave it to him on the proverbial silver platter."

I said, almost in a whisper, "He convinced me it was you."

"Only because you wanted to believe it." She shook her head. "Sweet Bay, but you never believed that I truly loved you."

Now I felt totally drained. I sat there, not moving, because I couldn't move.

She watched me.

I studied her face for the longest time. A face I had seen laugh. A face I had seen cry. A face I had loved. Eventually I sighed, and somehow pulled myself out of the chair. I walked to her door, opened it, then turned around to look into her eyes one last time.

"Do you remember that night when I asked you to run away with me? I said, we'll go some place, anywhere, we'll take the first plane out and when

410

we get there we'll get married. Do you remember that?"

"Lovely, tender Bay . . ." She nodded gently. "You were wonderfully mad."

I confessed, "I wish to God you'd have said yes."

And just like that I left.

By the time I got downstairs, all the anger that had built up inside of me – all the frustration, all the confusion, all the love I'd felt for her – came pouring out of my eyes. I didn't want to go home. I didn't want to have to explain any of this to Pippa. I didn't know what to say to her. So I found a taxi and told the driver, "Covent Garden." And when we got there I went to my office and sat on the couch.

The room was pitch dark.

Before long I put my feet up.

Patty found me sleeping there the next morning and sent me home.

There was a note from Pippa on the hall table. "I waited until dawn. When you're ready to be a husband and father again, you know where to find us."

I took off my clothes and crawled into bed. I didn't wake up until the middle of the afternoon. The first thing I did was dial the flat in Cannes. I needed to be sure they were there. Malika answered. I didn't say a word. I just hung up. Then I showered and went back to the office.

A message from Gerald gave me the name of the liquidators.

I rang Peter to tell him.

"That's show business," he said philosophically.

"Are you sure you're okay about this?"

He answered my question with his question. "Are you sure you're okay about this?"

"Theirs is theirs and ours is ours. That's not the problem. It's just the whole idea of a bunch of accountants coming in here and making off with the good times."

He started to sing, "No, no, they can't take that away from me."

"Is there anything you want from here? Anything you want me to send you?"

"What for?"

"I just thought maybe . . ."

"Listen, the guys in suits are merely taking the wicket. We never owned it anyway. They may even ask for the balls and the bats and the nifty white pullovers. But none of that is important. We both have enough money to last forever. You've come out of this with a terrific wife and my two godchildren. We've had a good innings. Bay, we've had a great innings. And we're healthy enough to play another day. What should we care about a few desks and your six line phone system? Good luck to them and the horse they came in on, as you would say!"

"I guess that's what I would say, if I felt better about this."

"Maybe it's congenital, this feeling sorry for yourself all the time."

"I don't feel sorry for myself . . ."

"Bloody hell, you're talking to someone who's had more than two decades of hearing you feel sorry for yourself. And frankly, Bay, it's bullshit."

"I'd convinced myself that this was all about Francesca getting even . . ."

"What do you care. It's over."

"Kind of wry that it turns out to have been Clement."

"It's time to call time."

"It's time to even that score."

"Why bother? Bay, forget it. There's too much to do tomorrow to worry about yesterday. If all you want to do is show Francesca you're still the man you want her to think you are . . ."

"No. It's to show Clement . . ."

"You know what your problem is? You're like the rich man who says to his son, 'Look at this very lush valley and all those wonderfully majestic mountains because some day they'll be yours.' Well, mate, it's time you were the poor man who said to his son, 'Look at this very lush valley and all those wonderfully majestic mountains. Period!'"

"I've got to go."

"You'll never change," he said. "Oh well, if you ever want to go back into business, ring me. And if you ever need a friend, you can even reverse the charges."

"See you soon, pal." And I hung up.

I took the Snowdon photo of my girls and the framed Einstein quote and the little plexiglass thing with the bag lady and the toy UPS truck. Then I looked around the room for a really long time and wondered if there was anything else I wanted.

Peter's quote about the rich man and the majestic mountains came back into my head.

I thought about the pens in my top drawer and the paintings on the walls and the pads of paper on a shelf. I unhooked one of my phones, to keep for old times' sake. And, once I'd decided there wasn't anything else, I rang Roderick. I instructed him to take whatever assets were left sitting in Golden Shores and make them disappear.

He wanted to know why.

"Because there's a payment due from the Golden Shores account to the bank on one of the properties."

He warned, "You don't want to meet it?"

I said, "That's right. Just get the money out of there. I'll speak with you soon."

"What happens when they bankrupt Golden Shores?"

I answered, "We're all going to plead insanity."

Chapter Thirty-two

On 7 August 1993, Pennstreet PLC was officially put into the hands of the receivers, which was tantamount to declaring it bankrupt. I happened to see in the papers that it was also the 36th anniversary of the death of Oliver Hardy.

There seemed something strangely poetic that we should both have suffered our ultimate another fine mess on the same day.

The creditors, who could have had a pound on the pound had they not been such pigs, rushed in and – thanks to the tab the liquidating accountants managed to run up – got 8p on the pound instead.

Oddly, they announced they were happy with that.

The press claimed that the demise of Pennstreet PLC officially put to rest the 1980s.

I admitted to Peter, "My ego is bruised."

He suggested that I remember one very simple truth. "Your bank account isn't."

I never heard anything from British Immigration. Not that there was much they could do, as I was married to a British national. But Gerald thought they might at least drop me a line, just to be nasty. Nor did I ever hear from the Inland Revenue. In the States, when you get your name in the papers, the IRS comes banging on your door. That's another nice thing about Britain. The tax man obviously doesn't read the papers.

By total coincidence, that fall, my passport came up

for renewal. I trotted along to the US Embassy on Grosvenor Square and filled out the application form as Bayard Radisson, no middle initial. I presented it to the guy behind the counter with my old passport, handed him my new photographs, paid cash and, in return, the United States of America agreed to call me Bayard Radisson, no middle initial, for ten more years.

I spent the next several months trying to figure out what I was going to do with the rest of my life. Eventually I decided there really was only one thing to do – spend it with my wife and children learning to look at wonderfully majestic mountains.

Now, on New Year's Day 1994, I lay perfectly still, curled up on my side, with my pillows tucked tightly under my chin, cheerfully considering the end of the world.

There'd been an article in the *International Herald Tribune* two days before, reprinted from the Science Section of the *New York Times*, that claimed all of the planets in our solar system would form a straight line on 5 May 2000. The immediate result of which, according to Professor J. C. B. Greenwald, a Harvard University soothsayer, was the total destruction of the universe.

To support his case, Greenwald cited the writings of the late Dr Immanuel Velikovsky, who had many years ago claimed that several events described in the Bible could be explained away by similar astronomical phenomena. For example, Noah's flood. Apparently many civilizations have, in their oral and written histories, made reference to a great flood that corresponds precisely in time with the event as described in the Bible. Velikovsky's hypothesis was that one of the planets – I think it was Venus, but it might have been Mars – entered the solar system by accident and came so close to the Earth that it knocked us off our axis. In fact, Velikovsky believed, the earth was actually turned upside down, switching poles.

Expanding on that, Greenwald claimed that the Indian file formation of the planets would create a magnetic field capable of throwing all the planets in our solar system off their axes, thus creating such havoc that it was doubtful the human race could survive.

I cut out the article because, now that I had time, I was intent on becoming one of those eccentric intellectual types who often quoted obscure scientists. Something told me that Velikovsky wasn't obscure enough. But Greenwald certainly was.

I'd already read Stephen Hawking's book – plodded through the whole thing – even though he lost me somewhere around page 11 or 12 when he wrote that time was affected by gravity. I'd also read everything ever written by Richard Feynman. While I didn't understand anything he said about nuclear physics, he'd instantly become my hero and I found myself spending hours trying to follow his detailed instructions in the art of safe cracking.

The Ferrari in the basement that I'd always intended to restore one day had taken a back seat to my new found passion for science.

What I appreciated most about Greenwald's theory was the myriad of possibilities it offered us. This was not an opportunity to miss. I kept thinking that if the world is indeed going to end on that particular day – I looked it up and it turns out to be a Friday — then sometime between now and early in the year 2000, I was going to insist that Visa, Mastercard, American Express and Diners Club change my billing date to May 6. That would give me much of March and the whole month of April to go absolutely wild, knowing that, when the time arrives to pay the piper, the final trumpets will already be sounding.

Not that I personally believe a perfect alignment of all the planets will cause some sort of immediate universal devastation. However, as I lay there – with my eyes still shut but otherwise awake – the mere thought of getting one over on the credit card companies elated me.

The twins finally broke into my early morning daydreaming when they rushed into the bedroom singing "Happy Birthday". Together they carried the breakfast, nearly spilling everything between the doorway and the foot of my bed.

Pippa was right behind them, with an armful of presents.

Once the girls gave me the tray, Pippa whispered something to Phoebe who nodded to Brenna who took one of the packages from her mother and said, "Open this one first."

"Are you sure?" It looked to me like some sort of can tied into Christmas wrapping with a pink ribbon.

"This one," Brenna said.

"You need it now," Phoebe pushed it to me.

I grabbed the paper and tore it off to find a jar of Welsh's Grape Jelly, straight from America. "Wow, this is the best," I gave the girls a big kiss. "Who wants some?" I opened it, took a spoon and put a big glob on top of a croissant. I pretended to savour it for a long time, then ate some and rubbed my stomach. "Mmmmmm. Made for croissants." I looked at the girls, "Want some?"

They both made a big face and went, "Uch."

"Next," Pippa announced.

Brenna took a package from her mother and handed it to me. "This is happy birthday from me."

"Me too," Phoebe said.

"No it's not," Brenna insisted. "Yours is . . ." She leaned over and whispered something in her sister's ear.

"Okay," Phoebe said, took another package from her mother and handed it to me. "Here. Merry Christmas and happy birthday and happy New Year," she started to giggle, "and happy Easter too."

Both girls broke up.

Brenna's present was a biography of Isaac Newton. I told her I loved it.

Phoebe's present was a biography of Albert Einstein. I told her I loved it too.

"And now mine," Pippa said, handing me an envelope.

Inside was a birthday card. But when I opened it, something else slipped out. I caught it just in time. It was a Polaroid photo of Pippa, wearing absolutely nothing but high heels and a red ribbon with "Happy Birthday" written across it in white.

The girls wanted to see it. I pulled it away from them, but had to know, "Do we own a Polaroid camera?"

Pippa looked at me with a slightly confused expression. "No, why?"

"We don't?"

She shook her head.

I tried, "Did you borrow one with a self-timer?"

"A self-timer? What for?"

I promised, "We'll discuss it later."

She stared at me. "Discuss what?"

"The camera with the self-timer."

From behind her back she brought another wrapped box and said in a very sultry way, "What do you suppose we'd do if there was a self-timer?"

Phoebe wanted to know, "What's a shelf-timer?"

I opened it and inside was a big, brand-new Polaroid, with six boxes of film.

Now Brenna asked, "Can I have a shelf-timer too?"

I smiled at Pippa. "Gee, there's even a built-in flash that works in the dark." Then I took all three of my girls into my arms.

Peter phoned. "Happy birthday, old man."

"Easy on the old bit."

He wondered, "You hear about Clement?"

"What about him?"

"Oh . . ." He seemed surprised. "You mean you haven't heard the latest?"

When I pulled the money out of Golden Sands, the bank moved against the company. Golden Sands went bankrupt, which panicked the bank holding the mortgage on the apartment house complex in Freeport. They went looking for funds and all they found was a bunch of worthless Golden Shore shares sitting alongside the title to the building in a company called Jura Mercantile Trading. They immediately foreclosed on the mortgage and that effectively bankrupted Jura. Having used that as leverage for some of his own deals, Clement suddenly found a queue of bankers at his door, looking for their money.

I said, "Last I'd heard, he was having some major aggravation in the Caribbean."

"It's better than Montezuma's revenge," he said.

"Montezuma wasn't in the Caribbean, he was in Mexico."

"Well, Clement's not in the Caribbean either. Two days ago he was in Zurich, in a courtroom, filing for personal bankruptcy."

I nearly grinned. "Hah."

"BFCS heard about his dealings and they fired him. So he's broke. Rumour has it that the bank is so upset with the damage he's done to their reputation, they'll announce sometime next week that they're closing London."

"No kidding." I wondered about Francesca.

"I don't know," Peter said.

"Don't know what?"

He'd been reading my mind. "About her."

"Is she all right?"

"Who cares?"

"She can always get another job. Or maybe she'll go back to Switzerland."

He changed the subject. "How's the beach?"

I thought about Francesca for a few seconds, then

told him, "Terrific. I love it. Can't get enough of it."

"You're full of crap."

"Well," I conceded, "the twins love it and Pippa says she doesn't miss London more than two or three days a week."

"And you?"

"I don't miss the weather, that's for sure."

"What about the action?"

"I'll get used to it."

"As I said, you're full of crap."

"No, no, no, really. It takes time. But I'll manage."

"The lady doth protest . . ."

"I'm doing my best. I've even gotten to the point where I can tell a waiter in a restaurant that he's made a mistake on my bill."

"So this is your idea of action, arguing with waiters."

"That's it."

"And you think this is what life is all about."

"Right again."

"Will you ring me when you come back to your senses?"

"I am back to my senses."

"No, you're living in cloud-cuckoo land."

"I'm retired."

"Tell you what," Peter suggested, "when you finally decide to get unretired, how about us sneaking back into the game?"

"Not interested," I said.

"What about the retirement party you always planned to throw on your 50th birthday?"

"It got rained out."

"Maybe not," Peter said. "You see, there's a small company I've just heard about in St Albans called Alleone Industries. They make plastics. Their borrowings are way up and the management is useless. Absolute wankers. But they've got a few good solid properties in the Midlands and a going concern in Lancashire. It would be a cinch to split up . . ."

"No thanks," I said flatly. "Bye."

"Wait a minute."

"I'm retired, bye." I started to hang up.

There was only enough time for him to shout, "You're full of crap."

Patty phoned to wish me happy birthday and happy New Year. She said retirement was the greatest thing that had ever happened to her and added that she was sorry she hadn't done it when she was 28. I reminded her that she was 28 when she first came to work for us. She said, "That's what I mean."

Then Stonewall rang. He sang "Happy Birthday" while his wife banged on the piano in the background. He said the two of them were great and that the piano business was booming. He'd just pulled off a deal where he bought a distressed cargo of bananas from Stevie Bridge, traded them for electronic components through a friend of Lee Lee's in Hong Kong, then traded the electronic components with a guy in Russia for a whole shipload of fine, pre-war pianos that had just been discovered in a warehouse outside Moscow. He figured he'd quadrupled his money. I told him I was proud of him.

Charles Patterson also phoned, to say that he was sending me my annual shipment of jams and jellies – a year's supply – and that he'd spoken to Roger Griffith-Jones who would ring me when he got back from holiday in Barbados to wish me a happy New Year too.

I didn't know it then, but a few days later I would get a card from Christopher Pepperdine to say he'd landed a job at Universal Studios, driving the tour bus, and that, so far, being a movie star was terrific.

When I put the phone down with Charles, mumbling

that all counties have now been heard from, I called out to Pippa, "Time for a café and ice cream."

"Me too," the twins said in unison.

"Us four," I said, walking into the living-room. "*Un, deux, trois, cinq.*"

"That's five," Brenna corrected.

"*Quatre,*" Phoebe said.

And together they counted, "*Un, deux, trois, quatre.*"

We walked along the beach side of the Croisette up to the Palais des Festivals, crossed the street and found a table at Le Festival. Now all the chairs had movie stars' names on them. Pippa got Catherine Deneuve. Phoebe got Jean Gabin. Brenna got Lino Ventura. I made a deliberate point of taking the one marked Michelle Pfeiffer. Pippa chided, "Dream on," before reminding the twins that ice cream wasn't lunch. So we ordered hamburgers for them, a salad for Pippa, and I worked my way through an omelette. Then we attacked the sundaes. Afterwards, we strolled up to the old port where the newsstand was open. Pippa bought a copy of Vogue and I picked up *Newsweek*, *Time* and a two day old *Financial Times*.

"Why the *FT*?" She asked.

"The baseball scores," I told her.

She said flatly, "This isn't the baseball season."

"You sure?"

"Bay," she looked at me straight in the eyes. "You told me it was over."

"It is." I raised my right hand. "Honest Injun."

"Then leave the *FT* right here."

"Where?"

She pointed to a bench. "Right there."

"No problem," I said and walked over to the bench.

"Leave it there," she called to me. "Go on."

I sat down. "I will, I promise."

She and the girls came to me. "Why are you sitting down?"

"Such a lovely day."

"We have a huge terrace," she reminded me. "We can sit there."

"Okay," I stood up.

"The *FT*," she nudged. "Go on. Leave it there."

I moved close to her and put my arms around her. "I love you."

She eyed me suspiciously. "What do you want?"

"I love you." I kissed her.

She moved away. "What are you doing?"

"Making love to my wife in public."

"What's going on?"

"I just wanted to know . . ." I pulled her back to me and kissed the side of her face several times. "You ever hear of a company in St Albans called Alleone Industries?"

☐ Burden Of Desire	Robert MacNeil	£5.99
☐ Unofficial Rosie	Alan McDonald	£4.99
☐ The Saga Tree	Hugh Noble	£5.99
☐ Oliver's Travels	Alan Plater	£5.99
☐ The Dangerous Flood	Derek Nicholls	£5.99
☐ Big Town	Doug J. Swanson	£4.99

Warner Books now offers an exciting range of quality titles by both established and new authors which can be ordered from the following address:

> Little, Brown & Company (UK),
> P.O. Box 11,
> Falmouth,
> Cornwall TR10 9EN.

Alternatively you may fax your order to the above address.
Fax No. 01326 317444.

Payments can be made as follows: cheque, postal order (payable to Little, Brown and Company) or by credit cards, Visa/Access. Do not send cash or currency. UK customers and B.F.P.O. please allow £1.00 for postage and packing for the first book, plus 50p for the second book, plus 30p for each additional book up to a maximum charge of £3.00 (7 books plus). Overseas customers including Ireland, please allow £2.00 for the first book plus £1.00 for the second book, plus 50p for each additional book.

NAME (Block Letters) _____

ADDRESS _____

_____

☐ I enclose my remittance for £ _____
☐ I wish to pay by Access/Visa Card

Number ☐☐☐☐☐☐☐☐☐☐☐☐☐☐☐☐☐☐

Card Expiry Date _____